To Love A King

To Love A King

The Yorkist Saga Book 2

Diana Rubino

Published 2019 by Liaison – A Next Chapter Imprint
Cover art by Cover Mint

Prologue

The Tower of London, January 1499

"Papa!" little Topaz shrieked. She pulled free of her mother's grasp and bolted after the bruised, bleeding prisoner.

Sabine grabbed her daughter. "No, stay back," she warned as two guards dragged her husband, his chains scraping over the stone floor. He fell to his knees and their eyes met. She froze in terror. "Ed—" His name clogged in her throat. He held up a grimy hand to warn her away. The guards jerked him to his feet and shoved him forward, ignoring the horrified woman. Watching him suffering like this tore at her heart.

"Where are they taking Papa?" Topaz's cries echoed off the stone walls. The torches pulsated in unison with her demand.

"I know not, little one. I know not." But Sabine did know. She dreaded this day. Her beloved Edward, imprisoned in this foul, stinking prison by the cruel King Henry the Seventh, was condemned to death.

Her mind spun her back through the years: the passionate courtship, the blessed marriage, God's gift of three precious girls.

As the dark maw of the stairwell swallowed him, Sabine slid to the floor in heart-wrenching sobs.

Seeing her mother like this, Topaz began to cry. That scene haunted her for the rest of her days.

Part One

Chapter One

Marchington Manor, Buckinghamshire, 1509

"Prince Hal and Princess Catherine's coronation is in two weeks, on Midsummer's Day," Lady Margaret Pole announced to her nieces, Topaz, Amethyst, and Emerald, as they sat in the solar tuning their lutes for a musicale. "You girls should attend. 'Tis a once-in-a-lifetime event."

Topaz looked up, knowing her aunt's last sentence was for her benefit. She stared the plump matron squarely in the eye. "Aunt Margaret, how can you expect any of us to attend this travesty? After all we have been through." Tears stung her eyes. "Oh, what a wasted childhood in that stark and haunted place, the hunger, the cold, seeing Papa dragged away in chains..." A stab of grief pierced Topaz's heart. Her mother's cries of sorrow echoed in her mind to this day.

"Why?" asked Topaz. "Why did King Henry have to kill Papa? He wouldn't have tried to take the throne away. All he wanted to do was play his lute and sing."

"Simply because he was his father's son." She strummed a minor chord. "No other reason."

Topaz knew Margaret was trying to appease the young girls with this simple explanation, to protect them from the evil thoughts that threatened their innocent minds. Topaz had spent hours poring over brittle books, studying the history of the Crown, trying to justify it all, but mostly injustices scarred their heritage.

"Your father was a gentle, harmless soul. The king was simply afraid..." Margaret hesitated, her words trailing off as she fingered her brooch.

"That was a bad choice of words, Aunt Margaret. The king—afraid?" Topaz let out a mocking laugh. At fourteen, she was the most outspoken of the family, heedless of the family's warnings.

"Not in that way... your father was a threat to the throne, to Henry's kingship. He never did anything wrong. But Henry was the king, and a king can do whatever he pleases, as you know." With a resigned sigh, her aunt returned to her lute-tuning.

"A cruel twist of fate, was it not, Aunt Margaret?" asked twelve-year-old Amethyst. "Henry killed King Richard. Had Richard won that final battle, then Topaz would now be queen. But God did not decree it so. So here we all are."

"How can you just sit and accept all this?" Topaz blazed. "It should have been our father. The throne was his birthright. That taffy pretender had no business taking it. He was a usurper as is his son, and Hal will never be my king." Topaz's hazel eyes filled with fire and her budding breasts strained under her tight bodice.

"No, no, Topaz," Margaret scolded her oldest niece. "It matters not what you believe, it happened the way it happened, and Prince Hal is to become King Henry the Eighth next week. And we're *all* going to join in the festivities."

"Well, I shall not go." Twirling round, Topaz stepped inside the empty hearth arching just above her head. "How can you, Aunt Margaret?" she cried into the gaping space. Her voice rebounded through the solar. "How can you celebrate the crowning of a king whose father killed your own brother? I want no part of this undeserving pretender." She pounded the wall with clenched fists. "I should be queen. Taffy Harry should have been bludgeoned and Father crowned king, even after Richard was killed. It just isn't fair!" She fled the chamber in a whoosh of satin, her copper hair flying out behind her. Amethyst started to go after her, but Margaret grabbed her by the sleeve.

"Let her go, there is naught you can do when she flies into one of her rages." She pulled Amethyst back.

Amethyst shuddered at a terrifying thought. Topaz had once told her a gruesome tale of a prisoner being tortured on the rack to extricate a confession. She recounted the sound of bones cracking and flesh tearing, the victim wailing in unbearable agony as the guards tightened the ropes, streams of blood oozing from the victim's eyes, nose and mouth, dripping onto the floor. Topaz was not supposed to be there. She'd wandered away from her mother while strolling the ramparts and groped her way into the Black Tower. Up a winding staircase she went and down a narrow hall to find her way back. She followed the wailing cries and found herself at the entrance to an alcove, lit by the harsh glare of torches leaning from their sconces. Two hooded torturers stood at each end of a prisoner lying prone, naked, his arms and legs stretched out before him. She turned and fled, but the victim's agonizing screams filled her nightmares.

"Aunt Margaret, Topaz thinks of naught but this," Amethyst said. "The news of Prince Hal's accession to the throne just made it worse. She tells Emerald and me of the horrors of the Tower... the moans of starving prisoners, the clanking of chains, the stench of body dirt and excrement. I am glad I was so tiny when we were freed, and remember none of it. But she does..." Amethyst sighed. "She relives it, again and again, relaying it all to us so clearly, as if we, too, remember it all."

Amethyst glanced over at the music scores on the brass stand before her, graced with the swirling treble clef.

Ah, music, such a healing blend of concordance and harmony. How she loved to strum her lute and fill the room with delicate strains. "Aunt Margaret, will nothing ever make her forget?"

"Only time will heal her, Amethyst." Margaret's gaze wandered round the chamber as she strummed random chords on her lute. "Time, that immortal force with neither beginning nor end, can comfort and heal as no physician or devout prayers or magic potions ever will. By morning she will have regained her appetite and be the first at the breakfast table as usual."

"Another tantrum, I do hope they lessen as she grows up, she is so old already," ten-year-old Emerald said to no one in particular. "Her tantrums used to frighten me. Now they simply bore me." Shaking her head, she returned to tightening her lute strings. "Does that mean I can sing soprano tonight, Aunt Margaret?"

* * *

Midsummer's Day brought forth a dazzling sun in a cloudless azure sky, enveloping London in warmth and the promise of a new reign. The city gates, flung open, welcomed every citizen to share in the joy of their new monarch. Crowds thronged the narrow winding streets. Rich and poor reveled side by side, in drunken ecstasy from the wine flowing through the public conduits. The gutters were swept free of the usual filth. No slop pails would be dumped onto any heads today. People nearly tumbled out of the second- and third-story windows of their crowded dwellings leaning into each other.

Lady Margaret, Sabine, and the girls had all been invited to the coronation, but Topaz stayed behind. "I shall stay here and watch the grass grow and the sun sink and the moon rise," she'd insisted when asked for the last time to join the party setting out for London. "Those are natural, honest acts. What you are going to witness is a travesty. And God won't smile down upon any of you!" She shook her fist as her family members and their servants entered their carriages. "May Henry Tudor meet a torturous end to his ill-gotten reign, just like his doomed father, the murderer."

Topaz watched the carriages disappear round the bend of the wheel-rutted path. "May he never bring forth an heir," she muttered to the twittering birds.

* * *

The carriages jounced down the rutted road. "I should have talked to her, I could have convinced her to join us," Amethyst voiced her thoughts over the clatter of hoofbeats, watching Topaz's figure shrink into the distance. No one had paid heed to Topaz's wearisome tirade, just as no one listened to Amethyst. They all tittered, in short spurts of half-complete sentences, of the splendid festivities they were about to witness.

"I wonder what Queen Catherine will be wearing…I haven't seen London in so long…I hear Henry the Seventh's Chapel is just magnificent…" all the way down the dusty road to London.

* * *

The procession marched into Westminster Abbey as the brassy tones of trumpets from the lofts rang through the air. Lady Margaret, Amethyst, Emerald and Sabine walked at the head of the procession, leading squires and knights in ceremonial livery, Knights of the Bath draped in purple robes, followed by the peerage: dukes, earls, marquises, barons, abbots, and bishops in crimson velvet. The officers of rank followed: Lord Privy Seal, Lord Chancellor, and assorted archbishops, ambassadors, and lord mayors.

Amethyst had never seen anything quite so grandiose as Westminster Abbey. The church in their cozy Buckinghamshire village was adequate to accommodate the villagers for Mass, but it was simple and modest, in need of repair, a mere repetition of their own austere surroundings. Westminster Abbey was the gateway to heaven itself. She vowed to walk through Henry VII's Chapel and pay homage to her late king, to kneel at one of these splendid altars and pray for his son, her new king.

Someday I shall come back here, she vowed. *I must…*

The little party took their seats along the North Aisle, facing the great nave, where the king and queen would make their entrance. Amethyst grabbed an aisle chair to get an unobstructed view of this once-in-a-lifetime event—and of Henry. Her picture of him was clear in her mind, from the many times Aunt Margaret spoke of him…the flaming hair that framed his intelligent gaze, the graceful gait of his stride, like a colt breezing over the landscape, that was Prince Hal.

Also a talented musician, blessed with a melodious singing voice, he was a lute virtuoso, a master of the organ and recorder. Ah, to engage in a musical interlude with the king! Amethyst thrilled at the idea. To strum their lutes and intertwine their voices in concordant harmony... she drifted away in a whirlwind of court festivities, draped in a billowing satin gown, alighting from a carriage at the palace gates, partaking in the elegant dancing and sumptuous banqueting, curtsying before her king... mayhap at some later date it would be reality, mayhap...

For an instant she thought of Topaz and all the hateful things she'd been saying about the Tudors all her life. Amethyst had never known her father, the man Topaz so brazenly defended, relaying that day to them so many times, repeating every detail. Amethyst paid heed every time Topaz recited the line of succession, and studied her sister's diagrams scratched on parchment.

"This is our family tree, and this is where the throne went wayward, *not* straight down to me, but detouring through the Tudors. Taffy Harry is a murderer," Topaz pounded into Amethyst's head incessantly, so she knew the routine by rote. "He murdered our father. He is not the true king and never will any of the Tudors be."

Amethyst was afraid for her sister—she knew the punishment for treason. She often wondered about her father, this blur of a figure stumbling through the Tower, dragged over the flagstones, suffering a horrid death just for being an heir to the throne. She saw the pain in her mother's eyes, the tears that never fell, the unspoken grief interred deep inside her, hidden by her murmurs, "the king's pleasure, 'twas the king's pleasure..."

But to speak out against the king—that was a death sentence in itself. She held in her own rage over the injustice.

She knew Topaz's reactions were extreme. To try to displace the king was akin to committing murder. Who wanted to rule a kingdom anyway? Amethyst pictured herself as a courtier, delighting in the intimate circle of royalty. That was good enough for her!

The procession finally ended and the Archbishop of Canterbury appeared at the Abbey doors. He strode down the aisle, nearly lost in the thick folds of his velvet robes. His appearance meant one thing—the king and queen were about to enter!

The spectators turned to the entrance and stood. Amethyst, leaning out into the aisle, saw two figures blocking the light at the entrance. As the organ music swelled and filled the ancient abbey, they began their march toward the altar. Henry walked on the left, closer to her. She glimpsed Catherine on the far side, waves of golden-brown hair spilling over her shoulders, her gown a cloud of virgin white. Amethyst fought a pang of envy for the young woman at Henry's side, about to become his queen. Then her eyes landed on him and she stood transfixed.

Henry was draped in a full fur-lined purple cloak, its train falling in gentle folds over an embroidered tunic of gold and glittering rubies, emeralds, and diamonds. The broad lapels of his shirt spilled over a crimson satin doublet, lined with diamonds and pearls. Breeches fit his muscled legs like a second skin, threaded with stripes of gold silk. Black leather boots reached his knee.

She studied his features, trying to drink him all in as he swept by—the shock of lustrous red-gold hair, the eyes betraying a wisp of wisdom behind the youthful playfulness. His stride was confident, his movements graceful. They came closer, closer—the end of his cloak touched the toe of her shoe and for an instant their eyes met. She wasn't sure she imagined it, but it seemed at that very instant he slowed his step to let his gaze linger upon hers. She held her breath and stood in adoring awe of this beautiful man who would within moments be her king. Then he and Catherine strode past them and approached the high altar. Henry went to the centuries-old coronation throne, its finish scratched and marred. He sat upon it regally as the High Priest turned to face the assembly and asked if they would have Henry for king.

"Aye, aye, aye!" Thundering voices rang through the openness, fading away into the high arches reaching towards heaven. The High

Priest anointed Henry with oil, then placed the glittering orb in his hand.

"All hail King Henry!" filled the hallowed space, rose to the high vaulted ceiling and died within the deepest recesses of the ancient sanctuary.

Amethyst, as did all his subjects in the very first moments of his reign, adored her new king.

Chapter Two

Marchington Manor, Buckinghamshire

Amethyst sat under her favorite oak tree strumming her lute. The clatter of hoofbeats approached and the instrument slipped from her hands as the messenger came into focus. Was that royal livery he was wearing? The red dragon of Cadwallader blazed on a field of white, and the same finery draped his horse. He dismounted, handing the reins to an equally startled stableboy. He approached her, looked down at her and gave her a smile that nearly melted her lute strings. "Is the Mistress Sabine about?" he asked.

Picking her jaw up off the ground, Amethyst stood and brushed the grass from her skirt. "Mother is abed, Sir, she's got a frightful summer grippe. May I deliver the message to her?"

"I suppose. It is from the king." He handed her a roll of parchment embossed with the royal seal.

"Indeed." Amethyst's heart gave a fluttering leap at the thought of holding in her humble grasp what had been touched by her great king. "I shall deliver it to her. It bears good tidings, pray God." She looked into the messenger's eyes, wishing he'd stay a while. How seldom they had company such as this!

"I am but a messenger, my lady. I know not what news the parchment betells." He tipped his hat and turned back to his mount.

"Uh—sir?" She dashed forward and faced him. "Would you like to stay for the evening meal? We have food aplenty."

"Nay, my lady. I must be on my way." He pulled on the reins and the horse turned and began trotting back down the path.

"Well, I bid you Godspeed then…" But he'd already galloped away.

She held the roll in her hands, stroking it with her fingers. *'Tis from the king, this actually came from the king…*

She dared not open it, but headed back towards the house. Now her mother would recover a lot faster.

Amethyst met Topaz coming from the animal infirmary she'd set up in the south wing of the stables, wisps of dog and cat hair clinging to her skirts. "What is that you hold?" Topaz peered at it more closely, her eyes squinting upon the royal seal. "From court? From Henry?" Never had she referred to him—or his late father before him—as king.

"Aye, a messenger just brought it. 'Tis for Mother."

"I shall read it then." Topaz reached out to snatch the roll from Amethyst's hand. "She's ill and if it bears bad tidings, 'twill only serve to make her worse."

"No!" She held her arm up out of Topaz's reach. "'Tis not yours! 'Tis for mother, and I shall deliver it unto to her. I'm sure it brings glad tidings. What bad would King Henry have to bring upon our mother?"

"You simpleton, it's probably our death warrants. He's planning to haul us back to the Tower just like Richard Humpback did to our poor little cousins." She made another attempt to grab the roll. "Don't give it to her, Amethyst. Burn it, be gone with it. We shall say we never got it."

"Oh, no, not again. Topaz, you're turning into a right lunatic." Amethyst flattened her palm to her ear and turned to ascend the stairs. "I'm bringing it to her and 'tis up to her whether she would open it."

"Take my word, Amethyst, when mother reads that note you will be facing one very disturbed woman," Topaz called after her.

"No, I won't, because you are staying down here."

* * *

Sabine sat up in bed, propped up against pillows, drinking from a pewter beaker.

Amethyst entered, approached the bed and fluffed her mother's pillows behind her. "Do you fare better, Mother?"

"Aye, but I would rather be out there enjoying the world." She wiped her nose with a linen cloth.

"Well, have I got glad tidings for you!" Amethyst could never imagine a message from King Henry being anything else. She held out the parchment, the seal facing her mother. "From the king himself. Open it, Mother, pray open it, I'm dying to see what good King Henry has to say. Mayhap he would invite us to court for Christmas!"

"'Tis but August, my dear." Sabine broke the seal and calmly began to unroll the parchment. Amethyst would have torn it to shreds. She sat on her hands in excitement. "Besides, why would the king want us..."

Sabine began reading, and just as Amethyst expected, a happy smile brightened her face. "Oh, Blessed Jesu!"

"What is it? God's foot, tell me before I scream!"

"Our great King Henry, our generous king, behold what he's given us!" She handed the note back to Amethyst and she read, in the king's own writing, the bestowing of an annuity of 100 pounds each to Sabine and to Aunt Margaret Pole to atone for the great injustice of his father Henry Tudor having had Edward Earl of Warwick executed. "In addition, he is... oh, Jesu! He's reversing the attainder against Father and..." She stopped to catch her breath, "full restitution is being made to the rights of the family! That means... oh, Mother!"

"Aye, my dear." Sabine clasped her hands and raised her head to heaven. "Thanks be to our good Lord, Warwick Castle is ours!"

"Do you know what that means, Mother? Lands! Our very own Warwick Castle! Titles! You're Lady Sabine, dowager Countess of Warwick, I'm Lady Amethyst, dowries for me and Topaz and Emerald! I must tell them! Oh, I must tell them!" She was no longer the simple village girl doomed to the life of a plain wench. She was now a lady, titled and landed, bursting with gratitude for her generous king. Once again the misty vision of court life unfolded from the remote fancy of her dreams to solid possibility. "Oh, Mother, King Henry is so good, so kind! How could we ever repay him, how could we ever—"

"How, indeed?" Sabine spread her fingers. "What do we have, save a few nights to rest at Warwick Castle, that King Henry could ever want?"

"Oh, I know not, Mother! I'll think of something!" She held out her arms and twirled on her toes. "I would send him one of my songs!"

"Aye, he should like that." Sabine nodded.

"I would give him something of myself…a part of me." Amethyst danced around the room, fed by a rush of joy.

"Hah!" Topaz lingered in the doorway and Amethyst, overhearing her sister's grunt of disgust, shook her head in perplexity. How could Topaz be so ungrateful to the man who'd saved her family from the doom of poverty?

Topaz turned her back and scowled. "That hypocrite," she spat. "I do not trust that wretch, his father's son down to the beady eyes." A stab of fear replaced her anger. Oh, God above, what was Henry up to?

* * *

Warwickshire, September, 1510

On this sparkling autumn morning, wispy clouds scattered and the sun struggled to share its comforting warmth.

Two wagons pulled through sticky muck. The last days' rain had left the road to Warwick splotched with pools of mud. The thin wheel ruts streamed with mud.

The carriage followed the wagons, carrying Sabine, Emerald and Amethyst. Topaz refused to partake in the family's sudden recovery of their ancestral home. She chose to stay behind and tend her animals.

Amethyst so much wanted her sister at her side on that day, to share in this joyous occasion, for they were finally being granted a home that was rightly theirs.

They approached Warwick through Westgate, one of three ancient city gates. As they entered the dark tunnel, the horses' hoofbeats and squeak of the wagon and coach wheels echoed off the inner walls. They emerged on the High Street, in the midst of the bustling town. To the left stood a timber-framed house leaning into the street, a wooden sign reading "Leycester's Hospital" swinging from a chain, clanging against its post with each gust of wind. More timber-framed houses huddled against the hospital, their peaked roofs pointing towards the clearing sky.

They passed through the market square, where merchants displayed their wares on shelves under rolled-up awnings. Villagers bustled about, grabbing and squeezing fruits and vegetables, loading their goods into wagons. The doughy aroma of meat pies encircled them, and Amethyst breathed in the rainwashed air mingled with the scents of fruits and spices. A pig scurried across the road, followed by a parade of clucking chickens. They left the bustle of the marketplace and at the end of the curved road, she saw the top of a round tower rising over the trees.

As they followed the curve of Castle Street, Amethyst halted the party and jumped out of the carriage, wanting to finish the journey on foot, alone. She rushed ahead and broke into a run. At that moment the sun burst through the last veil of clouds.

And there it was.

It lined the riverbank, rising from its ancient mound, the stonework echoing the sun in an earthy yellow mingled with a rosy glow. Curtain walls connected a myriad of round towers inlaid with arched windows, majestically topped with crenelations. The imposing fortress extended farther than she could see, and as she approached, it loomed bigger still. She could discern even more towers, walls, and barricades—on and on, far as she could see.

She scrambled up the hill, tripping over her skirts, laughing and whooping in a frenzy of emotion, threw her head back and gazed up at the massive structure. It towered into the heavens, so imposing, so impenetrable.

She entered a gatehouse built into the side of the hill under the raised portcullis. Standing upon the dirt floor in the dark, she inhaled the dankness in the whistling wind that sang of centuries past. Her tears fell and seeped into the ground. She stepped back outside, taking another sweeping look. Opening her arms, she embraced the curved surface of the tower, letting the cold stones absorb her body's welcoming warmth.

"My home, my home," she whispered, becoming one with her history. Finally, she knew where she'd come from. "Home, where I belong."

Chapter Three

Marchington Manor, December, 1511

Topaz and Lady Margaret received Christmas invitations to neighboring Kenilworth Castle from its lord, Matthew Guilford. Feeling the need for a diversion, Topaz decided to go, while Margaret declined, as she'd already been invited to court.

Topaz had never made Sir Guilford's acquaintance, but imagined him as a stilted nobleman bedecked in stuffy raiment and a graying pate. However, she mused, nobles sired eloquent sons, capable of engaging her in lively debate far beyond the scope of any common Warwickshire yeoman. Her new title could do well to yoke a worthy counterpart. She knew she'd been obscuring her title when she could be using it to her advantage.

She folded her lacy cloths and placed them in a traveling trunk. Mayhap a younger Guilford would pluck one of these up twixt his teeth in the triumph of a won tournament.

After two days' journey, Topaz and her small retinue of servers cantered down the final rutted road leading to Kenilworth. The charming castle paraded a sandstone glow and sprawling gardens, a striking ornament astride the velvety pastures and sparkling lake that lapped up against its walls.

A groom helped her dismount in the courtyard and a maid escorted her to a set of comfortable apartments. She dressed conservatively for that evening's meal in the great hall, her subdued blue gown devoid of ribbons or lace, and with a higher neckline than the fashion dictated. Actually, it was one of her mother's older gowns. She didn't want to outshine Lady Guilford–not on the very first evening.

As she descended the staircase, her eyes swept the entry hall for familiar faces. She tried to guess who old Lord Radcliffe could possibly be, but the guests milling about and entering through the huge oaken doors were of her own age group.

She halted halfway down the steps, spotting the tallest head in the crowd. A crop of dark blond hair caught the light like a cluster of glowing embers. He stood draped in blue, from his turquoise hat to the moderate tones of his doublet and hose tucked into indigo shoes. A satin undertunic peeked out, trimmed in gold. Sapphire rings glittered on his fingers. Swirls of aquamarines studded his doublet.

His laughter, resonant and confident, prevailed over the tittering and chuckling. A growing circle enclosed him. Guests clamored for his attention, especially the ladies. They threw their heads back in gaiety, headdresses bumping, as they nudged each other aside to get near him. A bejeweled hand stroked his sleeve and lingered. One of the more aggressive ladies clutched his arm and turned him to face her.

His eyes swept across the entry hall and over to the staircase. He looked in her direction. She stood, rapt. His eyes met hers. He turned away, but she kept a steady gaze on him. A moment later he glanced her way again.

This time their eyes locked. Smile met smile. He excused himself and his graceful figure glided through the growing press of bodies. He met her on the staircase, above the crowd. They stood detached from the rest of humanity as if they'd been swept away on a cloud.

"'Tis a pleasure to make your acquaintance, my fine lady. Allow me to introduce myself. I am your host, Matthew Guilford."

He took her hand and raised to his lips before she spoke a word. The image of the wheezing old man withered and died. "And I am Lady Topaz Plantagenet of Warwick Castle."

She couldn't remember another word either of them said...except his last question before he excused himself.

"Would you be so kind as to honor me with your presence for a stroll over the grounds after we sup, my lady?"

She heard her voice say yes.

While the music played and the mummers jangled, Topaz couldn't even think of eating. The sight of all the roasted fowl, meats and steaming dishes made her stomach churn. She barely said a word to those seated around her at the long table. She didn't give a fig about crops, weather, or even the explorations in the New World—not now. She could only stare at that dark blond head, that warm smile, and that exquisite body so magnificently dressed.

* * *

She perched on a seat in the winter parlour for quite a while before he finally arrived. He apologized for his lateness.

"Your faux pas is forgiven, of course." She lifted her hand to his lips and he kissed it. A thrilling shiver ran through her. Drowning in those green eyes, she heard his calm elegant voice speak of...she wasn't quite listening. His voice as smooth as the velvet of his doublet, he could have spoken his words backwards for all she cared.

She'd already decided that she would be the next Lady Guilford.

She found out all about him in the next few days, over the tournaments, card and dice games, asking casually of the other guests. Bred of good stock, he was landed and educated. His father, Sir John, had died fighting at Bosworth, the battle that brought Henry the Seventh to the throne. Throughout the entire twelve-day celebration, every slavish female in the shire flattered and fawned over him. He took it in good humour, brushed off his cloak and invited more. Though she ached for his exclusive company, Topaz acted aloof and disinterested, the opposite of all the other twittering wenches. It worked. She piqued his interest, for he asked to meet her again...and again.

He invited her back to Kenilworth, and she returned a second and third time. *Oh, yes, I shall become Lady Guilford before Hocktide,* she vowed.

* * *

"Tell me more about Topaz of Warwick. Who is she and where did she come from?" he asked one night as they sat before the fire in his solar. She'd just finished asking him more about the chapters of his life, learning of his love for hunting, ancient Rome, and his assortment of allergies.

Do I tell him the truth now or let him keep wondering? she asked herself. No, tell the truth. Spin a yarn and it'll backfire somehow, with these talebearers lapping up the juices of gossip like thirsty hounds. Besides that, she needed someone to talk to, to share her pain. Who better than her future husband?

"I know the Earls of Warwick go back several centuries." He stretched his legs and rested on his elbows.

"To 1088, to be exact." Her tone swelled with pride. "King William the Second created the Earldom. My father, Edward, was the son of the Duke of Clarence. My grandfather's brother, King Edward the Fourth, had my grandfather executed on trumped up charges and drowned in a butt of malmsey when he was twenty-nine years old and my father was but three."

"Why? What did your grandfather do that his own brother would have him executed?" His eyes widened in curiosity.

"He tried to take the throne a few times." She gave him the bare fact.

He nodded. "Ah. That will do it."

"My father never got to know his father," she revealed her sad history. "He was almost the same age I was when Taffy Harry killed my father." Her voice dripped resentment, and Matthew refilled her wine goblet in order to ease the pain these memories evoked.

"My father, the last of the Plantagenet line, was born in Warwick Castle. King Richard knighted him along with his own son. When King Richard's son died, he named my father heir. When Tudor killed King

Richard at Bosworth and seized the crown, my father was named *de jure* King of England, as he was the nearest in succession. So he was a threat to Tudor, being the rightful heir, by bloodline and all else."

"So that is why Tudor imprisoned your father for the rest of his life?"

"Yes." She nodded. "When my father was eight years old, Taffy Harry clapped him in Sheriff Hutton Castle, then had him brought to the Tower. He met my mother in the Tower when she went there to visit her father, the Earl of Ashford, who was awaiting execution."

"For what?"

"He fought on King Richard's side at Bosworth," she replied.

"So what happened to your mother then?"

"When Ashford had his land stripped from him, my mother was shipped off to live with an aunt. She had nothing. My father had Warwick Castle taken away and it reverted back to the crown. He and my mother fell in love and got permission to marry. She took up residence with him there in the Bell Tower and became a court musician and singing minstrel."

"So you were born and bred in the Tower?"

"Aye. A virtual prisoner. My only happy childhood memory was of the splendid Royal Menagerie they had there in the Lion Tower. They had monkeys, elephants, zebras, and giraffes, and huge tortoises, colorful birds, and all kinds of exotic animals from Africa." Her hands fluttered like wings. "The guards let me go there almost every day and I would stand and stare at the animals, fascinated with their behavior, their ways of communicating with one another, their rituals. I named some of them and the guards let me feed them. When Matilda the elephant had a baby, I named him Perkin, and he became my playmate. I would grab his trunk and he would curl it round my hand like a real friend would. Then one day returning from the menagerie, my mother and I climbed the stairs to the Bell Tower and I saw...saw them dragging my father away..." She stopped, not wanting to relive this scene. "Taffy Harry had my father executed when my mother was breeding with Emerald. Just because he was a threat to the crown. It shows how preposterous it all was. My father, imprisoned since age eight, who they said was so simple-minded he couldn't tell a hen from a goose, trying to depose the king! He was executed on Tower Hill. Didn't even have the honor of the green, where the nobles get their heads lopped off. We were all sent to live with my father's sister Margaret and her husband Richard Pole, and their brats. I began collecting animals, healthy ones as well as sick ones. I gave them names, I cared for them all, and learnt how to heal the sick ones in very much the same way our family physician cared for us. I made medicines for them and birthed them. That was my only escape, the menagerie they let me have. Animals were my only friends. It was my world."

Matthew sensed her pain permanently embedded within her soul.

But he understood. He held her and let her cry, and when she calmed down, he asked her to marry him.

* * *

Warwick Castle, October, 1512

Topaz strolled across the footbridge crossing the River Avon and headed for the Peacock Gardens where she was meeting her betrothed. Kenilworth Castle wasn't as grand as Warwick, but it was close enough to her rightfully inherited home that she could visit her family whenever she pleased and set up another animal hospital there.

She was now living at Warwick since Lady Margaret moved to court at King Henry's invitation, and took all her servers with her.

Topaz raised her left hand, and for the dozenth time that day, admired her betrothal ring, holding the cluster of rubies set in gold up to the sunlight. It glinted, twinkled and winked at her as if to commend her on her choice of a husband. No way would she succumb to any arranged marriage, as her sisters inevitably would. Marriages were for combining lands and titles, and the parties involved were merely vehicles to secure the claims. No, Topaz, Duchess of Warwick would bestow her generous dowry on the man of her choice, not her mother's, not that fraudulent Henry's, no one's but her own.

She watched the peacocks strutting proudly, the males displaying their brilliant tails. How much like Henry VIII they were, so pompous and haughty and proud! And what were they really, without that majestic splaying of feathers? Just ugly, scrawny birds, like Henry undoubtedly was under his royal regalia of ill-gotten jewels and robes. A pretender, nothing more. Males. Phonies, one and all.

Matthew was no exception. Handsome and comely as he was, he was there to serve one purpose: to sire her heir, her future King of England, Edward the Sixth.

She turned away from the peacocks and headed for the stables to check on her animals before Matthew arrived. As she crossed the moat towards the east entrance, she noticed an ornate carriage drawn by four white palfreys heading for the gatehouse. Surely that wasn't Matthew. Even he wasn't that extravagant. She broke into a run through the inner courtyard in order to greet them, excited at the prospect of a visitor, and a noble one at that. The carriage halted and the horseman dismounted to help his passenger alight. She didn't recognize his livery; mayhap it was someone calling on Amethyst or Emerald. Several noble gents were wooing the girls, the most persistent being the Duke of Norfolk, who'd had an eye on Emerald for some time now.

She gasped in delight when she saw the passenger daintily stepping to the ground was none other than her dear Aunt Margaret Pole!

"Auntie! God's foot, you look splendid!" And indeed she did. Her golden cloak was trimmed in fur, and the circlet on her head glinted with clusters of sapphires.

"I bring wonderful news!" She greeted her niece with a kiss on each cheek and a small box. "Don't open it yet. I have gifts for all of you."

"Gifts!" Topaz jumped with delight. Aunt Margaret always had a heart of gold and distributed a large portion of her annuity to the poor. "What is the occasion? Another betrothal party? But I just had one last week!"

"No, my dear, let us all assemble and I shall dispense the glad tidings. Pray tell me your mother and sisters are in residence."

"Aye, they are. I believe they're in the Green Drawing Room working on their needlepoint." She led the way.

They entered the private apartments and found Sabine, Amethyst and Emerald in the Green Drawing Room, chatting and sewing. A servant was lighting the logs in the fireplace.

After exchanging warm greetings, Margaret took four small boxes from the velvet sack she held and gave them out. "One for each of you. One for Sabine and one for each of my jewels."

Sabine opened her gift, a cross made of dark red rubies suspended from a gleaming gold chain. Amethyst's gift was a gold brooch inlaid with a round-cut amethyst, Emerald's was an emerald-cut emerald in a gold bracelet, and Topaz's was a teardrop-shaped topaz suspended from a gold chain. Sabine received a pearl choker.

"They're just magnificent, Margaret." Sabine slipped the chain over her head and held the cross up to the window. The rubies glowed like embers. "But pray tell us, what is the news?"

"I have just been created Countess of Salisbury by his majesty the king, ratified by parliament. He bestowed upon me the family lands of the earldom of Salisbury, as well as property in Hampshire, Wiltshire, and Essex!" As her words gushed forth, she beamed like a child with a new toy. Sabine squealed in delight, for now she and her sister-in-law were both wealthy, titled noblewomen. Amethyst and Emerald glowed like the jewels they beheld.

Topaz scowled.

"His majesty the king," she snickered. "No matter how many benevolences he conjures up, he cannot undo what his father did. Is this reversal of the attainder against our father, ten years after his death, going to bring him back? Lands and titles mean nothing to him, they are no sacrifice. Let him give up something that would hurt him to give up."

"Like what?" Sabine wondered why she even bothered to argue with her daughter anymore on this matter.

"Like the crown, mayhap," she retorted. With that she twirled away to meet her fiancé.

* * *

On the eve of Topaz's wedding, the three sisters sat in her bedchamber, appropriately named the Blue Boudoir, decorated in an array of blues: French blue silk wallhangings, a lapis satin covered the furniture, and velvet draperies the hue of bluebirds. The two younger sisters sat on the bed watching Topaz smear an oily concoction on her face.

"What is that?" Emerald wrinkled her nose.

"Lanolin, oil from lambs." Topaz poured some more of the greasy substance into her palm and rubbed her hands together.

"Are you going to do that every night after you're married, also?" asked Emerald.

"Why, of course. Just because I've landed a husband doesn't mean I'm not going to keep myself looking young."

Amethyst gasped. "God's truth, Topaz, you're only eighteen!"

"We'll be old hags before we know it, children." She smeared the oil on her throat in firm upward strokes.

"But I'm sure Lord Gilford finds you just as beautiful. You need not make your face all slippery and slimy for him."

Topaz looked at her sister in the mirror and laughed. "I do it not for him, nor for any other man, dear sister. I do it for myself. Once I am old and Matthew is gone and my looks are withered away by the ravages of time, I'll have naught but my wits to see me through. Men don't age as quickly as women, but I daresay look at your King Henry in the next few years, after a war or two and a few personal tragedies, and I can assure you he will begin showing his age. He won't be the pretty boyass he is now."

"Topaz! What a way to talk about our king!" chided Emerald.

"*Your* king, you naive child, *your* king. I referred to him as such as I feel generous tonight, and do not wish to insult him."

"I've heard you say worse things about your own husband-to-be," said Amethyst. "And he's the one you'll be abed with every night."

"Every night? Posh. I plan to maintain my own chambers, into which he will not set foot uninvited."

"Surely you won't lock yourself away in separate apartments on your wedding night, Topaz!" Amethyst was at that age where curiosity about such matters fairly burst out of her. "I look forward to my own wedding night."

"So you should, but to me, I have my own reasons for this marriage, least of which is the bliss of the marriage bed."

"But you love Lord Gilford, do you not?"

"Love, sister? No, I do not love him. But it matters not to him, because he has enough love in him for the both of us. He is a lucky man, for very few people find love within marriage. I am marrying him for reasons of my own."

"And what reasons may they be?" Amethyst asked, as Emerald had lost interest in the conversation and was now pawing through Topaz's wardrobe. "Surely 'tis not for Kenilworth Castle."

Topaz turned to face her younger sister and looked deeply into her eyes. "A son, Amethyst, that is what I want more than anything, more than these empty titles, castles and lands to build them on. I want a son, an heir, to carry my legacy through history. And I'll be breeding as of tomorrow night, pray God. This is my mission. And I shall carry it out."

Amethyst understood, as the younger Emerald couldn't, and what their mother Sabine dared not, Topaz's rants. She never quit this rampage about being the rightful queen. And poor Matthew Gilford, smitten as he was, was no more than the provider of the fuel.

* * *

Topaz's wedding day bloomed with a quilting of sunshine illuminating the clouds. The trees unleashed their papery leaves, carpeting the castle grounds with a matting of red and gold.

The great hall sparkled with Warwick Castle's magnificent array of plate. The butler laid the high table with gold cloth and set the salt cellar just below the middle of the board. The coppery tile floor shone like a mirror, reflecting each burst of candlelight. The massive stone fireplace housed the crackling logs. Sparks spewed forth and died within the fire's lustre. This was her autumn wedding, decorated with an autumn theme. Huge cutouts of leaves made from cloth of gold hung from the gallery and fluttered as the servants scurried about. A horn of plenty graced each table, a cornucopia of plump grapes, apples, nuts from Spain and colorful nubby gourds.

Matthew and 16 village lads wearing blue bridelace and sprigs of broom tied round their arms led the wedding procession into the tiltyard. A party of Morris dancers, musicians, and the village fool followed. Serving maids came after them, carrying spiced bridal cakes, and a village lad bore the bride cup full of sweetmeats, decorated with broom and streamers. Topaz rode atop a white stallion liveried in gold, gleaming in the sunlight as her horse's graceful muscles shifted in his noble stride.

When the noon sun had reached its zenith, the actual ceremony began.

Inside the small chapel sat their families in the carved wooden pews. Candles glowed in the chandelier above, sending their warmth to the arched stained glass windows above the altar. With Matthew at her side gazing at her, she stood at the altar before the priest, draped in white robes. She smiled lovingly at her groom. Matthew spoke his marriage vows as if reciting a prayer. She echoed them, thinking ahead to the day she would hold her first child in her arms.

They swept down the aisle, the kingdom's newest man and wife, her satin gown shimmering in splendor, her butterfly headdress fluttering as they glided through the corridors to the great hall.

The guests poured into the hall, the marshal seated us at their proper places, and the feasting began.

The minstrels played rondos and humoresques throughout the feast of autumn dishes of stockfish and red herring, fresh from the ocean. From the river they'd procured salt-eels and salmon. Topaz smiled in contentment at her new husband satiating his healthy appetite. She relished the garden gatherings, the delicious array of peas, squash, and carrots seasoned with cloves, ginger, saffron, and mustard. At the end of each course, servers brought a magnificent pastry to the table, shaped to represent the Holy Trinity watching over them.

There was no bedding ceremony; none of Matthew's attendants accompanied him to the bridal chamber singing bawdy tunes, preparing him for his wedding night. Topaz had always considered the tradition degrading to the sacrament of marriage, and especially to the bride, and would have none of it. The bride and groom simply mounted their palfreys and rode back to their new home at Kenilworth.

* * *

Matthew brought two silver goblets over to the fire where Topaz lay luxuriating on a pile of feather pillows, her hair splayed out like a fiery sunburst.

She sat up to take one goblet and clinked it against her husband's. "I hope to be breeding as of tonight, my lord." Her voice lilted in anticipation.

"Tonight?" A twinkle shone in his eye. "That would be a noble feat indeed."

"It would be, but I doubt your prowess not one bit, my lord." Topaz rested her gaze over her husband, her choice alone. She sat at eye level with his nether region. He lowered himself to his knees to tend the fire, and she scrutinized his every feature with discerning female curiosity. The dark blond hair brushed the top of his collar. A jagged gash interrupted the smoothness of his jawline. *And he's all mine!* Topaz displayed a racy grin as she anticipated Matthew hard and demanding against her, wanting her, begging her.

He lay down next to his bride with a leisurely stretch. She ran her hand over his nightshirt of fine Holland cloth, straining against his muscles.

"We shall create many beautiful children. We have time aplenty, our entire lives ahead of us. Oh, my darling." He stroked her hair. "I want to give you all the love in my heart."

"You are truly one of a kind, Matthew." And she knew he was. In a land of political alliances secured by wedding vows, love was as rare as spun gold. He held her tightly, and she'd never known such comfort and safety as in this man's arms. She returned his embrace and let his warmth seep into her.

He caressed her arms with his fingertips and slowly met her lips. She responded to his penetrating warmth. Closing her eyes, she pressed her body to his.

Her lips tingled from that teasing, too-short kiss as her fingers laced round his neck. She pulled him back down to her. Searching his lips, desperate to reclaim them, she begged, "Matthew, I want you now..."

He cut off her words with another demanding kiss as his mouth covered hers.

He removed her raiment piece by piece, more quickly than she could have done herself. In an instant, he was naked, beside her. His hands touched her everywhere at once, gently at first, then more probing and urgent as she responded. As her fingers explored, she sensed his urgency. She pulled him closer, to fuse his body with hers, in hers. But he stopped. She caught her breath. Volcanos erupted everywhere he'd touched her. He reached over to the table next to them and grabbed a small white jar. He opened the lid and waved it under her nose like a perfume bottle. She detected the faint aroma of mint.

"What is it?" Desperately wanting him to touch her again, she rotated her hips towards him.

He lowered himself to her side. "A special mixture of honey, herbs, and oils of hyacinth and sunflower, and will ease your pain, for I must break your maidenhead." He spread it over her breasts, down her stomach and twixt her thighs. It got warmer to the touch, and hotter still when he ran his tongue over where he'd creamed her. Her body a pillar of fire, her breaths came ragged and gasping as he pulled back and sat upright.

The delicate fragrance whirling round them, he laid her on her back once more. She wrapped herself round his body and eased him in, bit by bit. As he probed against her maidenhead, she thought again of the son she so longed for. *A brief pain tonight is a small price to pay for a future I deserve,* she reasoned. Then all reasoning gave way as Topaz slid her hands down the length of his back, gripped the taut flesh of his buttocks, and pressed him to her. As he breached the barrier, and they rocked against each other until they exploded together in a fit of passionate agony.

They lay touching on the soft pillows, her hand stroking his damp body. His solid muscles were the product of many years of vigorous athletic training. She opened her eyes and admired his powerful and commanding physique, smooth as marble and graceful in movement.

"Are you breeding yet, my lady?" He kissed the tip of her nose.

* * *

Kenilworth Castle, August, 1513

"Bring hot water, linens aplenty, and make haste, Topaz is about to birth!" Amethyst whirled round from her bedside vigil and ordered the chambermaids as Topaz's groans became high-pitched wails of agony.

"'Tis all right, love, the midwife is on her way, I can hear the hoof-beats now." Amethyst pulled the drapery aside and peered out the window facing the inner courtyard. There she could see Mistress Ellen dismounting. A servant now guided her through the front entrance. "She's here!" Almost afraid to look, Amethyst forced herself to turn and face her sister, to help her in this most crucial time. Even though she knew naught of the birthing process, she wanted Topaz to know she was by her side. Sabine propped Topaz up on goosedown pillows, her chambermaid running a cloth over her face, pushing back damp strands of hair.

"Here, I'll do that." Amethyst took the cloth from the maid and dipped it in the bowl of cool water. She looked down at her sister's face, devoid of the radiance that always graced her complexion. "There, there, is that better?" she soothed, trying to steady her trembling hand as her sister's cries of agony intensified.

"Oh, Jesu, it feels like I'm being torn... apaaaart!"

Though her sister's pain hurt as if it were her own, Amethyst couldn't help but wonder if a tiny bit of theatrics enhanced the scene—Topaz was the sister most gifted with the dramatic flair, after all.

Mistress Ellen burst through the door, ordered a fresh bowl of water and soap, and laid her black bag on the table next to the bed. She approached Topaz, swallowed up in that cloud of pillows and sheets. She sprinkled wallflower juice on the linens, to ease childbirth pain. That must have done it, because at that instant the midwife announced the appearance of the child's head.

"Take our hands!" Amethyst demanded above Topaz's screams. She squeezed Amethyst's fingers so tightly she thought the bones would break. In an instant, Topaz relaxed her grip and with a sigh, threw her head back on the pillows and laughed weakly, taking in deep breaths.

"You have a son, Lady Topaz," announced Mistress Ellen from the foot of the bed. At Amethyst's first sight of her nephew, the midwife held him by the feet, a bloody blue-red form covered with a glossy sheen. The midwife wiped him down, and the pinkish hue of healthy flesh emerged along with a loud squalling cry. Amethyst heaved a sigh of relief.

"Oh, he's just lovely, Topaz. Your son is just lovely. He's got a head of thick coppery hair, just like you!" she praised her sister, smoothing her sweat-soaked hair back.

"His name is Edward," Topaz whispered, so faintly that only Amethyst could hear. "Edward Plantagenet, King Edward the Sixth." She then turned her head away, and with a languorous smile, drifted off into oblivion.

* * *

Warwick Castle, Christmas, 1516

Sabine held her first grandson in her arms and swept through the great hall, watching the servants readying the castle for the holiday festivities. This Christmas would be like none other—King Henry VIII and his court were coming to spend the holidays! She placed little Edward on the floor and watched him toddle towards his pet cat. *He is so much like my Edward, who never lived to see his youngest daughter,* Sabine thought, unhealed grief bearing down on her heart. Now here was his first grandson, his namesake, that same deep brown hair laced with threads of gold, those same blue eyes, the dimple indenting his left cheek.

Amethyst entered the great hall carrying a necklace dripping with sapphires. "Mother, do you think this is too fancy to wear in front of King Henry? After all, we do not want to outshine Queen Catherine."

Sabine laughed. "I'm sure you will not, my dear. However, I hear the queen is very pious, and does not wear her jewels whilst on progress. Wear it if you wish. I trust the king will have much else to do than spend more than a few moments in polite conversation with you lasses anyway."

Amethyst lowered her head, her lips drawn tight. "But I so hoped he would listen to me play the song I wrote for him."

"If time permits, dear, we shall see."

"If only Father were here to meet the king." Amethyst seemed to have read Sabine's mood. Sabine gazed about the great hall, at the paneled walls, the ceiling that rose two stories, the galleries above. A stab of remorse shot through her, for her Edward had left here at age eight, never to return. But she knew he watched over on his grandson from heaven, enjoying every moment of the child's life here and at Kenilworth.

"How long will they stay, Mother?" Amethyst fastened her necklace and smoothed the blue stones over her chest.

"Just 'til New Year's Day." She followed little Edward as he skittered after his cat. "These royal progresses are very carefully planned, and they will be moving on to another noble's domain."

"Kenilworth mayhap?" Amethyst caught up with her nephew and knelt, taking his little hands in hers.

"God forbid." Sabine feared for her eldest daughter and her treasonable beliefs. "Windsor Castle will probably be their last visit on this progress, as the roads will be impassible ere too long. We've been lucky so far in that the winter's been mild, but it should be in like a lion soon."

"I trust his majesty will be spending much of his time with Aunt Margaret." Amethyst remembered Margaret's titters of delight when she broke yet another royal seal and unrolled one of many letters from the king, chirping, "His majesty says I'm 'the most saintly woman in England!' "

"I can't help but wonder if that was because Margaret had sent Cardinal Wolsey five thousand marks for the king's wars with France." Sabine knelt next to Amethyst and gathered Edward in her arms. "'Tis a saintly enough sum indeed. 'Tis good, though, the mutual admiration is still going strong as ever, and Margaret carries her newly acquired title and riches with aplomb, I must say. We've all got to stay in the king's good graces, my dear."

As they both stood, Amethyst understood the unspoken message in her mother's tone. She worried about Topaz, too. Topaz had her young son so convinced that his name was Prince Edward, 'prince' had been the child's very first word.

"The entire shire is buzzing with news of the king's visit here, Mother." Amethyst's throat constricted with excitement even after yet another sip of mead from the sideboard. "They'll all be trampling upon us like an invasion!"

Sabine smiled, cooing at her beloved grandbaby, and Amethyst could see her own excitement reflected in her mother's eyes. "Just consider our family very fortunate, my dear. A visit from court is a great honor."

"As much as I'm going to miss having Topaz here, in a way I'm glad she's staying with Matthew at Kenilworth. Who knows what kind of trouble she would stir up if she got on her high horse." Amethyst sipped her mead, licking the sweetness from her lips.

With the squirming Edward in tow, Sabine swept through the hall, heading for the door. "Oh, I don't think Topaz would dare cross the king. I'm sure she wouldn't want to see history repeated."

Amethyst put down her goblet, but on second thought, she refilled it one more time.

* * *

By mid-December the lower-ranked courtiers began trickling in—the jesters, privy chamber attendants, clerks of the wardrobe, queen's maid of honor and ladies-in-waiting, the king's Yeomen of the Guard.

Amethyst stood at the top of Guy's Tower at the southeast corner of the castle, searching the snow-blanketed landscape for any sign of the royal party's train of carriages. She hugged her cloak about her and pulled her ermine hat over her ears to block the icy wind whipping round the tower. Up here she enjoyed the sweeping view of Warwickshire, the winding River Avon and the surrounding countryside. Scattered among the spiky tree branches, the timber-framed houses of the adjoining villages stood bunched together as if huddled against the cold, thin streams of smoke trailing from their chimneys. Where the fallen snow had thinned, parcels of land were strewn with patches of brown. The sun offered a grayish tinge of light.

About to turn and go back inside, she glimpsed a gilded flash and heard a wheel squeak. The head of the procession lumbered towards the castle grounds, a parade of stallions draped in cloth of gold. Although the majority of the party had already arrived, this procession trailed on and on, snaking up the hill. She wondered if there would be enough food after all, for the party already numbered in the hundreds. When the gold-trimmed royal carriage reached the foot of Guy's Tower, Amethyst turned, ran along the rampart walk, down the winding staircase, and caught her breath at the bottom, forcing puffs of steam from her lungs.

As the procession entered the gatehouse, she ran across the courtyard and up to her chamber. Her maids fitted her with a much too cumbersome headdress, but in the presence of royalty, a sheer necessity. Ribbed bands of silk covered her forehead and let wisps of her hair show through. She pulled on her satin waistcoat, embroidered with seed pearls, over a purple satin gown. Round her waist she wrapped a beaded belt terminating in a silver pendant lined with rubies.

Checking herself once more in the looking glass, she twirled round in a rustle and swish of rich satins.

She quit her chamber and searched the private apartments for her mother and Emerald. "They're here!" she blasted the news when she found her mother in her chamber, her maid of honor securing Sabine's headdress.

With one more glance in the looking glass and a deep calming breath that did naught to soothe her jittery nerves, she raised her head and strode down the corridor, ready to meet her king.

* * *

Amethyst stood at the entrance of the crowded great hall. Her eyes landed on the magnificent figure. *Oh, Jesu, there he is.* She swallowed, her parched throat desperate for a sip of liquid. She stepped inside and took her first longing gaze at King Henry since he swept by her in Westminster Abbey. A page presented her to Queen Catherine first. From her pyramidal head-dress lined with diamonds to her purple robe turned up at the sleeves displaying ermine, she carried all the grace of royalty. Amethyst returned Catherine's smile with a practiced curtsey. She then faced the king. She dared to look into his eyes once again, those clear gold orbs, that playfulness yielding just a bit to maturity. A smile produced matching dimples in his cheeks. He nodded in recognition, yet his eyes questioned, as if he'd seen her before, but not knowing where. Those eyes sparkled with a lustre matching his cloth of gold doublet, trimmed with sable, the open front displaying a French chemay underneath. The shirt, open at his neck, exposed a mat of red-gold chest hair. The skirted doublet gave way to the sturdy legs adorned with slashed breeches to the knee, his hose woven with gold threads. His fashionable leather duckbill shoes showed gold silk within the slashings of the leather, gold hose peeking out. Diamonds adorned the slashings. Dazzling her, he sparkled from head to toe.

"Your grace, welcome to Warwick Castle." As she curtsied low, he held out his hand. It was large, yet graceful and slender, with fingers that could compel a keyboard into an exquisite blend of harmony, fingers that could run rivers through a harp…

She rose and grasped his fingertips. She and her king, that illusory object of her fancies, touched for the first time.

He smiled, obviously pleased at his adoring subject. "Lady Amethyst, the Lady Sabine tells me you are quite a talented lutist and organist." His light and amicable voice eased her. She let out a breath she didn't know she'd been holding.

Her hand still tingled where he'd touched it. She opened her mouth to reply, nodded and cleared her throat. "Oh, yes, your grace. I would enjoy performing for your grace during your visit, as I've composed several songs for the occasion." She hadn't meant to blurt it all out at once. But at this point she was beyond thinking, her mouth and brain two separate entities.

"We would be pleased. It would be an appropriate accent to these splendid festivities."

As the king moved on, she realized how cold and stiff her fingers were. She cringed in embarrassment, hoping he hadn't noticed. She scurried over to the fire and warmed her trembling hands.

The festivities began in earnest the next day. Servers cut the Yule log, and the king with the immediate members of his party attended Mass in the chapel along with Amethyst, Sabine and Emerald. Later they enjoyed masques, miming, songs and joking jesters and fools. The great hall glowed under thousands of candles in their talons fixed in the chandeliers above. Fine linen draped the royal dais, set with plates and goblets of gold. Fires blazed in the hearths. Minstrels played lively tuned in the loft overlooking the great hall. To Amethyst, this was the next best thing to actually being at court. Warwick Castle glittered like a palace, graced by royalty. She wished she'd been born into such splendor.

The king invited Amethyst to join the King's Musick, the company of court musicians, for a few pieces. Thirty members of the current

King's Musick made up the company: lutists playing the treble lute, the larger archlute, a theorbo and cittern. It included a harpist; a recorder and hornpipe player; two clarions; three musicians each playing the virginals; a dulcimer; three viola-da-gambas; two viols; and a rebec. The gallery also had a clavichord. Amethyst doubled as the clavichordist, and thrilled at its somber strains that echoed and swirled through the great hall.

When the king signaled his chief steward to begin the meal, the party took to the tables and feasted. Servers brought game upon gold trays: venison, crane, quail, duck, rabbit, goose, seafood: oysters, crayfish, prawns, and the king's favorite, baked lampreys. They washed this down with wine, and indulged in an array of sweets featuring a sugar sculpture of Warwick Castle.

When the servers cleared all that away, the dancing began. Amethyst flexed her fingers, stood up from the clavichord and came down to watch the courtiers dance to the sprightly tunes from the loft. She swayed and hummed to the music. Oh, how she wished someone, anyone, would ask her to dance...the thought of dancing with the king crossed her mind and she chided herself. How absurd! He led out the first dance with Queen Catherine in a pavane. Amethyst couldn't take her eyes off the king's strong leg muscles as he led the queen round the floor. The King's Musick then played a few motets composed by the king himself.

He now danced with Lady Margaret, bantering as they pranced along. Margaret had no trouble keeping up with the energetic king, and he led her back to her seat.

Then he crossed the great hall, taking long strides, closer, closer. She blinked to make sure this wasn't a dream. He approached her, reaching for her hand. Her heart simply stopped.

The music swirled round them and the candles' glow spun over her head, a galaxy of dazzling suns. "Would you care to dance, Lady Amethyst?"

"I—I—" she stammered, clearing her throat. *Come on, voice, don't quit me now!* "I would be honored, your grace, but my dancing leaves much to be desired."

"Simply follow me, then." His smile lit up the entire great hall.

As their hands touched, hot blood rushed through her veins. They moved together so naturally, as one with the music. His sense of rhythm and timing flowed through to her. The music captured their souls, aiding the spark already glowing between them. They danced and enjoyed each other as two young people sharing their love of music and movement.

When the music ended, he released her, his eyes twinkling in the candles' glow. "Thank you, my dear, you are quite the dancer. A superb array of talents." He excused himself, leaving her there, rooted to the floor in a daze.

* * *

The following day, a page brought Amethyst a message to her chambers. King Henry wanted her to meet him in the conservatory for a musical afternoon! She lunged for her lute, her music, and asked her chambermaid to lay out her burgundy velvet gown with the rabbit-trimmed square neckline. Simple and elegant, it wasn't flashy enough for eveningwear, just appropriate to join the king for an afternoon.

He had not yet arrived when she entered the conservatory. Of course, why would a king sit waiting for a subject? Protocol demanded that she arrive first. She spent the next few moments tuning her lute and practicing scales on the virginals with cold trembling fingers.

The door opened and he then joined her, alone, without an entourage, dressed in a cream chemay under a satin doublet, with velvet breeches and silk hose. He was completely devoid of jewels except for a square ruby ring on his thumb. He greeted Amethyst, commented on the lovely weather, and took his harp from its velvet-lined case. "I would play a little ditty I wrote whilst riding here to Warwick."

"You wrote a song upon your horse?" she marveled. "How do you compose without an instrument, my lord?"

"'Tis nothing." He shrugged. "The notes enter my head, the melody plays to me over and over, and by the time I can sit down to a sheet of parchment, I can write them down. There is no need for an instrument. Not 'til the actual playing."

"That is magnificent, my lord." She shook her head in wonder. "I cannot compose without the instrument."

"Ah, mayhap you shall learn." He gave her a glance and a smile. "Try it. All gifted musicians have the ability. Do you not ever have melodies playing through your head?"

"Oh, all the time!" She nodded. "Especially in dreams. Beautiful melodies visit me in my dreams. But I awaken and forget them so quickly. It would never occur to me to write them down."

"Try it next time," he suggested. "Keep parchment and pen by your bed. Write the notes down whilst they are still in your head."

"I shall try that, sire. I always had the desire to compose. I simply didn't think I had the ability."

He positioned his fingers on his harp and she noticed his ring didn't even touch the delicate strings. The harmonic strains of his simple tune filled the room. She began strumming chords with her plectrum, accompanying his melody. The strains blended, creating a complete tonal consonance that only musicians completely in tune with each other could deliver. His eyes closed and on he played, swaying with the music, a dreamlike expression on his face. His entire being became one with the instrument. On they played together, exchanging each other's music, adding notes here and there, changing a chord or two. He accompanied her on the harp while she played the virginals. She was especially proud of her singing voice, a clear sharp soprano, and prided herself on her ability to sing such high notes. A resonant baritone himself, the king harmonized with her beautifully, just as she had dreamed so long ago! To sit with the king and share her love for music...this was more of an honor that any titles or riches.

Later they sat on the plush chairs facing the windows overlooking the River Avon. "Now that we're aware we can share the language of music so well, what about a verbal exchange?" the king challenged.

Oh, she was up for this matching of wits. She wanted so badly to show off her years of tutoring. "On what topic do you wish to engage in discourse, your grace?" Besides horticulture, science and philosophy, would King Henry ask her feelings about being the daughter of a murdered heir to the throne?

"Have you any prospects of marriage?" That shot twixt the eyes caught her off guard.

She'd expected him to start with something superficial—her Latin studies or even her knowledge of Greek, but not this!

"Why, nay, your grace. I would like to continue my studies for a bit longer before I consider marriage. We have had wonderful tutors, several from Harrow and Eton. I so enjoy learning, about philosophy and science arithmetic because I enjoy numbers, but most of all I prefer music. 'Tis so much like arithmetic, the way the quarter-notes and half-notes all must add up to fit the time signature, the number of beats you must put in each measure. 'Tis very much a blend of body and soul."

"Aye, Lady Amethyst, 'tis a harmonious blend of science and art, but one need not be a scientist to enjoy it." He gave her a sly grin.

"So, with all my studies, attending services at five a.m. and falling into bed quite tired at night, I have not given much thought to a *parti*. I would finish one chapter ere opening another."

Now his grin brightened his eyes. Yet he had not a wrinkle. "Quite wise, Lady Amethyst. One or two more years will not hurt. Although my Queen Catherine was but sixteen when she married my departed brother Arthur, and royals are known to be betrothed virtually at birth, a matter of necessity. I always relished the idea of marriage following love, instead of the other way round."

"Aye, your grace." Very noble, indeed. Almost the same words spoken by Topaz. But coming from Henry, it seemed to have more credibility.

"I trust you will find a suitable *parti*, Lady Amethyst. For your dowry chest must be quite generous," he commented, as if he didn't know.

"Oh, aye, your grace. Thanks to you and your kind benevolences, having given us back...er, giving us Warwick Castle," she corrected herself.

"Aye, your grandfather might have been king," he admitted. "But I am king and I must do my best. You see, Lady Amethyst, my father ran the realm a different way than I. He won the crown by fighting. A poor, struggling pretender, he virtually plucked it from the head of Richard's corpse. I came into it in my own right. I was born to be king. If only it could have been that simple through history, had the crown been passed from father to son through the ages, instead of having been snatched through subterfuge and wars, it would have been so much simpler. Then again, I wouldn't be king at all." He chuckled, as if being king were just another occupation, like tinsmithing.

Oh, would Topaz have loved to hear that, she thought.

"My father selected his councilors for their loyalty instead of military prowess," he explained. "His was the last reign of his kind, and I plan to be known as the first king of what I like to call modern times. The Dark Ages are over, Amethyst. This is the rebirth...the renaissance, if you will."

"I am glad, your grace." She was proud of her ability to sustain eye contact with him and not turn to blubbering mush. "I would marry a man for love, rather than the union of our lands."

"And what of your sister?" His brow cocked in curiosity.

"Oh, Emerald is only—"

He cut her off. "Nay, your older sister, Topaz."

She hoped he wouldn't ask. Oh, if only he'd forgotten Topaz even existed. "She lives at Kenilworth with her husband Matthew Gilford. She runs an animal hospital and distributes alms to the poor."

"Ah, yes, Gilford, Duke of Lancaster." He broke eye contact and glanced out the window. "His father fought beside mine at Bosworth. Kenilworth and the title were granted to him at that time."

Topaz didn't seem to care how her husband's magnificent castle, lands, and title had been attained. As long as there was ample room for her animals.

"Topaz has a boy, Edward, named after our father," she informed him, not sure he knew every time a subject birthed another.

"Pray God he won't follow in your father's footsteps," he quipped. That was still a very touchy subject in her family, and she was surprised the king chose to jest about it. Yet that was just one of the things that enchanted her about him. His ability to laugh—at just about anything.

"I pray for the same, your grace." Oh, did she! Pray God Topaz had mellowed with the rearing of her son and the running of the castle and her animals and abandoned her so-called quest. "I believe Edward will become a faithful subject, as will my sons and daughters."

"Indeed. Well, my Lady, I must bid you Godspeed for now, for we must prepare for the New Year's festivities on the morrow and the journey back to London." He stood, took her hand in his, pressed his lips to it and released it. As he turned to leave, she curtsied, awestruck with this private audience, bursting to tell her mother and Emerald all about it.

As the king swept out of the room, she touched her hand to her lips, at the very place where he'd kissed her. She gazed out over the Avon, seeing nothing, only the delicate strains of his music running through her head.

* * *

On New Year's Day the entire household gathered in the great hall. With the king's gracious permission, Sabine collected all the servants, from her Maids of Honor to the stablehands, and they were granted the honor of spending a few hours in the king's presence. Sabine had gotten them all gifts, and they were distributed before the king and queen's arrival. When the royal retinue arrived, they exchanged gifts with Sabine and the girls. The king had presented them all with necklaces–pear shaped diamonds suspended on gold chains of varying lengths–the longest with the biggest diamond for Sabine, and gradually smaller sizes for the girls. They presented the king with a solid gold replica of the key to Warwick Castle's main gate mounted on a plaque depicting the Warwickshire arms of the bear and ragged staff. "This represents our eternal gratitude for granting us this land, your grace," Sabine told the king upon presentation of the key. "Warwick Castle will always be your home as it is ours."

He gracefully accepted the gift, kissing Sabine's hand.

"God willing, we shall meet again, Lady Amethyst." Henry took her hand as the retinue prepared to depart for London the following day. She curtsied, his cloak a flash of glitter as she dipped down and back up again.

"I look forward to it, sire." She tried to keep the quiver out of her voice. She wanted to say more, but he'd already moved on, for there were many good-byes to be said, and when the castle emptied of the retinue, her heart hit a bottom as hard as the stone floor. This brief taste of court life had been her most magnificent experience. *Oh, yes, this is the life I long for,* she sighed. But alas it wasn't her destiny.

Chapter Four

Warwick Castle, January, 1517

"So you met Henry then?" Topaz gave a disinterested sniff as she and Amethyst watched little Edward chase a butterfly through Warwick Castle's rose garden. They hadn't seen each other since before court visited the castle at Christmas. Edward, now a spirited, energetic three-year-old, looked like a miniature adult in his blue breeches and doublet, tiny gold buttons marching down his little breast.

"Aye, he was just fascinating. A marvelous dancer, superb musician, so easy to talk to..."

"He talked to you?" Topaz stopped in her tracks and pushed a lock of hair off her forehead. Amethyst peered through the cedars to watch Edward rolling in the grass, yanking clover out of the ground, chewing on it and spitting it out.

"Aye, we had a lovely chat. We even played music together, in the conservatory, just the two of us."

"How cozy." The breeze stirred the fragrance of roses. Topaz caressed one of the petals. "What could he possibly have found to talk with you about?"

"We talked about music mostly. His love for music is even greater than mine. We had a musical afternoon. We harmonized beautifully together," she gushed.

"Aye, so I heard the king has been known to harmonize with many ladies, but not necessarily in the musical sense." Topaz cast her a narrow-eyed sideways glance.

"The king's private affairs are none of ours," Amethyst said. "He is a modern man. He told me we should marry for love."

"Ha!" Topaz laughed without a smile. "That's a joke! Only because he wishes he will someday."

"Why?" Amethyst studied her sister's face, her brows knitted in ire. "Do you not believe he loves the Queen Catherine?"

"Surely you jest, Amethyst. He marries his brother's widow for an alliance with Spain and he talks about love." She sneered. "There is some talk that he isn't even legally married to Catherine, she being Arthur's widow."

"Oh, Topaz." Amethyst threw her hands up. "Where do you get such absurd ideas?"

"'Tis a well-known fact. The Pope erred in granting them a dispensation to marry. Therefore, they've never been married in the eyes of God. He is a bachelor and the Princess Mary is a bastard, just like his son by that whore Bessie Blount," Topaz stated, grabbing Edward's arm before he scampered away.

Amethyst gasped, openmouthed, at the cocky grin curling Topaz's lips. "Topaz, you may talk like this with me, for I am your own sister and I shall never let your words go farther than the two of us, but if anyone ever hears you speaking of the king like this—"

"'Tis no secret, Amethyst. God's truth, the man is not the Almighty. He's a man, a mere mortal. And mortals make mistakes. He'll make many more, no doubt, before he departs this earth." She straightened Edward's jacket. "Tell Auntie Amethyst all about the king."

Edward, his tiny fist full of daisies, thrust the flowers at Amethyst. She accepted her gift and breathed in their earthy aroma.

"The king is not really married to the queen," Edward recited in his high-pitched, yet carefully articulated voice.

"And what is the Princess Mary?" Topaz goaded.

"The Princess Mary is a bastard," Edward nearly sang.

"And why is she a bastard?" she coached.

"Because his marriage to Queen Catherine is a sham. The king longs for a male heir but is cursed with a female bastard." The boy giggled and as his another butterfly captured his attention, he sprinted off, a powder blue bundle of energy.

Amethyst shook her head in dismay. That wasn't her nephew talking. That was Topaz, talking through him, feeding his mind with this vile scandal about the king. She feared for his life as she thought of their innocent father locked in the Tower for life, nary a harsh word about any king ever passing his lips.

"Topaz, how could you?" she berated her sister. "How could you teach that boy all those things?"

"He knows of what he speaks, Amethyst." Topaz plucked a red rose from the vine and ran it down her neck, crushing it twixt her breasts. "He knows who he is."

* * *

Topaz gave birth to Richard George in November of 1518. Once again, Amethyst and Sabine both attended the birth, at Topaz's insistence. Yet this birth went much more smoothly, as if Topaz knew what to expect. She'd mastered the breathing techniques, the rhythmic pushing and bearing down, and brought forth a beautiful eight- pound boy. Just like his brother, a shock of copper hair crowned his head and his first squall of life could have been heard in the far reaches of Scotland.

"Richard George Plantagenet Gilford, Duke of Lancaster," Topaz recited in a resonant voice, so unlike her weak yet determined proclamation of Edward's name upon his delivery.

"Aye, Topaz, a lovely name." Amethyst smoothed Topaz's hair off her forehead. She turned to watch the midwife wash her new nephew.

"Richard after our mother's father, George after our father's father!" Topaz proclaimed.

Edward, of course, had been named for their father. He bore no middle name. He was simply Edward.

* * *

When Topaz completed her confinement, she fetched the leather-bound journal from her writing desk, a pen and some ink. The pen scratched across the pages just as they had when she began recording her thoughts at age 8.

"Now that my two heirs are upon this earth, the succession is secured. I shall engage Henry's enemies and begin my quest for the throne. And what a queen I shall be. I shall lift the heavy tax burden from my good subjects and distribute the Crown's fortune among the poor, the fortune hoarded away by the miserly old Henry Tudor, the profits he extorted under his false pretenses, the riches he reaped by digging up breaches of forgotten laws, the seizure of the property of his political offenders, my own father included!

I shall shorten working hours for the peasants and their children so that they will have time for learning. They may learn medicine to heal the sick of plague and sweat. They may learn law, to uphold justice throughout the land. They may learn drama, poetry and music, so that they may sing and dance and spend their leisure hours on refined entertainment. They may learn economics, to engage in equitable commerce, trade fairly, and watch their hoards grow into comfortable sums.

The prison will be a tolerable place to repent, a place to reform and prepare those convicted for another chance to live among society, to be treated like human

beings, a much more effective deterrent to crime than torture.

There will be wine and ale for everyone, and at the same time, no one will be fat and overfed, like these royal pigs who stuff their faces to corpulence with the flesh of the deer that roam the wild forests... the forests will once again belong to the animals and the lands shall belong to the people. My realm will love me and my son after me, King Edward the Sixth.

She clapped the book shut as Edward's governess brought him into the bedchamber. Tall and lanky, he stood straight, chin up, shoulders back.

He moved not with that gawky movement of four-year-olds whose undeveloped muscles undermined them, but with the grace and pomp of a man–a future king.

"And have you beheld your baby brother today, Edward?"

"Aye, Mother, he sleeps." The boy strode up to her for a hug. "He is such a quiet pup."

"So unlike his brother," Topaz laughed, reaching out to hug her son her heir.

"And what do you want to be when you grow up?" she asked him, as his tutor asked all the children, sons and daughters of nobles and gentry, who invariably answered, "Liege of many lands," or "Healer of the sick." Only one boy answered, "I shall be king."

* * *

Warwick Castle, June, 1524

Amethyst led her nephew Edward around the stablegrounds on his new pony. Upon the small compact animal sat the tall and lanky Edward, his feet stuffed into the stirrups, the reins wound round his long fingers. The pony was her seventh birthday present to him. Topaz nearly fainted when she saw her son mount the beast, but Amethyst checked her annoyance and chided her sister. "God's foot, Topaz, you were riding the back of the Royal Menagerie's camel when you were but a four-year-old. Why are you so worried about Edward?"

"Because he's my first-born son, and I don't want any accidents at his delicate age," she retorted, biting her nails.

"'Tis a pony, not a wild stallion. A sweet, gentle pony. What would you name him, Edward?"

"Oh, 'tis a him? I would name her Princess Mary if he were a girl." Edward stroked the pony's mane.

"Name him that anyway," Topaz scoffed. "I hear the bastard princess has a voice as deep as a well. She must get her masculine features from her mother."

Amethyst wanted to box her sister's ears for continuing this badgering of the Tudors in front of the children, but she did her best to stay out of it and not argue. She still harbored an odd respect for her sister for maintaining her belief, out of reverence for their father, but the family had long since given up trying. Reprimands, logic, and reasoning...all had failed.

Through the entrance of the stables Amethyst glimpsed a messenger riding towards the gatehouse. She recognized the royal livery, would know it anywhere. "'Tis a message from the king!" She broke into a run to meet him.

She stopped him halfway to the gatehouse. Remaining on his mount, he handed her a note embossed with the royal seal. "For Lady Amethyst from his majesty the king," he stated. The king had recently taken to being called "your majesty" as introduced by Cardinal Wolsey, a title to suit a monarch, as Wolsey felt "your grace" was beneath the king's dignity.

"I am Lady Amethyst." She broke the seal.

"The king wishes a reply by Tuesday week."

"A reply?" She tore into the parchment. The messenger began to rear his mount and begin his return journey.

"Wait!" she summoned him, and he halted the horse. "I can give you an answer right now. Tell his majesty I would be honored to attend court for his thirtieth birthday festivities. I shall be there." A sharp thrill sent a tremor through her as she ran her fingers over the creamy royal parchment. She imagined the glow of a thousand candles above her head as she and her king danced over the great hall's gleaming floor, lavishly dressed courtiers following her every leap and dip with overt admiration, her satin skirts rustling, her diamonds and pearls glittering...

"Aye, Lady Amethyst." The messenger touched the corner of his hat and trotted off.

Topaz and Edward, minus the pony, approached her. "Where's the pony?" Amethyst asked.

"Being bathed and perfumed." Topaz pinched her nose with thumb and forefinger. "He was rather ripe. So what does Bluff Prince Hal have to say for himself? More castles and titles await us? Or does he wish to reverse the attainder against our dead grandfather this time?"

"Nay, Topaz, 'tis an invitation to court for his thirtieth birthday." She held it up like a priceless artifact.

Topaz twirled round to face the stables, her back to Amethyst. "I shall not attend."

Amethyst was glad her sister couldn't see the smile brightening her face.

"I expect that would suit the king just fine, because it seems you were not invited, as was no one else in the family except mayhap Aunt Margaret, who is already there," she informed her sister's back.

Topaz faced Amethyst and fingered her delicate necklace of daisies interwoven with honeysuckle. "He invites you alone? What must he have on his mind, the lecher? Does he wish to make another addition to his harem?"

"'Tis nothing of the sort, Topaz." Amethyst fanned herself with the letter. "Your imagination is simply wild. He's celebrating his birthday and invites a representative of our family there to celebrate the occasion with him."

"Thirty, eh? The old toad is getting on in years." Topaz smirked. "Past his prime, I daresay. Growing older and feebler every day, and still without an heir."

"He wished for an heir and was cursed with two bastards!" Edward piped up.

Amethyst could stand it no longer. "Edward, listen to what Aunt Amethyst has to say and I never want you to forget it." She knelt till she was at eye level with her nephew. "Whatever you say about the king and Princess Mary in the privacy of your own home is your own business, but whilst standing on the grounds of Warwick Castle, do not ever speak ill of them again. I absolutely forbid it! And that goes for you, too, Topaz." She looked up at her sister, glaring down at her, the sun blazing behind her head.

But Topaz's glare vanished as she laughed it off. "That is your problem, not mine. Do becalm yourself, sister. He is but a child."

"A child with a poisoned mind at that, who will grow up to be an adult with a poisoned mind, and doomed to follow his grandfather's fate serving out his days for treason." She stood and faced Topaz with her dire warning.

"Never!" Topaz clenched her fists.

"Think what you will, sister, but mark my words, you are asking for trouble," she repeated her warning.

"And what will you do? Arrive at court and ask the king to sign our death warrants?" Topaz challenged.

"I need not. You are doing quite a good job of it yourself." Amethyst excused herself and crossed the drawbridge, deciding which gowns to bring on her trip.

* * *

Court convened at Windsor this summer after an exhausting progress through the shires, yet preparations for the king's birthday betrayed not one bit of weariness. Amethyst met him in the great hall the night of her arrival, three days before his birthday. She hadn't been invited to sit on the royal dais at dinnertime, but renewed their acquaintance after the minstrel show.

She approached and curtsied, her eyes roving over the athletic physique. Once again he glittered. His torso narrowed to the hips, the shoulders square and commanding under the doublet lined with diamonds, rubies, and emeralds. The crimson velvet cloak flowed from him with fluid grace. Silver-striped black hose adorned his legs. Glowing pearls lined his collar. His arms carried the slashed sleeves regally. He captured the light of each candle.

"'Tis a pleasure to meet you again, sire. Thank you ever so much for inviting me to share in these festivities." Her voice wobbled with excitement.

"'Tis a pleasure to see you again, Lady Amethyst. How fares Warwickshire?"

"It fares well, your majesty..." She began telling him of the harvest that had given way to the harsh winter, and as the conversation droned on, she beheld him. He showed not one sign of aging since she saw him last. His golden eyes sparkled. His skin glowed. His presence engulfed her; even if he were not the king, he would be the handsomest man in the realm. No man upheld himself with such grace and confidence.

"...and Mary is getting to be quite a bright child, she already speaks Latin..." He bragged about his daughter, but Amethyst stayed busy studying his features. A bit of golden stubble grazed his upper lip and chin. His exquisitely shaped lips curved, faintly amused. He lifted his hand and swept back a red-gold lock from his forehead. She couldn't stop staring at those hands, those slender fingers...how warm they'd felt in hers...

Although her voice betrayed her exhilaration, she was thankful that she was not trembling outwardly. Her poise verified her passage from blushing adolescence to womanhood, a titled lady of nobility with enough aplomb to keep a king's interest.

"And have you composed any songs brought to you with midnight inspiration?" he asked.

"Oh, aye, your majesty! I did as you suggested, kept some parchment by my bed, and when an idea for a melody came to me in the night, I wrote it down hastily at the virginals the next day, and was able to embellish it and create a lovely arrangement."

"Mayhap you would like to play some of your original compositions for me whilst you visit here?" His invitation stunned her. Oh, another private audience!

"I would be honored, your majesty. Although...I doubt my music reaches the standard of your discernment. You are a much more accomplished musician."

"Alas, these days I have less time for simple pleasures such as music. Affairs of state prevail and I find myself in the Council chambers more often than in the conservatory. A responsible job, this is. A demanding and imposing job," he added, but not in a complaining manner. "So you have not become betrothed since we last met?"

She didn't want to change the subject; she would rather have talked about music all evening. But of course, this was part of his imposing job also; to secure the marriageability of the kingdom's young maidens.

"Nay, your majesty," she answered frankly. "Several gentlemen have courted me, but none have yet sparked my... " She groped for an appropriate word.

"Passion?"

"Heavens, no. I was alluding more to... interest, your majesty. Passion I've yet to encounter."

"Mayhap here at court, then, you will find a suitable *parti.* I assure you, there are many young gentlemen worthy of your rank and... interest, as you say." His eyes roved over her, lingering at her breasts. She blushed to her roots.

"I doubt it not, your majesty." But how could she even look in the direction of a mere earl or duke when in the presence of the handsomest and most vibrant man she'd ever met, who loved music more than she, who just happened to be king?

"Do you care to continue our musical interlude during your visit to court?" he repeated, as if he needed to.

"Aye, your majesty, there is nothing I would like better," rushed out in breathless ardor.

"Very well, then, meet me in my receiving chamber following Vespers tomorrow. It is where my attendants meet to pass the time, and from there we shall find a quiet, private corner in order to play music together. I trust that suits you, Lady Amethyst."

"It sounds grand." Making music with the king again—something like this happened only once in a lifetime, not twice.

Then she remembered. "My lute has not yet arrived with my baggage, your grace."

"Never you mind, Lady Amethyst." The king touched her cheek with his fingertips, ever so gently. She shivered at the unexpected meeting of their flesh. "All the necessary instruments will be provided."

The king watched her hair tumbling down her back like spun gold, the way her erect shoulders squared off and her softly rounded buttocks swayed under the shiny satin of her gown as she exited the great hall. *Oh, we shall make music together, my sweet Lady Amethyst,* he silently vowed, tongue moistening his lips with a desire bordering on possessiveness. *We shall, my innocent, young maiden of Warwickshire. Sweet music will be ours, to resonate in a thundering crescendo.*

* * *

The king did not appear in the great hall the next morn where she breakfasted with some members of the King's Musick. She hoped they would invite her to join their practice session this morning, so she would be well rehearsed for the private duet with Henry.

She sat quietly nibbling on a slice of honeyed bread, listening to the musicians' idle chatter.

"Is Bessie out of the king's good favor again?" Mark Smeaton, a young musician, asked around the table as he dug into another slab of plum cake.

"Aye, she has been in and out for the last fortnight..." Ned, the citternist, replied.

"You mean the king has been in and out..." Mark quipped, and a conspiratorial laughter echoed round the table.

"She saw Catherine and went running like she'd been shot from a longbow."

"Aye, she keeps her distance from Catherine!" giggled John, the hornpipe player.

Amethyst had heard Bessie Blount's name more times than any other since arriving at court, even among the servitors, and always in a tittering way.

"Why, they were together the day after he married the queen, but I was not here yet. This is just what I hear," Mark repeated the gossip.

"Aye, I was here," George the organist affirmed. "'Twas not the day after the wedding, though. 'Twas the day after the honeymoon ended.

All Catherine has to do is turn her back to go to the privy, and he takes the opportunity for a romp with Bessie."

"Bessie hasn't been his only playtoy," Mark added. "He had that Boleyn wench…"

"He had 'er, all right," John joked, a lusty smirk crossing his features.

They all broke into laughter, but Amethyst sat expressionless, not wanting to participate in this prattle about the king and his dalliances. It chipped away at her appetite. She forced down the last of her smoked bacon.

"If you mind it not…" Her voice, firm but pleasant, rose above the others, "I would be honored if you would let me sit in on your practice session today," she intoned, desperately wanting to change the subject. She did not mention the king's invitation to his private apartments; after hearing the way these courtiers gossiped, she didn't dare.

"Aye, we would be pleased," the older gentleman said, and the others nodded. "What instrument do you play?"

"Which one would you like me to play?" she offered. "I play them all…lute, virginals, flute, harp…"

"Stop right there!" Mark Smeaton interrupted, obviously impressed, for he finally put down the tankard of ale he'd been so relishing. "It looks as if we have a virtuoso on our hands!"

The others smiled warmly, and her smile blended right in, as a rush of true belonging warmed her heart.

* * *

After a delightful practice session, the group disbursed. A page guided her into the king's inner chamber and she took a velvet-cushioned seat. The oak paneled walls intimidated her with their dark and imposing regality. She stood and circled the room a few times, taking gulps of air to calm her breathing. The rapid thump of her heart reverberated through her body. Another private audience with the king—she hoped he didn't expect too much. After all, she was nowhere as accomplished a musician as he.

The Yeomen of the Guard parted the doors and the king entered the chamber, illuminating its atmosphere with his royal presence. He was a burst of radiance in his waistcoat of cloth of silver, quilted with black silk, the sleeves puffed with wavy slashes at the wrists, his breeches drawn out with taffeta, his stockings a dark red, tucked into black velvet shoes. He approached Amethyst and took her hand. "Come, Lady Amethyst."

He turned and she followed. Through a short corridor they walked, a row of flambeaux glowing along the walls. Their feet padded over an Oriental tapestry threaded with gold. She would never use such an exquisite work of art as a floor mat.

They stopped at an oak door which Henry opened with a key he'd pulled from his belt. He stood aside to let her enter the chamber. The leaded glass windows were pushed outward to the whistling birds in the tree outside. Voices and neighing horses floated up from the courtyard below. The cool evening breeze washed over her as she inhaled. The fading sunlight threw lacy shadows on the floor through the delicate artistry of the table legs. Around the corner she glimpsed the massive bed, its curtains open to the velvet covers and plush pillows. A pallet lay crosswise at the foot of the bed. *Good heavens,* she realized as if hit with lightning, *he's invited me into his bedchamber!*

Snatches of the musicians' conversation ran through her head... *All Catherine has to do is go to the privy, and he takes the opportunity for a romp with Bessie... Bessie hasn't been his only playtoy, he had that Boleyn wench...*

She stiffened. She had to quit this bedchamber before the entire kingdom began tattling behind her back. Oh, God, how it would hurt her family...

"Your majesty, I mustn't..." She turned to face him and nearly fell into his arms. He guided her to one of the chairs before the fireplace and they both sat.

"Be calm, Lady Amethyst, I do not bite."

She gathered her skirts and took a deep breath. He reached into a velvet-lined box and lifted out a gold rope on which was suspended a teardrop pearl. The chain glimmered as it caught the firelight, and the pearl radiated the milky glow of a midsummer's moon.

He walked round her and fastened it behind her neck. The pearl nestled twixt her breasts. She quivered with delight as his fingers brushed her skin.

"A welcome gift. Welcome to court."

The shimmery gold felt like silk against her skin. She lifted the pearl and as if on demand, it gave off a rainbow of glimmers as it rolled delicately twixt her fingertips.

"This is lovely, sire. Thank you ever so much."

"Just a token. A groom will be in shortly with some wine." He must have sensed her apprehension because he moved his chair a trifle back before sitting. "Amethyst, you are a lovely woman. There are so few of your kind here at court."

"So few lovely women or women in general, your majesty?" She wanted him to clarify that.

"Both. You know your Aunt Margaret Pole is the Princess Mary's governess. She tells me she misses her family deeply and would like if one of her nieces could join her. Amethyst, I would like you to come to court. To be a court musician, just as your mother was when you were but a child." He leaned forward, clasping his hands. "You were no doubt too young to remember, but I recall several state banquets at which your mother played her lute and sang for us. I was quite young myself, but I remember her serene voice and how her fingers made the strings dance."

That word, serene. Her mother's voice *was* serene. She'd been looking for that word all her life to describe her mother's lilting voice, its rich tones of melancholy shaping every phrase. Then his unexpected invitation registered in her mind and it all converged on her at once—the glitter of court pageantry, the sumptuous banquets, the lavish surroundings, but with that came closeness to the king, the reputed womanizer—but of course she would accept. She wouldn't dare refuse.

"Aye, I would love to join my dear Aunt Margaret and even get to know the Princess Mary," she blurted. "But you would invite me to be part of the King's Musick, your majesty? Only having heard me play but once?"

"Oh, I've never forgotten that day in your conservatory at Warwick. You didn't merely play, my dear." His eyes closed and a dreamy smile curved his lips. "That instrument became a part of you, you gave it a life of its own. There is a place at court for as long as your love for music prevails. You may take a journey back home to bid your family farewell, then I shall expect you back in a fortnight."

He commanded her so gently, she realized what made these wenches swoon under his spell. Who would dare refuse such a charming man!

"Why, that sounds lovely, your majesty. I would be honored to take the position."

A groom entered with a pitcher and two goblets on a tray and headed for the table behind them. He started to pour, but the king, in a barely visible gesture, waved him away. He stood and poured them each a gobletful.

She took a small, cautious sip, for she'd never had unwatered wine before. She knew wine was a respectable, elegant drink, meant to complement meals, enhance the taste of meats and fish, and create a heady glow. But this wine was not merely strong, it was downright pungent. It burned a column of fire through her body. Her cheeks flushed with its swelling warmth.

"Port, from Portugal. The very best." He sipped at his, luxuriating in its aroma and verve. She watched his tongue roll languorously around his mouth. He was surely a man who enjoyed life's sensual pleasures and took his time to let each of his senses revel in the stimulus of the moment.

Before she realized it, he'd refilled her goblet. Now she took larger sips, warming the sweet liquid in her mouth, letting it burnish her gums and tongue before slipping down her throat, where it seemed to linger before warming her insides. She smiled at the comfort and warmth it provided, at the beauty of the man before her, of the raw maleness he exuded. He awakened the woman entrapped inside her.

Her inhibitions banished by the warm alcohol, she searched his eyes to detect any elusive force behind his gaze, which began to match hers with the same growing fervor.

Mayhap those chips of golden ice floating in the amber orbs had picked up her every thought, because he moved closer, put down his goblet and crooked a finger under her chin. She responded to his touch the way her body responded to the wine, invitingly, openly. She welcomed his mouth upon hers. He parted her lips with his tongue and slipped it inside. She tasted his warmth mingled with the wine's perfumey essence. He clasped her shoulders and she stood, her fingers playing through his hair, their mouths exploring, not yet having demanded that crushing possession. She knew not where she was going, but she no longer cared; he was the king and she was thoroughly at his command. The wine had dulled nothing; on the contrary, it had awakened her senses, making her more receptive to him. Their embrace tightened. In response to his fiery touch, a moan escaped the depths of her throat as his hands wandered and lingered.

"Why has not a beautiful creature like you been wed?" he whispered, his breath hot against her ear.

Not giving her a chance to reply, his tongue tickled her earlobe. "You are by far the loveliest woman at court. All the others look like tarnished silver in comparison."

She wondered if that comparison included the queen. "Why, thank you, sire," was all she could think of to say, flattered and embarrassed at the same time, a trickle of fear now teasing her.

"I would possess you as my very own, lest any other man lay eyes on you, and enjoy your beauty as I do."

She construed his choice of words. Mark's word 'playtoy' whipped through her head. "Do you propose to lock me up with the rest of the royal treasury, my lord?" She forced a playful lilt into her voice.

"Nay, I shall let you come up for air occasionally," he quipped, pouring them more wine, which she didn't make a move to touch. "But now that you are here, I don't believe I can bear to let you out of my reach." He sat and pulled her down onto his lap.

"I can't sit by your side on the throne with you, sire," she stated the obvious.

"But you can sit by me during private moments...like these." His lips, moist and hot with wine, nibbled at her neck. She fought the growing arousal churning inside her.

"I thought we were going to play music, sire."

"Ah, music. I love my music, but the music of lovemaking brings me rapture that a mere instrument never could. I make my best music with a the body of a beautiful woman, making her my instrument, creating exquisite harmony with my own. Let me put you to music, Amethyst." His voice dripped with innuendo, but she ignored his suggestive tone.

"I'm not feeling very...musical right now, my lord. 'Tis a trait peculiar to all artists, as you must know...the mood must be upon me." She doubted he'd heed her weak protest. She actually doubted what she'd just said. In truth, he was turning her body into a column of fire.

Her attempt to slide off his lap intensified his swelling passion. "I have within me strings vibrating strongly enough to create an outburst of sound, a duet of which you have never seen...or heard. We shall be within the throes of a fantasia you never knew existed outside a conservatory!"

"Nay, your majesty, this just is not right, 'tis so unexpected..." Her voice trailed off as she stopped trying to slide off his lap. Deep inside, a growing desire began to overpower her.

She feared he would order her abrupt dismissal, and in the same breath calling for Bessie, or whomever he fancied at the moment.

But he seemed too startled to retain her. She nearly fell out of his lap in a scramble to compose herself and scramble to her feet. "I must preserve my honor."

"Well, then, who better to honor you than your king? What better sword for your sheath than a royal one?" The twinkle in his eyes returned with the melodic tone of his voice as he reached for his wine and once again, partook of its pleasure almost as fervently as he'd done her.

"Please, sire, give me...give me more time. This came as such a...surprise!" Who wouldn't have been surprised? There was no lute or sheet music in sight.

"Very well. I shall wait. Patience is my greatest virtue. But I am also a man, and patience wears thin, so I don't expect you'll torment me again."

"Nay, sire, I've no wish to torment you." She spoke the truth although her voice trembled.

"Then you will return at my next invitation?" he goaded.

"Aye, sire." She found herself curtsying, nodding, eagerly anticipating their next meeting, but dreading it just the same.

Later in her own retiring chamber, she thrilled at the feel of his mouth against hers, almost ashamed of the way she'd responded. Then she thought of her family and her honor. No, she could not become one in a string of the king's mistresses. But, oh, how easy it would be to succumb to those kingly charms!

* * *

Warwick Castle, July, 1521

"You swine!" Topaz took Amethyst by the shoulders and shook her, nails digging into her shoulders. "You went running to court after him, that bastard of a king, you, my sister? He's the offspring of our father's killer." Her eyes spewed sparks of anger.

"You knew I was invited to his birthday festivities." She plucked Topaz's hands off her shoulders and smoothed the fabric.

"But I didn't think you'd actually degrade us all by attending. Promise never to associate with the likes of him again," she demanded.

"Topaz, you cannot tell me what to do!" But Topaz turned and strode from the room, leaving her scent of rose oil behind.

Amethyst dined alone that night in her bedchamber, stuffing herself with hot buttered scones, jellied tarts and delicate pastries. She needed the solace, the comfort, of hot sweet food. Then she began to feel dizzy.

Her mind simply ceased to function; she couldn't remember what day it was, where she was. A dense fog wrapped her brain, a cloudy curtain that would not allow clear thinking. She stumbled to her bed and fell atop it as a violent nausea rose to her throat. She leaned over the bed and retched. Her chambermaid rushed over to her, flung herself across the bed behind Amethyst, and held her hair back. Amethyst lost her dinner, and what seemed like her entire insides. With a weak groan, she lay back on the bed as her maid pressed a damp cloth to her face. Exhausted, she drifted off into blackness.

The next day, the sickening nausea rose to her throat with every breath. Sabine sat at her bedside, forcing some sweet gooey syrup twixt her lips, but the aroma made her retch more—what, she didn't know; she had nothing left inside her.

"Poison…she poisoned me…" she managed to whisper, for even using her voice was a major effort, an expenditure of energy she simply didn't have.

Sabine moved closer, stroking the hair off her face, fanning it across the pillow like the feathers of their great peacocks.

"What is it, dear? What about poison?"

"Topaz…she poisoned me…because I…went to see the king…" she mumbled through parched lips.

"Oh, no, no…" Sabine's soothing breath feathered over Amethyst's face as she rocked her gently. "She would not dare."

"She did, she did…"

The next day she could barely lift her head and still couldn't keep anything down. Sabine called for their physician, Dr. Stokes. He bustled into the chamber and pulled the drapes aside. A stream of sunlight flooded the musty room.

"No, please, shut out the light!" Amethyst groaned, her voice a cracked wail of pain. She doubled up as another stab of agony cut through her stomach.

The doctor jabbed a needle into her heel, bleeding her into a silver bowl at the foot of the bed, and forced some hot thick liquid into her mouth.

She gagged and spat, but he held her head twixt his palms with a vicelike grip, forcing her jaw shut. The nausea rose to her throat, and she retched violently, arms and legs jerking under the covers, her head thrashing from side to side, but barely able to move under his confining grasp.

"You will swallow that, my lady, or I shall open your gob like a bird's beak and force it down your gullet with me fingers," he shouted above her moans of protest and pain. Finally, a breath of the fresh breeze allowed her to relax. Her throat gave way, the warm liquid coating her tortured, twisted insides.

The doctor relinquished his grip on her jaw and pushed her head back onto the pillows.

"Give her that every sunup and sundown and at high noon. Make her swallow it." He handed the bottle to Sabine, grabbed his black bag and dashed from the room.

Amethyst's lids closed. The soft breeze and sunlight faded farther away as her mind drifted into an empty void of. She saw nothing, felt nothing, and heard nothing.

The pain was gone and her body felt delightfully lithe and supple. Nausea was no longer a burden enmeshed within the confines of the flesh and bones she dragged about. She was a feather, a lucid puff of vapor with no eyes, yet able to see a radiant glow before her, colorless, but brilliant. She felt herself smiling, but she had no mouth with which to laugh, and when she wanted to retreat, the light itself faded to dimness and she once again faded with it.

The drapes were drawn, the window pulled shut. A candle flickered in the corner. The bedcurtains were parted to a narrow crack for Sabine and the priest could see the withered body lying still under the sheets.

Matthew entered the chamber behind Emerald, both wiping tears from their eyes, their faces contorted with grief. Topaz was tending some sick animals on a nearby farm.

The priest said a few words and sprinkled holy water on the slight figure. Sabine heard her daughter breathing and beheld see the expression of pure peace on the drawn face.

"She will leave us peacefully," the priest whispered. "She will enter Heaven tonight and there will be no pain."

Shattered with grief, Sabine turned and fell into Emerald's arms. Mother and daughter wound their arms round one another, each lost in her own private grief.

Amethyst sighed and her eyes opened. She saw shadowy figures at the foot of the bed, the priest in his black robe, holding up a chalice of some sort, chanting softly in Latin, his head bowed, and beyond him, Emerald's honey beige hair piled on top of her head, her face a confused contortion of grief.

She turned away and drifted off.

When her mind again opened to the real world and she knew she was not in some faraway dreamland, she opened her eyes, sensing a presence in the pale golden light of the candle on the bedstand. Topaz sat at the edge of the bed, smiling down upon her. The nausea began to recede, to cease its cruel and savage racking of her weak body. "Topaz, please bring me a cool cloth." Her words came out in a croak. Topaz wrung out the cloth and wiped her down. The cleansing made her feel almost human. The next morning, her throat muscles loosened and allowed her to swallow a few spoonfuls of soup or porridge without heaving it all back up again. Topaz always seemed to be there, keeping a vigil by her bed, hugging Amethyst close, and she could hear Sabine at the foot of the bed murmuring prayers of thanks.

"Amethyst, you almost left us, He almost took you, but He gave you back to us," Topaz whispered as Amethyst's eyes fluttered open, welcoming the warm sunlight that spilled into the room.

"Please open the window, I want to breathe air," she pleaded, "Bring me flowers, 'tis so stuffy in here…"

She opened her eyes to a basket of hyacinths, pansies and marigolds mixed with roses from the garden. She took one soft petal twixt her fingers and let its velvety smoothness soothe her.

As she regained her strength, she lifted her head without that blast of dizziness, and as soon as she was able, began directing her maids to pack precious belongings. She was leaving, and would escape at midnight if she had to, in order to avoid Topaz. She could not let her sister know she was going back to court.

A messenger arrived with a polite summons from the king. She sent her regrets with the explanation that she'd been very ill, and that she would commence her journey as soon as she was able. Her hand trembled as she penned the note, her heart astir in anticipation of her new life at court.

Over the next few days, her appetite returned and that sickening rise of bile gave way to the hollow gnaw of ravenous hunger. How good it felt to hear the familiar rumble, to actually crave a sweet sticky tart, to enjoy those spurts of mouth-watering when the aroma of a roasted chicken wafted through the room.

She took her first swallow of solid food, a plump drumstick, as she'd requested something she could eat with her hands, to gnaw at it like a starving animal. She sank her teeth into the warm roasted flesh and chewed, savoring the smoky taste, happily letting the grease smear her chin. Her stomach filled to the point of satiation, and she later fell into a contented, satisfied slumber, her body efficiently nourished.

* * *

The day before her planned departure for court, she took one last walk through the rose garden, touching the petals with her fingertips, inhaling their sweet scent, glancing back at the castle with a wistful sadness. Her eyes misted over, blurring the rows of towers and protective walls. Although she was leaving to start a new and exciting life in the intimate circle of royalty, she would miss the close familiar warmth of home. She plucked a white rose from its stem and twirled it twixt her fingers. She would take this rose with her as a reminder, hoping that by the time the rose withered and died, court life would obliterate her homesickness.

At the clatter of hoofbeats, she looked up and glimpsed a gray stallion saddled with the Gilford livery and its handsome rider. "I hope I haven't come at a bad time," Matthew shouted across the field, and she began running towards him. He waved, gesturing her to stay put and not move on his account. Since that evening of the priest's visit with the cold fingers of death at her throat, he'd visited her on two more occasions, bringing her peaches and apples from his orchard.

"Nay, but Mother has gone to visit Aunt Margaret with Emerald." She looked up at him, saddled on his mount, his eyes as green as the carpet of grass beneath them, his skin aglow in the sun.

"'Tis you I care to speak to. Shall I stable the horse?"

"Please do. Join me back here." She patted the ground next to her.

He galloped off and returned on foot. He sat and removed his shoes, digging his feet into the grass.

She gazed admiringly at the man Topaz had chosen for a husband. His sandy hair, sun-bleached to a platinum, was now clipped short in the French style that fashion demanded, brushing his shirt collar. A dark blond brow introduced a pair of brilliant green eyes expressing merriment, displaying laugh lines in the corners. His ruddy complexion flaunted daily rides in the fresh country air. She'd been so enthralled by the king, she hadn't even looked in another man's direction. Matthew was charming and attractive—but he was no King Henry.

"I need to speak with you, Amethyst. Please hold this in the strictest of confidence."

If it was about Topaz, which it invariably would be, who would she tell? Who could possibly be interested? "What did she do now?"

"She did nothing yet." He raised his eyes to meet hers and she noticed that they lightened with the sun to a bright green in contrast to how they darkened in the blaze of their great hall's candles. "It's what she's about to do."

"What else can she do? Come over here and stuff me into the oubliette?" she chuckled, her tone sardonic.

"Nay, 'tis not against you. 'Tis much more serious. She's talking of engaging Wolsey's services for a tidy sum and going round the realm to raise support for her cause."

A stab of fear shot through Amethyst. Her mother was the only person who knew she'd been invited to court. What would happen now? She thought quickly. "Fear not, Matthew," she spoke calmly, for his sake. "I don't believe she means it. She's has no way of rousing that much support. Besides, Wolsey's a feeble old man. His days are numbered. The king would never see him as a threat."

"She's already got followers. She constantly reminds me of your family history and how strongly she feels about reclaiming her birthright, as she calls it." She twirled a blade of grass. "I tried to reason with her; to talk her out of it. I tried to stop her by forbidding her to go anywhere without my permission."

Although she tried to put Matthew's mind at ease, Topaz's success was what Amethyst feared the most. She had no doubts of her sister's capabilities. What her mother had dismissed as mere talk, Amethyst recognized as careful planning, maneuvering, and organizing. That took years, and mayhap now Topaz was ready. Her time had finally come.

"I'm sure it will not come to anything. She'll see how hopeless it is and give up before any blood is shed," Amethyst tried to appease Matthew, though she dared not betray her fears.

"That's not only it." Matthew yanked a clump of grass out of the ground and kneaded it. "She's talking of poisoning the Princess Mary."

"Oh, dear God." Amethyst hadn't expected this. Fighting against Henry's armies was one thing, but harming an innocent child? "No, she couldn't. Mary is surrounded by guards, moves from residence to residence. It couldn't be done."

"It has happened through the ages. Didn't Topaz once tell me that your father's own mother and brother were supposedly poisoned? 'Tis nothing new. Poisonings have been taking place since the beginning of time. I doubt she would personally dispense a cup of hemlock to Mary.

It will be done slowly, painstakingly, in stages. Henry has enemies. Mary has enemies. Don't put it past her."

The thought of her recent illness sent a shudder through her. Although she would never know for sure if Topaz had poisoned her, her mind believed she had, but her heart fought the evil judgment, pushing it into the past, leaving it there. Matthew did not know about her confrontation with Topaz over her last visit to the king, and she did not wish to tell him.

"Matthew, I used to worry about Topaz a lot more when we were younger, because it never seemed like merely talk, the way we all spew forth our lofty dreams and ambitions when we're children. To her, it was going to be a lifelong quest, one that she'd never given up."

"She talks of reforms." Matthew lay sideways, resting on an elbow. "She's like no one I've ever met. She lets the servants dine and sup with us, she invites the stablehands in for Mass in the chapel, she tore down the high board in the great hall, she turned the dungeon into an animal shelter and...believe it or not, she forbade the consumption of meat and fowl in the house. I finally convinced her that the lads' bones would become fragile as birds' wings should they not have meat."

"Topaz always felt this way about animals." She laughed, picturing a menagerie, creatures of all sizes wandering among the chains, irons and instruments of torture strewn about the dungeon.

"Mayhap I can talk to the king," she said more to herself than to Matthew. Mayhap it was about time Henry found out. She and the level-headed king would come up with a reasonable solution. Their minds worked so well together.

"Talk to the king?" He sat up and blinked.

"Matthew, I haven't told anyone this, but King Henry invited me to court to join the King's Musick. Had I not had this...illness, I would have gone already."

"Were you planning on telling Topaz?" he asked.

"Nay." *Of course not* remained unsaid.

Matthew nodded. "This much of Topaz's personality I know how to handle."

She folded her hands and leaned forward. "I was going to write her from court and tell her…Matthew, I have an admiration and respect for King Henry like I have for no other human being. I also love my sister. But I shall obey the king's orders. I am also very much looking forward to life at court."

"I'm sure you are. I am so excited for you…imagine, one of our own Warwickshire folk, a courtier!" His smile warmed her, his company comforted her as their hands reached towards each other and touched precisely in the middle. Their eyes locked upon one another, Matthew's imploring, confused gaze pouring into Amethyst's, searching for an answer. "I don't want to see her harmed in any way. But…" His eyes darkened as his grasp on her hand tightened. "If something happened to either of you, I could not live."

"Oh, Matthew…don't even think that way. I can talk to the king. He really is an understanding man."

"Just be careful there at court. Although it is intriguing and luxurious, it can be a dangerous place. And please do write." His brows darted up and down as his eyes reviewed her features, tucking her image into his memory.

"Of course I shall." A wave of melancholy clouded her face as she held Matthew's hand. As much as she wanted the court life, to be near the king, she would surely miss her cozy realm right here with her beloved family, and those who loved her.

Chapter Five

Whitehall Palace, 1525

Amethyst gathered a stack of sheet music from the minstrel gallery and headed down the corridor to her apartments. On this hot and sticky day, the remaining courtiers either went riding or for a dip in the pond. The king and queen departed the day before on a summer progress. As much as she would miss him, a strange relief calmed her when his royal coach passed through the gates. A few weeks without his presence meant time to herself, to learn court etiquette, and to indulge her grand passion, music.

She decided to take her lute out to the gardens and practice under the sun among the colorful array of flowers and clipped hedges.

A page scurried towards her as she ascended the staircase. "Lady Amethyst, Lady Amethyst, you have a visitor." The lad's shoes scuffed along the polished floor. The royal crest emblazoned on his skinny chest looked overbearing and incongruous, but no doubt made him feel like a grown man.

"Who visits me?"

"Lady Topaz Gilford." He caught his breath. "She awaits in the garden, Lady Amethyst."

Topaz! What on earth was she doing here at court? A stab of apprehension shook her as she considered telling the page to send her away. She did not want to hear more of Topaz's tirades, stand captive to her accusations, her disparaging remarks about the king, and worst of all, another possible physical confrontation. Her life was at court now and Topaz would have to accept it. Now what excuse to use?

"Tell her I am not in res…" But visions of her mother and Emerald appeared in her mind as they did every waking moment and in her dreams. Court life was a whirlwind of activity, singing, dancing, feasting and heated discussion, and the king captivated her to a point of breathlessness. But at times, especially during the long nights in her dark chambers, she longed for the comfort of her Warwick Castle, her dainty boudoir, and the sweeping view of her beloved countryside. So she decided to see Topaz, her only link with home.

"Tell her I shall be there presently," she told the page and entered her apartments to fetch her lute. Once Topaz left, she would have some time to practice alone before the eve's rehearsal with the King's Musick.

Amethyst found Topaz sitting on the fountain wall dipping her hand into the pool of water. Polished as always, she displayed perfect posture, her hair tucked into a white coif trimmed with daisies, her brows plucked, her pink gown slashed in front over a richly embroidered kirtle. A canvas sack lay at her feet. "Amethyst!" She stood and flicked water off her fingers. Amethyst approached her sister knowing that behind the smiling pink lips lurked a sinister temperament about to be unleashed.

They exchanged two-cheek air kisses. "What brings you to court, Topaz?"

"I trust you are enjoying court life?" Her light and airy tone showed no hostility or sarcasm. Yet.

"I love it here at court," she conveyed her feelings in all sincerity. "I can imagine no other life. I am sorry I left without saying goodbye, but I did not want another confrontation."

"Amethyst," she interrupted. "I am not here to condemn you. If you wish to live with these…people, I cannot stop you. We are all grown now, and must lead the lives we choose. Your presence here is short-lived. When you realize what that king is really after and get a glimpse of his lecherous ways, you will flee in disgust. So keep your distance. He is a Tudor. Trustworthiness does not run through Tudor veins," she warned, her tone low and menacing.

"So what are you here for, Topaz? The king is not in residence." She glanced at the palace gates. "He and the queen left for progress. You must save your tirade for another time, if he will see you."

Topaz *tsk*'d with a dramatic eye-roll. "I am not here to see him. I've nothing to say to the man."

"For what, then?" Amethyst inquired, not truly curious. "A tour of the palace?"

"Nay. I am going on a visit to St. George's almshouse in Whitechapel and wish you to join me." She gestured to the satchel on the ground. "My quarterly progresses take me through the poorest parts of as many shires as I can reach, where I distribute food and alms to the beggars, offering any other help I can. St. George's, one of the most desperate, is one of my favorites because many children live there."

"Is that not a dangerous area?" A twinge of fear niggled at her. "Could you not just send them food or money and restrict your travels to the shires round Warwick?"

"Nay. Parts of London are poorer, more destitute than almost any shire near Warwick, you naive little goose. Have you not seen any of it? God's foot, you've been here long enough." She raised her chin and looked down at Amethyst with a frown. "Does not the royal barge float far enough down the Thames to see the other side? Is Henry not even aware of the poverty and starvation his subjects have to endure?" she prodded in a haughty tone.

"Aye, he is on progress as we speak, traveling through Ipswich and Norwich, then up the coast of East Anglia to Kingston-upon-Hull. These royal progresses are quite exhausting. He carries out his royal duties," Amethyst informed her.

"Aye, and then where does he go?" Topaz tossed her head. Sunlight glinted off her hair. "To the royal forest for a few weeks of hunting. To slaughter the innocent round-eyed doe and stuff its young flesh into his chubby face. What good does that do the poor?"

She let out an impatient huff. "Topaz, King Henry has done a lot for the poor since becoming king, and so has Queen Catherine. You know him not, you have no right to stand here and judge."

"I know there is still much too much squalor and hunger about, and I do my part to correct it. Now, go and change into a simple frock." She eyed Amethyst up and down. "That billowy satin thing will never do. I know you courtiers dress pompously to impress one another but you must look genuine when you visit the squalid slums or they will spit on you and throw rocks."

So that was it. Her sister had made up her mind for her. Refusing to accompany Topaz would be tantamount to refusing the poor. Giving Topaz a few coins and a sack of food wouldn't suffice. She had to physically accompany her, to see the hunger and filth for herself. And she knew what her crafty sister had in mind. She did not merely desire a traveling companion. She was going to try harder than ever to sway Amethyst to her way of thinking, hoping to spread her beliefs throughout court. Oh, Amethyst knew her sister intimately. Now that Amethyst was a courtier, Topaz planned to use this to her utmost advantage. She knew how convincing and persuasive Topaz could be. How else could she have snagged an unassuming country gent like Matthew Gilford?

She looked down at her robe, a simple garment cut square at the neck, the full sleeves pushed up unfashionably against the oppressive heat. Her hair sat piled atop her head under a coif. She wore no jewelry. "I'm hardly the picture of a pompous courtier," she commented to Topaz. "But I will change my raiment."

She turned towards the palace to change, but into what? The traveling gown she'd worn to court was simple enough, but far too heavy for a day like this. She then realized she owned no simple attire; since living at Warwick Castle and especially since arriving at court, her clothes were made for her by seamstresses, and the king had generously provided her with bolts of rich satins, cloth-of-gold and silver, delicate brocades, laces, and velvets for her sumptuous court wardrobe.

She dug through her chest of drawers, choosing a simple linen tunic. She pulled it over her head and belted it with a tie-back from one of her curtains. It was green velvet, but all she could find in a hurry. She bloused the garment to conceal her curves, slipped her feet into her scuffy slippers, and went back down to join Topaz.

She was already saddled atop Alice, her favorite mount. Amethyst went round the stables to fetch Blossom, her birthday gift from Henry, a gentle gray palomino that loved to breeze through the countryside. Two grooms she recognized from Kenilworth accompanied Topaz. One lad was delicate and slight, the other a burly bully type, more than able to guard them all against any adversary. All three horses were laden with bulging sacks.

"We will ride the mounts to the barge and take the barge to Tower Bridge," Topaz instructed. "Mitchell, you will watch the mounts at the riverbank and Peter, you will escort us. Most of the folks know me there, but poverty does bring out the worst in even the sweetest disposition. Let us depart."

Amethyst took a few breaths to calm her jittery nerves. She'd never ventured to this side of London before. For Henry's coronation, they'd entered the city through the Ald Gate, the easternmost of the city gates, and had ridden through narrow, shabby streets thronged with unwashed beggars in rags. But on the way to court, they'd approached from Highgate. On that dark eve, she'd seen only the tall dwellings leaning into each other and above the street, dotted with flickering squares of light. This world of poverty and privation was foreign to her, and she knew after today she would have a much different perspective on her own situation. Mayhap she wouldn't need Topaz's convincing; she would see it all for herself.

The barge glided down the Thames, and looking past the Gothic spires of Westminster Abbey behind her, she glimpsed the blue-green hills of Hampstead and Highgate unfurling dreamily over the horizon. Fishing boats, barges and ships crowded the waterway, all winding their way round one another much like a network of busy ants. Ships lay at anchor at either bank, packers unloading their cargo into lighters. Hundreds of boats traversed the river, each with a direction and purpose. The boatman of their barge shouted and waved to his fellow watermen, their voices fading into the industrious bustle of trade and negotiation. A tangle of masts and tackle lined each bank. Great cranes swung to and fro, conveying parcels of goods from ships to wharfs. From the Tower in the distance beyond stood quays and warehouses and the cluttered aggregate of the Steelyard. On this tranquil day, the heat mollified the bustling commerce, but here on the river she lifted her face to welcome the refreshing breeze. She spied the shiny black skin of a pair of porpoises leaping about, playfully dodging the barge and disappearing back into the murky depths, as carefree as the spangles of sunlight glinting off their oily backs.

London Bridge's two pinnacled towers flanked them as the barge glided beneath it. The sunlight cooled to a soft blue-gray as they passed under the vast drawbridge. She looked to their left as they swept past the imposing Tower. Topaz turned her head away and Amethyst gazed upward at the unsightly fortress where she'd spent the first two years of her life. The dusty spires rose into the sky like dragons, their pointy flags fluttering in the breeze like forked tongues.

They rode parallel to the bustling Thames Street, past dingy warehouses and cranes for unloading cargo, their graceful necks swooping down. Along the bank stood the stately mansions of the wealthy merchants and bustling wharves. Sailors and fishermen strolled about, all moving in their own busy circles. A cacophony of voices filled the air, the light lilting of French, the singsong Italian, the guttural German. Inns and taverns stood tucked twixt towering warehouses and graceful mansions, their wooden signs swinging in the breeze. The aroma of fresh strawberries rushed by them as they passed a cook-shop, a gang of housewives converging upon it like a gaggle of geese, stuffing themselves through the door.

The barge veered to the river's left bank, and the boatman eased it in twixt two weatherbeaten fishing vessels. Well-dressed merchants, frazzled wenches and haggard seamen merged on the wharf, haggling, exchanging coins for bales of cloth and nets full of fish, their scales glimmering like heaps of silver.

Topaz disembarked and handed the boatman a few coins. She waited as Amethyst gathered her skirt and clamored from the barge, dragging her sack of offerings, skinning her knee on the barge's jagged edge.

"We are going to Whitechapel," Topaz called over her shoulder as Amethyst slung the sack over her shoulder. The coins at the bottom smacked against her hip and she winced in pain. She would have handed it to the groom to carry, but he carried two bulky sacks slung over his own back.

They left the bustle of the Thames commerce behind and headed north up the Tower Bridge Approach. The Tower loomed ahead of them. A semicircular bastion cut off its thick eastern wall, the structure blackened under centuries of soot and grime.

The sky above became a blanked-out pattern of blue patches as they trudged up the narrow lane. The shabby timber-framed dwellings leaned over the street, the windows flung open, threadbare curtains tumbling out like ratty strands of hair. Merchants peddled their wares—meat pies, fruits, sheep's feet, pigs' trotters, ale, lemonade. Stalls on either side of the narrow street displayed more wares. The stench of fish filled the close, hot air as they passed a stall hanging with gutted cod twirling on their strings like a grotesque puppet show. Merchants shouted out offers of their products in sharp, piercing voices: "Smelts an' salmon, flounder an' pike, fresh from the Thames!" "Sides 'a beef!" "Ale 'ere!" "Pigs' feet, 'alf p a pound!"

They made a left up Leman Street, where more dwellings huddled together. The sun did not penetrate the peaked roofs here either. Chickens squawked as a group of grimy urchins, no more than four or five years old, rags hanging off their emaciated bodies, matted hair coiled about their necks, scampered past them. One lad held out his hand to Amethyst. She summarized his features, the already hardened face, the squinting eyes, never having known pleasure, only hunger and misery. She reached into the bag and tossed him a coin. He bit it with rotted teeth and scampered away.

More shops lined the streets. Merchants called out, trying to lure them in to sample the wares. The odors of fish and the stench of refuse turned Amethyst's stomach as Topaz yanked her out of the stream of slops poured from a second-story window. "These people don't have garderobes, Amethyst, this is not Warwickshire. You will be very lucky indeed if you get through today without having to comb a turd out of your hair." After that, she kept her eyes riveted to upper-floor windows for flying slops.

"The almshouse is on the corner of Whitechapel Road," Topaz called over her shoulder. Amethyst heaved a sigh of relief. The bag weighed her down, straining her muscles, and it banged against her side with every step. She nearly tripped over a pile of excrement as she witnessed two men fighting in a narrow alleyway twixt two shabby houses, tearing at each other's filthy shirts and breeches. The sound of bone cracking against bone sickened her. What could they be fighting over? With so much poverty and starvation here, it could have been a piece of stale bread.

They reached the corner of Whitechapel Road. Topaz kicked open the door of a run-down timber-framed house. A bit larger than the others and freestanding, it still exuded that rancid air of poverty. The odors of unwashed bodies and urine hit Amethyst in the face as they entered the dark hall single-file. Topaz turned into a small room, Amethyst and the groom following. They dumped their bags on the dirt floor, strewn with dry rushes. In an instant, a crowd of stinking ragged bodies converged upon them, tearing into the bags, stuffing handfuls of bread and cakes into their mouths with filthy hands, as if they hadn't eaten in weeks, and they likely hadn't. It reminded Amethyst of Topaz's animal shelter—these souls were as animals, having lost all human dignity and pride long ago, or never having known it at all, born within the confines of this pathetic squalor.

"Topaz, do they live like this?" Amethyst whispered, watching the scene all around her, people of all ages, from babies barely crawling, to the middle-aged and beyond.

"What do you think, you innocent ball of fluff?" she retorted. "They are born this way and die this way, with no hope for escape whatever, through the howling winds of winter and the searing heat of summer. They eat what they can beg, steal, or what I and those as kind as I bring them."

"But...there are so many farms in the kingdom. Why is there not enough for everyone to eat?" She knew how ignorant she sounded, never having known hunger, not even in the Tower. Topaz had told her of the hard straw pallets, the lack of firewood and the cold they'd endured, but somehow there had always been enough food at mealtimes.

"Because they haven't the money to pay for food because they haven't the work to do in order to earn any money. 'Tis a vicious circle, Amethyst, and one which I plan to break. If they are lucky, they can be apprenticed to a chimney sweep or a blacksmith or scale fish for the fishmongers, but there is no steady work here. None of them can read or write, they live by their wits. The girls become whores round age eleven and the boys—why, they either kill or steal for their sustenance, or they die out in the streets, mostly in the winter. Do not be surprised if you see the corpse of an infant on a rubbish heap along with a dog or cat carcass. I told you it would be a shock."

Amethyst fought down the sick churning inside her at the sight of these wretched creatures. She watched a girl and a much younger boy smacking each other, rolling to the floor, kicking and gouging. "What are they fighting over, Topaz? Stop them!"

"You stop them, I'm feeding this infant here!" she called out from across the room.

Amethyst glanced over at her sister, a tiny baby in her arms, gently spooning food into its mouth. She sprinted over to the fighting children and threw herself on top of the girl, yanking her off the boy, his face beaten and bloody, a few teeth knocked out, on the floor beside him. "What is your problem? Is there not enough for all of you?"

" 'E took me jar 'a pickles, the bleedin' sod!" The girl scrambled to her bare feet. She was scrawny and emaciated, her ragged skirt torn and bloody. She wiped her hands on the hem. The boy sat on the floor, whimpering.

"Here." Amethyst reached into the pocket of her robe and took out some coins. "Take this, go to the shops and buy yourself a decent meal." Amethyst's heart cried out for this poor girl. She would have given the robe off her back if she'd had something else to wear. "Buy something to eat for your friend there, too, and no more fighting."

"'E ain't me friend, 'e's me brudder," she mumbled, holding her hand out for the boy. He grasped it hesitatingly. "C'mon, Jack." She turned back to Amethyst. "Ta, Lady, for the silver."

The crowd by now had quieted down. Several more urchins entered the almshouse from the street, but many left after Topaz gave them sufficient money to buy food or cloth or shoes or whatever they felt they needed most. Amethyst crossed the room and found Topaz sitting among a circle of children, their grubby but captivated faces turned up toward her as if she were a princess right out of a fairytale.

She inched closer and crouched next to Topaz to hear her tale. It was probably the story of Robin Hood, one of her childhood favorites. It always brought her back to the magic and intrigue of the enchanted medieval forest.

But Topaz was spinning no tale. "...and we were born in that horrible dungeon, that place crawling with rats and bugs, the cries of torture echoing through the dark and musty halls. Then when I was four and my sister two, we went to visit my father, who was a handsome young man, a dashing lad indeed. I saw them dragging him in chains, and screamed 'Where are you taking my Papa!' I never found out, for my mother never told me, but I never saw my Papa again. Then we left the Tower, and I had my first glimpse of the countryside. I did not find out 'til I was a big girl, what had happened to him. King Henry the Seventh killed him." Her voice rose in a dramatic crescendo. "He chopped off my father's head."

A collective gasp filled the room.

"Topaz!" Amethyst gave her sister's arm a slap. "What are you telling these children that blasted story for?"

"So they will know the truth," she hissed. "I am giving them a history lesson."

"History lesson, my arse!" Amethyst's blood ran hot.

The circle tightened, the curious ears poised for a juicy story. "You stop poisoning these minds right this instant or I shall never help you again, do you hear me? I shall not plead your case before the king and I shall not give you one ounce of support. Ever," she spewed forth her threats into her sister's ear.

"Then I am sorry I brought you here," Topaz replied evenly, her arm protectively around a dirty little boy sucking his thumb. "If you have no compassion in your heart then I shall not seek your help."

"I am leaving," Amethyst announced, "for I am not getting mixed up in this. If the king finds out you are spreading these treasonous tales, he can have your head."

"And who is going to tell him? My dear sister, his future concubine, if not his present one?" she snarled.

She smacked Topaz's arm. "How dare you. I am not his concubine. I shall not have you coming here spreading your treasonous beliefs round London and round court, as if I didn't know your real reason for coming here to see me."

Topaz glared with narrowed eyes, turned her back to her sister and addressed the children. "Wee folk, I must go away and gather up some more food and cloths and coins for you, but I shall be back ere long."

They gathered round her, tugged at her skirts, begged her not to leave. Amethyst's eyes welled up with tears at the touching, pathetic sight. Even the adults looked sorry to see her go, if they could ever look more forlorn than they ever did.

Amethyst emptied the contents of her other pocket into the hands of a middle-aged women who gave her a toothless grin and many blessings for her generosity.

They exited the almshouse, but the air still carried the cloying stench of the streets. The odors clung to her robe, her hair, her body. She couldn't wait to get back to her apartments, burn the robe and slippers, and scrub her body down in a hot steamy tub.

The heat had given way to a cooler breeze as the sun began to sink, throwing long pointy shadows of the peaked roofs into the narrow street. The bustling pace of business hours had quieted down, but the gutter still ran with refuse. The denizens still trudged along, staring straight ahead, seeing nothing. It weighed on her heart, and she wanted simply to be alone with her thoughts, to talk to no one.

They turned back toward the Thames and waited for a barge to take them back to Whitehall.

* * *

The king and his retinue returned a month later. The first eve after his return, she sat up in the gallery with the King's Musick and played her much-practiced renditions of several of his own compositions. The king and queen danced, surrounded by the admiring, fawning courtiers.

Henry and Catherine did not dance together all that much, however. She noticed the frosty distance he now kept from Catherine but concluded that affairs of state burdened him.

He challenged Amethyst to a game of tennis one afternoon and she accepted, having played a few times on Matthew's court at Kenilworth.

He arrived in a light linen shirt and white breeches over white hose, a striking vision of athletic endurance. He sprinted round the court with his hard muscled legs. His strong arm whacked the ball with a graceful, practiced swing. She was no match for him as he had her dashing to and fro, chasing the ball, barely able to return it. At the end of the match he wiped his brow with a linen towel, laughing as she loped off the court, spent.

"So tennis isn't your game, is it, Lady Amethyst?" he teased.

"I scored but one point, and that was because you weren't looking!" she shot back her defense.

"You put up quite a fight, and as the only female member of court who dared challenge me, you must be rewarded."

A bolt of excitement pierced her. Her heart leapt. But he refused to reveal his surprise.

Her reward was the seat to his right on the dais that evening in the great hall, in the absent queen's place.

Amethyst felt all eyes upon her as she picked at the sumptuous dishes of pheasant, quail, partridge, steaming vegetables, and the luscious pastries and tarts, ten courses in all. But under the intense scrutiny, her appetite eluded her. *This isn't worth it*, she decided.

Proudly displayed round her neck was a three-tiered strand of gems, diamonds alternating with rubies, emeralds and sapphires with a pearl clasp. Circling her wrist was a bracelet of the same design, and two rings of fiery amethysts and diamonds set in gold circled her fingers, rewards for having challenged him to tennis.

"I cannot imagine what you would have given me had I won," she marveled at her new gifts, setting off the radiance of her new crimson velvet gown sprinkled with tiny pearls and diamonds. With the feasting courtiers no longer staring, her discomfort eased at having taken the queen's seat. But she admitted Henry made her feel like the queen of his own heart. Once again they danced, and he leapt and twirled, not missing a beat of the lilting music from the gallery above.

As the great hall emptied, he invited her to his chambers.

With a fluttering heart, she dressed for him in her new pale blue silk robe, creamy chemise and matching white gown, slashed in front to show a frilly blue underskirt. She basked in the comforts he'd provided her, pinching herself to make sure it wasn't another of her girlhood dreams. Aye, she would see him tonight, for another of their delightful chats about astronomy and religion, to laugh with him, to enjoy his charismatic personality, but in the end she would not give in to his carnal demands. She was here for the King's Musick, but no more. She'd finally encountered the elusive Bessie Blount at a distance and glimpsed nothing more than the torches' light glinting off her platinum hair. Every practice session of the King's Musick produced another wave of juicy items—he and Catherine were indeed estranged, he was now wooing a sister of a former mistress, planned to bring his and Bessie's illegitimate son to court, on and on.

With all these rumors swirling through her head, she spread her skirts about her and waited, for she did not want to seem too eager. By now she knew if she continued to ward off his advances it would only be a matter of time before he banished her from court. According to the King's Musick, he'd dismissed many an unwilling maiden. Sorrow darkened her heart as she gazed upon her opulent surroundings, the richly paneled walls, the oaken carved bed with its richly embroidered canopy and coverings, the glittering jewels about her neck, wrists and fingers. Why did he pursue her? Didn't he have enough women? Even though he was the king, he was still a man—and how much could a man possibly handle?

Why couldn't things be simpler, why couldn't Henry have been an ordinary country gent with whom she could enjoy the ritual of courtship instead of being another object of the king's desire? As badly as she wanted to stay here at court and enjoy his alluring presence, his image still frightened her. She stood for several tense moments, her fingers clamped round the door handle, torn by her hesitancy and her desire to please the man she'd grown to adore. Her hesitancy won.

She did not go to him. She scribbled a quick note and gave it to a page. "Deliver this to the royal chamber, please."

She undressed, folded her skirts and robe. She pulled on a linen nightdress and climbed into bed, calming herself as she nestled into the feathery down mattress. *Henry is a gentle, understanding man*, she assured herself.

He *had* said patience was his greatest virtue.

A few minutes later, her inner chamber door opened. Thinking it was one of the grooms coming in to kindle the fire, she ignored him. Then she felt the bed sag as someone sat at the edge.

She sat up and saw his figure illuminated by the fire's soft glow.

"My lord!" she gasped, pulling the cover up around her throat. "What…what brings you here?"

"What indeed?" His voice, smooth and even, hinted at annoyance. "Why did you refuse my invitation, Amethyst?"

"I...I thought it better this way, my lord." She inched away, bumping the headboard.

"What way? To remain untouched for the rest of your days? Why do you refuse me? Do I not appeal to you?"

"Aye, of course you do! But my feelings...they are so jumbled." She spoke the truth.

He crept closer and she inched back.

"Tell me of these jumblings, Lady Amethyst." His voice came to her, low and soothing. "I do not want you to be unhappy in any way. What bothers you?"

"Well, sire, 'tis..." She pulled the bedcovers up to her chin as his eyes burned even more intensely. "...many things, namely, you're a married man."

"Lately it has been in name only, Amethyst. Catherine and I are at the point of estrangement, as you can plainly see for yourself."

"I knew that for some time, sire, but still, she is your wife. Then there is Bessie Blount..."

"What of her?" He gave a one-shoulder shrug.

"Is she not your mistress?" she probed.

"She had been, on and off, for many years. No longer. In fact, Wolsey is about to marry her off to a gentleman named Tailbois within a fortnight. You will no longer be seeing Bessie Blount at court. She and I are finished." His tone remained low and conversational, devoid of anger or passion of a man speaking of a decade-long affair.

"But you have a son by her." She inhaled the woodsy fragrance of his cologne as it tickled her senses.

"Aye, so I do. But Henry Fitzroy is illegitimate. I made him the Duke of Richmond, but that is all he can ever be. Besides, Henry is nearly six. I sired him before I even knew you existed. Why would you resent him?"

"I do not resent him," she clarified. "It's...all these things I'm finding out about you, I find out through others. I would so much rather hear them from yourself."

"Ah…now I see." He nodded with a cocked brow. "You want a ritual courtship. You want a gent on bended knee to woo you in the garden and serenade you under your chamber window in the moonlight."

Her laugh came out throatier than she'd liked. The bedcovers fell to her waist as she relaxed her grip. "Aye, that would be nice."

"So that should serve to unjumble your thoughts?" he persisted.

"When you invited me to join the King's Musick, I thought my sole duty would be to perform with the King's Musick." She pulled her legs up under her, keeping a tight grasp on the covers.

"You think quite a bit, don't you? Then I shall put all thoughts out of your head but thoughts of our bodies uniting and belonging." Only a king such as Henry would presume to purge thoughts from someone's head.

"But then there is tomorrow," she attempted to put him off.

"Aye, I was never one to refuse an early morning romp." He stripped the covers from her with his eyes.

So much for putting him off. "Nay, that is not what I mean. I mean the courtiers will talk behind my back, and the queen will resent me." She grabbed the pillow beside her and placed it twixt their bodies as a barrier.

"Catherine cares not what I do, Amethyst. Our marriage lost its lustre long ago. I want you, Amethyst. I do not want Bessie, or Mary Boleyn, or anyone else. Just you. So let me make you mine, my darling." In a graceful pounce, he captured her in his arms. His lips crushed hers and she inhaled the sweet scent of his lavender shaving water as she went limp in his arms. As the kiss intensified, she fought the urge to respond. Pulling away, she disengaged their mouths and caught her breath.

"What is wrong now?" He shoved the pillow aside.

"Please, my lord, your visit was so unexpected…" She wiped her lips and moved to slide off the bed.

"Do not play games with me, Amethyst." He stood, towering over her. "I can plainly see the way you look at me, the glances we exchange, the touches, the innuendo in just about every word...then when I come to your bed you refuse me."

"But I came here as a musician, not as your mistress," she made another weak attempt at logic.

He smiled, though his eyes remained two golden beams of anger. "Your innocence is utterly charming, Amethyst. It makes me crave you even more." He ran a finger along her jawline. "But how can you have been so...innocent? You are unlike any woman who's ever come through these palace gates, who have literally stumbled at my feet and let me whisk them off to my bed for the thrill of a royal romp. Mayhap the values in Warwickshire are pure indeed."

"I like to think so, sire." Still clutching the cover, she sidestepped to the glowing embers in the hearth. "I am not even a Londoner, though I was born in the Tower I suppose I am a native Londoner. But since you gave us back our castle, Warwickshire has been the only place I've ever called home."

"Aye, you are pure of heart indeed." He followed her across the chamber, stopping within kissing distance. "You may not realize it, Amethyst, but your body gives one signal while your mind speaks another. When you get them synchronized, then we shall continue."

He kissed her on the hand and straightened his robe.

"Does that mean I can stay on at court, sire?" She didn't dare let a hint of entreaty invade her tone.

"I shan't have it any other way." He nudged her cover aside and admired her curves under the thin nightdress. Standing there under his scrutiny, she began to enjoy it. With a brush of her lips, he strode out of the chamber.

"Of course!" she hissed. He planned to make her the next Bessie Blount. Her resentment dueled with her growing attraction to him. Oh, why did he have to be so desirable?

* * *

He was in and out of council meetings over the next few days. Amethyst glimpsed him once from her perch in the gallery. He didn't return to her bedchamber. She took his frosty indifference as his message that he was indeed waiting for her to come to him when ready. They ran into each other in the hallway late one night as she returned to her chambers and he roamed the palace, as he often did, unable to sleep.

"Good evening, Amethyst." Through the semi-darkness she could see his tousled hair, as if he'd been to bed and risen again. Flames danced in the torches on the walls, creating a ghostly shadow around his regal figure.

"Sire." She bobbed a curtsey. "I trust you found the music enlightening tonight."

"As always," came out flat.

"I heard the queen was ill?" She wanted to remind him that he still had a wife, but her genuine concern for the queen overshadowed her need to make conversation.

"She's...not feeling quite right, she's been confined to her chambers." His tone sounded genuine enough despite what she'd heard of his waning interest in his wife.

"Is it serious? Mayhap I can go to her and sing some songs to cheer her up," she offered.

He waved that idea away. "Nay, she sometimes feels the need to retreat from the fanfare and delve deeply into her scriptures and Masses."

She could tell he didn't want to talk about his wife. Catherine was becoming somewhat of a nonentity at court. Even when she did join the king at the high table, she seemed to be in a world all her own, talking to no one, simply eating her meal and leaving.

"My lord, I thought about that last evening when you...entered my chambers," she voiced this now, rather putting it off.

"I do not plan to wait forever, Amethyst, but I shall never force myself upon you." His eyes bored into hers and she didn't dare break that contact.

"But how can you expect me to be like all those others, sire?" She wanted to hear his answer to that, truthful or not.

"If by now you still think I consider you a mere wench, you are more obtuse than I ever thought possible." His eyes narrowed with a spark of indignation. "I would have banished you from court long ago had it been mere lust."

"But it is so perverse…" She grappled with her belt, cringing under his gaze.

"What on earth is perverse?" His voice rose and the flames seemed to jump in response. "What is perverse about two people who are genuinely attracted to each other expressing their feelings? 'Tis the most natural act God has given us humans the ability to perform."

"Not when one of them is married," she reminded him, as if he needed reminding, as if he cared.

"Are you saying you plan to wait 'til Catherine dies before you will let me take you?"

His bluntness hit her like a lightning bolt. She blanched. "Nay! I simply do not want to hurt her."

"Catherine does not come into this. We no longer live as man and wife. Do you understand that or must I spell it out for you?" His tone became condescending.

"Are you and the queen truly estranged, my lord? I wish to hear the truth from you, to quell all those rumours floating round court."

"We have been having many problems for quite some time now. Long before you ever arrived at court." He smoothed his hair back.

"Is it because of…your other affairs, my lord?" she probed, expecting the naked truth if she was to become entangled.

"You are a presumptuous one, are you not?" His eyes sparkled like two stars in the flickering torchlight. "Our problems go much deeper than that. My affairs were never any of Catherine's concern. You know very little of court life, my dear. It is as natural as breathing for a man to engage in extramarital affairs. You must expect whomever you marry to do so as well."

"My father never stepped out on my mother," she informed him.

"He was a prisoner in the Tower." He shook his head as if correcting a child He spent most of his life in chains. It was not as if he had many opportunities."

"I would expect my husband to be faithful to me as I shall be to him, my lord. I take marriage vows seriously." Surely no lady had ever spoken to him in this manner. She wasn't sure where she'd gathered the nerve.

"Then I suggest you find yourself a saint, Lady Amethyst." He turned and left her standing there as the torch nearest her sputtered and died out.

* * *

Several evenings later, Eustace Chapuys, the Imperial Envoy, arrived at court. They entertained him lavishly, and the King's Musick played throughout the fornight-long visit. Catherine appeared, as she and the Envoy were close associates, and the king danced, but not with the queen. They kept an even greater distance, Amethyst noticed. She found it easier to believe they were estranged, and it wasn't a court rumour or a mere ploy to lure her to his chambers. When the musicians took a short recess, she crossed the great hall to partake of a repast before the next session.

She glanced in Henry's direction. Deep in conversation with his council members, the Dukes of Suffolk and Norfolk, he did not see her. When she again looked his way, she caught him staring at her, and their gaze held. That unspoken signal shot through the noisy hall. Desire glowed in his eyes; they glittered more brightly than the gems trimming his doublet as he regarded her, beckoning.

She returned that gaze with a barely discernable nod.

He came to her after all the courtiers had retired.

She met him at the entrance to her audience chamber. "Something told me you would come to me tonight, sire," she whispered.

"You have me." Hand in hand, they strode through the labyrinth of passageways, reached her bedchamber and entered.

They sat by the fire and he poured each of them a gobletful of mead from the pitcher on the sideboard. She developed a taste for this strong sweet liquid that turned her insides aglow. Once again the king set her heart aflutter, as she was so in awe of his regal bearing, his vigorous, yet gentle manliness. But her fear stood in the way.

He filled his goblet after every few sips, fingering the clasp of his girdle, the fireglow creating a halo about him.

"Your majesty, Topaz and I made a visit to an almshouse in Whitechapel recently." She opened the conversation with a matter now dear to her heart, not only to put off the inevitable. "It was so sad to see how the poor must live."

"I am aware of that, Amethyst." He nodded. "In our society there will always be rich and poor."

"Is there anything the crown can spare to help these people?" She circled her fingers round her goblet. "They literally starve, kill each other for scraps of food."

He gave her a sad smile. "Aye, tomorrow, just for you I shall dip into the treasury and send a delivery to Whitechapel."

"Oh, thank you, sire." She reached forward and clasped his hand. "It is not just for me, but for your subjects. They will be so grateful."

"It is done." He drained his goblet and glanced at the sideboard, likely for something to eat.

"Now, I would challenge you to a game of tennis tomorrow, but alas I have no jewels with which to gift you," she joked, but dead serious about the game.

His gaze fastened onto hers. She wished he would tell her what bothered him; she wanted to be his confidante. But was that even possible? "Amethyst, you do have a gift you can bestow upon me."

He leaned over and she nodded, knowing. He'd been right; her body sent signals independent of her mind. Her mind continued to tell her that he was a married man with a string of mistresses and she was next in line. If only they could share intimacy and each other's lives without this stigma, without the entire court tittering behind her back.

Resigned to her fate, she asked, "What would the arrangement be, my lord?"

"Arrangement?" He sat back and tilted his head.

"Aye. Would I need to make an appointment to see you? That is court protocol, is it not?"

"That is preposterous." He disregarded her questions with a sweep of his hand. "Nay, we would see each other when time permits!"

"In other words, when you can fit me in," came out sounding more sarcastic than she'd meant it to.

"I am a king, Amethyst, not a yeoman farmer. Affairs of state take precedence over my personal life and always will. If your body's desires exceed those of mine, then you will have to deal with it accordingly."

"I did not mean it that way," she huffed, exasperated at the way he summed everything up to carnal animal desires. "I would be taking a huge step, a step I am not sure I wish to take."

He leaned forward 'til their knees touched. "You torment me, Amethyst, and you know it. You have been driving me wild with desire for you, and it seems you are basking in it. Why do you enjoy torturing me so?"

"I do not wish to torture you, sire. You will never know what it is like to be in my position... a virgin, never touched by any man, now with a king courting me... already the court thinks I am your mistress, they think things that aren't even true. People are cold to me, and snicker when I walk by." This was far from true; although she'd noticed a few furtive glances, no one outwardly treated her with any less respect than the day she'd first joined court. But she had to exaggerate her plight to drive her point home with him; nothing else seemed to work.

"Who snickers, who is cold to you?" he demanded. "I shall banish them immediately."

"Nay, do not do that." She held up a hand. "It is expected. It is human nature. Especially in as close proximity as court. I am beginning to realize that. Courtiers love to gossip... they spin what are obviously tall tales, just to keep themselves amused. They are worse than country folk. That is easy enough to live with. Being your mistress is not."

"All right, then. I shall do what I must do." He stood, slammed the goblet down, and left in a swirl of ermine and lavender shaving water.

"My lord…" Now what did he mean by this ambiguous statement? She knew. This was the end of her stay at court. He'd waited long enough and she'd given him her answer. She stood, ran her hand over the fine velvet chair, and turned to face the wardrobe. Tomorrow at this time she would be on her way back to Warwickshire with a bruised heart, but with her honor intact.

* * *

The following afternoon, before Vespers, a page greeted her and led her into the king's closet. *This is it,* she thought. *This is goodbye.*

He sat before the fire on his lounging sofa, draped in a satin robe of burgundy, a gold goblet in his bejeweled fingers.

"Come sit beside me, Lady Amethyst." He patted the seat.

"I know what you want to say." She dreaded the thundering outburst, the banishment from court and the rest of her life as a Warwickshire wench who'd had the gall to rebuff the king.

He offered her wine and she declined. He took another sip of his own. "You do, do you? Are you a mind reader as well?"

"Nay, my lord, but after last night, I am aware that you have ended your wait for me, and wish me to leave." She sat, but a bit farther from the spot he'd patted.

His eyes bored into her, but she avoided his gaze. "Well, this time you are dead wrong."

Her muscles went stiff. "You do not wish to send me back home?"

"Nay. You refuse to become my mistress, and I cannot tell you the enormous respect I harbor for you because of that. You are a special one, indeed. Not only beautiful and talented, but honorable as well."

Relief flooded her, but apprehension forced her to remain at the edge of the seat. "Thank you, sire," she whispered twixt parched lips.

He sat back, crossed one leg over the other and grabbed his ankle. "Amethyst, you know very well Catherine and I have been estranged. It is not because of my other mistresses, as you thought. That is no reason for an estrangement. The reason is that I have ceased to love Catherine. We've grown apart, our ideals and goals have long since parted their ways and have followed diverse paths. We cannot talk, cannot see eye to eye on any subject, she is as bent on her beliefs as I am on mine." He gazed into the fire and sighed. "The other reason is much more mundane." He looked into her eyes. "I need an heir, a legitimate male heir, and Catherine is past her childbearing stage. It was when I came to the realization that Catherine and I shall never produce an heir together, I knew what I must do."

"And what is that, sire?" She tensed up, afraid of what was coming next.

"Set Catherine free so that I may pursue a mother for my heirs."

Amethyst tore her gaze from the two piercing chips of gold that held her fast. This was hard to take it all in at once. She dared not ask him what he had in mind. She wasn't even sure she wanted to know. But she was here, in private audience with the king, pouring his heart out to her, as any common man remorseful over his mistakes. She now knew that kings made mistakes, too. "Set Catherine free…but how, your majesty? She is your wife."

"I looked into the matter most carefully, Amethyst, spent many, many sleepless nights poring through many sources, mulling it over in my mind, talking to our great Lord himself, pleading for answers like the most common street beggar, for as I am your king, he is mine." He glanced up toward heaven. "It matters not what Catherine thinks, for the succession of the crown must continue, and continue naturally, so that I may leave legitimate and uncontested issue, so that the crown will not roll upon the ground to be plucked up by the nearest or most ambitious pretender. I plan to put an end to my marriage to Catherine."

He set his goblet down with a determined thud, as if vocalizing his plans officiated them; the first step to carrying them out.

"How, your majesty?" she blurted, for lack of anything else to say. But of course he would find a way. She froze, half expecting to hear what she most feared. But then, he'd said he wanted to put an end to his marriage, not to Catherine.

"I did some research with Wolsey and came upon the most startling conclusion, quite surprisingly." He poured himself another goblet of wine and munched on a handful of grapes, popping them into his mouth one after the other, extracting the pips and flicking them into the fire. Once more, he offered her wine. This time she accepted. "Catherine and I were never married. We were never man and wife. As the widow of my brother Arthur, our marriage was never valid in the name of God."

She'd heard that before; it sounded vaguely familiar. Of course, Topaz, who'd spat it out so vehemently with all the other venom she spewed about the king, Amethyst had forgotten it within minutes. So it was true—and how surprised could the king have been then?

"Your majesty, I cannot see how that can be so." She didn't want to throw cold water on it, but raging fires always needed cold water.

"It is simple. Read Scripture. It states clearly in Leviticus, 'Thou shalt not uncover the nakedness of thy brother's wife; it is thy brother's nakedness.' and 'If a man shall take his brother's wife, it is an unclean thing: he hath uncovered his brother's nakedness; they shall be childless.' We are not married. It is that simple. I shall approach the Pope and obtain an annulment."

How simple could it be? she wondered. But then again, he was talking as if the Queen Catherine were a fly he could brush off his cloak. How simple it had been for Henry's father to purge her father from the face of the earth. *Please, God, don't let Hal turn out that way,* she mouthed a silent prayer.

"Then I shall be free to marry again and bring forth the heir this country so desperately needs," he concluded, as if explaining how he'd won a chess game.

"The country needs? Or you need, your majesty?" she challenged, once again, fascinated with his mind, eager to explore it further.

He licked wine off his lips and plucked another handful of grapes off the vine. "You are getting to know me, you feisty little spirit." He smiled at her, his twinkling eyes echoing the jewels glittering on his every finger. "What man, from the king down to the lowliest stableboy, doesn't want a son? However, for me it is more than a personal wish. I have a duty to carry out, an obligation to my kingdom, to the ages."

"And how does Queen Catherine feel about it?" As if it mattered. But still, she was curious.

He cleared his throat and for the first time since she'd entered the chamber, his gaze left hers. He stared into his wine goblet. "She doesn't know yet."

Her jaw dropped. "You discussed it with me, a mere court musician, a servant, before bringing it before your wife, the queen, the victim?"

His eyes returned to hers and bored straight through to her soul. They blazed, fiery, his temper piqued. "I am the victim here, not she." His voice, though remaining calm and even, rasped with scorn. He was not one to shout to make a point; it would be ever so un-kingly. He needn't ever shout. "'Tis I who shall suffer, along with my realm, because she cannot produce an heir. She will be well provided for. She will not want. What more would she have of me?"

"Why, I do not know, your majesty. I know the queen not at all. I've not met her more than three or four times, and we've exchanged no more than the most simple of niceties. But if it must be, then all I can think she would ask for is dignity."

The smile returned but did not touch his eyes. "And that she will always have, my dear, for Catherine is true Spanish royalty. That she will always have."

She sipped her wine, the king's gaze warming her.

"Besides, you are no longer a mere court musician, Lady Amethyst. You are my special confidante. One to whom I can turn when this great matter goads me, and goad me it will, knowing Catherine, who will probably fight this to the death. I feel I can trust you, and you will never judge me."

"Thank you, sire." She gave him a reverent nod. "I shall always be here for you should you need someone to confide in."

"More wine?" He gestured to the pitcher.

"Nay, thank you." Amethyst could not handle any more wine now; her mind was reeling too much. What the king talked of seemed like an impossibility. She'd always thought marriages were forever. Her mother had stood by her father throughout his entire life, as a prisoner just as he was. No matter how much misery and sorrow she'd suffered, Amethyst knew her mother would never have ended her marriage. "How will you convince the Pope that your marriage should be annulled should he use the fact that you and Catherine have a daughter?"

"Mary is a lovely lass, but a punishment, a well-deserved punishment for my sins did God bring down upon me for marrying my brother's widow, and also by giving my mistress a son. I shall use the precedents throughout history. There have been several..." He explained, "Henry the Fourth of Castile was granted a dispensation to discard his first wife for not producing an heir. He was given the right to try a second wife, and a third, and even to go back to his first, 'til he was given his rightful heir. I am sure Pope Clement will do the same. He is a man; he realizes how important it is for a king to have an heir. We do not want another Battle of Bosworth, do we?"

"Nay, sire." Certainly she didn't. Topaz's wishes were another story. It was what her sister lived for—a virtual reenactment of the Battle of Bosworth, only she would emerge victorious, head held high, to be declared queen as the crown rolled out from under a bush to be placed on her head, Henry's corpse flung over a horse, as Topaz had repeated Richard III's fate in that Bosworth scene so many times... she shuddered at the thought.

He began pouring, then stopped with his goblet half full. As he took a deep breath, she could see he was carefully planning his next words.

"What I feel for you is not only lust. You are a gentle, sincere woman, so different from the others. I do not want you to be my concubine. I want you to be my wife, Amethyst." How more simply could he have said it? It wasn't a flowery romantic proposal on bended knee in the moonlight as she'd always dreamed. But then, what she'd never dreamed, never in all her years of endless reverie about the king, was that he would ever want her to be his wife!

It wasn't a question at all; it was another kingly command, as he commanded his servants to carry out his orders: "Trim my beard, fetch my doublet, become my wife." It was all within the power of his birthright to make demands on his subjects. He didn't have to ask anyone for anything. Nevertheless, his words thrilled her all the same.

"Your majesty…I…" she stammered, dumbfounded. "I know not what to say."

"Say aye and be done with it." He shrugged, palms up. "Would you not like to be queen?"

"Like to?" Simple, oh, so simple, was King Hal's life, from the crown placed on his head at birth. "Your majesty…you're…still married." She couldn't get over that simple fact. She reached for her goblet, nearly knocking it to the floor, and gulped the wine like water.

"I am not married, have you not been listening to a word I've said?" His voice boomed. "An annulment is all I need. Then I shall be free."

"But, sire, you need a princess, someone of royal lineage, one of your peers. I am not worthy of the honor." She looked down her body to her shoes. "Look who I am; look who my father was!"

"You are not who you are because of who your father was."

But his answer hardly assured her. "You are who you are because of who *your* father was," she replied with as much conviction.

He nodded and pointed a finger. "And that is the sadness of it all, Amethyst. That is the burden I must bear. But I am still a man, and am falling in love with a beautiful woman whom I wish to marry."

"Please, sire, give me some time." She closed her eyes and opened them again to make sure this wasn't a dream. "I need to sort through my feelings."

"I do not want to rush you, Amethyst, but our lives on earth are pitifully short. I am a mortal, just like everyone else, although the courtiers and subjects look upon me like some type of God."

"It is because you are so imposing, so regal..." She gestured up and down his magnificent form. "That is what brought me to you at first. I hadn't even seen the warm, sensitive side to you yet, not 'til that first day at Warwick Castle when you met me in the conservatory. If only all the others could see that side of you."

"Nay, they never shall." His lips tightened to a thin line. "They shall never see the anguish I suffer, the decisions I agonize over for the betterment of the kingdom. You understand now why I need someone at my side, not another Wolsey, but someone to whom I can open my...my heart."

"Oh, sire, I shall always be here for you," she vowed, knowing her wedding vows wouldn't be any less heartfelt.

"Then sit beside my throne as my queen," he urged, grasping her arms.

"Please let us wait until these other matters are solved," she hedged, knowing she could push him off the edge at any moment. But still—this was so sudden!

"But are you now convinced of how badly I want you? I am willing to make you my queen, not a mere mistress. Amethyst, I want to make love to you." His grasp on her arms tightened.

She raised her lips to meet his in a painfully short kiss. With his hand flattened on the small of her back, he led her to the bed. They lay down together, and he gently removed the wimple from her head, letting her hair tumble in a golden waterfall through his fingers. "Your hair is like silk," he murmured into her ear as she responded to his soft caresses and the tiny kisses he was planting on her neck and throat. His breathing became more rapid as she felt his manhood stirring beneath the satin robe. Her thighs parted and her hips began that slow primitive thrust against his. It all felt so instinctual, so natural; she'd never done this before, yet she knew it was right.

He removed her bodice and skirts and they lay in a glossy pool upon his satin sheets as she opened the front of his robe and unlaced his shirt. She shivered in the cold air against her bare breasts for but a moment, until he tore off his shirt and covered her with his torso. She whirred dizzily with the touch of his warm skin. His fingers fanned her breasts and she pressed up against his throbbing urgency. "Such lovely rosebuds," he whispered, and his mouth closed on one breast, causing her to gasp, bringing her to soaring heights.

"I am afraid, sire," she whispered as his lips trailed a hot blaze down her abdomen, then nestled twixt her thighs. She wound her fingers through his hair, her legs clasped round his head as her body spasmed in ecstasy.

She pulled his head up and moved down to meet him. "But I really do want you," she sighed, running her hand down the smooth mat of curly red hair on his chest, down to touch his member for the first time. It throbbed, just as she did inside, with urgency. She gasped as he pushed through her maidenhead, a sharp stab of pain giving way to a burst of fireworks as he thrust gently, slowly, and her hips joined his in an erupting surge of passion. He was hers, all hers, helplessly entranced within her, stripped naked of his jewels and velvets and satins. He was a beautiful, rugged man pouring his passion into her, but he was still the king, whom the entire realm bowed to and obeyed. She closed her eyes, each breath a gasp, each exhalation a cry of rapture, and nothing existed but their bodies, their closeness, their bodily fluids as well as their cosmic beings mingled, entwined, united.

He exploded inside her and she cried out, then retreated into dreamy delirium, his head upon her breasts, his body spent, his breaths rapid, yet subdued.

"My lord, I have never been with a man before," she confessed once more, feeling ashamed at her lack of ability to please him the way she thought she should have.

"'Tis all right, Amethyst. You gave me a most precious gift and I appreciate it."

"What if Queen Catherine finds out about us?" Her small voice betrayed her fear.

He laughed, reaching over and pushing a few strands of hair out of her eyes. "Surely you jest. She has nothing to say. I can bed whom I please. It is she who prefers to remain chaste and spend the best years of her life with priests and Bibles. She has never held a tennis racquet nor tossed a pair of dice in her life. She knows not how to live."

"Neither do I, sire. This whole life is so new to me."

"Ah, you will get used to it. Already you are looking more courtly, with the new gowns and jewels I have given you. You are the pride of the King's Musick. Do not worry about Catherine. Leave that to me." He patted her arm.

"And I want to stay the pride of the King's Musick, in the eyes of court," she said. "Please do not tell anyone of us... yet."

"As you wish, dear lady."

* * *

Upon returning to her chambers at the other end of the palace, she grabbed a leaf of parchment and a pen and began scribbling a letter to Matthew. She knew no one else in whom she could confide. Desperate for an outlet, she trusted Matthew, the one she could always turn to, as he had to her. She wrote her first letter to him whilst the king was still on progress, and recorded her immediate impressions, the polite yet impersonal mingling in the great hall, the magnificent Windsor Castle with its gateways and central round keep. "My chambers are sparsely decorated yet tasteful, my bed soft and feathery, my chambermaids cordial and sincere... " She'd kept it light and chatty Matthew wrote back that Topaz behaved cool and detached as of late. He took it as an ominous oracle—she'd been distant and aloof ever since that last revelation of her plans. She now spent all her time either with the animals, with the boys, or locked in her study—conspiring, as they both knew.

"Fret not," she'd written back. But, God's foot, did this stream of events go topsy-turvy! She now found herself pouring her heart out, baring her personal feelings about the king, and the pen flew across the parchment as she expressed her doubts and fears as well as her fervent desire to please the king in every way.

"Now do not let this shock you, dear Matthew, but the king is determined to free himself of Catherine by having the marriage annulled... and has asked me to be his wife. Me! Amethyst, the daughter of the murdered and martyred Earl of Warwick, the future queen consort! He cares not about my background, but most importantly he knows not of Topaz. I cannot in good conscience consider marrying someone who engages in endless dalliances with every maiden of his fancy, while still married to the queen! No doubt he would carry on the same pattern of behavior should I ever agree to marry him... but does anyone dare refuse the King of England? But dear God, Matthew, I do love him so. Please pray for my soul.

Who knew what would be happening by the time her letter reached him? Oh, how she wished he were there for her, just as she had been there for him that day in the rose garden.

Chapter Six

Richmond Palace, 1527

"Sire, I simply adore being your personal musician," Amethyst declared, her fingers poised over the keyboard in Henry's conservatory while he tuned his lute. "But..." She hesitated, turning to him.

He looked up and held her gaze, urging her on. "Yes...but what?"

"I believe the other minstrels are a bit slighted. I do not want them resenting me, too, for they are my closest companions...apart from you."

"Oh, is that all?" He chuckled, his voice touched with relief. "The other minstrels aren't as gifted as you, dear lady. They cannot sing like you, they cannot pour their hearts into the strains of my own compositions as you can. You have what they do not—a feel for my music, an understanding of why I wrote it, the emotion behind the busy runs up and down the scale..." His hand traced triangles through the air, as if conducting a troupe of musicians, "...taking trouble to add the pretty mordants, the significance of writing one piece in a major key and another in the minor."

"Do I, sire?" She took a step closer. "I've noticed, lately..." she lowered her voice to an intimate tone. "...your music's been losing its gaiety, its lightheartedness. It's transforming itself from light entertainment to an expression of your deeper emotions, becoming more sorrowful, more sullen. Lately your music seems an outlet, not only of your creativity, but of your anguish."

He eyed her with scrutiny. "Very observant, my lady. What I've told you, I have not shared with another.

You do seem to know me to the depths of my soul, and you know what?" A smile brightened his eyes. "I am fine with it. Mayhap I need the confidante you want to be. I've never shared my feelings with a lass before..." He hesitated, his eyes searching the room. "Come to think of it, never with anyone before."

"Tis an honor to be your confidante, sire. And you can rest assured, I'll never repeat a word of what you share with me to another soul." Taking another step closer, she noticed for the first time a furrow in his brow she'd never seen before. *He is troubled*, she thought. *We both are.*

* * *

After several days of torrential rain, the sun burst through the clouds and Amethyst dashed to the stables, eager to ride. Henry joined her in cantering through the fields east of Windsor. She raised her face to sun in the warm October breeze dotted with pockets of coolness. The landscape lay spread before them, a tapestry of vivid browns, burnt oranges and muted golds. The bursts of color blazed in radiant rejoinder to the sun's golden rays, the sky a clean blue backdrop. The wind sighed through the trees, and they obeyed its command. They spurred their palfreys to gallop over the lush fields.

"Shall we picnic here?" He signaled to the grooms and servants trailing them. They settled under a sprawling oak, its burnished leaves fluttering to the ground like fragile shreds of parchment, and spread a linen cloth on the ground. The grooms busied themselves with their repast out of earshot while Henry and Amethyst enjoyed a private interlude.

"I told Catherine," he stated simply, flipping open the basket lid and extracting a small drumstick, which he handed to her.

"Told her?" Her stomach churned and she clasped her hands around her cup to steady them. "I must confess, I…I've dreaded this inevitable day. What did she say, my lord?" She tried to keep her voice steady.

"There's naught to dread." He tore into his drumstick, looking more interested in feeding himself than altering his wife's life. "After an emotional outburst that quite unnerved me, she began screaming and raving, half in Spanish, no less." He talked as he chewed. "Eventually, when she became coherent, she refused to believe me. She looked at me as if I were making the entire thing up, for my amusement, like I'm a bloody mummer." He wiped his chin with his hand and rummaged through the basket. "I explained it all to her…how the Pope erred in issuing the dispensation for us to marry." He took out a linen napkin and swept at his face with it. "I told her how it was torturing my conscience that we were not truly man and wife, and I explained that all the theologians and canonists agreed that we were living in mortal sin. She refuses to believe any of it." He took another gouge out of the drumstick and chewed. "Catherine, of all people, the one I thought would understand, all she has to do is re-read the Scriptures for the millionth time. God's truth, she rattles it off like she wrote it herself."

"Does she doubt the credibility of all the churchmen you'd consulted, a woman a pious as Catherine?" She bit into her own drumstick, though this conversation didn't do much for her appetite.

"That is what makes it all the more difficult." He pulled another drumstick from the basket. "She blamed Wolsey for the whole thing, for instigating a plot, and for influencing me into believing our marriage is not valid, for delving too deeply into Scriptures and misinterpreting them, twisting them to serve his own dogmas, and finding things that simply weren't there." He gnawed at that one and chewed it with gusto. "Then she accused him of wanting to cast her aside so I can marry a French princess and produce an heir to reign over France and England. I must say, her accusation on that point may have been valid a few years ago." He swallowed and washed the meat down with a swig of wine. "Wolsey has always believed that the King of England should rule France, as in the past. But in the end, she believes we are both victims of Wolsey's cunning devices. The truth is, Wolsey was as shocked as anyone when I first approached him with the idea. I would suppose telling Catherine that it was entirely Wolsey's idea would ease this strain a bit." He took another generous bite. "But Wolsey has been such a faithful servant to me, my naming him the perpetrator would just turn him against me...and God knows, I do need Wolsey more than ever."

"There usually is one partner who does not desire the annulment. 'Tis rarely a mutual break, my lord." She barely nibbled at hers. "But despite all her reasons, I am sure she will see that it is best for both of you, and your agenda can no longer include her." She hadn't meant to sound vindictive towards Catherine. As a reasonable person, she thought everyone should be reasonable.

"When, Amethyst, when?" He stopped chewing, clutching his half-eaten drumstick in mid-air. "I cannot see her backing down without a long, hard fight. She is adamant, she insists she had never been married to Arthur, she guards that virginity she maintained in their marriage bed as if the crown jewels were 'twixt her thighs...then I tried to convince her we were without issue, all our children had died..."

"But what of the Princess Mary?" She sipped her wine, wishing she was more hungry.

"That is exactly what she said!" He held up his pointer finger. "What of her indeed? A daughter cannot rule. She will marry into foreign royalty, and with it goes the entire kingdom. Why cannot you women see that?" With that patronizing inquiry, he went back to his gnawing and chewing.

"We women see certain things differently, my lord," she gave him his answer, though she knew he hadn't expected one. "We think differently. More logically and less impetuously."

He turned away and slapped his palm on his thigh. "Are you with me or against me on this, Amethyst? What is your choice? And I want it before we go any further."

Another demand. Why did every question have to be put this way? "Why...I wish whatever will make everyone happy, sire..." Merely telling King Henry what he wanted to hear wouldn't work in this instance, it would catch up with her in the end, she knew it. "I want you to be happy, as well as the queen."

"That is impossible, that woman will never be happy." He hurled the gnawed bone into the distance, shaking his head in exasperation. As he focused on a faraway point, he looked helpless, even mortal, in a way she'd never seen him before. But of course—it was the first serious dilemma he'd ever had to face in his life.

"You will work it out, my lord. I know you will. You have that special way of doing everything." A twinge of hunger made her take a bite into her drumstick, enjoying its juiciness. Before, she'd nibbled at it without tasting it.

He reached over and embraced her. "I pleaded with her not to repeat any of this to anyone, lest her nephew Charles stick his nose into it."

She swallowed and took a quaff of wine. "Then surely you will not require my answer for quite some time, my lord."

"Ah, you wish to keep me in suspense for the duration of the untangling of this travesty of a marriage?" He wiped his hands on his napkin and rummaged in the basket, coming up with a loaf of brown bread.

"No, sire..." She shook her head. Why did he have that uncanny knack of making her sound like the villain? She hoped to eventually master her way round that. "I just meant that we should take one step at a time. I still have a lot of thinking to do."

"What is stopping you, Amethyst? You know how badly I want you, and I daresay you want me. We are well suited for each other, we appreciate each other's talents and beauty and style and grace," he listed what sounded like his own virtues, easily lifting her to his lofty heights with him. "Come, what is really stopping you? There is something, I know it. Why do you not wish to be my wife—and my queen?"

Escaping his impatient gaze, she turned to the beautiful day, the pearly ribbons of clouds above her, the orange clusters in a distant pumpkin patch, felt the soothing shade of the graceful oak under which they sat, their horses grazing contentedly beside them, the servants at a comfortable distance. She placed her drumstick on the plate and thought carefully. "I want very much to be your queen, sire, but several things stop me...you may not believe you are married in your heart, but in the eyes of the Church and the kingdom, and most of all, the queen, you are still very much her husband. And until this matter is solved, either by the Church or whomever you must consult to end it, I do not feel you should expect me to consider marrying you. And to ensure that I wouldn't bring forth an illegitimate child to trouble things further, I've been to a physician in Richmond. He inserted a pebble into my womb."

"And it bothers you not?" He tore off a chunk of bread and stuffed it into his mouth.

"Nay...I am not even aware of its presence."

"Well, if it begins to give you any kind of pain, I want it removed immediately...mayhap to replace it with a prince." His lips curved into a smile as he chewed.

"Not while you are still married," she insisted—again.

"I daresay the very day this marriage ends...so will that pebble." He pointed with his fistful of bread at her nether region.

"Another obstacle is a problem of mine..." She took a breath and prepared for a confrontation after this. "My sister Topaz. I've been loyal to my sister all my life, and always empathized with her when everyone else ignored her, but she believes she is the rightful heir, by way of our father. Our father would have been king hadn't your father dethroned Richard the Third."

He dismissed my father's fate with a casual wave. "Well, that's quite a moot point at this point in time. For my father's army did defeat Richard, because some of Richard's men deserted him at the very last second. It was a precarious victory, but a victory nonetheless. The crown itself has no loyalty, no respect for bloodlines. It sits upon the head of the latest victor."

"Aye, you are right, sire. Your father did kill Richard and take his crown, altering the succession. But Topaz never recognized it as such. She believes she's still royal and Henry Tudor was a mere pretender." I hastened to add, "This is what she believes, certainly not me."

"So she must believe you are royal as well." Amusement lit up his eyes. "She must enjoy living in her fairy tale."

She relaxed in relief at his refusal to take Topaz seriously—so far. "It matters not what she believes. I respect her but I do not agree with her."

"What about her lads?"

His question made her wonder if he'd go so far as to bring the lads to court for questioning. She hastened with, "I know not, sire. They're far too young to understand any of it." She had enough to tell him without bringing her two brainwashed little nephews into the picture. "She has been talking of this for years, since we were children." She shuddered at the thought of Henry's reaction—treason, it was, pure and simple treason, and punishable by torturous death. But she hoped her growing closeness to Henry would be Topaz's salvation. "Please, sire, she's a country lady who harbors great resentment, yet she is my sister, and I love her dearly…I want to help her get over this madness. If you truly love me, please forgive her and pardon her."

"'Tis all right, Amethyst." He calmly continued eating his bread, now breaking off a wedge of cheese. "There is nothing to forgive. I fear not the likes of her. I've got real enemies, these religious heretics who refuse to support my break with Catherine, the Pope for one. We might see civil war before this decade is out. But worry not. I shall handle it."

The bread and cheese gone, he wiped his hands on his linen napkin and dug into the basket once more. "Hmm.…some sweets would have been welcome to top it all off."

"But sire…that is my problem," she went on, caring less about sweets. "You must stay safe. You must also protect the Princess Mary and keep her safe."

"I worry not about Mary," he said between chomps on a raw carrot. "She is safe enough. If Mary were a boy, well…" he chuckled through his chomps. "However, I understand your dilemma. She is your sister and I am your king. I shall respect your wishes and not pressure you to make up your mind this minute. Such a beautiful day calls for a ride in the country, not affairs of state. We will discuss it at length on the morrow, mayhap. But for now…" He stood and she gazed at his lean body as he stretched, the taut muscles straining under the riding doublet and hose. "Let us continue, for it will be dark soon."

So relieved at his calm reaction, she took the last remaining item from the bottom of the basket, a red apple, and dug in.

* * *

"Sire, how is the Princess Mary? I trust she's faring well?" Amethyst asked that night as they dismounted and the grooms led the horses away.

"I have not spoken or written to her in some time," came his casual reply as they headed towards the garden for a quiet stroll before the evening meal. "But I must invite her back to court for a lengthy stay." Now his voice betrayed a hint of remorse, as if he hadn't even thought of his daughter before Amethyst her name.

"Does she know anything of your great matter?" she asked.

He shook his head. "I doubt not that Catherine has been writing her, telling her all kinds of prattle. God only knows what kinds of ideas she has put in the girl's innocent head."

"I would very much like to meet Princess Mary," Amethyst mused as they followed the winding garden path, and she plucked a red rose from one of the many bushes. They headed for the marble fountain, three marble birds streaming water out of their bills, and sat at the edge.

"She is with your Aunt Margaret at Ludlow Castle at the moment," Henry said. "I sent her there to keep her away from Catherine, and to begin her duties as Princess of Wales."

"May we go visit her?" she asked.

"I think we might," he answered noncommittally, making it obvious that a visit to his daughter was not on his immediate agenda. Bringing her to court was much more convenient—for him.

"When, sire?" she badgered. "I really want to meet her."

He cocked his head at her and pulled an end of his cloak that had fallen into the fountain. "Whenever you wish."

"How about tomorrow?" She knew she was pestering him, but her meeting Mary would create a family atmosphere she knew the girl longed for.

He laughed, wringing out his cloak on the fountain's edge, watching the stream of water run back into the pool. "Amethyst, I cannot go visiting round at whim. My appointments have to be carefully planned. I have a full itinerary these next few days that precludes any social calls. You may go and acquaint yourself with Mary, visit with your Aunt Margaret. You have my blessing."

"Very well. I am most eager to meet her. Is there any message you wish to convey to Mary?"

"Nay," he replied without thinking. "There will be plenty of time for that when she is a bit older. Then I shall tell her everything."

She couldn't help but wonder what 'everything' was.

* * *

She traveled to Ludlow in the royal carriage with gifts of silk cloth for Mary and her Aunt Margaret. Her heart went out to the little princess—did she understand why her father separated from her mother and why she was shunted off to faraway Ludlow?

Mary would be eleven now, she figured, and in light of the conflict between her parents, very much on the defensive. She had to explain to the child that she was a trusted friend, and meant no harm to the queen or to Mary.

Amethyst entered the formal gardens among flower beds spilling over with lavender, rosemary and thyme. She walked down a narrow path twixt two marble fountains to where Margaret sat working at needlepoint. Next to her sat a young girl, her hair pulled back and tucked under a white headdress, her face strained with deep concentration on her own needlework. They both looked up as Amethyst approached. Margaret dropped her work into her lap in surprise, and Mary looked up curiously, her face showing a pleasant but guarded expression.

"Aunt Margaret, 'tis so good to see you!" Amethyst and her aunt embraced, and as usual, Margaret was exquisitely dressed and jeweled, her gown a light blue adorned with pearls and gathered to show off her trim waist. Mary rose, and Amethyst curtsied to the princess.

"So this is the Princess Mary."

Mary, head held high, carried a mature countenance for her age. Amethyst saw Catherine's determined scrutiny mixed with Henry's jovial vitality in her eyes and in her smile.

"It is a pleasure to meet you, Mistress Amethyst. Please join us."

Amethyst sat on the marble bench next to Mary, bursting to tell the little girl she wished to help her through these difficult times, to share her own troubled childhood, to assure her that she would indeed be queen someday. Then realizing that would be too overwhelming for an eleven-year-old to absorb in a first meeting, she decided to ask Mary about herself.

"I am betrothed to a French prince, but I like it not," was the first revelation about herself to Amethyst. "I want to marry a prince of my own choosing." *How much like Topaz she sounds*, Amethyst thought. Mary's words sent her soaring back to their childhood.

"I have two little nephews," Amethyst told Mary, knowing they would never meet, feeling that sad pang for the lads who were living Topaz's brainwashing ideals. "Edward is fourteen and Richard is but nine."

"I would be so happy to have an older brother and a younger brother." Mary's wistful longings broke Amethyst's heart. The poor girl had no children of her own age to socialize with.

She then asked a question that took Amethyst totally by surprise. "Have you seen my mother?"

Amethyst in fact hadn't seen Catherine more than a few times in her life; she was still at court but isolated, keeping to her chambers and attending her many daily Masses.

"Nay, Mary, I do not see her much. I am a court musician, a very loyal subject of your father's, but I haven't the chance to talk with the queen much at all. Have you not heard from her?"

Margaret sat and listened carefully to the conversation, not interfering.

"She writes to me, and I write to her, but her letters are sorrowful. She says father is trying to end their marriage. He no longer loves her." Mary's voice dragged with sadness.

"Oh, nay, Mary, he still loves her, very much." That could not have been a lie; Amethyst knew Henry still bore feelings for Catherine, but not the way a man loved a woman—the way he now loved her. "You see, she is simply past the age that she can bear children, and you know the king thinks he needs a male heir to carry on the royal line. 'Tis a complicated matter, a matter I myself do not fully understand, but I am sure everything will work out."

"He thinks a wench cannot rule. He does not read his history books. There was Queen Matilda, and Queen Eleanor, and even my grandmother Queen Isabella. So why not I?" Mary implored.

Oh, if only that had a simple answer. "Some people think differently, but I have a feeling things will change, Mary. Would you like to be queen someday?"

Mary's eyes brightened and she smiled, showing young straight teeth, just a bit big for her face, which would certainly fill out to more even proportions. "Oh, aye, I wish to do all the things my mother cannot do."

"Then mayhap you will someday." Amethyst hoped with all her heart that Mary would get her rightful wish.

* * *

After a quiet dinner in the great hall devoid of musicians, Mary retired to her chambers to study.

"So how are Topaz and the lads?" was the first thing Amethyst wanted to know as she joined her aunt in the solar. "Is she behaving herself?"

"So far. She has been all talk up to this point." Margaret's tone sounded hopeful enough but her eyes betrayed a hint of fear. "She can put your life in serious danger if you continue there at court, Amethyst. The king may turn on you at any time."

"Henry would never do such a thing." She stated with the conviction she truly felt. "He cares for me a great deal, as I do him. He knows about Topaz. I am the one who told him. I told him, hoping he would pardon her out of consideration for me. He was not a bit disturbed. So concerned is he with his great matter, Topaz is but a joke to him."

"Lord knows I and my lads are in enough danger, being the only living rightful heirs to the throne." Margaret's hands shook as she lifted her goblet of mead.

"Not that we would ever try to rebel against Henry…especially since I am like a mother to Mary. But that can work against me, too, in light of his problems with Catherine. It is all very scary."

Amethyst leaned forward and gave her aunt a hug. "Worry not. Catherine will break down and give him his divorce. She has naught to gain by staying married to a man who doesn't want her. She's virtually powerless. 'Tis a shame, especially since he considers himself the victim, cursed for not being blessed with male heirs."

"Poor Mary, she tries so hard to be strong." Margaret buffed her ruby ring on her satin robe. "I do hope she will not grow old and bitter like Catherine."

"I am sure she will marry a man who will love her dearly," Amethyst said.

"We can only hope." Margaret gazed up at a crucifix on the wall. "Our line ended tragically enough. Who knows how long the Tudor line will last."

* * *

Upon ending their visit, Amethyst promised Mary that they would correspond, and offered any help she could give the girl. She had a troubled life ahead of her, but she certainly was better off here on the Welsh border than anywhere near court and once Amethyst was married to Henry, she'd be a devoted and loving stepmother.

* * *

The eve she returned to court, Amethyst joined the king on the dais in the great hall, at his insistence. As the queen's seat stayed conspicuously vacant for longer and longer periods of time, Amethyst felt that Henry wanted her up there not to honor her or dangle another enticement over her head, but out of plain loneliness. A king sitting alone at the high table among two hundred families at court wasn't exactly presentable.

She joined the King's Musick for her usual session after the evening meal, although the king wanted her to rest, but when she insisted, "I am a court musician, sire…" he sent her on her merry way up to the gallery. She waited the respectable amount of time for the courtiers to settle into their chambers, then agreed to join him in his sanctuary.

She wore her new satin underclothes, the chemise pure white, soft and buttery to the touch. She brushed her hair until it shone like spun gold, then pinned it up with the ornate ivory combs she'd received from the king. She dabbed Topaz's rose petal oil from a delicate glass bottle onto her pulse points, then on a plucky impulse, lifted her skirts and dabbed the scent on her inner thighs. She strolled at a leisurely pace as not to let her skirts rustle too noisily, swept through the hallways, up the staircase, past the erect guards, and through Henry's private apartments to his inner chamber.

He took her in a soft but demanding embrace, as if he'd been waiting a long time.

"Do you not want to know how Mary is?" she opened the conversation with a topic she believed even more important than his difficulties with Catherine.

"Ah, yes, and how is Mary?" *Now that you mention it* trailed in the air unsaid.

"She asked me if I'd seen her mother," Amethyst informed him, leaving the floor open for him to address that matter with his daughter.

"None of us has. Catherine is more secluded than the abbey monks." He turned and gestured for her to sit with him before the fire.

"She is a strong-willed lass and I believe she will come through this just fine." Amethyst walked over to the chair at his side, lifted her skirts and sat. "I made it clear to her that I am not the reason for her parents' divorce."

"Oh, hell's bells, she knows that." He fanned the air with his fingers. "With your auntie there as governess, I'm sure she is getting the truth. I am worried not about Mary. In a few years she will understand the facts about childbearing, and how short that fertile time really is."

"Oh, that she must learn, sire." She gave him a knowing nod.

"She will also understand why I need a male heir." His eyes quit roving over her breasts and met her steady gaze.

"That I am not so sure of. She is Catherine's daughter, you know." Amethyst settled back in the chair as a server brought her a cup of mead.

"Which is precisely why I must keep them apart. I do not want Catherine putting ideas into her head." Henry took a quaff from his tankard and wiped his lips with his hand.

"You must not alienate Mary, my lord. She is your only living legitimate heir." A subject ordering a king was grounds for dismissal and a stiff penalty, but they were far past subject-king protocol.

"I shall have sons, many sons, before I depart this earth. While I still have any life in me, I am going to give this kingdom a male heir." He stood and brought her to her feet. "Oh, Amethyst, darling child…" he breathed, his hands moving up to the combs just like she knew he would, pulling them from her hair, tossing them on the rug. Her tresses tumbled down around her shoulders. He took her face in his palms and claimed her lips, wordlessly, for there was no need to speak any further.

They glided to the bed, its velvet curtains open to the plump pillows and satiny coverlets, the pallet empty. They were alone in complete privacy, their bodies prolonging a desperate embrace. As he lowered her to the feathery mattress, she wanted to melt away and consume his patient passion for her. She reached up and ran her hand through his hair. As their kiss came to an end, she ran her lips over his neck, his warmth blending with the glow of the surrounding candles. She reached out and he was there next to her. His arms wound round her waist, and she caressed the smooth satin of his nightshirt. Her fingers found the buttons clasping the shirt and started to undo them, one by one. When she reached the bottom button, she slipped her hand inside his trousers. He moved closer and she felt his body against hers, warm, hard, impatient. Her hands explored, caressed, felt his swelling desire. He slipped her gown and chemise over her head. As his hands slid over her curves, she melted into the warmth of his bare skin. His breath came hot and demanding as his lips crushed hers, his tongue seeking, savoring her taste, her essence.

They kissed and explored and stroked. She pulled him closer, closer, until he was all hers, in her, with her, hers in every sense of their being. Together they soared and drifted, gasping their desperate need for each other. Finally, when she felt as if both their bodies would burst, she screamed, she cried, caught up in the most blissful rapture she'd ever felt.

Afterward, she reclined in his arms, drifting on tiny wavelets of pleasure, on that magic cloud on which they both lay.

She stroked the damp hair away from his eyes. Bathed in the warm golden light, he appeared the picture of peace, yet still so regal and majestic.

Beyond speaking, she drifted in that magical trance during which the very world had exploded around their bodies. She smiled, closed her eyes, and once again, they floated away together.

He placed upon her finger a magnificent ruby ring, sending out deep red bursts of light from its richly faceted depths, set in a delicate gold band. "This is an exact replica of the Regal of France." He held up his thumb, a perfect likeness of her ring glittering in the candlelight. "Thomas à Becket wore it, I wear it, now you and I have matching rings."

"How magnificent it is, sire." She held it up to the candlelight and the wine-red ruby glowed from within.

"Will wedding bands be next?" he asked.

"That is not entirely up to me," she gave him the simple fact.

"Neither is it up to me, alas," he whispered.

* * *

She opened her eyes to the silver-blue moonlight cascading through the windows, diffusing like diamond dust on the tapestry rug. She sensed the warmth of Henry's gaze enveloping her.

"Do you love me, sire?" she asked him through sleepy, dream-clouded eyes.

"As the bees love the honey, my lady."

* * *

The next evening, as Amethyst entered the king's outer chamber, she detected an ominous buzz that did not speak of an ordinary pleasant evening in the palace. She caught snippets of sentences, the words "Rome" and "The Pope" prevalent among them. *It must have something to do with Catherine,* she guessed. The attendants did not turn to her as she entered; no one greeted her.

She approached one of the king's gentleman ushers. "What is amiss?" Half expecting to see an enraged Catherine storm out of the king's privy chamber in a swirl of satins, crucifixes and tears, she kept her eyes riveted to the door.

"Rome has been sacked, Lady Amethyst. Charles the Fifth's troops have taken Rome and imprisoned the Pope."

"God Jesu!" She looked past the usher at the Flemish tapestry on the far wall. All thoughts of Catherine vanished. "Where is the king?"

"With Cardinal Wolsey and the Council in the Council chambers." He gestured with his head in that direction.

She left the king's chambers and returned to her own. She made a mad dash for her desk and began a letter to Matthew. Her writings to him resembled a journal; she recorded her reactions to the events of each day, and related her feelings about life at court, the courtiers around her, the sincere friends of the king as well as the enemies-in-the-making.

Now all she could write was "Catherine's nephew sacked Rome." She could write no more until she saw the king.

* * *

She faced Henry the following evening. After his invigorating tennis game, his mood was light, bordering on jovial. It seemed to bother him not that the Pope was a prisoner of Catherine's nephew.

"But my lord, this gives Catherine an uncanny advantage. She can manipulate the Pope ruthlessly through Charles in order to secure her marriage to you. How can you be free of her now?" As much as she respected the queen, she'd begun to see Henry's side. No one deserved to be forced to live with someone out of spite—the heir apparent excuse notwithstanding. After all, he had Mary, but she planned to give him many sons.

"Bah." He wiped sweat from his brow and tossed the towel aside. "I am sending Wolsey to France to help free the Pope. If the Pope cannot be freed, I shall get Wolsey to appeal to the other cardinals and make them see that if the Pope is in no position to consider my problem, I shall hand it over to Wolsey for final judgment." He plucked up a handful of grapes and chomped on them. "Aha! It will work out after all. See, Amethyst, there is always a way. That is something every king must know, in order to keep his kingdom alive, free from invaders, and thriving. There is always a way."

But even when Charles let the Pope escape from the Castle San Angelo where he'd been prisoner, and the Pope slipped out in disguise, the Pope dragged his heels in fear—fear of turning Henry against the Church.

So Henry's divorce proceedings once again screeched to a halt.

* * *

A messenger brought Amethyst a folded note the following eve. She squealed with joy recognizing the slanted penmanship.

She broke the wax seal and unfolded the parchment, her eyes sweeping over Matthew's letter before returning to the top and reading it through once again. "And do you truly want to be Henry's queen?" he asked at the end, after all the newsy bits about the harvest, his orchards strewn with juicy apples, her nephews' progress with their lessons, always saving their confidential correspondence for last. She penned in response:

"Aye, dear Matthew, I do truly love him, and I do want to become his queen. After all the misgivings I harbored these last months, in dread of hurting Catherine and my family, I am convinced that the king is doing all he can to dissolve what he feels was never a marriage to begin with, but it has become increasingly frustrating. He runs into one wall after another; the Pope refuses him, Wolsey drags his heels, and there is Catherine's relentless cloying when she comes out of hiding. I feel we are all dancing an endless rondo, going in circles all the time, like a dog chasing his tail, and I wonder if it will ever be solved. I shall let you know, Matthew, but please, do not tell a soul...no one must know until Henry is completely free."

* * *

She found Henry in the gardens late that night, his sleepless nights more frequent. "What troubles you tonight, sire?"

As he embraced her, his arms beneath the velvet cloak obliterated every trace of the brisk autumn chill. "The usual. What about you?"

"I am just very apprehensive of how the kingdom would react to me if I did become your queen someday." She smoothed her skirts and sat with him.

"Any woman who displaces Catherine will suffer a bit of disfavor throughout the kingdom," he said. "But you do not have to live to please the kingdom. I must, of course, but you do not have to."

"Still, my lord, it is quite beautiful the way it is." She leaned into him and he wrapped his arm round her shoulders.

"I must agree with that. But you realize I must have a wife who will bless me with a legitimate heir."

"Of course, my lord." She snuggled more deeply into the folds of his cloak, the soft ermine trim tickling her cheek. "How much longer do you think your great matter will take?"

"That depends on so many people." He sighed, frustration tightening his voice. "But most of all on God."

* * *

Amethyst sat at her desk reading Matthew's last letter to her. "I am a melange of emotions, so relieved to be unfettered from Topaz's yoke, yet fearful for the lads, over whom she still wields such manipulative sway..."

A rap on her chamber door startled her. Puzzled, she wondered who would be visiting so late. Her maid of honor opened the door. Amethyst watched her jump and dip and swoon and bow her head so much, it appeared as if strings from the ceiling crossbeams controlled her.

"Who is it?" Amethyst called out, looking up from the letter.

She gasped at the sight of the king standing there. She swept the letter into a drawer and slammed it shut. "Sire! I didn't expect to see you. I thought you would retire early, all the... activity going on lately."

"Aye, it will have taken a day or two off my life before it is resolved," he replied with a droll cock of his head. "That is why having someone like my Lady Amethyst makes it all the more bearable."

He sat upon the velvet cushioned window seat. She followed his gaze out the window at the river, a black void in a moonless night, the twinkling candles aboard the barges and boats so faint they could have been distant worlds.

"What happened today, my lord?" She sat beside him and that familiar warmth penetrated her being. Aye, he would tell her his problems, vent his frustrations with the Pope and Catherine. Then he would take her, gently at first, then with a growing burst of passion, he would release all his pent-up energy and obstructions, and all would be well until the cold light of another day plagued them.

"I ambushed several letters Catherine had written to her nephew Charles in Spain. I caught the messenger just as he was about to climb atop his mount. I'd followed him all the way from Catherine's chambers through the halls and down to the palace gates. Mayhap banishment is not the answer. Once she is removed from court, this will go on rampantly. Must I employ spies for lack of trust of my own w…" He halted, as if at a loss for what to call her. "The princess dowager?"

"You may as well say wife, my lord. 'Tis merely a matter of semantics. For appearances' sake, at least, until this has been resolved."

"You are forever the pragmatic one," he gave her another of his endless compliments. "But were you in my place, your determined heart would dispel all so-called logic and would yearn to be free. I shall continue to expound my belief. She is not my wife. I am as much a bachelor as the day I was born."

She knew two instances when she was not to argue with the king. When he was angry or when he was hungry. If he was both, she simply left the room.

"What did her letters to Emperor Charles say, my lord?" she asked.

"Pathetic, actually, just beyond the boundaries of laughable. Like a sad joke, as when our court jesters imitate beggars and carry out an entire performance around the beggar's routine. 'Tis real life exaggerated to the point of laughability. That is what they reminded me of. She begs him to sway the Pope to declare that our marriage is valid." He stretched his arms and yawned. "She appeals to him with memories of their childhood together, how strong the blood ties that geographical distance will not weaken, the strength of the family bond, the sacrament of marriage, then she goes on to quote Scripture…as if the Emperor has nothing else to do than read paraphrased Bible quotes. She should respect the sanctity of marriage! She is a widow, Arthur's widow!"

"She has no one else to appeal to, sire. It is an act of desperation. You needn't intercept any more letters. The Pope will soon see it your way. It is not necessary to thwart Catherine's ineffectual attempts. Then once we are married he will realize how wrong he was to delay ending your first marriage."

"Aye, you are right, in the end I shall prevail, but who needs any more interfering fingers plunging into this pie?" He focused his tired eyes on her. "I want this to take not one more day than necessary to be done with. As it is already, Clement has refused my request to try the case in England. He insists that it be tried in Rome. Now I've got Charles to contend with. Soon the entire world will be sticking their noses into it. All I want is a divorce, not a reenactment of the bloody Crusades!"

"It will all work out, my lord," she gave him the assurance he craved. "Queen Catherine knows what's best for the kingdom. But I won't be queen at her expense."

She noticed the cynical twist of his lips. "She knows I am not divorcing her because of you. She knows plainly enough that I need an heir."

Stabs of anger at Catherine shot through her. "Oh, why cannot she simply let you go with dignity instead of making such a pathetic attempt to hold on to what is nonexistent?"

"You ask her, not me," came back in a weary tone.

"By trying to spite you she's hurting the entire kingdom—and depriving it of a future king. She's holding back the natural progression of history," Amethyst spoke her feelings to Henry as she did with more frequency.

You're singing to the choir here, dear." He glanced out the window, pushed it open and took a breath of the chilly air.

She shook the anger away and took the hand of her future husband. "Come to my bed, my lord, I shall make you feel better."

This was the first time she'd made the first move, and it was worth seeing the king's surprised and delighted expression when she began unlacing the front of his shirt. A look of amazement softened his rugged face. He stared into her eyes, the new revelation brightening up the dimly lit room, sparking his aura. *Had he never been seduced before?* she wondered. Nay, mayhap not, he was the king, and simply demanded whatever he wanted, not waiting until it came to him.

She felt not like a wanton, for she and Henry had grown so close, everything seemed natural and proper, naught was out of line with anything they said or did. On one obscure level, in their most intimate moments together, they were equals.

A hint of playful eroticism emanated from behind his tired, care-worn features. His magnetism immediately warmed her blood, drawing her even closer. Within the next instant, she was encircled in his arms. He stroked her hair and face, whispering words of love into her ear.

"My love." The ambiguous inflection in his voice prompted her to look into those questioning eyes, past that ever-present confidence gleaming from within.

"You know I've always dreamed of meeting you, when I was a child, the first time I saw you at the coronation," she told him of her fantasy. "Sometimes I become embarrassed when I think of how…how much we're…"

"Compatible?"

"That is a very regal way of putting it, my lord." She gave him an inviting smile and a flutter of her lashes.

"There's nothing embarrassing about it. We are two passionate people, and we should be thankful that we can fall into each other's arms and you can make me forget the chaos in the realm around us."

He led her over to her bed as he unfastened her bodice and ran his tongue lightly over the swell of her breasts, causing a gasp of desire to shudder through her body.

"Henry…" Another gulp of air enabled her to speak his Christian name for the first time as his dexterous hands wandered over her flesh. He brushed his fingers over her breasts, weakening her senses, and lifted his body off the bed. He strode over to the window and closed the heavy drapes, shutting out all but a slice of moonlight that spilled in a cone on the rug. The entire chamber was now enshrouded in semi-darkness. Soon a comforting warmth began to radiate from the hearth as he lit a fire. Returning to the bed, he finished unfastening his shirt.

"Are you still embarrassed?" He playfully ran his fingertips over her neck, her stomach, her thighs, until she could hold back no longer.

"Make love to me, sire! Take me right here on the bed, on the floor, on the trestle table, anywhere, just make love to me!"

He emitted a flirtatious laugh, teasingly slipping his shirt from his torso. She watched behind half-closed eyes as if she'd never seen him before. Every session of lovemaking was different; he made love to her in each room; atop the virginals in the conservatory, one hand tickling the ivory keys as he brought her to the heights of effulgence with the other, on the trestle table in his inner chamber while feeding her a luscious puff pastry, in his bathing tub full of warm fragrant water. He was deliciously decadent just as she'd always imagined a king should be. He was now standing over her, sliding his hose over his thighs, tormenting her.

Her arms encircled his head, pulling him down to meet her lips. She could no longer bear to watch him disrobe without touching him.

"No...not so fast..." He broke the kiss and ran his hand over her body before rising, causing her to arch towards him. He stepped out of his tights as the bulge beneath his undergarments grew before her eyes. He was now naked except for the sheer undergarment that barely concealed his loins. She reached out once more. He leapt back, out of her reach. "Henry, come here, please!" she begged, yanking at her bodice, exposing her flushed chest. Her mouth ached for another of his sumptuous kisses. Yet she could not move as pangs of desire tortured her. "Come here now," she breathed, tilting her head upwards to savor the hard maleness.

"Not so fast, I'm not quite finished." He went over to her tub, returning instantly with her bottle of coconut bath oil.

"I'm going to spread this all over our bodies." He flipped the cork off, knelt before her and poured the slippery liquid on her chest, massaging it over her skin lightly with two fingers in a circular motion. She closed her eyes and let his hands usurp her entire being. He tugged at her skirts and they gave easily, until the garments were on the floor. Only her undergarments remained, which he slid off as smoothly as the oil had slid on. "Let me do something to you," she whispered in short gasps as his fingers traced wavy patterns over her legs, her inner thighs, deliberately avoiding her center of passion. "Let me touch you, please."

"No!" he commanded, tickling her stomach, her thighs, her feet. The silky fluid enveloped her heat like a cocoon. Waves of desire engulfed her with every skilled stroke. He stayed just out of her reach, so only her eyes could touch the imposing physique from below.

He inserted his thumbs into his undergarments and pulled the garment down just so that it revealed the dark shadow around his pubic region. He fanned his fingers over the prominent bulges, came to her and kissed her deeply.

"Now you can make love to me, my Amethyst." Their bodies met, their heat mingling with the slippery oil. The exquisite sensation made her want to melt into him.

She sprang up, pushing his hand away as it slinked over her thigh. "I would just love to. But you'll have to catch me first." She sprinted across the room, shouting over her shoulder, "Once you've caught me, I'm all yours!"

"I already caught you!" He heaved himself off the bed and chased her across the chamber. She leapt over the bed crouched behind it.

"You're not fast enough," she chanted. He finally reached her, grabbing her mane of hair as she twirled to face him. With orgiastic frenzy and wild desire, she yanked at his undergarment, tearing it off his body and flinging it to the floor. He turned to face her and she threw herself into his arms, their slippery bodies sliding against each other, drenched with oil, perspiration and need.

Lifting her by the buttocks, he wrapped her legs around his back and took her standing, in the middle of the chamber, candlelight glowing over their glistening bodies.

Later they flopped on the bed and she lay coiled around him, running her fingertips over his wide chest.

"Did you enjoy the chase?" She lifted her face to look into his eyes, still darkened with passion, yet bright with satiation.

"Not as much as the prize." He found her lips and recaptured them in a deep commanding kiss.

"Please, sire, don't ever call me your mistress," she mumbled, falling into an exhausted sleep.

* * *

Richmond Palace, 1528

Wolsey's cunning suggestion to send another Papal legate convinced the Pope to hold a trial in England. So, while the impatient and frustrated king washed down meal after meal of boar, game, fowl and sweets with quaff after quaff of strong wine, Cardinal Lorenzo Campeggio arrived in London—in his own sweet time.

Henry met Amethyst for a quiet supper in his privy chamber after his first meeting with the Cardinal. This feast was no smaller than what he'd gorged on while waiting for the Cardinal, but at least the king no longer paced in circles tearing his hair out.

"And how fares Campeggio? Was he as awe-struck and overwhelmed with admiration as everyone else who is graced with your presence?" Amethyst knew which of his buttons needed pushing and when. Right now she sensed he'd enjoy lapping up her flattery along with his cherry tarts and mead. Flattery had become a sort of foreplay; it actually seemed to arouse him.

"He is a senile, bent-over old bird with two filmy eyes each facing in different directions, coughs up into an old linen cloth every two minutes, and who has the gout so bad, he has to be borne through the streets upon a litter." He signaled for the steward to fetch another bottle of mead. "Not only that, he hardly speaks a word of English. Wolsey acted as an interpreter, for even I could not decipher his obscure dialect, and I possess quite a command of the Italian language."

"You believe this brainchild of Wolsey's will bear fruit? Will Campeggio's presence here work in your favor?" She broke off a piece of cherry tart and nibbled on it.

"Aye, I truly believe so." Noticing one lone oyster left on the dish, he plucked it up and slid it into his mouth. "The best news he brought with him was that Clement suggested to Catherine that she enter a convent. He would banish our marriage like that," he snapped his fingers, "should she take that route."

Amethyst emitted a gasp of delight. "Finally, something that resembles a solution. Why, that is wonderful news, sire. Catherine is so devout already, she may as well have taken her vows at birth."

"My sentiments exactly." He nodded. "She will continue the religious life, I shall be free to remarry, Campeggio can go on his merry way, and Clement and I can resume our... heh, heh... amicable terms." He wiped his hand on his napkin and tossed it on the table. "I so dislike being on the wrong side of His Holiness." A belch erupted at the mention of the Pope, the timing impeccable. They shared a quiet laugh as the steward poured them each a refill from the new bottle.

Later he stretched out at the window seat sipping wine. The setting sun's glow drifted in through the diamond paned windows.

Gliding up to him in her black satin nightdress, Amethyst slid her arms round his shoulders. "A beautiful view of the hills, isn't it?" she cooed as they shared the dying day. "The entire kingdom is yours, and the entire night is ours." She dug her fingers into the soft satin of his robe, kneading his hard muscles underneath. She reached around and touched his lips. He pulled her onto his lap as his tongue met hers, teasing, tormenting, causing her breath to diminish into short gasps. "Henry, I want to make love to my king."

Now, in reality just as in her dreams, he lifted her into his arms and carried her to the bed, placing her on the edge. He climbed in next to her, reclaiming her lips. Closing her eyes, she beheld soaring fireworks behind her lids. She caressed his golden red hair with one hand and his lean muscled form with the other, opening his robe to reveal the taut waistline and the red gold hairs on his chest. Lowering her head to his torso, she ran her tongue over his stomach, opening his robe along the way. His breaths increased, harder, faster. He moaned and turned to face her, his fingers playing her body as if strumming a harp, arousing every strain of sensuous passion, in a sonata of love.

He halted her and pulled off his robe, hanging it over the edge of the bed. "Now it is my turn to disrobe you." He smiled down at her, lowering his head to reunite their lips, his hands everywhere, expertly touching her most sensitive areas. He slipped her chemise over her head. Her fingers sought his hose and tugged; now all that was left to conquer were the undergarments, which slid off as easily as if they'd been oiled. He arched his pelvis, moaning her name softly as his fingers traced thin lines of fire over her curves, and down twixt the soft sensitive flesh of her thighs.

She felt his heart pounding against his chest in perfect rhythm with his breathing. Her senses took leave of her with every inch she explored. She slipped her hand beneath his hose. As her fingers brushed over his manhood, her heat seeped into the hardening member. She clasped her fingers around him and caressed him, feeling his arousal mount with increasing intensity. She slipped her hand farther down, twixt his legs, fanning her fingers over the entire area. He moaned with pleasure as his body shuddered. She slipped the hose off his legs and moved downwards, her lips throbbing from his demanding kisses. As her lips touched the tip of his aroused member, he clutched her shoulders.

She wanted all of him, everything he had to give. As she pulled the pins from her hair and let the ends tickle his neck, their explosive coupling shattered the night.

Chapter Seven

Richmond Palace, 1529

"Damn that woman, curse her and her self-righteous Spanish smugness!" He hurled a pewter plate through the air. It crashed against the wall, missing Amethyst's head by a safe distance as she reached his retiring room. She lifted her skirts and tiptoed round the bits of pastry and clumps of fruit on his Oriental rug.

"What happened now, sire? What scheme could Catherine have possibly contrived within the last twenty-four hours?" Amethyst's own impatience made her voice tremble. "Oh, my lord, I'm empathizing more and more with you at her tenacity. Your ire is contagious, believe me in that."

He swept his hand through the air in her direction. "Come hither, just close that door and come hither and let me look at you!"

She shut the door and attempted a calming breath. "It cannot be all that bad. I'm here if you want to, uh...to borrow from Vulgar Latin...vent." She glanced round the empty chamber. At this late hour, the servitors had dispersed, and the Yeomen of the Guard stood way down the hall flanking the outer chamber door, out of earshot. All was quiet, but Henry's anger issued forth an intensity she could sense from across the doorway. Her eyes followed him in the candles' glow as he flopped on the bed, flung his shirt off and sat, bare chested, heaving great angry sighs. His mat of chest hair narrowed to a tantalizing pattern towards his hose, which molded to his thighs. He ran a hand over his chest and with one swift stroke swept off his hose. A thrill rushed through him. Whether he loved it or hated it, the king was never indifferent to anything. Her desire overpowered her, to hold him close, feel his warmth seep into hers, gather his hair in bunches, smooth it back from his face, kiss his searching lips.

He held out his hand and she rushed into his arms, giving in to her desperate want for him. As she melted into him, he fondled her breasts over the silky material of her chemise. A mad rush of desire coursed through her, starting with her fingertips, shooting down to her toes. She let him devour her hungrily. As he blanketed her with his powerful body and poured all his pent up frustration into her, she knew she'd fulfilled his needs, and afterglow once again subdued him.

"Now tell me what Catherine did...calmly, my lord," she whispered as they shared his pillow.

"Catherine...I've forgotten." He placed his arm over his eyes. "I do not care to bring her into my bedchamber, in body or in spirit."

"The problem will still be there tomorrow." She snuggled up to him. "I only want to unburden you. So if you tell me now, it will become my problem. I shall hold it for you tonight so that you may sleep. After all, we do share these endless disappointments together. Mayhap if we divide it twixt us, it will be half as frustrating."

He removed his arm from his eyes, kissed her forehead and bunched her hair in his fingers so tightly it pulled at her scalp, releasing it just as fast. "She refused the Pope's suggestion to enter a convent. Then she displayed the first I've ever seen of her attempt at humor since I've known her...she actually made a joke, deliberately this time."

"A joke? Catherine? I wasn't aware she had a sense of humor." She nudged him, "Well, carry on, what was it?"

He shifted so that he lay on his side. "She wasn't attempting levity, believe me. I mean it was amusing in its sheer audacity. She refused the suggestion of taking the veil, saying she would live out her days in holy matrimony into which God had called her, and nothing would change her mind. But, she said...and this is the part that brought a moment of comic relief…she said she would enter a convent only if I took monastic vows and lived as a monk. Mary would be the sole heir and would reign over the kingdom."

Amethyst didn't laugh. "I'm glad you found levity in it. But it's her way of thinking. She knows you need an heir. How in God's name could you possibly produce one while living as a monk? It's her self-serving solution that would allow her to save face." The irritable edge to Amethyst's tone voiced her returning exasperation.

He looked at her with that hint of annoyance as he did whenever she questioned his judgment. "I must take it as a joke, Amethyst. I cannot take that proposal in the least bit seriously. Or I shall not retain my own wits. She knows bloody well I could never take vows of poverty, chastity, never to hold a woman in my arms again, to forsake my kingdom, the kingdom I was born to rule." He raised his hands and they landed on the sheet with a thump. "She has no credibility with me now. No matter how she meant it, I took it as a pathetic attempt at humor, had my little guffaw, and now I must move on to the next step. The Papal court meets tomorrow. I shall have my say and there will be no further joking."

"I pray the court won't take long making their decision." Too restless to remain lying down, she sat up, folding her legs beneath her.

"What can we do short of eloping to one of those wild rugged islands of the New World and living among the savages where no one knows us?" he thundered, punching his pillow.

She turned to face him, glowing in the candlelight—his narrowed eyes, his knitted brows, his lips tight in frustration. "Henry, I do not mean this as an insult, just an observation. You are letting your subjects walk all over you."

He hissed out a breath through clenched teeth. "The Pope is not my subject. It is his hands that hold my life!"

"And Catherine's and her nephew's and Campeggio's," she added the obvious.

He sat up and jabbed his pointer finger at the door. "Remove yourself, Amethyst, before I put you over my knee and spank you. I've enough people trying to lead my life without listening to your whining. Now be gone."

She threw on her raiment and swept out of the room in a swirl of angry tears, her hair streaming out behind her.

Oh, he will forget it all in the morning, she assured herself as she headed to her chambers to order a warm bath. She was getting used to his tirades. *How did Catherine put up with it?* she pondered.

* * *

As Henry departed for the trial at Blackfriars, Matthew stopped at court to pay Amethyst a visit.

"Oh, 'tis so good to see you, Matthew!" Without reservation, she threw herself into his arms. "A visitor from home, oh, how homesick I've been!" He smelled of the woods and lavender soap. She sighed into his cloak as he swept his hat off and tossed it onto the nearest chair in her receiving chamber. Dark circles hung 'neath his eyes. His short French haircut had grown out and a lock of hair fell across his forehead. She reached up and pushed it aside, looking into his eyes, as green and shiny in the glinting sunlight as the newly sprouted leaves of spring. She eased the cloak from around his shoulders. "You look tired, but so relieved," she observed.

"My looks deceive you." He followed her down the corridor. "I am still worried sick for the lads."

"And I also. I would ask the king to invite them here, but court is no place for children. They are better off at Warwick." She led him through the palace halls until they reached her chambers.

"I beg to differ." He stopped as she opened her door and stepped inside. "With Topaz's toxins permeating their minds, how can being surrounded by a bunch of capering courtiers be worse?"

She offered him a seat in her audience chamber and sat across from him. A servitor brought in a wedge of cheese and hot buttered bread along with goblets of ale. Matthew picked at it and sipped the ale.

"I am anxious for you to meet the king," she said. "I believe you will find much to talk about, hawking, hunting, tennis, all the outdoor sports that you both love. Just do not mention Topaz."

His eyes darkened at the sound of his wife's name. "Do you take me for an oaf? I wish my journey to take me back to Kenilworth, not through Traitor's Gate."

"The king is not in the least bothered about Topaz," she shared the cheery news. "He believes she is all talk. He knows her not. That is a great relief to me; I thought he would certainly restrain her somehow, take her much more seriously than he has. He has been so caught up with this divorce, he has not had a moment to give to much of anything else... except his most basic needs, of course." She lowered her lids and looked away.

"I have heard nothing in weeks," Matthew said. "Topaz has said naught since her visit here to you."

"I cannot help but think the longer she delays, the more organized and devastating it will be." She took a bite of bread.

"She has but few supporters." His tone lightened. "The king has few enemies, but I daresay with the divorce proceedings, tongues are beginning to wag. There is a great outpouring of sympathy for Queen Catherine."

"And rightly so. I dare not say it to the king, but I hardly believe the Pope is going to bend. I am there when he needs me, I comfort him in his time of need, and make him forget his troubles, but I am becoming as frustrated as he." She took a swig of her ale. "Every time it looks like we've opened a door, another slams in our faces. It's gotten to where we've been short with each other, not meaning it, of course, but these times are so tense."

He sat forward and rested his elbows on the table. "Amethyst, it has been some time now. Do you truly believe he is going to attain this divorce?"

"Sometimes it seems hopeless." She shook her head. "But Henry is a strong-willed man. I believe he will achieve his goal."

"And you?" He cocked his head.

"Well...when the divorce is final, I shall wait a respectable time, then I shall accept his marriage proposal. But not before." She broke off a piece of cheese.

"Don't you think you'll have done enough waiting?" He circled his fingers round his goblet but didn't raise it to his lips.

"Oh, by then the frustrating part will be over with." She sat back and slipped her shoes from her feet, wiggling her toes. "Once Henry is free, nothing will stand in our way."

He asked, "And how long do you intend to wait out this frustrating part, as you say?"

She shrugged. "As long as it takes."

"It may be years." His dire warning alarmed her.

"Years?" Could it take that long? She'd never considered that. Here at court twas impossible to think so far into the future, activities occupying every moment. "Oh, nay, Matthew. Something will happen soon..." Her voice trailed off, lacking any conviction, as she pondered what Matthew had just said. She'd never thought of putting a time limit on it. Years? Her beloved Henry needed a brutal shove to get things moving faster. "...if indeed Catherine ever lets him go. But I'm confident she will."

"Will it not be the Pope's decision?" Matthew asked.

"Oh, 'tis so many people," she sighed. "Emperor Charles the Fifth, Holy Roman Emperor, is Catherine's nephew and does not take to the idea of his aunt having lived in sin. With this working against Henry, it makes things very difficult."

Matthew shook his head and gazed past Amethyst out the window.

"I want to be everything to him, his lover, his friend, his confidante, the mother of his heirs, and his queen. But I must expect repercussions."

Matthew's gaze returned to her. "I still haven't told anyone. Not your mother, no one."

"Thank you, Matthew, for your trust. I shall tell them in good time. And Lord knows we have plenty of it. But I still fear Topaz and her plans. She is willful and stubborn, but she is still my sister and I love her."

"Aye, you are safer here on the king's side." He finished his ale. "If this plan of hers ever does come to be, at least she can't kill you."

That word shot through her like the pierce of a knife. "And what makes you think the king would? He loves me!" She jumped on the defensive.

"He's the king, Amethyst." His gaze landed on her, sharp and focused. "He can do anything he pleases."

"Dear God, you sound like mother and Aunt Margaret did through my childhood about my father's fate. Henry would never do such a thing to me, just as no one could ever conceive of the king's frustration over the powers thwarting his need to be free of Catherine," she berated him, mostly to assure herself. "But of course no one can understand. No one knows my Prince Hal as intimately as I do."

* * *

That evening, a subdued tone enshrouded the great hall as the court supped, listened to music and dispersed. A page presented Matthew to the king. Henry stayed polite enough but he feigned interest in Matthew's ramblings-on about his estates, falcons, and tennis game. Amethyst felt badly for Matthew, but felt worse for the king. She could tell by that certain look only she could discern, the deepened furrow in his brow, that he'd had a most difficult day. She knew he would knock at her chamber door tonight.

And indeed he did. As they embraced he tugged at the combs holding her hair in place. He loved to feel her locks tumble through his fingers.

They sipped May wine as he stared into the fire. "I am so sorry I yelled at you the other night, my darling," he said.

"'Tis quite all right, my lord. I did my share of yelling as well."

"Did you? I did not hear you. I was so wrapped up in…oh, this bloody mess!" He threw his hands up and they fell into his lap.

"'Tis just as well. What bothers you tonight, my lord? What took place at Blackfriars?" She hoped someday he would share his troubles without her asking first.

"Amethyst, that woman I married is relentless. She rose from her seat when called, and without replying, strode up to me, bearing her royal countenance, got on her knees before me as if I were God almighty and implored me to recognize her as my humble and obedient wife." He blew out an exasperated breath. "She went on to declare that she had come to me a virgin, with God as her judge, implying, of course, that for me to say the opposite would make me a liar. She went on to beg for a Spanish court to hold the trial, as all of my subjects, of course, were partial toward me. After making a complete fool and a liar of me before Wolsey and Campeggio and the entire court, she didn't return to her seat…no, she walked out." He rolled his eyes toward heaven. "Simply said what she'd come to say and swept out of there in a regal fashion and failed to reappear when summoned…three times, no less, but she had finished and as far as Catherine's concerned, so is the entire matter." He raked his hand through his hair and rubbed his eyes.

Through her growing resentment of Catherine, Amethyst marveled at the queen's boldness with a wonder bordering on admiration. "What an audacious thing for her to do. How did the court react to her entreaty?"

"It seemed to move no one but old Bishop Fisher. He continued, in his stubborn tirade of senility, that Catherine and I are still married in the eyes of the law and the Lord. The only one against me, against Wolsey, all the other bishops…Fisher, whom I'd been born and raised with, that aging, arthritic old infirm. Catherine got to him, all right." He grimaced, glancing round the chamber, no doubt for something to eat.

"Mayhap Wolsey can appeal to him, my lord," she offered.

"I hadn't planned on coming up with an answer to this tonight, but the end must justify the means. Whatever it takes, I shall prevail and I shall produce an heir!" He glanced at her over the rim of his goblet. "Er…we shall produce an heir, pray God," he corrected himself.

"Aye, my lord. Meanwhile, it has been a tiring day for you. Would a good night's sleep be in order, mayhap interrupted once or twice by a pair of caressing hands?"

"Oh, Madam, you do treat me like a king!" His gaze landed on her and his smile brightened his face.

She woke in the middle of the night and ran her hand over his warm sleeping body. She took his wrist and ever so gently brought his hand up to her neck and guided it over her breasts, very slowly, until her nipples grew erect under the sheer silk of her chemise. She cupped his hand over her left breast and continued, her voice softer and inviting: "Wake up, sire." She lowered her arms and wriggled free of the chemise as she continued to run his hand over her breasts. The silk slid off her shoulders and she guided his hand over her soft pink flesh. He was beginning to awaken now. She guided his hand through her hair, over her face and lips and back down to her breasts.

"What a way to wake up," he murmured.

She touched his half-open mouth with hers, forcing his lips apart with her tongue, kissing him deeply, leaning against him until he rolled onto his back with her pelvis straddling his, her knees aside his ribs. His hand now slid up and down her thigh, the strokes faster, more urgent.

She rotated her hips, easing him into her, slowly, brushing her breasts over his lips as she rode him, thrusting and undulating gently at first, then more furiously as her passion intensified.

He clutched at her hips, drawing her more deeply into him. His lips were upon hers in a second, searching, showering her with kisses. She wanted to hold him close, feel his warmth seep into hers, smooth the golden hair back from his face, kiss his forehead, nibble the searching lips. She didn't think about the next hour or the next morn. Their bodies, their want for each other filled the momenet. As he moaned softly, she melted into him, and they lay back against the pillows. He fondled her breasts as a mad rush of desire coursed through her, starting with her fingertips, shooting down to her toes. It was a want close to pain. He exploded within her.

Then quickly, too quickly, he pulled away, leaving her hungering for another of his cushioning embraces, his ravishing kisses. He cradled her in his arms, and she felt herself floating away into a dream. "You are so beautiful." His voice was anticipating, hopeful, his hands lightly brushing her shoulders. She felt her body heat seep into his, warming her. Their bodies touched, sending thrills through her, as if the glowing fire in the hearth come alive, breathing its heat into them. He brushed her forehead with his lips, then his mouth closed on hers, his tongue seeking, drinking her in with mounting passion. She responded instantly, her breath in short gasps as his hands glided over her cheeks. His fingers fanned out around her breasts. She shuddered under his fiery touch. She embraced him as the ecstasy and fervor they'd shared came rushing back to her. Once again his mouth met hers and reclaimed the magic they'd drawn from the heavens and called their own. A warm glow of desire nestled deep within her and churned a flow of long-forgotten emotions.

All this from a mere kiss! She longed for the touch of his hands; she wanted to bestow every facet of her being upon this man. A moan escaped her lips as he ran hot kisses over her neck and soft, sensitive earlobes. His hot breath in her ear made her shiver as she pressed closer, feeling his growing desire against the scanty film of cloth separating their bodies.

"Oh, Amethyst, be my queen just for tonight," he breathed, showering her with kisses, down her neck, twixt her breasts.

She placed her palms against the sinews of his chest, fluttering her fingertips over the brawny musculature.

Henry stroked her cheek and gently brought her face close to his. He boldly gripped her wrist and rested her hand against the fount of his desire. With a will of their own, her fingers began to slowly stroke him. She watched with mounting pleasure as his eyelids closed, and he threw his head back, groaning through lightly clenched teeth. As she continued her caresses, his hands began an exploration of their own. She felt them grasp her shoulders, then slide down her back. His fingers played along her spine, and she arched towards him, pressing her taut breasts against his chest, trapping her clasping hand twixt their locked bodies. For a moment, they were crushed together, and her senses spun dizzily out of control.

She lowered herself to the pillows, onto her back against the cushiony fluff, and waited in panting wonder, her heart pattering against her ribs.

Her eyes locked on his face and his features came into sharp focus. Just looking at him sent a surge of excitement through her. But her vision blurred when his mouth descended to fasten over her eager lips. A moan escaped from deep within her, and she surrendered to his demanding kisses. Her arms stole up around his neck, and she felt his pulse match the rampant pace of her own.

"Please," she begged as his mouth left hers and trailed a fiery path along her jaw, down her throat. His hot, exploring tongue licked the salty slickness of the skin twixt her breasts. His lips moved to cover a pink nipple, and he nipped it gently. Then his hand kneaded the flesh of her other breast, his mouth following to suckle at the rosy tip.

Amethyst sighed and entwined her fingers in his tousled hair, tugging his head lower and lower. He darted his tongue over her abdomen, making her muscles clench spasmodically, and a flame ignited in her soul as he sought and found the nucleus of her desire.

She would never be more ready; she craved for him to fill her, to make them one. He seemed to sense her immediate need, for he covered her trembling body with his and parted her thighs with his knee.

He looked into her feverish eyes as his virile hardness invaded her tender flesh. The roar of an exploding star swelled in her mind and tore through her senses. The muscles of his back flexed beneath her clutching hands as he surged into her again and again. The world spun in a swirling vortex joy swelled her heart. She sensed he had denied his own satisfaction until she achieved hers, and now she knew he was at the threshold of fulfillment. He called out her name, and she held on tightly, as feverish thrills ripped through her soul.

He was hers.

They lay entwined, their bodies warm and moist, the soft sheets clinging to them, their fingers laced. "Amethyst, you will take occupancy of the adjoining apartments to my own, so I do not have to traverse the entire palace to reach you," Henry demanded.

"Oh, sire, I couldn't. That would brand me as your mistress for sure, and that I cannot have."

"But you are my mistress," he affirmed.

"I would have hoped you regarded me as much more than that, my lord." She enjoyed tossing out these cheeky taunts.

"You are, love. But you are my mistress, too. You fulfill my desires to the point of satiation. I need no other woman. You are the object of my desires. My soulmate and bedmate. And floormate and tubmate..."

"But only while we are alone, like now. In the eyes of the court, I wish to be but a minstrel, a servant." She stretched her legs.

"Do you not think the court has ears and eyes, Amethyst? By God, the very walls may as well be of parchment, for all the good they do to conceal the goings-on and the cavorting."

A stab of hurt went through her and she snatched her hand from his grasp, wrapping the coverlet around her. "You consider our time together cavorting, sire?"

"Nay, you know my feelings for you go much deeper than that, Amethyst..." He waved his hand about. "But the rest of the court...they all know by now how I feel about you."

"She sat up. "Whom have you told?"

"I've heeded your wishes and not told a soul. But when this great matter of mine is settled, I shall announce our betrothal to the world among the fanfare of trumpets, the clanging of every churchbell in the realm, the booming of a thousand cannons!"

"They know I am your close companion and confidante, sire, but do they know what goes on in the privacy of our chambers?" She drew her knees up to her chest.

"Oh, Amethyst, by now how could they not know?"

"I come to your apartments very late at night," she near-whispered, wondering if anyone lurked about. She knew all about court spies...

"And you do not leave till morning. They are not blind, Amethyst. Or deaf," he added under his breath.

"But I do not want to be known as the king's whore," she stated, looking away, hating that vile word, never wanting to be associated with it.

"Anyone who dares to call you that will be banished immediately. I find that now, as it has become obvious that we have grown close, you are treated with more respect. The king's confidante and special lady is a far cry from his whore. Especially now that I have banished Catherine from court, no one sees you as her rival."

"I just wish to preserve my honor, my lord." She turned to face him and traced a finger along his jawline.

He smiled. "As you wish, Lady Amethyst. We shall keep our apartments at a distance. Lord knows, I need the exercise."

* * *

As the first rays of light floated through her windows, she gradually surfaced from her delightful dreams. Disoriented at first, she realized she was in her own bed. Alone. The king had probably been up for hours. She pictured him dressing quietly, slipping out of her chambers before the servants were up, taking special pains to keep from waking her. She turned and faced the pillow he'd slept on. A strand of his hair lay on the pillowcase. She reached out and placed her hand on the fabric, pulling his pillow to her, hugging it. The realization spiraled within her, like tulip petals fluttering through her insides. She was no longer enamored of the bejeweled and powerful monarch reigning over the kingdom from a velvet-seated throne known to his subjects as King Henry VIII. She was simply in love with the compassionate, sincere man that few subjects would ever be privileged to know, the man named Henry Tudor.

* * *

Several weeks later, while practicing with the King's Musick, the door opened and in walked Mark Smeaton, late for rehearsal. On his heels was a young dark-haired girl, her hair tumbling down about her shoulders, a bright yellow satin gown in striking contrast to the blackness of her hair and eyes, like a striped bumblebee, all black and yellow. Amethyst had seen her before; she'd been one of Catherine's ladies-in-waiting. But what was she doing here in the music chamber? The court had more than enough minstrels.

As Mark rushed to his place and adjusted his music stand, his companion sat quietly near the door.

"Mark," Amethyst spoke up, putting down her lute. "Aren't you going to introduce us to your lady friend?"

"Oh, I'm sorry." he looked up from his sheet music, as if he'd forgotten she was there. "This is Anne Boleyn. She loves music, and wishes to watch us rehearse."

"Well, if it is all right with the other musicians." Amethyst glanced round the room at the disinterested nods and shrugs.

"'Tis a pleasure to welcome you to the King's Musick, Mistress Boleyn." Amethyst remained standing.

Anne bowed her head ever so slightly, as if a full bow and sweeping curtsy was inappropriate for someone she considered of equal rank, even though the entire court knew Amethyst was the king's closest confidante.

"'Tis a pleasure to meet you, Lady Amethyst." Her voice floated through the air low and soft, a bit uneasy, with the slightest shade of a French accent. The dark slanty eyes continued to stare, and the thin lips curved in a forced smile.

"Do you have aspirations of joining the King's Musick?" Amethyst asked.

What else could Anne Boleyn do now that Catherine was being banished? she wondered. Mayhap the king would consider placing Anne in Amethyst's service. She needed no more ladies-in-waiting, however; she was fully staffed. The king could do well by sending Mistress Anne back to wherever it was she came from. She'd felt a tinge of uneasiness when Anne walked in and settled down like a piece of the furniture.

Anne shot Amethyst a wary glance as a hand reached up to clutch a lock of her dark hair. Her billowing sleeve fell away and Amethyst saw a tiny nub jutting out from her little finger. "I am not sure, although I feel I can contribute a great deal to your troupe."

"Well, that will be for the king to decide." Amethyst dismissed Anne's presence by strumming the opening bars of her favorite song on her lute.

* * *

"Who is this Anne Boleyn?" she asked Henry as they dined in his chambers late the next eve.

"Oh, just one of Catherine's former ladies-in-waiting," he waved a hand through the air before plucking up a wing of pheasant.

"Why was she sitting in on our rehearsal today?" Amethyst asked.

"Was she distracting you?" He answered her question with a question.

"Not in the least. She came in with Mark Smeaton and sat—"

"Mark Smeaton?" he cut her off in mid-chew.

"Aye. They came in together, he being very late for rehearsal." She sliced through a mushroom.

He'd stopped chewing, his eyes narrowing to the calculating slits she'd become so used to. "Ah, well, she loves music. I told her she can stay on at court for a while longer, then she'll be going back home to Kent. Anne beholds a mystique that the courtiers find intriguing, but if she does not wish to stay at court, she need not stay."

"But who…who is she, Henry? And why the French accent? I'm deeply curious." The meal forgotten, all she wanted to digest was the mystery that was Anne Boleyn.

"She spent a great deal of her childhood at the French court," he explained. "The Boleyns are direct descendants of Edward the First. Her mother is Elizabeth Howard, whose grandfather died fighting for Richard at Bosworth. Her father Tom was an envoy to the Netherlands when I became king."

Now the name registered. "Her sister was Mary Boleyn, was she not? One of your mistresses?"

"A fleeting spark of my energetic youth many years ago," he replied airily. "She is now safely married to William Carey, a gentleman of the royal privy chamber. I also gave her brother George a position at court."

"So the family is united in their goal, that is, their social climbing efforts." She smirked, chewing on her mushroom.

"The Boleyns are good people, Amethyst." He looked up at her as he dug into his sprouts. "Her stock is solid, she is talented and well-read. Not as much as you, of course. I would be so pleased if you would let her sing with you once or twice...she does so love to sing. She plays the virginals as well."

"We do not need another musician, my lord," she stated firmly.

"My Lady Amethyst, are you jealous of an insipid little buttercup?" he teased, a smile playing on his lips.

"Nay! Of course not. She was just rather hostile to me, that's all." She fluttered her lashes.

"She feels very out of place now that Catherine is gone. Just make her feel welcome, 'tis just a while longer." He took another huge bite and a swig of ale.

"Speaking of a while longer, what of your divorce proceedings?" This was far more important than keeping Anne Boleyn occupied, though it wasn't table talk.

"What of them? Nothing has happened since you last asked me twenty-four hours ago." He tore into the wing more voraciously, shutting her out.

"I know how her questioning irks you, Henry. But it's been so long since we've heard anything, if only the Pope would say aye or nay, at least. Have you thought of any more solutions?" she probed, her appetite waning, not from the delicious meal, but from the topic of conversation.

He did not answer right away, but glared at her, took another swig from his goblet, and continued chewing. "Aye. But I do not care to discuss it right now."

"Is it about the break with Rome?" She'd heard, not from Henry, who discussed his matter with her less and less, but from talks among Cardinal Wolsey and others, that a break with the church was the only solution. "I know you are disinclined to create your own church," she went on, despite his protest. "'Tis such a grave matter and must be handled very delicately. But, sire, as your closest confidante, I can help you sort details out. I can give you another point of view. A church that is not purely Catholic in all its dogmas may be the solution for all." She pushed her plate away. "A more progressive doctrine can be adapted without being considered heretic. Wolsey is an old man who may not be as sharp as someone younger, someone who can mayhap come up with more modern ideas and—"

"I am sick of this whole bloody matter!" he roared, spitting out a small bone.

"Well, how long can I can sit and wait, sire?" She knew she was a pest, but this was her fate he held in his meaty hands.

"As damned long as I have to sit and wait!" His retort echoed through the chamber.

"I am not the one who is desperate for an heir, my lord," she shot back.

"Nay, you are desperate to drive me crackers!" He tore into a slab of pie and belched.

"Sire, if this is not solved, our lives will be wasted. I am not getting any younger, as you can see. You will tire of me and cast me aside for some pretty young thing just like you are doing with Catherine." Her eyes filled with tears and her vision of him blurred to a reddened head and ever-fattening face surrounded by piles of food. The sound of his chewing suddenly disgusted her.

She threw her napkin to the table and stood. Waiting another few seconds for a reply and getting none, she turned and stalked out of his apartments, nearly knocking down Anne Boleyn in the corridor.

Chapter Eight

The next day Henry brought the Boleyns, Anne included, on a hunting trip to his lodge in Oxfordshire. With this opportunity to visit her beloved family, Amethyst tossed some garments into a trunk.

A knock at her chamber door brought her chambermaid in.

"Lady Amethyst, you have a visitor in your receiving chamber. Lady Topaz."

Topaz! Her first reaction was elation on seeing her sister after all these months. Then logic set in, and she began wondering... what does she want this time?

It's not a social visit, she suspected. "I shall be glad to receive her. Do sent her in."

One of her ladies-in-waiting sat on a footstool doing needlepoint and attendants gathered in the outer chamber chatting. If Amethyst's suspicions about Topaz's visit were correct, they'd best be alone. The chapel was the perfect place. It was empty from morning Mass until Vespers.

Moments later, the chambermaid returned. Topaz pushed past her through the doorway to Amethyst. Her svelte form was a forest of deep rich green satins. Her eyes echoed a circlet of green flowers gracing the burnished copper that tumbled freely to her buttocks, windblown, yet looking wild and natural. Her gown glowed, setting off the spring green of the flowers strung round her neck, nestled twixt her uplifted breasts. "Amethyst!" They embraced lightly.

Amethyst voiced her wariness. "Why do you visit me at court, Topaz? Is there a problem at home? How are the lads?" She ushered Topaz from the apartments into the hallway towards the chapel.

"All is well in Warwickshire. And where are we going?"

Amethyst linked her arm through her sister's. "To the chapel where we will have complete privacy."

At the chapel, Amethyst leaned on the ancient wooden door. It squeaked on its rusty hinges as they entered. Colored bands of light streamed in through the stained glass windows and the aroma of burning incense hung in the air.

They took seats in the back. Topaz glanced round and sniffed. "So Harry the Great is away. And where is the queen?"

"She is preparing to be removed to Ampthill." She regarded her sister's casual gaze and stifled yawn. "Topaz, would you have come had the king been in residence?"

"Mayhap. Just to see how fat he's gotten." She gave her sister a smirk that slanted her eyes like a cat's.

"He's not gotten fat; he's...muscular, that's all," she jumped to Henry's defense. "Not only that, he is wise and intellectual and well-read. We sit and discuss many topics, sometimes until the wee hours of morning."

"When does he have time to consort with the likes of court minstrels?" Topaz raised her chin and looked down her nose at Amethyst.

Ignoring the gibe, Amethyst heaved a sigh of relief. So the news of her closeness to the king hadn't reached Warwickshire and Matthew, bless his heart, hadn't told anyone. She was sending all his letters to his other manor house in Evesham, to keep them away from prying eyes.

"The king is a cordial host and has time for all his courtiers," she kept up her defense.

"But of course," she quipped. "What else has he got to do?"

She didn't dignify that with an answer. "So what other tidings do you bring, Topaz? Have you finally brought your cavalry of rebels to storm the palace?"

"Hardly." Her smile displayed her straight white teeth. "I wish to bring you tidings from the family, bring you their regards, see how court life was treating you, and tell you that Matthew and I are separating."

Her mouth fell open. "What?" This was even more of a surprise than the king's revelation. "What happened?" Her heart went out to Matthew. The poor gent had given this woman the best years of his life, only to be tossed aside like a used rag having outlived its usefulness.

"He decided we cannot go on living together as man and wife while he does not support my cause. I wished him well, took the children and left a fortnight ago." She sat back and spread her skirts about her.

"'Twas his idea?" Amethyst probed, shaking her head in disbelief.

"Aye, but we both could see it coming." Topaz rested an arm along the back of the pew. "The marriage became nominal only. We ceased sharing our bed months ago. 'Twas not a shock, believe me, when he finally sat me down and requested that we separate."

A burst of relief pervaded the abrupt shock at the news. Amethyst now shared Matthew's long-awaited peace of mind. "So where do you make your residence now?"

"Warwick Castle. Where else?" She stared at Amethyst, her eyes bright and well rested.

"What about the lads? How are they taking this?"

"They are fine." She held up a reassuring hand. "They sensed something was amiss long ago. We both explained that we cannot live together as man and wife any more, but that does not diminish our love for them. They are with me, being tutored as always and well protected."

Over-protected, Amethyst itched to say. *And brainwashed into believing your ideals like a pair of puppies.*

"There is no longer any reason for us to live together, Amethyst. I have my heirs, and he refuses to support my cause. He is no husband of mine." She gave a resolute nod.

Amethyst had to know or she'd burst: "Are you divorcing?"

"Nay." She shook her head. "I shall not live that dishonor. I shall retain the title. I brought him the dowry, I shall not let him off that easily. It would be too traumatic for the lads. We shall remain married, but in name only."

Amethyst knew she'd be hearing from Matthew any day now. "Well, I hope you have done the right thing. What did you do with your animals?"

"I'm having an addition built to the stables with a huge fireplace and clean straw mats. So where does the king stand on his own great matter? Pray it was much easier for me to rid myself of Matthew than it will ever be for him to dispense with Catherine, banishment or no."

Amethyst didn't mind sharing Catherine's rants with her sister. "She insists she was a virgin through her entire marriage to Arthur, so she and Arthur were never married."

Topaz threw her head back and laughed, her eyes crinkling in delight. "How utterly typical of court knavery. How genuinely amusing. In order to keep Henry within her clutches, Catherine insists she was never married to Arthur and Henry turns round and insists he was never married to Catherine, because she was married to Arthur. What a vicious circle indeed." She scattered a few chuckles twixt her words. "The poor Pope must feel like a tennis ball during an endless volley. Catherine and Henry each pleading their wretched cases before the Holy judgment of Rome. Well! Did Arthur leave his young bride pure and untouched or not?" She spread her hands with an exaggerated shrug. "That is one mystery that will live unsolved through the ages: did she or didn't she? If I remember correctly Aunt Margaret's recollections, Arthur was a frail lad indeed. Notwithstanding his bragging from the marriage bed about having been 'six miles into Spain,' I tend to believe Catherine. Sometimes the best of them are duds when it comes down to the rigors of a command performance. Kings included."

How many kings have you bedded? she wanted to ask her smug sister.

"So where does that leave them, then?" Topaz continued. "At an impassible stalemate, like the king and queen on the proverbial chessboard, stymied by a pawn. Who can ever prove whether Catherine was a virgin during her marriage to Arthur? That truth has followed him to his grave as it will follow Catherine."

"The king believes she is Arthur's widow and on that belief is appealing to the Pope for a divorce," Amethyst explained.

"And what odds does the court lay on his success?" Topaz's smirk returned, this time spreading into an amused grin.

"I know not." She looked up toward the altar. "I do not engage in court gossip. I do not even know why I am discussing this with you. Is there nothing else you have to report, Topaz?"

"Well, yes there is..."

Here it comes. Amethyst braced herself.

"I was hoping you would return home to Warwick with me," Topaz stated, as if inviting her to sail down the Thames.

Her eyes widened. "Whatever for?"

"Court can be very corrupt and the king may act impetuously one day. Just the way he is handling his marriage is a good indication of his capricious character, little sister," she instructed in that patronizing tone she'd used since Amethyst could understand the language.

"Oh. You want to try goading me into fighting for your cause again? I did what I could to get the king to dig into the treasury to help your dejected Whitechapel. He's got enormous expenses, building the navy, to guard against those relentless French and Scots. Do you not have enough support among Henry's enemies? Pray God he doesn't need another one, least of all me."

Topaz thrust out her chest. "You are my sister and I am worried about you, here at court in such a vulnerable position. I fear for what will happen to you, caught in the middle like this, he may use you as a scapegoat once this gets under way."

"And Lord knows I am worried about you," she replied. "But why on earth would he do that?"

"The same reason his father killed our father. Does that hold any more logic?" Her tone intensified.

"He is not his father, he is a kind and gentle king and I trust him," Amethyst mimicked her sister's authoritative voice, quite well, she reckoned.

"You are playing a dangerous game, Amethyst." Topaz rose and rubbed her hands together. "This air is growing chilly. Can the king not afford heat?"

Amethyst stayed on the subject at hand. "When is your great rebellion going to take place?"

Topaz shot her a look of perplexity. "I cannot tell you that. 'Tis not going to be on the morrow, that's all I can say. I must wait until the timing is just right, when the king is at his most vulnerable. Then I shall proceed."

"You are the one inviting danger, Topaz." Now her tone carried foreboding. "You are endangering the lives of your children as well as ours. You have signed your own death warrant already. The king does not take you seriously now, but once your rebellion begins to materialize, you will not last one day. Either way, it would tear the country apart, shed rivers of innocent blood, and ruin more lives than you would ever salvage as queen."

"We shall see." Topaz flicked her wrist. "But I am doing what I feel is right for this kingdom. Now this is your last chance. Do you return home with me or not?"

"Nay. I am going nowhere with you." Her tone made it clear that her sister's request was simply bonkers.

Topaz rose to her full height and swept past her down the aisle, her palm flattened against the chapel door. "Very well, then. Then this is farewell, for I doubt we shall ever see each other again upon this earth." She vanished in a whoosh of green, furious as the whirlpool of the ebb tide swirling out of the Thames. The door slammed shut behind her.

Amethyst did not let Topaz's theatrics affect her. Topaz could never bid her own sister farewell in such a flippant way. Amethyst wished the king would return. He could talk Topaz out of this madness; she knew he could. He could even get her to like him; that was the beauty of Henry's charm.

As she returned to her chambers, she realized this would be a bad time to visit home. If Topaz's rebellion happened any time soon, Henry would surely hold Amethyst partly responsible, even though her return home had nothing to do with Topaz or her loony plans.

So she stayed on—waiting for the Pope's next move.

Chapter Nine

Hampton Court Palace

The trial was suspended until October, further frustrating Henry and Amethyst. Catherine, as smugly as her position would allow, and in her mind, remained queen.

On the advice of Henry's council, and because Henry could no longer rely on him, he arrested Wolsey. The charge—treason. Wolsey never made it to the Tower for sentencing. Guards seized him, he relented—and died.

With Cardinal Wolsey gone, Hampton Court Palace, with all its splendid gardens, mazes and furnishings, now belonged to the king. He held court here, and gave Amethyst apartments much closer to his own chambers, but still not adjoining. The Boleyns, permanent fixtures now, kept apartments at the opposite end of the palace.

"I am bringing the case before the universities of Europe and soliciting their advice. A theologian at Cambridge, Thomas Cranmer, came up with the idea. He believes this will sway the Pope," the king told her on their first full night at Hampton Court. "I was at my wits' end, at the complete end of the road. Cranmer is a godsend."

"Mayhap this is finally our answer, my lord." She unbuttoned his undershirt and brushed her fingers over his chest, as she always loved to do.

"I am overjoyed that another answer has come." He breathed more deeply, his voice more husky as she aroused him. "I only wish I had been the one to think of it."

"You may be potent, my lord, but you are not omnipotent," she purred into his ear.

"Only you can make me realize that, my lady," he said as she wrapped her arms around him.

"So how long do you think it will be?" she asked through his kisses.

"Please, Amethyst, don't talk. Just make love." His breath melted her, hot against her neck, but she managed to push him away.

"And why is Anne Boleyn still here?" She had to know. It distressed her, day and night. "I thought you were sending her back to...wherever she came from."

"Anne...who? Oh, God's foot, I've forgotten all about her." He made an attempt to capture her lips.

She turned her head away. "Well, she hasn't forgotten all about you. On that last hunting trip you took, she asked just about every courtier in sight when you would be back."

"So, mayhap she has a thing for me."

"And do you have a thing for her? Like this thing in your trousers?" She gave him a fast squeeze.

He pushed his hardness into her. "Are you accusing me of a dalliance with—what's her name?"

"Nay, but it would be much more comfortable if she would just go home." She felt the swell of his desire now shrinking. He looked round the room, and she knew he was looking for a goblet of wine. "Just tell me." She gripped his forearms, the pads of her fingertips yielding to hard muscle. "What is she to you?"

"Nothing!" He shook her hands off and smoothed down his thinning, but still very golden red hair. "You can shrink the most throbbing male member to a sheer mushroom cap, do you know that? You have completely obliterated any tinge of desire in my body by your incessant whining about this bloody divorce, and now..." he sputtered. "What's her name!"

"You well know what her name is, and until your great matter is settled and she is in a litter on her way back up the River Styx, you shall not touch me," she declared, knowing she was taking a great risk. But her honor was worth it.

"Wench!" he spat, searching for something to hurl against the wall.

Without another word, she returned her chambers to pack—for good this time.

* * *

Warwick Castle, 1530

Amethyst and Matthew took a stroll round the grounds of her beloved home. She hadn't heard a word from Henry since her departure six weeks ago, but her arrival had thrilled Matthew. "This is where you belong," he'd said.

She knew deep down that Henry would be back for her. The divorce had taken its toll on his health, causing Henry to overeat to the point of sickness.

"Oh, Matthew, you were right, 'tis so good to be home!" She gazed at the castle, its towers proudly jutting into the sky. They strolled across the Pageant Field and headed for the Peacock Gardens. "I miss the king so, but mayhap with me away from court, he can concentrate on resolving this matter. I know it will happen much faster with no distractions."

An unsettling thought trampled upon her once more, as it had pervaded her mind during the entire journey home—Topaz would be arriving tonight. She was visiting the local shires distributing alms to the poor, and making her rounds of "house calls," caring for sick animals along the way.

"Matthew, I am so sorry the turn your marriage to Topaz took," she gave her condolences, though Matthew hardly looked grief-stricken.

"'Twas simply one of those things, Amethyst." He spoke lightly with no hint of remorse. The sadness rendering a voice ragged was simply not there. "We have different outlooks on life, on what is good for the kingdom, on who should be on the throne." As he turned to look at her, the sunlight glinted off his hair, which had turned to platinum in the brilliant gleam. The breeze tousled his hair, sending his sharp woodsy scent through her head. His jaw was relaxed, his facial muscles pleasantly slackened.

"Shall we sit?" They'd reached the edge of the Peacock Gardens and a few of the birds were lazily basking in the sun.

They sat upon the grass and she lifted her face to the sun.

"I am not sure she ever loved me, Amethyst," he confessed. "She never told me so."

She could never tell Matthew about Topaz's breezily selfish reasons for marrying him. That would hurt him terribly. "Topaz does not show her emotions. She has always kept a distance from others, even when we were growing up. She was usually off on her own, studying or attending to her pets, as if she didn't belong to the family. Especially when Warwick Castle became ours again, she became more defiant than ever, calling the king a hypocrite. Her lifelong passion is to reign as queen and to rule the realm according to her beliefs."

"I daresay she is a devoted mother." The praise lightened his tone. "Those lads have everything they could ever want; the best tutors, the finest clothes, toys and ponies and pets galore, but she never gives herself to them totally, as she'd never given herself to me. She only went so far, and up went the wall I could never penetrate. Mayhap it is not love that she needs as most of us do."

"Nay, Matthew. We all need love. I need it, you need it, God knows the king needs it. But Topaz was always above that. Her heritage is her passion. I've never told anyone this, Matthew, but...part of me wants so badly for her to succeed, because I can see why she believes so strongly. I love my father, although I never knew him. But of course, Henry is our king and so will be his son. 'Tis a terrible feeling I harbor every time I am with the king. It's as if Topaz is looking over me, chiding me, like I'm betraying her. I want to be queen, but his queen. I dread to think of what Topaz will do when Henry and I finally do marry."

Matthew smiled down at her. "Well, your being queen consort will not be much of a threat. 'Tis not as if you are trying to become queen in your own right, as she is. She tried to convince me." He plucked some clover from the ground, twirling it in his fingers. "But I believe if your father had meant to be king instead of Henry Tudor, 'twould have happened that way. But it was fated to happen the way it did."

She nodded her agreement. "Aye, I'd heard my father had been a simple-minded man. He may not have been a good monarch at all."

"So few are," he said over a sigh.

"Do you believe Topaz would be?" she asked, for the first time, really challenging Matthew to dig into his conscience.

"I believe she would make a fitting queen" He plucked more clover from the ground. "She carries herself royally, she possesses strength and a willful nature that few of us have. Her ideas are radical, the changes she proposes would be sweeping. But not now. She was born too soon, much too soon. This simply is not her century; it is not her time. England is not ready for a queen like Topaz. I just do not know why she cannot see that."

"She will, I assure you. It will take a rebellion and a failure for her to see that the natural course of history will not accelerate because of the actions of one woman from Warwickshire."

"So tell me more of this Nan Bullen anyway, speaking of mysterious women," Matthew said. "You told me the Boleyn family had managed to get themselves court appointments, but that is all."

She fought to keep the grimace from her lips. She didn't want to spend her precious time here with Matthew discussing Nan Bullen. "She was one of Catherine's ladies-in-waiting, who spent half her life at the French court. Their name was originally Bullen but they Frenchified it, to appear more genteel, I suppose. She speaks with this dapper French accent, throwing in a 'oui' and a 'c'est bon' or two every now and then. Saunters about with her nose wrinkled up like vinegar is wafting through the air. Nearly her entire family's bouncing round court, but I have not seen much of her. She sits on the sidelines quietly. I really believe the king fancies her. Not in the way he loves me," she hastened to say, "but she is such an enigma, he seems fascinated by her. He gazes at her not with the love two people share, but with an open curiosity, as one gapes at a distant star, or something he does not understand."

"Have you seen them alone together?"

With that question he stepped into territory she'd avoided till now. "Nay, never. He does not desire her physically. His life is just so fraught with these divorce problems, and hard as it is to keep my patience, I try to be there for him. He sometimes forgets he is the king, only in front of me, of course, and I can sense his helplessness in dealing with all these outside powers..." She waved at the land in the distance. "Rome, for instance, and Catherine's stubbornness. I do pray his disposition will relax when we are finally married, and when I am with child, and the sooner the better, I say."

"But how can he think he is not married to Queen Catherine?" Matthew now asked a question only the king's intimate could answer.

"In his eyes, he insists their marriage never was. In the beginning, he insisted it was a question of conscience. He appealed to the Pope with this angle, telling him...and me, that he could not in all good conscience stay married to Catherine, because she is his brother's widow. The conscience part sounds very convincing when presented to the Pope, but deep down, his motives are selfish. No one else knows this." Their eyes met. "Ironically, Cranmer's idea of soliciting the advice of the universities turned out to be a good one, for it made the Pope even more adamant against the king's divorce. This is exactly what Henry needed, for the Pope to refuse him when he was at the end of his rope, to provoke him to take this final, most drastic measure."

"What is that?" He tossed the clover to the ground.

"He has chosen a London lawyer, Thomas More, to replace Wolsey as Chancellor, and has chosen a Thomas Cromwell, one of Wolsey's henchmen, to help him carry out an elaborate scheme, one which I believe the king is executing out of desperation, for I do not believe he really wants to do this."

Matthew sat silently, waiting.

"He is planning to declare himself head of the Church. His own Church, with nothing to do with Rome. Cromwell even suggested dissolution of the monasteries, for they are corrupt agents of the greedy Roman sphere of influence."

"Are you saying the king would be like the Pope?

As well as the king? That is rather ambitious," Matthew spoke the understatement of the century.

"He can handle it, Matthew, believe me. He is planning to take all the money the church has been sending Rome throughout the ages and from now on deposit it in the royal treasury. He talks of destroying the abbeys and monasteries, throwing the monks out into the streets to fend for themselves, melting down bells in order to make cannons and building coastal forts to defend against the French. He is not doing this out of power, hunger or greed," she went back to her defending of the king. "He simply wants a divorce, a divorce attainable only through a break with Rome, and being the determined soul that he is, always used to getting his way, he will stop at nothing to get it."

"What will this do to the kingdom?" Matthew, gazing upward, asked the universe, rather than her.

"I shudder to think of it. Just go along with him, Matthew. Do as I do and you will always be safe."

"What of Queen Catherine in all of this?" His gaze fell back upon her with that more immediate question.

"She's even more insignificant now. She has been banished from court and has been languishing...oh, I do feel so bad for her. Henry will not let her see Mary, and although I have tried to convince him that they would both be so much better off together, he storms out of the room."

"But you always come back and appease him every time," he spoke the truth. Oh, yes, he knew her as well as she knew her Henry.

She smiled to herself. "But he is going to come back to me now."

* * *

Topaz arrived late that eve, a blood-splattered apron covering her burgundy skirt. Amethyst looked upon her sister, staggering backwards in shock. Her imagination began to run wild. "What happened?"

"Dear sister!" Topaz approached Amethyst for a warm embrace, and Amethyst backed away, the red-brown stains coming into focus just as they'd soaked through the apron. "I daresay I doubted we would ever meet again. I am glad you came to your senses and left that wretched court."

"Topaz, pray what happened to you?" She held out an arm, palm out. "Are you hurt?"

"Nay, one of the mares at one of our neighboring farms gave birth to a beautiful white colt named Robin. I was the midwife," she bragged, chin raised, displaying her razor sharp jawline.

She linked her arm in Amethyst's and walked up the staircase to the library, their favorite room to chat and browse through the books, write poetry and dream.

She removed the apron and tossed it into the garderobe outside the library.

"So why did you leave? Did the palace run out of food?" Topaz flaunted a smug smirk.

"My leave is temporary." She didn't want to discuss court or her relationship with the king until his divorce was final. "Do you…have any plans yourself?" she asked Topaz, not really wanting to know, just fishing for some kind of hint.

"Nay, no plans to date." Topaz sat in the leather chair she'd claimed the first time she ever entered this room.

Amethyst breathed a sigh of relief, although she knew the longer her sister waited to carry out her plans, the more devastating it would be. Too worked up to sit, she paced the room, running her hands over the spines of the books lined up on the shelves.

"So what is going on with Henry and this Boleyn night crow? According to the tittle-tattle of the nobles who met Henry on his last progress, he forbade her to marry Henry Percy. I still know not whose loss that is," Topaz said breezily.

"You hear quite a bit, don't you?" Amethyst retorted, desperately trying to deny that her beloved king had any feelings for Anne Boleyn other than deep curiosity. "She is a fixture at court, nothing else." She preferred to explore the bookshelves and caress the thick dusty volumes, slide one out at random, wondrously scan each frayed page, fragile as autumn leaves, breathing in the ages of knowledge contained within the leathery covers.

"I think his taste is abominable," Topaz voiced her opinion, and for the first time Amethyst agreed with her.

She turned to face Topaz. "Come to think of it, you and Anne are alike in many ways. She, like you, distributes alms to the poor." *She's also a pompous witch,* Amethyst thought, but kept any further comparisons to herself.

"Ah, yes, she tosses an urchin a few guineas from her traveling litter when she's in a generous mood." She swept a hand at the air. "Nay, I have never met her and I never wish to. None of those court people are worthy of my company."

How easily she dumped all the courtiers together, including the king, in that general category.

"When I become queen, they will love me," Topaz remarked, and Amethyst shut off her ears.

"Where are my nephews?" She turned to Topaz, just as eager to see the lads as she was to change the subject.

"At Kenilworth. I shall fetch them in the morning. They know you are here, and are equally eager to see you."

"How they must have grown," she mused. "I cannot wait to see them."

"Edward is as handsome and noble as any king will ever be, and Richard George is coming along, not quite as tall and statuesque as Edward, a delicate lad, but he is not a big eater. I try to compensate with plenty of fresh vegetables and milk."

As Amethyst walked along the bookshelves, her fingers brushing the spine of each volume, she noticed several old books shoved off to the side and piled atop one another to make room for a set of what looked like new volumes: the covers in bright reds, greens, and rich browns, gold lettering embossed on their spines glinting in the sunlight. She pulled one out at random and flipped open the cover. "Utopia" read the title page, "by Sir Thomas More."

"Utopia? What is this, Topaz?" She held the book out.

"It is an ingenious volume by Sir Thomas More, a brilliant London lawyer," Topaz replied. "You should read it. Anyone with any intelligence round here has."

"I know who Thomas More is. He just replaced Cardinal Wolsey as Chancellor. Of what does he write in this book?" She scanned the pages.

"Utopia is a whimsical little island in the New World where everyone lives together in harmony, and shares equal portions of everything, which is available in abundance. There is no greed, for no man asks more than he can possibly use, there is no money, therefore no profits, no extortion, no bribing, no stealing." Topaz sang its praises. "The only use for gold is not as a measure of currency, but to craft beautiful objects, ropes to be worn about the neck and wrists, plates, goblets, and chamber pots."

"Chamber pots!" Amethyst blinked in surprise.

"Aye, gold at both ends! The communal storehouses maintain a healthy reserve, so there is no hunger. Each adult works but six hours a day on agricultural endeavors, to further ascertain adequate production. There are no lawyers, for each man is required to plead his own case." Topaz stood and came up to Amethyst, taking the book from her. "Those who violate the law are not simply tossed into a stinking dungeon, but are required to serve the community." She held it in her hands like a beloved family Bible. "There is no adultery and young people are permitted to inspect each other's naked bodies before marrying to avoid disappointment and are permitted annulment if the spark does not fly, and even heretics are treated with respect and are accepted by members of the society, as long as they do not presume to judge the others' beliefs about the established religion. He wrote it many years ago. Surely Henry has a copy of it somewhere."

"It does not sound like the type of thing the king would find entertaining. It sounds too irrelevant," Amethyst replied "I've read a few books belonging to Henry. He's a self-proclaimed theological expert. His tastes of late run according to the new books dealing with the papacy that he seems to enjoy reading and discussing with the more learned and outspoken courtiers." She'd noticed a few books on Henry's nightstand, in Anne's clutches, and in the hands of several of the courtiers.

Topaz replaced Utopia and said, "This is my favorite." She slid out a thin volume entitled 'A Supplication for the Beggars.' "Simon Fish wrote this while in exile, when he fled after ridiculing Wolsey in a play. It speaks out against the clergy, where the poor complain that they are dying of hunger because the clergy has seized one-third of the kingdom's resources." Topaz flipped through the pages, her eyes brightening at certain passages, as if remembering them fondly. She could see Topaz identifying with the author. "The monks and priests seize women in the dark corners of the confessional and seduce them. The monasteries are a hotbed of corruption in this book. Does it bear a striking similarity to a kingdom we're all familiar with, Amethyst?"

"Aye, it does. And if I remember correctly, the king did read that volume, and liked it."

"Ah! Mayhap he's coming to his senses after all. For I could have written this book myself. It expresses my sentiments exactly." She turned to the front page. "Alas, poor Fish died last year. I would loved to have collaborated with him on another book. Mayhap I shall simply write one myself."

"No book of yours would ever be allowed in print," Amethyst stated.

"When I am queen, I shall write and publish and circulate any book I so desire," she answered defiantly, sliding the volume back into its slot and giving it a gentle shove until it hit the back of the bookcase with a thump. "Heretics one and all will be welcome to write and argue anything they wish. I shall hold court parties where Catholics and Lutherans and heretics and anyone with a self-concocted religion will be welcome to speak his peace and acquire as many followers as he can carry on the tail of his robe!"

"Let me read this, if you do not mind." Amethyst slid "Utopia" out once again. After seeing nothing in the last few years other than these heretical and reformist books, and hearing Henry's incessant dinner hour debates at the high table on vernacular versions of scriptures and whether the Bible should be printed in English, she was in the mood for some easy, light fiction.

* * *

The lads arrived the next day, delighted to see their aunt, as she was to see them. Edward, nearly tall as she, held his head high, his posture and carriage that of a true nobleman. Richard George, smaller boned, lacked Edward's regal aura, but beheld Topaz's mischievous twinkle in his eye, that gleam no one could decipher. They were both dressed in identical brown velvet doublets trimmed with ermine, sleeves slashed and turned up to expose an ermine lining. They both sported the closely cropped French haircuts. She wondered if Topaz always dressed them up like twins.

Richard George sat beside her and asked her all about court, while Edward, the first born, sat quietly and listened carefully, asking no questions. *What has Topaz been teaching him?* she wondered, but dared not ever try to undo Topaz's dogma. It was not her place. Still, she wondered, and tried to gain some insight from the impressionable adolescent mind.

"I would like to talk to you lads, Auntie to nephew, and keep this twixt us." She kept her voice low. "Neddie, how do you feel about our king?" she asked the lanky youth, old enough to marry, have children and ride into battle, nearly the age of her beloved Henry when he swept down the great aisle to his coronation and captured her heart. Her nephews had not seen as much as a boarding school. Topaz educated them with tutors from Oxford and Cambridge, paying them great sums to sit in the comfortable solar and teach the boys mathematics, natural science, music, philosophy, the classics, Latin, Greek and French. They'd never shot an arrow at an archery target; they'd never been hunting or hawking—much too dangerous. All sports save lawn bowling were too threatening to their precious lives.

"Henry Tudor needs an heir and regrettably, Queen Catherine cannot give him one," he recited.

"Do you still believe the princess Mary is a bastard?" she asked.

"It all depends on whether the marriage is valid, just like any other marriage," he gave his practiced answer.

"And do you believe it is?" she probed, wanting to know if this young man, already sporting a neatly clipped but light beard, still believed the words Topaz had introduced into his very young mind, that he'd once spewed off by rote.

"I shall never know if Catherine and Arthur consummated their marriage. No one will ever know. I say it would be cruel to bastardize Mary now, after thinking her parents were truly married. But once the divorce is final, it will be a moot point, will it not?" He regarded Amethyst as a student he needed to teach.

"Very clever thinking, Neddie, but the king wants a male heir. Mary doesn't seem to count," she instructed him.

"Once he is dead, it will not matter to him. I believe a queen can reign just as effectively," he informed her—*from his intellect or from Topaz's teachings*? she wondered.

She so hoped he was thinking for himself.

Edward smiled, and she remembered Henry not much older than this age, the strong teeth, the look that spoke of sheltered privilege, never having lived the excesses of pain or passion—not quite yet. "Auntie Amethyst, we know mother has her beliefs. She always made sure all our scholarly tutors never taught us English history past the crazed old Henry the Sixth and Margaret of Anjou. That is where she commanded them to stop abruptly because that was where she always picked up where they left off. Both Richard George and I do not think Grandfather Edward would ever have made a good king. He was a feeble and simple fellow. How can someone spending all his life in the Tower ever be a strong leader? He knew nothing of the world. Also,

King Richard could have killed Henry at Bosworth but it happened the other way round because Richard had traitors. Henry Tudor was lucky, that is all. He went on to become a strong king. That is the way it was. Besides..." he chuckled and his voice cracked a bit, riding the cadence of the high-pitched laugh, "I would not make an effective king. I would let my subjects get away with murder. I would not fight for our borders. I would let the French come in through the front door and the Scots through the back door and the entire kingdom would be one big orgy!"

So relieved she was to hear her nephew talking this way, she reached over and hugged him, bringing Richard into her embrace as well. "Oh, Neddie, I am so relieved you are not going to fight for this dubious claim to the crown. Your mother has made this quest her entire life's dream, but you must stay by her, help her, and always remember she loves you both very much."

Now that the lads were growing into proper young men in their own right, mayhap they could talk some sense into their mother, to abandon this lunatic cause for their sakes, to continue helping the less fortunate citizens of the kingdom keep warm with full bellies, which even Henry admitted he appreciated.

"Tell me, Neddie, have you ever told your mother about your beliefs?" she asked.

Edward shook his head and grinned. "Never. She would have me head!"

"I enjoy helping Mother tend to the animals and feed the poor and go about the countryside distributing blankets and food and I don't even mind shelling peas now and then," Richard George piped up, "but I wish she would just forget about wanting to be queen. With her outlawing hunting and letting all the animals multiply and roam free, England would become quite uncivilized, wouldn't she, Ned?"

* * *

Warwick Castle

A fine mist sprayed Amethyst's face as she stood atop Guy's Tower. Her favorite spot in the entire castle, no one ever came to bother her, No one ventured the dizzying climb up the steep stone steps, even for the reward of the sweeping view.

Basking in her family's love and warmth, she missed one special person. She longed for the king with every beat of her heart.

In all these months, he hadn't sent a word from court. No messengers came, no scuttlebutt wound its way up the rutted paths and worn roads to Warwickshire. Topaz's cronies always showed up empty handed.

She considered writing to him, and sat down one day to begin a letter that bared her emotions: the loneliness without him near her, the crushing letdown every time a messenger arrived without a message from him, the heartache...the shame. *I was wrong*, she wrote, quill scratching over parchment, *I never should have treated you so cruelly. You are my king and I hold the utmost respect for you, sire. I beg you to find forgiveness in your heart.*

But she knew Henry's temperament. He didn't tolerate much, especially from subjects—and much as he purported to adore her, she was still, in the eyes of the kingdom and the world—a subject.

Her mind told her the stark possibility, but heart told her another: *he'll come back to me.*

She heard the sound of soft footsteps and turned to the staircase. Who would venture up all those steep steps in the cold rain to speak with her unless it was important? Her heart leapt in anticipation. A figure appeared in the shadows—a white headdress, a slim neck, a graceful pair of shoulders covered in white fur and blue velvet.

"Emerald! What are you doing here?" Amethyst abandoned the shrouded view of the countryside to greet her younger sister.

"I just wanted to talk to you." Her breath came in rapid puffs of vapor that collapsed in the cold droplets swirling around them. "Why on God's earth do you come up here in the cold, Amethyst?" She began to catch her breath. "You'll catch your death!"

"'Tis peaceful and quiet and I can see the world from a different perspective. It gives me a sense of immortality to see the earth from such a lofty perch." She turned back to face her beloved Warwickshire.

"Please, we have enough lusting for immortality in this family already." Emerald stood beside her, running her hands up and down her arms, blowing on her hands. "'Tis colder up here than I thought it would be. Come back down to the solar, there's a cozy fire there, we can sit and sip some ale."

"If you want to talk, we shall talk here," Amethyst cut her off with a stern reply. "No one will interrupt us or hear us, you can be sure of that." Taking a few paces, she returned to her spot overlooking the winding River Avon, the narrow footbridge in the distance. "If William the Conqueror could have stood here in the most inclement weather to build this castle, then we can certainly stand here and talk."

"He built only that section down there." Emerald pointed to a mound way below them. "And they had their fires on days like this."

"Aye, a poxy central hearth with a hole in the ceiling. They must have frozen their culls off in winter. We are fortunate enough to have a fireplace in nearly every room. Imagine having lived during those primitive times," Amethyst mused, holding her face up as the mist replenished the moisture the dry fires had robbed of her skin.

"Amethyst, you have not been yourself since you've been home," Emerald said. "You were always so attentive of me, willing to teach me new things, singing, playing our music together. You have not touched your lute or harp since you've been back. Music has always been such a passion with you. Why do you not play anymore?"

"Because it reminds me too much of court, Emerald, and it depresses me so. I do not want to be reminded of my life there, I see it enough in my dreams, I do not need to hear it, too." She placed her hands on the stone battlement and leaned over, taking a deep breath.

"Are you never going back?" Emerald asked.

"Aye, I shall go back." She glanced at her shivering sister. "When the king comes back for me."

"But why would the king do such a thing?" Emerald badgered. "He has a kingdom to rule, he cannot be taking time off to chase after maidens."

Amethyst regarded Emerald's bright blue eyes, shining with starry innocence. She was yet untouched by the driving forces of love, of the tangle of emotions it aroused, including its antithesis, hate. How closely they were related, how they both made a person act in the same way!

"You are right," she admitted. "He has got a kingdom to run. But he also has numerous personal problems. He is trying to divorce the queen but the Pope and Catherine's allies are giving him a very difficult time of it. He will come back for me because we share a special bond. We grew very intimate since my arrival at court, and he needs me the way I need him. I have no doubt at this moment, he is sulking in his chambers or playing a solitary game of cards with nothing but a pitcher of wine to soothe him." *Oh, would that were true!* she could only hope.

"Do you love the king, Amethyst?" Emerald probed.

"Aye, very much, dear sister," she spoke the truth. "But it is a special love that has only been strengthened by our separation. I miss him now more than ever, but I had to leave, in order to give him more time to sort out his problems and contend with his great matter. I know King Henry and I hold a piece of his heart right here with me. It will not be long before he comes back to claim it."

"What if he claims it and brings it back to court with him, leaving you here?"

Amethyst laughed, wrapping her arm round her sister's shoulders. She could feel Emerald shivering under her cloak. "I shall not give it back, for he has a piece of my heart as well, and that he will never give up." She guided Emerald towards the doorway and they headed for the winding descend.

* * *

"Amethyst, you were right." Emerald's voice echoed through the hallways and down the stairs to the great hall where she breakfasted with her mother and some holiday guests.

"He's here!" Emerald burst into the great hall, pulled Amethyst from her chair and breathlessly dragged her out into the courtyard. "Come! Greet him at the gatehouse!" she called behind her and they broke into a run. Amethyst caught up and led the way.

"No!" She halted.

Emerald nearly knocked her over as they collided. "I mustn't let him think I've been waiting all this while for him. Let me go to my chambers and have a servant bring him to me." As anxious as she was to see Henry again and throw her arms around him, to feel his body against hers and to gaze into those golden eyes, she knew she couldn't behave that way. "He's come all this way, he can come another few hundred paces," she declared. Taking her sister by the arm, she strode back through the courtyard to her apartments. She chose the most lavish velvet gown from her wardrobe and yanked at her headdress, replacing it with Henry's favorite ivory combs.

The castle buzzed with excitement over the royal visit. Sabine ordered the servants to rustle up a banquet for that eve. Cleaners hastily swept the floors and scattered fresh rushes down. Laundresses washed linens and chambermaids readied the elegant King's Bedroom for his stay.

Sweeping through the corridor towards the solar, Amethyst trembled with excitement. Keeping her emotions under cover, as she had in the very beginning, would require some serious acting.

He sat before the fire, sipping a tankard of ale. A few minstrels lingered about, his fool stood in the corner talking with the grooms, and a light chatter hummed through the air. The room fell into a dead silence as she entered, filling the doorway with her white satin skirts, her long billowing sleeves trimmed in white rabbit fur, gleaming in a milky sea of pearls. The teardrop pearl he'd given her nestled twixt her breasts. He fixed his eyes directly on it.

Her heart thumped with every step she took closer to him. Finally she stood before him and curtsied deeply. As she rose, he turned to his retinue, and with a wave of his hand, they vanished as if by magic.

"My lord, it is such a pleasure to welcome you back to Warwick Castle." Thank God her voice came through without a tremble or a break.

She wanted so badly to hurl herself into his arms, to tumble with him to the floor, to make up for all these wasted months of yearning. But she stood rigidly waiting for him to speak.

"Why did you leave so abruptly, Amethyst?" His tone was flat, devoid of all emotion.

"I got terribly frustrated and tired of waiting," she told him the bare truth. "This divorce was taking forever, and I thought my leaving would prompt you to speed up the process."

"You got tired of waiting?" he thundered. "You? And what do you think I have been going through, you selfish woman? Do you have any idea how this matter has tormented me? Look at my eyes, look at my hair…" He pointed with his huge fingers as he spoke. "I have been applying the daftest of salves and ointments to my dome every bloody night to prevent any further of this hideous thinning. And you think you are frustrated?"

"But, my lord, I realize how I missed you!" She rushed up to him till they stood within kissing distance. "I've made up my mind. I want to marry you! I accept your marriage proposal…I do not want to keep you waiting a moment longer. I do not care if you are not yet divorced. I accept and I shall wait as long as I need to."

He looked away and the orange citrines in his cap caught the fire's glow. "I have put the preliminary steps of my break with Rome into effect."

"Which means what?" He never got right to the point, one of his annoying traits.

"I shall be free to marry in a few months' time," he said.

"Oh, sire!" She went to grab his arms, but held back. "That's grand, sire. We shall be married by spring!"

He shook his head. His eyes darted everywhere. "We cannot be married at all, Amethyst."

Her heart crashed. She fought a rising sickness. "Why not?" she managed to choke out.

"I must marry Anne." He spoke so low she could barely hear him. "She believes she is with child."

"Oh, no." She shook her head, and his gemstones flew from side to side in a dazzling blur. "No...no, it can't be...she's lying!" Now she grabbed his arms and shook him, abandoning all protocol, all etiquette, all manners. "Why must you marry her? You bedded Nan Bullen and after making me wait all this time, now you are going to turn round and marry her?"

He jerked out of her grasp. "You ran away, you silly wench. What was I to do, live like a monk, the way Catherine wants?" He took a few paces to the table and picked up a goblet. "The only reason I turned to her was because you'd left, without so much as a word." He took a long pull of the ale and replaced the goblet with a thunk. "I do not love her. She is merely a breeding mare, more than willing to give me an heir, which you did not have the patience to stay around and do." His eyes narrowed at her. "My divorce is finally in sight, you know how badly I need an heir, and you couldn't wait another few months." He swept his hand through the air. "No, you had to come running back to home and hearth, back to the castle, expecting me to come back to you, begging on bended knee. A king does not beg." His eyes narrowed to beady slits. "I have come to tell you I want you to return to court. I am admitting what you so desperately want me to admit. I want you back there with me. That is why I journeyed here. To bring you back."

Her wish, her prayer, now answered after all this time...but now it hit her like an insult. "To play second fiddle to the night crow? After you asked me to be your queen? What kind of fool do you take me for? You no longer love me." She placed a fist on her hip. You want me under your thumb so you can keep me as a spare for when Nan gets too swollen and ugly for you to bed." She turned away, unable to look at him.

"Holy Jesu, Amethyst, would I have left court and the future mother of my heir if I did not love you?"

"At this point I don't know what to believe." Her fists now clenched before her, she wished she could strangle that harlot he'd bedded.

"How dare you refuse me." He strode to the door and flung it open. "I shall give you until tomorrow, when my retinue and I leave. If you have not agreed to come back with me, do not ever return to court again."

At the door he dismissed her with the same wave of his arm befitting his servants. She left, not in obedience to him, but because she no longer wanted to see his face. The thought of him bedding that scrawny little hawk sickened her.

Tears blinded her as she returned to her apartments and found Emerald sitting on the bed waiting for her.

"Be gone, Emerald, I wish not to speak with anyone." She tumbled into her bed and drew her knees to her chest.

"Did he ask you back just like you said?" Emerald handed her a lacy cloth. Amethyst swiped at her hot tears.

"Aye, but he has gotten Nan Bullen with child and is going to marry her," came out over a mournful sob.

"Why…what is so bad about that?" asked her sister, in all her innocence.

She couldn't tell Emerald—until now no one knew about the king's marriage proposal to her, and to tell anyone now would have been unthinkable. "He does not love her, as he just admitted." She sat up and looked at Emerald through her tears. "He loves me."

"Then go back to court, Amethyst." Emerald came up to the bed and sat beside her. He can't love Nan Bullen if he came all the way here to take you back."

Mayhap Emerald wasn't so naïve after all. Amethyst considered her sister's reasoning, way beyond her years. Staying absent from court would not spite anyone but her. She had to return, to reclaim his affections, to keep Anne at bay. Sometimes the young were wiser at times, she admitted to herself.

"Then do you think he will ask you to marry him?" Emerald's eyes glowed.

"Oh, I have never even thought of that, little sister." She felt her face burning. "Nay, why would the king want to marry the daughter of the Earl of Warwick, a mere pretender to the crown?"

"According to Topaz, Henry Tudor is another mere pretender." She gave Amethyst a sly grin.

"Aye, and according to Topaz, she is the rightful queen," Amethyst said. "But alas, there can only be one queen at a time."

* * *

Before her twenty-four hours were up, she gave her king answer. "I shall be returning to court with you, sire." She spoke evenly, not betraying any of the garbled emotions swimming through her.

"I shall be so glad to have you back, Amethyst." He took her hand and pressed his lips to it. "If only you'd waited. I told you how I needed—"

"You need not explain, sire." No one dared interrupt the king in mid-sentence, but they'd passed that. Nan Bullen wouldn't dare interrupt him. Ever. "I carry no jealousy toward Anne. I understand that the royal line needs to be continued. But…why her?"

He hardly looked happy. A frown tugged his mouth down at the corners. His eyes sat above dark circles. "In my desperation, I thought she would make a good wife. I did not look very far."

"Nay, I daresay you didn't," she agreed. "The end of the Catherine's hairbrush handle is certainly not far."

"This does not change a thing twixt us." He squeezed the hand he'd just kissed. "I so much wanted you to be my queen. The first choice was yours, but you ran away like a frightened doe. So please understand that I did what I had to do."

She nodded, not knowing who she was madder at—him or herself. "I fully understand, my lord," she had to say. "Have you told Anne where you and I stand, and that she should bear no ill will towards us because of our relationship?"

"The entire court knows how we feel about each other, Amethyst. It is no secret. With her royal duties as queen consort, and her subsequent pregnancies, and pray the Lord there will be many, she will have no time for petty jealousies or resentments. My goodness, that is a child's game. We are adults. Anne seems mature beyond her years. Her youth abroad has given her a fiery independence and strong will. She is secure in who she is and becoming queen consort will reinforce that security." His assessment of Anne hardly came across as bragging about his new liaison. It sounded as if he was suggesting her for a court position. "She will not see you as a threat. You and I shall continue to see each other just the same. This will work out, I know it will."

"Well, I shall never run away again." They stood for a silent moment, looking into each other's eyes, making up for lost time. "If you must marry Anne, will you divorce her once she has the baby? That is a lot to ask, but after all, you're asking a lot of me."

He let out a long breath. "Amethyst, please, I am not even completely divorced from Catherine yet. One divorce at a time."

"Then no more talk of either one of them." She leaned against him and rested her head on his chest. "I missed you so much, Henry."

"And I missed you." His arms wound round her waist. "I turned to Anne only in desperation. She was so willing—"

"Never mind her." She was already sick of the name. "Anne will be a thorn in my side until you dispose of her. Why must you marry her at all?" she insisted, forever wanting answers to everything—simple logical answers in a complicated illogical world.

"Because she is carrying my heir, and he must be legitimate," he explained, smoothing her hair down her back.

"She may have a girl," she said, knowing that was the last thing he wanted to hear.

"The chances are fifty-fifty, and I must not gamble," was his answer to that.

But that did not satisfy her. She looked way farther ahead than he seemed capable of. "If she gives you a son, I shall never give you your heir."

"We shall see," he gave her his pat answer. "Let us not talk of these matters any longer. I am finally back with the woman I love, and I want to enjoy it."

She bade farewell to her family and returned to court, willing to wait as long as she had to this time.

* * *

Hampton Court Palace, Christmas, 1532

The familiar rumblings of the season were underway, and the court prepared for the festivities. The palace glittered with gold, silver, red, and green hangings in the shapes of stars, angels, and trumpets. Amethyst's heart burst with joy when the king invited Matthew and the lads to court for the holiday. If the roads stayed passable and no more snow fell, they would be on the palace grounds by nightfall.

While she sat in her solar with three other musicians, playing "Greensleeves", the door swung open and banged against the wall. Anne stood there, surrounded by ladies-in-waiting. She wore a tight-fitting coif tied under the chin. The billowing sleeves of her lemon yellow gown fluttered like a ghost. A three-tiered diamond choker wound round her throat. *A gift from Henry?* Amethyst wondered, hit with an ugly pang of jealousy. Above Anne's plunging neckline, her breasts sat pumped up and pushed together. It created a rather questionable effect, for if she made one fast move, out they'd pop like charms concealed within Christmas crackers.

This was the first time she'd seen Anne since returning to court. She felt no warmth or cordiality, only a simmering jealousy and resentment. She gathered every ounce of willpower to act polite. "Good day, Mistress Anne, what brings you to my conservatory?" She used the word she now used for her solar, since Henry had given her the virginals and music stands.

"When does Sir Matthew arrive, Amethyst?" No greeting, no apology for barging in without knocking.

"He should be here after supper, weather permitting." Why would she be interested in Matthew? Amethyst wondered, but she refrained from asking Anne, for she wanted to keep their exchange to the bare minimum.

"I was hoping he could bring me some of his luscious apples that he grows at Kenilworth." Anne glanced round the room with disdain, as if assessing which furnishings needed updating.

Matthew's gift of apples was a favorite at court, for his orchard produced an abundance of plump, juicy apples matched by virtually no one throughout the kingdom.

"I expect he will bring some. He always does." She returned to her music to signal an end to this unannounced visit, but Anne waltzed over to Amethyst, peered over her shoulder at the sheet music and tittered.

"Greensleeves! One of the king's more simple, mundane pieces, but you may master it someday, Amethyst."

The entire court was aware of Amethyst's musical talents, no one more than Anne, whose homespun melodies were given to courtiers' children to learn the rudimentary basics of music, whilst Amethyst's compositions enchanted foreign dignitaries as well as the king himself. "Do you wish to sing with us, Lady Anne?" Amethyst asked, knowing Anne liked to sing solo, but when it came to harmonizing with a group, her ear proved itself made of tin.

"Nay, I must find some apples! I have such a longing to eat apples! Do you know what the king says?" Her voice intensified, as if she were singing a capella, "He says it means I am with child! But I tell him no. No! It couldn't…no!"

Before any of them could reply, Anne burst into laughter and dashed from the room, taking two of her ladies by the arm, slamming the door behind her with her foot.

"God's truth, you do not think she is with child!" Mark Smeaton stared at the slammed door. Apparently, neither Anne nor Henry had announced their impending arrival to any of the courtiers. Amethyst certainly didn't intend to be the one to herald that declaration.

"I am not sure, but she likes to tease people, keep them guessing about her. The king finds it awfully amusing as well." Amethyst rummaged through the sheet music for more carols. "But we shall see how amused he is when Anne delivers him of a girl," she murmured, voicing her desperate wish, but more to herself than to the others.

* * *

Matthew arrived that eve with the lads in tow, two trunkloads of clothes and gifts, and baskets of apples. Anne did not hesitate to demonstrate her appreciation. She bit into one apple after another, tossing them aside after one bite, gushing as she pawed Matthew's doublet, "Oh, how luscious is the fruit, nearly as luscious as you, dear Matthew!"

Amethyst lost her appetite there and then.

At supper, the great hall glittered with candles, gold-and-silver tissue gracing each table. Golden plates and goblets twinkled as wine flowed and servitors brought in tray after tray of steaming meats, game, and vegetables.

The courtiers joked, laughed, and danced joyfully as the King's Musick played jaunty motets upon their lutes and recorders.

"Matthew Gilman, the handsomest man at court," Anne flirted openly as they sat upon the dais, the king preoccupied with Cromwell in discussing the divorce, their heads together in deep discussion.

"Uh, that's Gilford, Mistress Boleyn," Matthew corrected her, keeping his distance by using her formal title. This relieved Amethyst, though unsure it would discourage Anne's advances.

Anne gushed forth, "Thank you so much for the apples, for they are the most scrumptious in the kingdom. So red, so juicy, so succulent." Her ubiquitous touch of French played about the vowels, elongating them, rolling them round her tongue like fine wine.

Anne's long fingers cupped his chin, ran down his arm with a casual brushed of his knee, while Amethyst sat on his other side. Patiently letting Anne embarrass herself, Amethyst sipped her wine, clasping her goblet twixt thumb and forefinger. Her other hand enfolded Matthew's, his fingers tightening round hers in a reassuring squeeze—hidden 'neath the tablecloth.

* * *

As Matthew and Amethyst shared a nightcap in her receiving chamber, he mused over the incorrigible Anne.

"What a flirter she is!" He sipped ale from a goblet. "The king will have a jolly good time keeping her in tow."

"Anne has been wearing Catherine's jewels and acting very much like a queen when in the presence of court. How she behaves alone with the king is a different matter." Amethyst chuckled, remembering Henry's bellyaching one evening. 'She squawks and bellows and balls her fists and throws things to the floor whenever I mention Catherine, Mary, or Wolsey,' he'd said. 'At first I found it so girlish and pretty. Now I remove myself from her presence when she flies into these tirades. 'Tis my fault,' he'd sighed. 'I have been neglecting her, but now I must train her to act in a more royal, subdued fashion worthy of a Queen of England. She's just too Continental…too Frenchified!'"

"But how about his need to marry a princess?" Matthew asked. "She's no more than the daughter of a Kentish knight. Tom Boleyn is far from royalty. You are more royal than she. The milkmaids are more royal than she!"

"Aye, mayhap I was born closer to the crown," Amethyst replied. "But the Boleyns do have some royal blood in their veins. They are direct descendants of Edward the First. Her father was his envoy to the Netherlands. He holds Thomas Boleyn in high favor. So the family's well connected. She's not a serving wench he stumbled upon in the buttery," she informed him, her resentment waning. Matthew's presence changed her entire mood—and outlook. "When I decided I could wait no longer for him and returned home, she caught his eye, mystified him with her aloofness, and he, in that characteristic Henry style, plucked her up, decided she was the most suitable of the eligible court wenches to breed his heirs, ordered Wolsey to forbid her marriage to

Henry Percy, and here she is." She shrugged, sighing. "She's not much to look at, with that black hair and all those gowns with the cinched waists she brought over from the French court. Such a contradiction to her dark, enigmatic disposition. Did you see the clawlike nub jutting out from her little finger?" she asked, knowing Matthew must have noticed. She just thought it amusing to mention it.

"Nay," he replied. "Her hands were touching parts of me that were not in full vision."

"Well, those who like her not call it a witch's mark. Imagine!" Amethyst laughed. "If it were I in that position, I would be the witch of whom the scandalmongers tatter."

"So what does he see in her, then?" Matthew asked her to solve the kingdom's most baffling mystery.

"According to him, a conquest first, and a son. He sees in her the heir to this throne. What else, I know not. But we shall see what she does bring forth."

"I know you want him back." Matthew lowered his voice, his tone intimate and inviting.

Sharing her feelings with him lightened her emotional burden. "Aye, with all my heart. But tis just a matter of time." She refused to relinquish that thread of hope.

* * *

Richmond Palace, 1533

The king married Anne Boleyn in January. Her bride's cryptic prediction had come true. She indeed carried the royal child. No one outside court's intimate confines was privy to the information. They held the ceremony in secret, should the Pope refuse the bulls for Cranmer's consecration. Since the king's case was still pending in Rome, Cranmer could by-pass the papal authority and declare the marriage null.

The king finally carried out Cromwell's plan. England was now declared an Empire under a monarch supreme over Church and State. Many of the monasteries were demolished and lay in ruins. Monks fled and scattered throughout the kingdom. The king still insisted he had been living in sin with Catherine, now banished to Ampthill, demoted to Princess Dowager by an act of parliament. In May, Archbishop Cranmer gave the sentence for the king's divorce.

Then came Anne's coronation, hardly a celebration. The masses ventured out for the solemn affair and watched out of curiosity rather than reverence for their new queen. A hostile hush hung over London like a dark thundercloud as the procession wound its way toward Westminster Abbey.

Festive flags, streamers, and banners decorated fifty barges for their trip down the Thames to Greenwich. There they met and escorted the queen's barge to the Tower. The lead barge carried musicians playing trumpets, clarions, cromhorns, and viola-da-gambas. Next to the Lord Mayor on this barge was Anne's device, a white crowned falcon, sitting upon a root of gold with roses. When the barges reached Greenwich, Anne appeared, dressed in cloth of gold, attended by her retinue of ladies. The blast of guns rang out as her barge glided downriver. She arrived at the Tower to a booming of cannon shot. The Lord Chamberlain escorted her inside.

Amethyst joined the king and Cromwell at Baynard's Castle and watched the endless procession of gentlemen, knights, judges, Knights of the Bath, doctors, abbots, noblemen and bishops, but the mood was not the same as at Henry's coronation. She sat there, bored to tears. The royal purple, blue, and crimson velvet banners, canopies, and caparisoned horses were all there, but without the jubilation, the drunken revelry. Tapestry, carpets, arras of tissue, gold, and velvet decorated the streets. The crowd turned to stare at Anne as if eyeing an oddity. The sheer silence spoke volumes as she rode by upon a glittering litter under a canopy, led by two palfreys in white damask. She was clearly with child by now, but dressed in pure white, as if defying anyone to question her honor at this point. She wore a surcoat and mantle of white cloth of tissue furred with ermine, her hair hanging under a coif with a circlet of stones.

The City of London certainly had made an attempt at revelry. Pageants adorned the streets, fountains sprouted wine. But none of it came from the heart.

The next morn, Amethyst and Henry went to Westminster Hall to await the queen's arrival. At nine o'clock, draped in a robe of purple velvet, Anne entered the hall, then began the procession to Westminster Chapel. The archbishop of Canterbury began the service, and she lay prostate before the altar. He anointed her on the head from the ampulla. The singing of the Te Deum rang through the chapel. After the service, the procession returned to Westminster Hall, and the banquet followed.

Amethyst, with the king and several ambassadors, sat in a private closet in the cloister where they observed the banquet. "This will be you in a few months' time," Henry assured her, reinforcing his promise with a tight embrace. Her heart fluttered with hope. But her mind told her otherwise.

When the time came for Amethyst to be formally presented to the new queen, she curtsied, knowing it should have been the other way round. But she could not in good conscience resent Anne; she had no one to blame but herself. What kept her going was hope. This got her through each day. The hope that Henry would divorce Anne as soon as this child entered the world, and the next coronation would be hers.

* * *

As Anne approached her confinement, Amethyst observed Henry and her heart went out to him. He was uneasy and edgy; his hearty appetite had greatly diminished and he drank more than he ate. Goblets of wine, mead and ale flowed while trays remained piled with food, on the dais, in his chambers, as he told his Lord Steward's servers to "leave it, I'll eat it later."

He discharged Margaret Pole from her duties as Mary's governess when Margaret refused to give up Mary's jewels, but she continued to look after the princess at her own expense.

"I was only going to give those jewels to you, Amethyst," the king said one early eve as they picnicked on the grounds of Hampton Court in the setting sun. This was a rare treat, for she hardly got to see him alone anymore. As they relaxed together, she realized for the first time in her life, she'd eaten more than he in one sitting.

"Please, my lord, I do not want any more jewels. They belong to Mary. Give them to her, and let my Aunt Margaret and Mary enjoy each other's company. Mary needs that motherly companionship, and Margaret is so good with her." Her tone bordered on begging, but she'd beg on her knees for the princess. Her heart ached for the poor girl.

"As you wish," he gave in. He took another gulp of wine and looked at the simple pearl around her neck, the first token gift he'd ever given her. "Why do you not wish lavish jewels and radiant gold shimmering from your neck and wrists like Anne does? She thrives on it the way normal people thrive on basic foods. She devours the gemstones faster than I can have them made up for her."

"Mayhap Anne will not feel that way in the next few weeks," Amethyst offered, "when she is feeling the pangs of childbirth, I am sure glitter will be the last thing on her mind."

"Amethyst, you are truly the earth's most glittering jewel," he lavished the praise she craved, and as she reached over to kiss him, his eyes brightened for the first time in months. "And to think I almost lost you. Look at the punishments I have had to endure so far. A feeble daughter, a strong, healthy bastard son, a wife I do not love, and a woman I do love whom I cannot marry. Lord knows, Anne is praying for a son as if her life depended on it."

She detected an ominous note, but did not question him about it. They simply reclined under the sky striped with fingers of alabaster purple and pink, listened to the crickets chirping, and said nothing more. The only thing tearing at her heart was that it could have been her. Now she had to wait even longer.

* * *

Greenwich, September 7, 1533

The king burst into Amethyst's rooms in a fit of rage.

"What is it, my lord?" It couldn't be Topaz. No, Topaz blathered of battles, cavalry and armies. This night was as peaceful as the hyacinth-scented breeze wafting through the window.

"A lass! A wench! Nan brought forth a girl! What the hell am I to do with another female! Useless, useless, female, aye, I am cursed, I am convinced now!" He stomped round the chamber, flinging his arms up and dropping them to his sides, clenching his fists, punching walls.

"Calm down, my lord." An immense relief washed over her. Her prayers had been answered! The king still had no male heir. A burst of happiness exploded in her heart. He was now free to divorce Anne and they could begin their lives together—finally! But she did not dare voice her feelings. He was much too distraught right now.

"Oh, Amethyst." His fury spent, he dragged himself over and plopped down beside her, the only human being capable of comforting him. His rage had given way to defeat. He buried his head in his hands. "My spirit is crushed."

How would he ever handle Topaz's charge? With more composure, she hoped.

"What is the baby's name?" she ventured a conversation.

"Oh...Elizabeth, I think. Aye, Elizabeth, after both our mothers."

"Pray God she is healthy?" She knew Henry had a heart in there, and wouldn't wish harm upon the innocent babe.

"Healthy as a horse." His voice carried a hint of pride. The baby was a Tudor, after all.

"With your blazing red hair?" She knew just which buttons to push.

He looked at her sideways and dared to grin. "How did you know?"

"I am sure you will grow to love the Princess Elizabeth as she will grow to love you," she gave him that reassurance he longed for.

Chapter Ten

Warwick Castle, 1534

Thomas More rode through the gatehouse and dismounted. A groom led his mount away as a server greeted him and led him through the courtyard. They climbed the stone steps to the state rooms where Topaz waited in the Green Drawing Room.

She rose from the overstuffed chair and placed the specially bred Persian kittens from her lap to the chair. Her pink satin gown with billowing sleeves and trimmed with tiny pearls whispered of gentle meekness. She'd chosen the room graced with the pale green walls as a sedative to the eye. She didn't want to appear as the overpowering revolutionary he'd been hearing about. Not at their first meeting.

"Sir Thomas," she greeted him, her sleeve swaying as she extended her arm. He clasped her hand and swept off his plumed cap.

"Lady Topaz, 'tis indeed a pleasure to finally make your acquaintance."

"This shall evolve into more than a mere acquaintance, I trust," she assured him, motioning for him to sit in the satin chair opposite hers. She sat, cuddled the kittens in her lap and rested her feet on the footstool before her. A servant brought bread, cheese, fruit and ale, backed out and closed the doors. She waved a hand in the direction of the bookshelves flanking her desk, where she'd propped up a copy of

"Utopia" inside the glass cabinet doors. "As you can see, 'Utopia' is in the place of honor, as always."

"Aye, I am glad you enjoyed reading it." His eyes lit up. He looked chuffed, all right. *Score one point,* she mentally conjured up a scoreboard.

"I enjoy reading it more each time, and so do my sons," she flattered him. "The ideas you explore are reminiscent of many of my beliefs about how the ideal society should be run. I identified with it quite strongly. Our society is so oppressed, so entrenched in the dogmas of Rome, where it is a sin to do most anything that is pleasurable. I so agree with your belief that youngsters should see each other naked before marriage, to avoid the prospect of disenchantment later on. After all, the body is so hidden by our cumbersome robes and doublets and billowing sleeves and petticoats and breeches, we cannot begin to wonder what is underneath it all." She gave him a dazzling smile, for she'd polished her teeth that morn.

More snickered, gulped at his ale, and let Topaz speak on, for he was beginning to wonder what was under all *her* skirts and petticoats.

"To take a step further, I condone premarital lovemaking as well, in order to avoid the prospect of incompatibility in the marriage bed. You may find yourself attracted to someone who lights your fire by day, but fairly bursts your bubble by night! Looks deceive, do they not?"

"To a great degree, they quite do. When a fine gentleman, Sir William Roper, came by to ask for my daughter's hand in marriage, I led him upstairs where she slept, on her back fortunately. I tore the sheet away, and when she flipped over onto her stomach, Sir William said, 'Now I have seen both sides!' As a result, he and Margaret have been quite happy ever since."

"Ah, but that was not fair, Sir Thomas, and that was not consistent with your writings. She should then have had the chance to take a gander at his credentials, fore and aft!" Topaz's tone was chiding and playful.

"Aye, well, Margaret is but a shy girl." More sipped his ale. "No one rule applies to every one of us."

"And that is one of the reasons for my summoning you here. Sir Thomas, I invite you to this rather informal atmosphere to discuss a matter that is paradoxically very grave. I believe you know of what I am speaking." She sat forward, ready for business.

"Aye, I believe I do, Lady Topaz, but I have been wrong before."

"But first, tell me what goes on at court," she goaded. "I hear nothing from my sister Amethyst, for she refuses to repeat what she considers 'tittle-tattle.' "

"'Tis only tittle-tattle when it is not true, is that not so?" he questioned.

"Aye. However, she feels it is beneath her to be the bearer of second-hand news. I wish she would. The way rumors spread about this kingdom, it needs someone who will repeat truths and not malicious lies." Her gaze penetrated his dark eyes.

"You are so right, Lady Topaz." He returned her gaze with open admiration.

"Warwickshire could certainly use some news from court," she went on. "These poor villagers are starved for tidbits about their king and his new queen."

"As starving as the landed gentry for a unified kingdom under a unified church, my lady?" he asked.

She laughed. They were going to be equals in this endeavor. Nothing was going to get by Thomas. "Aye, Sir Thomas. We have a right to know, after all, we are all his subjects. What has transpired twixt the king and the gog—I mean his fair queen?"

"They have been estranged for some time now, Lady Topaz. The king has been in a bad way, oh, he has been suffering greatly. Not even your dear sister, his closest confidante, or his loyal old fool Will Somers, have been much comfort to him."

"What is amiss then?" Her toes in her satin slippers curled round the edge of the footstool in anticipation of goodies More was about to spill. The more she knew about the king's emotional fragility, the more acute her advantage, to surprise him while at his most vulnerable. "If you wish me to keep this in confidence, I shall, Sir Thomas. I confess

I am asking you for my own selfish reasons, which we will discuss at length after you reveal to me what kind of havoc Queen Anne wreaks over our king."

More laughed, took a breath and sat back in the chair, crossing his legs comfortably.

Aye, do be comfortable, Sir Thomas, Topaz thought, *for we are becoming fast friends.* "Is more ale in order, Sir Thomas?" She plucked up the bell she used to ring for servers.

"Nay, this is as much as I can handle." He held up a hand. "You needn't loosen my lips with ale, Lady Topaz. I shall tell you all. And you needn't keep it secret."

"That was not my intention, Sir Thomas." She managed to keep a straight face.

"Indeed. So...about the king. I am greatly worried about him. Not only because of his disenchantment with me over of what transpired twixt us, but because of the effect Queen Anne has had upon him...this is nothing new. It has been going on for some time now, since before their marriage."

"So I heard," she pondered the crumbs of gossip thrown her way since Nan became queen. "First she drove Henry daft with intrigue over her, then she presented him with a wench. Not a very lucky card she drew that time."

"The poor king is fraught with worry and unease. He believes Anne is a witch." He lowered his voice as if the walls had ears and he'd be dragged off to the gallows for even speaking of such treachery.

"A...what? A witch?" Elation simmered through her like a bubbling pot of potpourri. "Why, I hadn't expected anything quite this absurd! I've always known Henry would snap under all the pressure he's unequipped to handle. He's not the warrior his father was. His victories over France notwithstanding, he spends more time blowing deer to bits in his royal forests and prancing about on tennis courts than he ever does in the council chamber. Now it's happening—he'd finally gone scranny." She looked at More. "Whatever makes him think that?"

"Anne herself."

"Anne told him she's a witch?" She couldn't believe her ears.

He shook his head. "Nay, she does not have to tell him. She shows him. Look at the turn of events since his marriage to her. First it started with her lies. She lied about being with child. She claims Mark Smeaton is no more than her personal musician, but the entire court believes otherwise. The king... he tends to side with the court but dares not admit it. Then the murders—"

"Who has she murdered?" Topaz gasped as her heart leapt with lusty glee.

"Her malevolence towards Bishop Fisher caused the king to execute him five months ago, his parboiled head still rots upon a spike on London Bridge," he gave her the gory details. "Fisher had been poisoned before that, at his home. Some of his servants had died, but Fisher lived a while longer only to lose his life on the scaffold. Then there were the mysterious deaths." He counted on his fingers. "Wolsey, who fell from grace at Anne's doing and died a mysterious death. Warham suddenly died, when Anne decided she wanted him out of the way. Her former lover Percy is now dying of a mysterious wasting disease. The king's sister Mary, who'd refused to attend Anne's coronation, fell mysteriously ill and died. The king's son Henry Fitzroy is gravely ill. Then there's the king's leg ulcer..."

So many! Topaz reckoned he'd run out of fingers and take his shoes off to count. "My sister Amethyst mentioned something about the king's trouble with his leg, at about the same time he began putting on weight. At first he told no one but her. He always managed to escape state affairs and banquets and retire to his chambers so that she or Dr. Butts could change his bandages and place a draining cup against the wound," Topaz explained. "She learned that technique from me, having watched me tend my animals. Now it is helping the king..." her voice trailed off as she thought *the blasted despicable king! How ironic!* "And Henry attributes all these mysterious deaths to the workings of Anne who he believes is a witch?" she asked him, still stunned from all this.

"You must admit, Madam, it is too bizarre to be coincidence." He raised a brow.

"So you also believe she's a witch?" She flipped her hand at him. "Oh, Sir Thomas, never would I think you would be so credulous, especially since you speak out against fortune telling, astrology, and all those supernatural phenomena in 'Utopia.' "

"Nay, madam, I do not believe that at all." He folded his hands and placed them twixt his knees. "She may be dispensing poisons, aye, that is quite possible. But a witch? No, it cannot be. I am a scientist. An astronomer. I gaze out at the stars," he glanced out the window, "and am fascinated at the idea of other heavenly worlds beyond our own, but I do not believe there is aught beyond what we can see. Granted, the stars are in the heavens and we shall never reach them, but with a good telescope, we can certainly see them. Witchery or demons..." He shook his head. "We see those in our minds. They are not of the same flesh as we, we can never touch them, they are not material as we know it."

"I should not think you would believe something so preposterous. That would never stand up in court, would it, Sir Thomas?" They laughed together, the level-headed realist and the scientifically minded lawyer, united in their common bond—a desire to end the Tudor dynasty and a fond longing for Utopia.

"The king is not thinking straight." His eyes wandered round the room. "He sees the queen only during affairs of state, and retires to his chambers immediately. He avoids her constantly. He has been known to say on more than one occasion that he believes he will be Anne's next victim."

Topaz tapped her lips with her fingers. "Hmmm, that is intriguing. As one so close to court, what do you think, Sir Thomas?" She looked at him. "Will Anne choose Henry to be the next victim of her 'spells' or does she wish to live out the rest of her days as queen consort?"

"It will be interesting to see, Lady Topaz," was his noncommittal answer.

Mayhap I should bide my time just a bit longer, she thought. If Anne did plan to weave a spell over the king and cause his demise, it would save Topaz some trouble. The chronically ill and neurotic Mary would be much easier to oust from the throne, given her dubious legitimacy. But she wasn't ready to share these thoughts with More. "Yes, let us see," she agreed with his assessment.

"Aye, no need to jump to conclusions." Despite Topaz's reticence to share, More knew exactly what she was thinking.

"This indeed ties in with the matter I wished to discuss with you, Sir Thomas. I hear you are one of the few of the king's subjects who refused to take the oath to the Act of Succession." She let a slice of a smile curl her lips. "Let me commend you on your strength and ability to uphold the courage of your convictions."

"I was not able to bring myself to sign it simply because I could not compromise my principles. I do not agree with his position as head of the Church and as fond as I am of the king, I believe his tyrannical ways will not serve the best interests of the kingdom."

"Indeed. And we know what will. As official sworn enemies of the king, as you now must admit you are, we must not stop here. You are aware of my background, that Henry the Seventh killed my great-uncle King Richard and later executed my father. My lifelong quest has been to restore the crown to its rightful recipients, the Plantagenets. I trust you are of the same belief, Sir Thomas." She needn't ask him. There was no question about it. She was speaking with the man who was destined to be her closest ally—who, having defied the king by refusing to sign his name to Elizabeth's right to the crown, was willing to sacrifice his life for his beliefs.

"I always felt that way, Lady Topaz. Several of my family members fought beside Richard at Bosworth, but not so much *for* Richard as *against* Henry Tudor."

"Very cunningly put," she praised him. "You are a true lawyer." She took a breath and waited a beat. "So then you will help me oust Henry and his Tudor bastards from the throne that they never should have seized to begin with?"

"Aye, I shall help you in any way I am able, Lady Topaz. The kingdom deserves to be ruled by its rightful heirs. Henry is a tyrant and as such will not last long anyway."

"Unless the wicked witch gets to him first." She gave him a sly smile which he returned.

"You are with me, Lady Topaz." His smile widened.

"As such, we shall wait. Keep a close eye on the queen. Either way, Henry's days are numbered." She focused in on him and captured his gaze.

A grin approaching that of lechery broke out on Thomas' sullen face and he held his goblet out to clink hers.

"That is why I asked you to bring the list." Her inquiring glance scanned his person.

"Ah, yes, the list." His blue-gray eyes twinkled as he patted his doublet in a quick search and extracted several sheets of parchment. She glimpsed the edge of a hair shirt as he leaned over and detected a grimace of pain as he moved. Why some people went to such preposterous extremes, she'd never know.

"Here it is, Lady Topaz, direct from the king's personal archives of the Chapter Library at Windsor Castle, a comprehensive list of every nobleman and knight who fought in the Battle of Bosworth...for Henry Tudor. Also, from the personal archives of Eleanor Essex, a granddaughter of King Richard's sister Elizabeth, a list of Richard's peers and proclaimed traitors."

He held it out to her and she snatched from his hand, hungrily scouring the list, her teeth scraping over her lips.

"Ah, yes, Sir Thomas. Whom have we here...traitors, let us see Richard the Third's traitors..." She let out a peal of laughter at the first name on the list. "Henry Tudor, Earl of Richmond, top of the traitor list! So the list is in descending order? I expect my father was at the top of Tudor's list of traitors, or was he not meticulous enough to have recorded such a list?"

"I know not if Henry kept a list of his traitors, Lady Topaz." More showed not a hint of a smile. "Mayhap he kept the list in his head."

"Nay, impossible, there were too many, no one could keep a list of that length in such a pea-sized head." She returned back to the top of the list, which she found infinitely amusing. "Henry Tudor, Earl of Richmond, indeed," she snorted. "He never even was Earl of Richmond. His father was attainted and the title reverted to Richard. Just shows what a fraudulent humbug he was, all the way down to his bogus title. All those Tudors are frauds." She flipped the page over and scanned the next. She turned the second page over, her lips moving as her finger trailed the page. "...Sir William Cheney, John Cheney, Sir William Noreys, Richard Beauchamp of St. Mand, William Knyvett, Sir William Hunter pardoned, Sir George Brown of Bletchworth executed at Maidstone, Sir John Gilford...hah!" Her eyes widened in recognition and she looked up at him. "The dear old father-in-law I never met, gave his life for the old Tudor goat. No wonder Hal suckles up to Matthew like a piglet at feeding time."

"I expect most of these soldiers are deceased, Lady Topaz. Those of the living are old men now." He pointed at the papers with his chin.

"That matters not." She turned another page over. "They have sons and grandsons. They were brought up hating the Tudors for the frauds that they are. Then there are the sons of those who fought *for* Taffy Harry...ragged urchins who grew up without fathers, because they died to put Taffy Harry on the throne...I venture to say there is more than a little resentment on their parts. Not to mention all the enemies this present Henry has collected with his banishment of Queen Catherine and his taking up with the goggle-eyed—uh, with Mistress Boleyn."

"Why not bring France into this, then?" More, the intellectual but frustrated military man, suggested.

"Nay, I wish not to bring them into this." She shook her head. "'Tis a domestic issue, a very English issue, done for a specific reason, for nationalistic reasons. We are not fighting for land or religious reform. We are trying to regain our claim to the throne. This is something France would not appreciate, could not fully understand. Besides, I never trusted the French. They spend too much time romancing to be effective, serviceable allies. Leave them to their flamboyant art and their romantic theater. We are too stolid for them. We would not fight well side by side."

"But the best mercenaries are from the Continent," he argued. "We would never be able to raise an army to defeat Henry's forces with Englishmen alone."

"Whom do you have in mind?" She raised an inquiring brow, never one to miss an opportunity.

"Oh, I can rustle up a band of soldiers, never fear," More assured her. "Just leave it to me. You can retain your men of noble blood. Leave the other ranks to me."

"Aye, I shall let you know if we need reinforcements. I have a strong leader in mind already. He is old, but he is experienced. What he lacks in bodily strength will be made up in sheer military genius." She left it at that. More would meet her general soon enough.

She folded the parchment carefully and slipped it twixt the pages of her Latin Bible. "How does Thomas More, Duke of Richmond sound?" She batted her lashes at him.

"The title that Henry's bastard son holds? Absolutely magic!" He rubbed his hands together.

"Then it will be yours, when I am Queen Topaz the First and my son is the Prince of Wales. Let us engage these other true believers and fulfill our mission."

The clink of pewter goblets faded into the folds of the velvet drapes.

* * *

Hampton Court Palace, 1535

"Henry, what are you saying?" Amethyst moved away, darting across the chamber, afraid of him, a fear very different from the reverence of her younger days. Her fingers grappled and found the door. She grasped the knob in case he decided to attack her, too.

"I am saying I must be rid of her. Cromwell will not divorce us, so I must rid this earth of her evil, her demonic ways. I must have her executed!" Spittle glistened on his lips and he wiped it away with a sweep of his hand.

Now that the startling realization had begun to gnaw at her conscience—all the warnings, Topaz's rants about Henry inheriting his father's violent temper and his ability to end a human life at whim. She now realized it—he was her friend, her lover, her equal in the bedchamber, at her mercy and under her control, submitting to the powers of his desire as helplessly as any sexually aroused male, but he was still very much the King of England, and as such had the authority of no other person in the land.

She took short gulps and dared not speak. In the past, he'd awed her, thrilled her, and astonished her. Now he simply terrified her.

He seemed to have detected her fear, for his features softened immediately and he kept his distance. "I shall not hurt you, Amethyst. Don't you understand? She is a witch. The Imperial Envoy just confirmed it."

"Chapuys? How?" She gasped, realizing her mouth was so dry, she could barely form the words. Her throat closed up as if it doused in the dust of rutted roads on parched summer days.

"He just delivered the message that Mary is deathly ill." He held the letter, bunched up in his fist, and waved it at her. "Mary wants Catherine to nurse her back to health. This is Anne's doing." An ugly sneer marred his features. "This is the next spell she has woven, but God's truth, it will be the last."

"Let Catherine go to her daughter. Please, sire, I implore you," she added for effect. "What harm could she do?"

"What harm indeed! I should give in to her silly whims!" he hissed, smacking the letter against his leg—his bad leg—at the utterance of each word. "She plans to depose me. In a letter she wrote to the Pope, she urges Charles and Francis to invade England. She is a traitor, naught more."

Is Topaz in on this? she couldn't help but wonder. Topaz had never mentioned Spain or France, her involving them, or their wanting to be involved. Her deposing of the king would be her triumph and hers alone, an English victory, shared by no other nation. Nay, it couldn't be.

"Then let me go to Mary, please, I beg of you." Amethyst didn't mind begging.

"Go, go to Mary." He flung the paper to the floor. "You will not poison her mind the way Catherine would. Go to her if you want to so badly."

"My lord, you are her father, she needs you, too." Her voice gentled.

"I am much too busy, you go. Bring her money, cloth, and whatever else you think she would want," his voice was down to a consenting mutter.

"How about your love, sire? May I bring that to her?" she asked softly.

He glared at her. "Amethyst, you will melt me like an ice sculpture in the July sun, you will melt me yet!" His tone didn't match his glare, though. He tipped a wine goblet to his mouth, his signal to end the conversation.

She implored him once more before she left, "Please, sire, think this over. I've told you time and again. Anne cannot be a witch. There are no such things as witches. Just convince Cromwell to divorce you and be done with it so we can finally marry."

"We shall see." That old noncommittal brushoff again. But this time his voice was too placid, too calm, frightening her now with its cold composure. "This will be the test, and the final test. If the Princess Mary dies within a fortnight, Anne will follow her to the grave."

With no way to answer that, not wanting him to elaborate on it, she quit the chamber.

* * *

Amethyst and her small retinue rode all the way to Ludlow Castle, stopping at an inn on the way. Upon entering Mary's chamber, she sighed with relief that the girl was sitting up in her window seat, tuning her lute, looking pale but healthy enough.

"Hello, Mary." Amethyst rushed into the chamber and embraced the young girl. It was like hugging a bird. Mary's gown hung at the shoulders and sagged at the neckline, but her face brightened upon seeing her ally. "Are you well?"

"Aye, much better." She nodded with a smile. "'Tis this recurring sickness, I know not what it is, the physicians know not what it is. It comes over me suddenly, one minute I am reading or studying or at the virginals, the next minute I am deathly weak, and in bed with fever and complete loss of appetite. Today is a good day. And all the better for having seen you."

Amethyst sat upon the window seat next to Mary. "I came here on my own volition. Your father did not send me."

"I fear he will not be sending my mother any time soon either." Her voice dragged, breaking Amethyst's heart.

Oh, how to console her? "They have divers problems they must work out," seemed the best she could do.

"What problems?" She looked Amethyst square in the eye. "His only problem is Anne Boleyn, and he is already tiring of her. If only he would take my mother back, once Anne is out of the way." She rested her head against the window, gazing wistfully outside.

"I sincerely doubt that will happen, Mary." Amethyst glanced at Mary's sheet music propped up on a stand. "He still needs that male heir, or so he thinks so." She longed to tell Mary about her love for the king, about their desire to marry, but not while the girl was still so vulnerable. She wondered if Mary would resent her for marrying her father, vowing to regard Mary as her own daughter.

Mary let out an ironic chuckle. "I cannot help but feel sorry for Anne." She plucked her lute strings aimlessly. "She signed her own death warrant by not giving my father his male heir." She stopped plucking. "How fares my baby sister? I regret to say we have never met. Who does she look like most?"

"Oh, she's got the Tudor red hair, the Tudor sprightliness—"

She broke in with, "The Boleyn arrogance and stubbornness as well?"

Amethyst wasn't sure herself. "She is but two years old. Her dominant traits have yet to form one way or the other."

"I trust she is being brought up as a Tudor, if my father has anything to do with it." Mary turned one of the tuning keys on her lute, tightening the string.

"She is at Hatfield being attended by governesses and nurses," Amethyst replied.

"What is to become of Anne now?" Mary set her lute aside.

"I know not, Mary," Amethyst gave her honest answer. "It is up to the king. Anne's fate is no longer in her own hands. I must admit that I am afraid for her. If only they can have a simple parting of the ways. I do not want to see anyone die. Your father…scared me. He's never been so enraged."

"In that event, we shall see whether she truly is a witch," Mary's tone lightened as she turned towards the window. "She has not yet been able to curse me, I am still alive. But I am worried she will bring harm to my mother."

"She is not a witch, Mary." Amethyst tried not to chide, but why would someone as intelligent as Mary believe in witches? "Anne Boleyn may be a lot of things, but a witch is not one of them. She is as mortal as you and I."

"Just pray for my mother, Amethyst. I have the most terrible feeling about Anne Boleyn. Just say an extra prayer."

She reached out and patted Mary's hand. "If it will make you happy, then I shall. But believe me, no one has to worry about Anne Boleyn." She knew if Anne had any supernatural faculties, she would have used them to do what Amethyst had already done without any powers but those possessed by every woman–make the king love her.

* * *

Richmond Palace, October, 1535

Within two weeks, Anne announced she was with child once more. Amethyst's jumbled emotions poured out of her pen in another letter to Matthew. She counted the days 'til her holiday visit to Warwick Castle, as the mood at court was quite sullen indeed. It was no atmosphere for a twelve-day Christmas celebration. "Mayhap this is Anne's salvation," she wrote to her dearest friend outside the palace. "For I dread to imagine her fate should she not produce Henry's desperately needed heir. Unlike the kingdom's disdain for Anne, I pity her. First the object of the king's curiosity, then a breeding mare for his heirs, now branded as a witch...her fate is literally in his hands."

She pitied Anne more than Catherine, although both were helpless victims. But Catherine, she rationalized, could live out her life in comfort without shouldering accusations of witchcraft. Amethyst considered offering Anne her support and sympathy, but with her better judgment, dismissed the thought. She and Anne had never exchanged a civil word since the day Anne popped in at court. Anne well knew Amethyst was first in Henry's heart. But all these illnesses, all these deaths...it made her wonder.

Anne Boleyn was as mortal as any human being crawling the earth, the proverbial fly caught in the tangled web of the monarchy, unable to escape, even with her esteemed wits.

* * *

Amethyst saw Topaz briefly over the holidays, preoccupied as she was with her heated animal hospital within the stables. She bumped into Topaz in the kitchen wearing a filthy apron, shelling peas for the poor with the servants. "Oh, Amethyst, I heard the latest," Topaz breezily mentioned as she poured another podful of peas into a bowl, "it seems the king gave Anne the heave-ho."

"Where did you hear that?" Amethyst approached the butcher block where Topaz sat. "I'm not sure that's exactly true." Oh, but would that it were! Her heart danced a pitter-patter of hope.

"From a reliable source I do not wish to name."

Amethyst didn't badger her sister for her "reliable source". She'd find out soon enough. After all, her own "reliable source" was the king himself, not some messenger bringing tittle-tattle to the midlands.

Topaz stayed mum on her rebellion, she pitched no tirades about her right to be queen...she seemed to have settled into a mellow routine that occupied her time and energies. Amethyst found her almost...pleasant.

But she wasn't naïve enough to believe her sister's silence meant she'd abandoned her quest—mayhap she'd tired of her own rants and realized even the lads had turned a deaf ear.

Amethyst joined the lads on their journey to Kenilworth to see their father the next morn.

That eve they relaxed in his solar before a roaring fire, sipping sweet red wine. The lads and the servants were already abed. After midnight seemed the only private time they could secure together.

"Topaz wasn't herself on this visit," Amethyst voiced her misgivings to Matthew. "The mood was strained and subdued. We exchanged our gifts, ate and drank as usual, sang, played music...I actually managed to enjoy her company for once. But she was quite aloof."

"Thank God." He raised his head to heaven. "Mayhap she's realized her folly and decided not to carry through with this absurd charade after all."

"I entertained that very thought—briefly, before I realized I was thinking about my sister." Amethyst looked deeply into the eyes of the man who had been Topaz's husband for too short a time. What she could tell him about that woman could fill volumes, all her quirks and moods that he never could have beheld during a mere few years of marriage. It mattered not, because Topaz was no longer his problem. But he did have the lads to think about, being reared and groomed by Topaz alone, not sent away to other nobles' homes to be educated, as most boys. She was shaping them her way, and that bothered both their father and Amethyst.

"You do not know her the way I do." Amethyst set her goblet down and warmed her hands before the fire. "She showed you the side of her that she wanted you to see during the time that you knew her. I've known her all my life, and her restrained tone this last week is concealing an agenda. I fear she's finished talking and is now getting ready to act."

"I was so glad the lads hadn't spoken of any rebellion or evil words against the king or Mary, or anyone in so long, I had begun to believe it was a forgotten issue," Matthew said.

"The lads do not agree with her, thank God they've formed their own beliefs, but Topaz will never change." She shook her head, sorrow weighing down her heart. Oh, her poor sister—she was in for a tragic ending.

"Have you discussed this any further with the king?" Matthew asked.

"Nay, he's got his plate full at the moment, with the recent deaths, and with Mary being ill, and his disgust with Anne..." She looked over at him. "You should have heard him talking of executing her. I'd never seen the king behave like this. He was not the Henry I've come to know." That last horrific scene with Henry made her shudder.

"Mayhap he was venting his anger," Matthew offered. "I mean, look at Topaz. Look how worried I was when she spoke of poisoning the Princess Mary..." He stopped dead in his tracks and his hand flew to his mouth as his goblet slipped from his grasp and clanked to the floor. A flood of wine splattered onto the rug.

"Oh, no, Matthew, no! It couldn't be—" She sat up, alarm tightening her muscles.

"I would never wish that it could," he muttered.

"Queen Anne and...Topaz?" Her eyes bulged with disbelief. "No, that plot would fit a horror tale."

"Mayhap Anne is not the only witch of whom the king speaks, Amethyst." His eyes narrowed to sharp pinpoints in the fireglow.

A fear she'd never known drenched her. Needing his warmth and comfort, she slid over to him, nestling into his embrace. "Matthew, just hold me, don't let me go." She heaved a long sigh. "The king was so livid, he'd never scared me so. He's become someone else, he's been plagued because of all this, all these deaths, all these illnesses...he blamed Anne for it all. He barely remembers Topaz exists."

He held her in a light but warm embrace, and how different he felt from her King Henry, how unfamiliar were the contours of his body, how strange it felt as he clasped her arms and rubbed her back.

But she forced herself to break away, sensing Matthew was as reluctant to let her go, his hand lingering a bit longer than deemed proper. Later in bed, she denied how much she enjoyed his closeness, talking with him, laughing with him... but mostly, her stirrings of arousal.

* * *

Richmond Palace, January, 1936

Upon her return to court, Amethyst entered her retiring chamber and faced her sobbing, grief stricken maid of honor. "My Lord, Bridget, what on earth happened?" She approached her maid and, laying her arm round the distraught girl's shoulder, pressed a handkerchief into her hand.

"Queen Catherine died, Lady Amethyst. She expired at two in the afternoon, day before yesterday." She took a ragged breath "She was so kind to me all my life. I feel I've lost a dear aunt. She'd been gravely ill for quite some time." She swept at her tears and blew her nose into the square cloth.

"I know that." Amethyst stood back, head down, flooded with sorrow for the poor queen. "I hope she did not die alone." A sudden anger at Henry tormented her. "The king wouldn't let Mary visit her dying mother..." She purged those thoughts. Now was not the time—she needed to concentrate her energy on praying for the queen's soul. "But to expire so suddenly." She looked into her maid's moist eyes. "Is the king in residence?"

"Aye, my lady." She nodded.

"You go and pray for the queen, I'm releasing you from your duties for the next few days." With a pat on her maid's cheek, she offered, "Use my prayer beads if you haven't your own. " She gathered her skirts and, without pausing to bathe away the journey's dirt and grime or change from her traveling garments, she tossed her cloak on the bed and hurried to the king's chambers.

The Yeomen of the Guard halted her at the entrance to Henry's privy chamber.

"The king is receiving no visitors," the guard stated, his eyes straight ahead, focused on some distant pinpoint.

"But I am... you know who I am! Let me through!" She tried to hustle past him.

He shoved her aside. "We have our orders, Madam."

Just then the king appeared, waving the guard aside. He looked as if he hadn't slept since she left him. Dark rings circled his bleary eyes.

"Sire!" She rushed up to him. "I just arrived back and I heard..."

He held his hand out to her and swept past the guards as they parted for the king. They entered his bedchamber and he sat on the edge of his bed. It sank under his increasing weight, the sheets rumpled, the pillows strewn about the floor.

"I am so sorry," she offered her condolences, but deep down unsure of how sorry he was.

"She is to be interred at Peterborough Abbey." He turned away, as if needing her touch, but not the sight of her. Still holding her hand, he continued, "I received this letter but a moment ago..." His voice, so strained, barely reached her ears. The wind rattled the windows and the fire crackled, each vying to defeat the other.

"A letter?" She searched the bed and glanced at his desk, but saw no letter. "What letter? From whom?"

"From Catherine."

She shuddered.

"She wrote it before she died." His voice cracked. He seemed more shaken up about the letter than the queen's actual death.

"I would think she did, sire."

"She knew the end was upon her, and she made a few requests of me." He stood and strode over to his sideboard, glanced at the half-eaten bread, cheese and leg of a bird, but turned away in disgust, swiping up a goblet instead.

"And what were her requests, sire?" She didn't sit, not out of respect for protocol, but because her rump was killing her from the long ride—astride, like a strong woman, as Topaz taught her.

"After pardoning me…pardoning me…" His voice indicated that he'd acted in a fashion that demanded a pardon. "…she asked me to provide for her maids. She asked something else of me…she asked me to be a good father to Mary."

"Not unreasonable at all, my lord." She mouthed a silent word of praise to Catherine in heaven for her astute request.

"Nay, you are right," he admitted, and an admission from the king was rare indeed. "Your Aunt Margaret is like a mother to her, and for that I am grateful. Mayhap I can summon her to court, along with Elizabeth, and we shall be just like a family."

Like a family, he'd said, for a solid family he never really had.

"We shall have a family of our own someday, sire." Voicing it out loud made it seem more feasible.

"Aye, someday," he sighed, and relief lightened her spirit, as he'd omitted the "mayhap" to sanction her hopes.

Desperate as she was to give Henry that first heir, she knew Anne was even more desperate. Anne had much more at stake—her life. For if her son lived, then she would live.

"Chapuys thinks Anne poisoned Catherine." The quiver in his voice validated his own suspicion.

She drew in a short breath. "Oh, no, my lord, she wouldn't have done such a thing. Anne may be self-centered and impetuous at times, but I do not believe she would ever take such drastic measures."

An uneasy smile parted his lips as he seemed to see her for the first time that day. "You are so trusting, Amethyst, seeing the good side of everyone."

"If Anne were to poison Catherine, she would have done so long ago, when the divorce was pending." Amethyst reasoned, feeling like a defense lawyer. *But why am I defending Anne?* she wondered, even as she spoke.

"Anne easily could have poisoned Catherine any time when she was still at court. Chapuys is wrong," she added her unsolicited judgment to her defense. "Of course he has his own reasons for accusing Anne—he was devoted to Catherine."

"Anne's behavior towards Catherine's death was not exactly mournful, either," Henry rebutted, sounding like the prosecutor now, in this seemingly mock trial.

"Did you expect her to be?" she countered. "Anne is no doubt greatly relieved. She is only being true to her feelings. You know even better than I, she is a greatly troubled girl, sire. She is under enormous pressure to produce your heir."

"Then why doesn't she give me my heir and be done with it?" He followed his outburst with refill of his goblet to the rim, not spilling a drop. He slammed the decanter down, the gold liquid sloshing inside.

"Mayhap now she will." Amethyst approached him, taking the goblet from his hand and twining her fingers through his. "And then you and she can part amicably so you and I can officiate our love."

"Enough about this, how is Warwickshire?"

He changed subjects more abruptly these days, as if unable to cope with his increasing troubles. But, she saw clearly, who had brought on all these troubles? No one but himself.

"Oh, just grand, sire, the lads are growing into fine young men..." She rattled off a string of pleasantries about the holiday festivities, carefully keeping Topaz's name out of the monologue.

He didn't inquire after her. Amethyst hoped he'd forgotten Topaz still walked the earth.

* * *

Torches blazed through the biting cold as Catherine's funeral procession approached Peterborough Abbey. Anne stilled wagging tongues by claiming her pregnancy kept her abed.

But of course tongues wagged as tongues will. "Ah, what a lame excuse, that heartless wench," buzzed round the court including up to the dais, where the king spat his disgust at every meal. Yet Amethyst sensed the validity to Anne's absence. Henry didn't need elaborate further when he declared "I am at the end of my rope with her." Anne's life hung in the balance. Losing this heir would mean losing her head.

Amethyst sat at the king's side during the two-day journey to Peterborough. They followed the black hearse groaning mournfully on its wheels over the frozen rutted ground. Mary, draped in black, clung to Amethyst's arm, sobbing pitifully. Her heart broke for Mary, forbidden to see her mother during her final illness. To further humiliate her, Henry had her bastardized, her claim to the throne shoved aside to make way for Anne's as-yet-unborn son. Bursting with grief for Mary, bearing her sorrow over Catherine's wasted life, harboring rage at the king of his neglect of Mary, coupled with her devotion to him...it all converged on Amethyst during this bleak and sorrowful occasion, rendering her an emotional wreck. Knowing she was some comfort to Mary was her only solace. She stepped aside, clearing the way for father and daughter. At her urging, they reluctantly made eye contact across the empty space, and with grudging acceptance, fell into an embrace.

* * *

The next morn as she rehearsed a motet with musicians in the conservatory, a page approached her. "His majesty wishes to see you in his apartments, presently, Lady Amethyst."

The pages never knew the reasons for the summonses—they were equal to carrier pigeons, only finding out later during the gossip sessions.

A list of reasons went through her head. The first reason had to do with Anne. She was his "great matter" now that the divorce was behind him. Way down on the list was his need for a morning romp, which happened more infrequently these days.

She set down her lute and plectrum and followed him down the corridors, across the great hall and up the staircase to his chambers, past the guards, and knocked on his door.

Most times, he answered it personally, as he knew her knock, but this time a Yeoman of the Guard opened the door. A few glowing candles stood scattered about the shadowy bedchamber. He lay upon the bed, eyes closed, his ulcerated leg propped up on pillows.

"What is it, my lord?" She rushed up to the bed and grasped his hand. It was cold and clammy. He returned her grasp, giving her great comfort.

"I had a…a small accident," he explained, his usually resounding voice now small and strained. "I was preparing to run at the lists and fell off the horse."

She gasped as her heart lurched. "Oh, my lord! Are you all right?"

"I sustained no serious injuries. It is not necessary to go into detail."

"Can I help you at all…with anything?" She glanced round, her eyes landing upon the empty table. "You must be hungry."

"Aye, but not for chicken legs. See if my manhood is intact." Before her astonished eyes, he propped himself up on an elbow, a lecherous leer twitching at his lips.

So relieved he wasn't badly hurt, she slid in next to him. "Gladly, my lord." She let him pull her towards him, his arms still powerful and muscled. She lowered her head for him to remove her caul. Her hair spilt over his fingers. "Take off everything but the jewels, and go to that velvet box over there and take whatever you want," he commanded, but in an amorous tone.

She crossed the bedchamber and opened the velvet box. Closing her eyes, she chose a dazzling diamond-and-ruby pendant with pearl-encrusted gold rope, two more necklaces of diamond and emerald, and a three-tiered choker fastened with a huge pearl surrounded by three rows of diamonds, at random. She draped them round her neck, slid three glittering diamond-and-ruby rings onto her fingers, and stepped out of her chemise, skirts, and petticoats, winding a golden braided girdle round her waist. The rings caught the firelight as she wiggled her fingers. Now she truly felt like a queen.

She climbed upon the bed, stood up, and spread her arms, each hand winding about an ornately carved bedpost, her hair tumbling down around her shoulders. She placed a foot on each side of him and lowered herself onto his erect manhood, straining against his breeches, which she pulled down to his knees, as not to disturb the bad leg. Straddling him, she eased him into her. He grabbed her buttocks and arched his back, letting her set the pace. She began thrusting slowly, then faster as their passion mounted. That delicious fire spread deep inside her as the rumblings of an explosion swelled up within her. He placed his hands on her breasts and caressed them softly, bringing her to a frenzy of desire. She wished she could cease breathing, she wished the burden of their flesh and mass would simply disperse in order to let their souls mingle and pulsate together. There was no food, no wine, no water, no fragrance, nothing but their throbbing heartbeats and delighted moans as they coupled. He pulled her head down to him and crushed her lips to his, his tongue exploring, darting round her mouth with his surging frenzy. She thrust in circles, and finally spent him. He lay her on her back and kissed her all over, lingering at her breasts, her sensitive buds rising like rubies beneath the glittering jewels, down past her navel and to her inflamed nether parts. She writhed under the touch of his tongue and lips within her sensitive folds, wrapped her thighs round his head and exploded once more.

Chapter Eleven

Greenwich Palace

Amethyst entered the king's inner chamber. He hadn't summoned her this time, but the guards let her through. His ushers and pages bowed to her, with the usual reverence, but with solemnity.

"Do you wish to sup with me, sire?" She approached him, sitting in his favorite velvet seat before the fire, reading a book. "Utopia" read the title on the spine. Who wrote that? she wondered. "Matthew sent some barrels of dry-salted beef and mutton from his neighboring farms along with his delicious apples."

Rubbing her hands up and down her arms, she chased away goose-bumps in the damp, chilly chamber, for the fire was sputtering out but he hadn't bothered ordering his chamberlain to refuel it. He put the book down and faced the dying embers, deep in thought.

Not wanting to disturb him, she waited. Wishing to make herself useful, she picked up two logs from beside the fireplace and tossed them inside. A spray of sparks shot up and flames began to dance into life.

A moment later he turned to her, an ominous half-grin splitting his lips. He harbored a tangle of emotions she couldn't discern. "Anne did not attend the funeral rites I held for Catherine last week." His voice was dry, flat.

"I know she didn't. She didn't attend the funeral itself either. She claimed her pregnancy kept her abed. Does that come as a surprise, my lord?" She sat on the rug at his feet.

"At this point, no. But when I entered her apartments afterwards, I thought I'd stepped into a May Day feast." His voice dripped bitterness and scorn. His eyes glittered diabolically in the firelight. "She was all dressed in the brightest yellow like a goddamned tulip. Dancing with her courtiers, also clad in yellow, a field of jonquils swaying in the breeze. I include the males in that description."

"Mayhap she is not one to mourn death," she gave an educated guess. She herself hated the dreary black of mourning attire.

"Death is only mournful to those close to the deceased. In Anne's case, Catherine was nothing to her." The bitterness in his voice instensified.

"Did you reprimand her?" She secretly hoped he had. Then she mentally slapped herself down. Here was Anne on the cusp of life and death, what good what a chiding do?

"I did not bother. God punished us both. She dances no more." The diabolical glitter in his eyes blazed into raw hatred.

She stiffened. A tentacle of fear crept up her spine. "What do you mean?"

He looked at her, his eyes slits of contempt. "She lost my son, that is what I mean. Four months along, and she danced him right from her womb. His features contorted into a mask of revulsion. In the firelight he resembled a grotesque parody of himself. "It was deformed, a hideous, half-formed creature that could only have been borne by the witch that she is!" He pounded his fist on the arm of the chair, causing her to jump.

A wave of dizziness overcame her as the stark truth hit her: Anne had played her last hand.

"Oh, I am so sorry, so very sorry. But you know that cannot be true, my lord. Catherine was delivered of a deformed child and she was no witch." Why she continued to defend this now-detested woman, she didn't know. Deep down she clung to a thread of hope that she'd talk

Henry out of executing Anne. Executions repulsed her, after a lifetime of hearing about her father—but never had she witnessed it for herself. Would Henry force her to attend Anne's execution? she wondered. The thought made her flesh crawl.

"Nevertheless, Anne had conceived a son within her womb, my son." He jabbed his thumb at his chest. "My only hope for an heir. And she expelled him...she thrust him out into the world to die."

"Not purposefully, of course. Why would she endanger her own life?" She tried to talk sense into him, but in his state of mind, her efforts were useless.

"That I do not know. But I suspect it. Too concerned about our unborn heir to attend Catherine's funeral, but cavorting about her apartments to bright, joyous music, jeeringly scorning Catherine's memory, as well as her very husband," he scoffed, crossing his bad leg over his good one and grasping his ankle.

"Anne never really understood how to make you happy, my lord. She never loved you, she is a young and ignorant—"

"It matters not!" he interrupted her sharply, for this time he didn't need her soothing. So she shut her gob. She realized he needed to fume and rave, and wanted her to just listen. "But she blames the miscarriage on the fright she suffered when hearing of my accident at the tournament."

"Well, that may be, sire. I was quite shaken when you told me about it. Any sudden shock can cause great turmoil in an expectant mother." She couldn't help countering his twisted logic.

"Five days later?" He, slapped his hand against his thigh in exasperation. "She conveniently used it as an excuse. I would not put it past her to deliberately kill my child, being a boy, of course, to twist the knife she's already plunged through my heart. What could she possibly do to torture me more brutally than to kill my prince?" He spoke as to the flames, wanting an answer from their sharp licking tongues. "But she failed this time. This sinister plan of hers did not succeed. I cannot be totally outraged, nay, I cannot, because I feel the strangest jumble of gladness and sadness, all mixed together like those crazy concoctions

Dr. Butts mixes and grinds with his mortar and pestle." He heaved a sigh. "Sad because I lost my prince, but glad because Anne just forfeited her last chance. It is the end for her. I am free." But his voice didn't carry any joy or elation of a man suddenly set free.

"You will divorce her now?" She tried to keep the eager rise out of her voice. At least divorce meant she'd live. Relief lifted her spirits.

"Divorce…bah! Divorce is too good for her! She is to be tried and convicted."

Her temporary relief vanished. "But…how? As a witch?" That's so…archaic. You're a much more worldly man than that, Henry. You are the quintessential Renaissance man," she heaped praise and flattery upon him, still clutching that shred of hope that he'd change his mind and do the sensible thing, as he'd done with Catherine—simply cast her aside—but for God's sakes, let her live.

"No…" He stood and limped about the chamber in circles, favoring his bad leg, his hand flattened to his forehead. "Think fast, Hal," he muttered to himself, "faster than the crafty Anne can." He turned to her. "Something more earthly, more mundane, something more fitting for the deceitful, lying, scheming, treacherous whore that she is…" He held up a pointer finger. "That is it. Adultery," he announced as simply as if they'd just composed a song together. "I shall accuse her of adultery, bring her up on charges, throw her into the Tower and be done with her."

"How will you find someone with whom to charge her, sire?" she needled him, hoping he'd throw that idea out, simply because he couldn't prove it. "Anne is usually pregnant and ailing. When could she commit adultery? It does take two, you know."

"It can take two." His smirk glowed from across the room. "But in this case it will take three. No; four, five! I shall accuse her of having five lovers!" He smacked his desk with a flattened palm, his eyes shut tight in calculation. "One will be no more incredible than five, so why not? Let her go to her death in shame and degradation. I need not look far to round up conspirators." He glanced round the chamber, as if hapless suspects sat about. "That Smeaton pouf is just as good as dead, always fawning round Anne's ankles like a lovesick poodle waiting for a pat on the head, strumming his lute with those pretty fingers and pared nails," he held up his hand in mockery, "singing his way into her heart with that shrill voice like a mastiff with his tarriwags whacked off. Then there is that poet, Thomas what's-his-name, though I use the term loosely, when I saw the kind of mucus that spurted from his pen."

"You mean Thomas Wyatt, my lord?" She blanched in horror at these insane accusations.

"Wyatt, aye, he's the one." Henry opened his top desk drawer and yanked out a sheet of parchment, torn and creased, as if it had been opened and closed many times. "This is the kind of muck he has been writing to her. 'The lively sparks that issue from those eyes, sunbeams to daze men's sight… ' " he read. "Yecch!" Spittle ran down the side of his mouth and he wiped it with the parchment. "Sickening, that is what it is. It makes me want to puke. I would use it as a privy wipe, for a better use it could never have. However, I must keep it as evidence."

"My lord, why did you feel it necessary to snoop through Anne's personal effects in order to incriminate her? Why did you have to stoop so low? 'Tis beneath your station to resort to snooping." Never would another subject dare to voice these words. But his abhorrent behavior demanded an answer—not just of her, but their maker.

"I am the king, and as such, every single item in this land belongs to me. Every house, every stick of furniture, every scrap of cloth, every shoe, every crop—'tis all my property. A king cannot snoop." That was his answer to that.

Then, just when she assured herself that he would lower himself no further, he spoke again, as if she wasn't even there, "Then there's her brother George—"

"Adultery with her brother?" Her hand flew to her throat as her breath stuck. "Oh, sire!"

"Ah, yes. Why not?" An devilish mirth curled his lips. "Any witch who would expel a half-formed monster from her womb when she is supposed to be carrying the heir to the throne of England would not be above incest. It is perfectly credible. He could very well have been the father. Who would dare question it, in the light of everything else she has done?" Now he grinned maliciously, and she knew he was enjoying this plotting of Anne's disgraceful and torturous death along with a roundup of innocent men. "Is there anyone you wish to dispose of, my dear?" He addressed her as if asking her what she'd like to sup on.

Amethyst reeled in shock. "No! Never could I presume to take another person's life…no matter how they hurt me. Please, sire, think this over. Just divorce her and be done with it. Then we can marry," she begged, dropping to one knee, then the other. "But this…charging her with adultery! Think of the scandal."

"You must excuse me, Amethyst, for I must now speak to Cromwell."

He strode past her, and she grabbed on to the sleeve of his robe, but he yanked himself out of her grasp and slammed out of the chamber.

She got to her feet and fled to the chapel to pray.

* * *

The council, which included Anne's own father and uncle, inquired into the activities of the queen and her alleged lovers. Finally they charged Anne with adultery, poisoning Catherine and Mary, and of injuring the king's health. After her trial, Anne was taken by barge to the Tower, and a jailer led her to her lodgings there. Amethyst later heard that Anne had laughed and wept, her remaining time on earth reduced to days.

* * *

Warwick Castle

Set in gold candlesticks, hundreds of candles glowed atop the horseshoe-shaped table at the center of the great hall. Fires blazed in the hearths. Place settings of gold chargers, cups and ewers sat in perfect symmetry. The Venetian glass wine goblets sparkled in the candlelight like star sapphires, throwing blue shadows on the tablecloth. As the future Queen of England, Topaz was giving her guests a fanfare to rival a royal banquet. She'd planned this ambrosial feast down to the last detail of the marzipan molds of Warwick Castle.

Topaz's ladies-in-waiting piled her hair atop her head, brushed to a coppery sheen, adorned with a diamond tiara, a pompous but appropriate statement. She wore her rich royal purple velvet gown over a gold chemise. She did not need jewelry, for her radiant skin and gown sparkled more brilliantly than any gems that could have adorned her fingers and throat. On this eve, her subjects' first preview of her as their queen, she would show them what a generous queen she would be.

She made one more inspection of the kitchen, a bustling but organized affair. Cooks attired in white checked the roaring fire in the central open hearth and two smaller hearths on either side. Above them were suspended huge iron cauldrons billowing with aromatic steam. The master cooks scurried about, shouting orders to their apprentices, stirring, churning, pouring batter into mixing bowls, beating eggs, turning the roasts on spits. A young scullery maid swept a sprinkling of flour from the floor, and the bakers slid loaves of bread and cakes into the brick ovens.

The long worktables were strewn with carving knives, strainers, sieves, whisks, ladles, and shiny copper pots. Platters were piled with cheese tarts, pastries, cubes of jellied milk, meats and game, including turkeys, recently introduced from the New World. Bowls were heaped with peas as green as the countryside, sunny yellow squash, bright orange carrots chopped into round coins, earthy turnips and radishes, luscious apples, plump pears and succulent grapes spilling over the platters like waterfalls. She had a few surprises for her guests in the exotic fruits in their first season in her gardens; raspberries, black currants, and melons, all germinated and raised from seeds imported from the lush gardens of Portugal, Spain and Italy. In addition, each guest would find a 'love apple' from Mexico on his plate—a delicacy the brave explorers brought back from the South American colonies.

The kitchen help, her personal maids and servitors would cater to these brave soldiers' and warriors' every need. She'd planned dancing, music, archery, lawn bowling, uninhibited lovemaking, as she'd invited all her guests to bring companions, and on the final day, a staged tournament with jousting, knights and horses clad in armor, wielding blunt-edged swords, charging toward each other with their ladies shrieking in glee. For this weeklong feast, she'd sent her mother away to visit Margaret Pole.

Dipping her finger into a bowl of cream and dabbing it on her lips, she nodded, turned and swept out of the kitchen. All was going well. At any moment, guests would begin arriving at the gatehouse, and she planned to greet each one personally.

Thomas More was the first to arrive, as expected. She'd told him to come early.

"How many guests do you expect at the castle, my lady?" He handed his reins to the groom who trotted his mount off to the stables.

"At least two hundred, not counting their retinues." She walked him through to the inner bailey. "Every room in the castle will be occupied, although the sleeping arrangements may be a bit awkward, since I know not who is bringing whom and who wishes to share a bed with whom, but that will add to the fun of it."

Indeed, close to two hundred guests did arrive, some with as many as ten servants, maids, and ushers. Her ladies-in-waiting checked off the guest list upon each party's arrival at the gatehouse. The great hall filled with all the glittering jewels, furs, embroidered velvets, satins and noble bodies that could have graced Hampton Court Palace for a royal wedding feast.

After the final course ended, she stood and hushed the musicians in the gallery. The hall grew quiet. Dancers stopped in mid-stride or mid-leap, goblets halted halfway to open lips, and all heads turned to face their hostess.

Thomas More sat at her right, gazing up at her with open admiration.

"My dear guests, some of you may be aware of why I invited you here for this week of merrymaking," she announced, her voice resonating through the great hall. "Every one of us has something in common.

We all share a common history. We are descendants of the brave soldiers who fought at the Battle of Bosworth and lost their lives fighting for either the Yorkists or Lancastrians. The two houses are now united under Henry Tudor. But we must remember how this battle was won, and who won it. And we must remember who my father was. He was Edward, Earl of Warwick. He was the last Plantagenet, and as such, he was in direct line for the throne."

She went on to explain her family's claim to the crown, how Harry Tudor, the current king's father, had snatched it from her father. She brought their history right up to the present, condemning Henry the Eighth "for his cruel treatment of Queen Catherine, for his heretical abandonment of Rome and the Pope, for his adulterous affairs and bigamous marriage to Anne Boleyn. I denounce his dissolution of the monasteries and his declaration as head of the Church," she declared, "for his hypocritical heraldry of the continuation of his father's policies to bring the kingdom out of the feudal systems of the dark ages into a radiant outburst of Renaissance culture and finery while his subjects starve."

By the time she had finished delivering her speech, her guests were no longer scattered about the dance floor or pouring wine down their throats. Their thunderous burst of applause showed their enchantment with this captivating woman, born in the Tower of London, witnessing the horror of her father, the rightful king, dragged to his death at Henry the Seventh's request. By evening's end, she had the lords of many shires—and the pledges of their sons and tenants—willing to fight for her cause.

They approached her one at a time, bowed and kissed her hand as if she were the queen herself.

And so I shall be, sooner than you think, she vowed silently as the last of her followers bowed his way out of her presence.

She dashed up the stairs before any of her servers bothered her with the morrow's meals or appointments. Digging through her wardrobe, she found what she'd been looking for: an item she never told a soul she owned—a glittering crown, albeit with fake stones, which she'd fashioned herself out of base metal, but she relished placing it on her head. "Queen Topaz the First," she proclaimed in a steady, yet quiet voice—servers hovered everywhere. "Off with Henry Tudor's head," she ordered, not so quietly this time.

Part Two

Chapter Twelve

St. Annes in the Fylde, district of Lancashire

"I am about to do what no woman has ever done in the history of England—I am going into battle for the crown that is rightfully mine," Topaz wrote in her diary that morn.

Refusing to give in to weariness, she returned to the cliff-top as the sun finally set. Her horse stumbled once again on the unsure footing of long-abandoned trails. This glorious clear day finally yielded in a blood-red haze to darkness. Her brow furrowed as she squinted out to sea but it was not the setting sun, in its last dying throes, to the west that troubled her. "Where are they? Why are they not here yet?" she mumbled, stomping her foot in frustration, rooted to this desolate spot for three days now.

When plotting around the table with Thomas More, safely ensconced within the walls of Warwick Castle by a warm fire, this had seemed a perfect choice, but she second-guessed herself now. The isolated cove, nestled back down the trail and surrounded by jagged sentinel cliffs, was a cursed place the living seldom visited. Even the bolder veterans in her party seemed to sense it. They all refused to pitch their tents within the bounds of the ancient ruins. She shuddered, not from the westerly breeze, bringing with it another night edged with chill, but in this forsaken atmosphere. A virulent breeze swirled round the cliff, the sweltering sun drifting away to cast its heat upon another land. Her heart leapt at every rustle of the wind in the gorse and ferns, sole inhabitants of this barren cliff-top. With foreboding, she sensed that they wished her gone.

"Cease this silly fear, woman!" She chided herself out loud, patting her horse on the side of his neck, not so much to comfort the animal as to reassure herself. Railing at phantoms! If her warriors could see her now, after she'd mocked their fear of the troubled spirits rumored to walk these bleak cliffs. A thriving seaport two hundred years ago, the cove was now a tomb. Even before the final deathly raid, when the French landed in the mist slaughtering every last unwary villager in taking their plunder, the accursed place had been blighted. It had suffered the lawless butchery of countless pirate raids and twice been stricken with the Black Death. The hangman's noose was seldom empty, for when no other enemy was afoot, the village fell about its own with accusations of witchcraft, conspiracy or smuggling.

Small wonder, then, that mortal men had finally forsaken, but not forgotten, this grim place. Even now, few folk dared walk this coastal path by day and none ventured forth by night. The devil himself had been spotted here just two years hence, leaving cloven hoofprints in the barren earth—or so they were told by the fisherman living in the cottage by the coastal road that had led them here.

"Bad rum, superstition and wandering goats have conjured up many a devil!" She'd laughed, and in the warm summer breeze her men had laughed with her. Now they clustered uneasily, cheek to jowl, about their campfires in the twilight, taking courage from strong ale. They added new embellishments to the well-worn tales of their own bravado that would see them to their bedrolls. No, the choice had been a good one, a perfect one, to shield their venture from prying eyes. Who cared if dead men did roam these ways. Dead men could not warn King Henry!

A few feathery lavender bands now streaked the sky. She dismounted in order to gently turn her steed and descend the steep course back. She planned to walk ahead and lead the creature safely down the derelict path as she had the last two nights. Could she stand another day's wait? She would have to, for if she abandoned this quest, her lifelong dreams would be as ruined as this town.

After she took a dozen steps, the glint of a solitary lost ray of sunshine on polished steel caught her eye. Her pulse quickened. Were they come, or were these Henry's ships about to thwart her desires, somehow made aware of her treachery? Had she been a fool to trust old man Bridgeman? She'd made him Captain of Arms at Thomas More's insistence, entrusted him with a fortune in gold and charged him with raising an army abroad, and on what basis? His only references came from his own mouth. He could not account for his whereabouts for almost half of his seventy-eight years—rumored to have been spent in prisons, not least of which was Newgate. Yet she couldn't help but trust the rogue. No one else had any use for the old wretch, and he knew it. Without her cause he would have no purpose left but to wither and die, this she knew. He could never betray her. Beyond his gnarled ugly husk and broken gait, she'd found rare qualities, not all goodly but certainly useful. He had an eloquent manner, a practiced poise, a charm that she had never seen before. He could bargain, too, all but pick a man's pocket and be thanked for the deed! He spoke many languages, or so he claimed. She could test only his flawless Latin and French, but the guttural growls he claimed he'd learnt in the East beyond the edge of her maps. As she was a bear, he was her ragged staff! Even as she thought it, she glimpsed her standard raised high above the nearer vessel, now looming in the approaching night's dimness. The bear and ragged staff, and with good reason to fly proudly. With all caution cast aside she leapt, most unladylike, into the saddle and spurred her mount to full gallop down the incline.

The rowboats, oars skimming the water like a restless waterbug's legs, slid ashore at St. Annes on the west coast, fifty miles north of Wales as the crow flies. Ah, the mercenaries, here at last! She ran to John in her first general's tent to relay the good news. She burst in on him having his nightly shave before a cracked mirror.

"That is bad luck, dear friend, but this news should quell any suspicions, for today, anyway. They are just about to land. They've come, finally!" She clasped her hands in glee, jumping up and down.

"Good." He swiped at his soaped-up face with a knife. "Just remember, they think they're in Ireland now to extinguish a minor dissension."

Topaz and John strode to the edge of the campsite and could see the two vessels being anchored at the shore. Men began spilling down the gangways in twos and threes, tripping over each other to set foot on land, looks of muddled perplexity on their faces.

A swarthy seafarer swaggered towards John and Topaz, mumbling to himself. The bedraggled men behind him looked round at the unfamiliar landscape, faces screwed up in puzzlement, heads turning in every direction.

"What idiot picked this landing spot?" their leader shouted over his shoulder to the confounded group, shoulders shrugging in reply.

A few of them curled their fingers around their hilts, swords at the ready. Others appeared on guard, prepared for an ambush.

The captain approached Topaz with an uneasy gait and shot John a passing glance. "Wench! Where is thy master? I'll box his ears…nay, I'll run him through. What better place for an ambush, we're lucky the rebels didn't slay every last one of us."

Topaz folded her arms across her chest and glared at the captain. He took a tiny step back. "Call me wench, do you? You will speak to me with the respect due the rightful and future Queen of England!" she bellowed.

His mouth hung open. "England? I have no quarrel with Henry and his legions. Hell's teeth, that Methuselah Bridgeman tricked me! We spent the entire voyage playing backgammon and following the stars, when I should have been checking the rogue's charts to find out where we were really going!" He turned to leave. "I want nothing to do with any war against Henry, son of the Tudor warrior tribe," he called over his shoulder. "I only have my regulars. You would need the entire army of Spain to put down Henry. He will vivisect us!"

"Well, take your scurvy, pox ridden pond-scum and go back whence thee came, you worthless band of brigands!" Topaz spat.

The captain reeled back in shock and turned to face her, his eyes darkening to the color of the blackened sea. "Where's Bridgeman?" he tossed a command to his men. "He promised Ireland, he promised more gold and bountiful treasures…fetch him. Clap him in irons and bring him to me. Fetch the knave, let him tell me where his thirty thousand good men and true are. Let him show me his gold!"

"No wonder he wanted to be last off the boat," one of the men, on the outskirts of the group, spoke up.

Just as the words left his lips, an explosion shattered the air about them. A flaming blaze lit up the coastline as if the very sky had shattered before their eyes. All heads turned. The men hurled themselves to the ground, and the captain threw himself before Topaz, shielding her from the flying debris, chunks of wood and canvas that had been the mercenaries' ships.

"There he is, the bastard!" one of the sailors barked.

A withered figure silhouetted against the flames emerged from the billowing smoke in a small rowboat. Stooped over the oars, he laboriously rowed toward shore.

The men scrambled to their feet and the captain relinquished his hold on Topaz. She straightened her skirts and adjusted her headdress.

His rowboat skimmed up the beach and several of the men sprinted up to old man Bridgeman, rocking the boat til he tumbled out, sprawling onto the sand. He stumbled to his feet, brushing off the barrage of questions the men hurled at him. His watery eyes skimmed the group and fixed on Topaz. He smiled cheerily and waved.

"Ireland? By Jove, do I have a terrible sense of direction. It must be my poor befuddled brain, did I say Ireland? I never could read charts properly since I lost the sight of my left eye." He approached Topaz and took her hand in his, kissing it gallantly.

He turned back to the men and waved a withered arm. "Don't worry, lads. One war's as good as another, you'll die just as easy here as there. What would you have from Irish peasants anyway? Steal the peat from their bogs, would you? Nay, there's richer plunder here. To London and Henry's treasure chests say I. Thirty thousand. No! No! I'm quite sure I made it clear at the outset we would have three thousand men, not thirty thousand."

"Gold…hm…maybe this is worthwhile after all…" Topaz could hear the men muttering among themselves, clustering into a tighter huddle. "Aye, I've heard something about these Crown Jewels…"

Bridgeman turned to the sea captain, a crooked grin brandishing his weatherbeaten face. "Well, Captain Vogts, it seems your sailors have made your mind up for you." He twirled around to face Topaz, his sodden doublet slapping his skin in the breeze. "Now that that's settled, let me introduce you formally. Captain Franz Vogts, this is Lady Topaz of Warwick, the rightful and future queen. Lady Topaz, this is Captain Vogts, recently a commander of the Swiss Guard."

The captain flashed a look in Topaz's direction, scratching his head, then threw another glance at John. Gathering himself to his full height, he regained composure, scanning his huddle of men. "We'll rest here tonight but we'll have none of this madness. We march south tomorrow and by God we'll not stop 'til we reach the channel, and then just long enough to board a ship to Calais."

Topaz took a few haughty steps up to Vogts. Even at his full height, she was at exactly his eye level. Her stern gaze bored into his. "I'll not be sorry to see you go." She jabbed him in the chest with her finger. "Why, our poor village fool is a braver man than ye. Why not trade your fancy doublets and polished armor for his fool's garb now? The bells would become you better."

"'Tis an army well suited to fools, my dear," Vogts replied. She saw his cheeks flush, his pale sallow skin turning blotchy with rage. "I'll not be one of them!"

They glared at each other for another silent moment and stormed off in opposite directions.

She saw Bridgeman out of the corner of her eye strolling over to the campfire, emitting an amused guffaw.

"Just what entertains you so, you old vagabond?" Topaz shouted over the crackling fire and the men's confused mutterings as they set up camp. "What manner of men are these that you brought me? They possess naught but cowardly swagger and loud mouths, which will be hungry come morn, no doubt."

Bridgeman rubbed his hands and wriggled out of his doublet. It hit the sand with a soggy plop. "Men you wanted, Lady Topaz, and men you have got. They are the best Europe has to offer, strong men with bold hearts, each one worth four of Henry's men." He touched her cheek. "Worry not, dear lady, I have not gotten to this age by poking at lions. Give our captain a good night's sleep on solid ground and methinks you'll find his manner much improved by dawn."

"I hope so, Patrick. The whole kingdom rests in your hands." She left the old man to dry out and went to join John in his tent to partake of the strong ale undoubtedly flowing by now.

* * *

Vogts appeared at Topaz's tent at daybreak. She was already awake, having bathed in the sea among the driftwood of the destroyed ships before the first light of dawn and was now sipping the last of her breakfast ale.

"You come to bid farewell?" Topaz eyed the smooth linen shirt slashed at the sleeves, light breeches tapering to fine glossy hose. "Be off with you. Not a groat more will you get from me."

"I do not come here for the balance of my retainer. I've been thinking, Wales is South, a Tudor stronghold and fierce loyal to Henry. I'll not tangle with the Welsh. For sure those flames were seen last night, old Bridgeman is not so daft. He knew we would have no choice but to join your venture and so we shall. Your middleguard we will form, so I can keep my eye on you and protect our interests. We'll lead you to London but don't stand in the way of our plunder when we get there, Lady Topaz," he warned.

She smiled to herself, draining her ale cup, pouring yet another for herself and her new ally.

* * *

Whitehall Palace

The Duke of Norfolk, stricken with panic, bustled into the king's audience chamber, maps clutched to his chest. He spread them out on the largest table in the chamber and waited for his majesty to wake up and appear. After an hour, Henry, roused from sleep, blankly followed Norfolk's finger as it traced the movements of Topaz's army.

"She left Warwick with three thousand men, marched them up past Chester to St. Annes. Two days after she arrived there, fiery explosions came from the ghost hamlet and ripped into the night," he explained to the king.

"The place where they saw the devil's hoofprints?" Henry asked. "I'm surprised they did not find Anne's footprints right alongside his."

"Aye, my lord." Norfolk nodded. "The next day, she left with almost six thousand men. The locals think Topaz did a deal with the devil himself and that these extra men came from hell; the flames were let out when the gates of hell itself opened up to spew them forth!"

Henry's mind cleared and he stabbed his finger at the map. "So she will likely take the road through Shrewsbury." His eyes followed the map's rendition of the well-worn road to London. "She's not about to trample through Sherwood Forest. So she has to come through Chester to Shrewsbury and then on to London."

He swept the map out of the way, as it was lying on top of his breakfast, and turned to Norfolk. "Send word to Denbigh, Ludlow, and Stokestay."Have them raise troops and cut the rebels off at Shrewsbury. That will put an end to the matter. Now…" He began stuffing his mouth with the roasted partridge heaped up on the pewter platter. "You sure you won't partake?"

Norfolk held up a hand. "Nay, sire, I've already broken my fast."

Henry chewed and swallowed. "Then on to more important things. Has the Lord Steward brought in that elk I shot yesterday?"

* * *

Whitehall Palace

Amethyst sat supping with the king, alone. As he chomped away on his leg of pheasant and swilled his wine, she pushed her plate away.

"Is the fare not to your liking, my dear?" He chewed and asked, and chewed and chewed. "Three apprentice cooks have just entered our employ, but I wouldn't have known it hadn't the steward told me. Would you care for another variety of dish?" He pointed at the feast before them.

"Nay, sire," she sighed, fingering the brocade trim of her gown.

"What ails you then?" He wiped his mouth with his third linen napkin of the meal.

"Topaz and this uprising of hers." She turned away to gaze out at the setting sun. A trickle ran down her back with the cloying humidity. A rumble of thunder in the distance made her shiver. She took the gathering storm as an omen.

"Uprising? 'Tis no uprising. 'Tis merely jousting exercise for my troops," he brushed it off like a fly.

She turned back to face him. "Sire, I need to ask you something honestly."

He finally pushed away from the table and began twisting a gold toothpick twixt his teeth.

"What are you going to do about her?" she asked, dreading the answer, but needing the truth, to prepare for tragedy.

He placed the toothpick down and sucked at his front teeth. "Amethyst, I have not even given it the slightest thought. I've got much more on my mind."

She blinked in surprise as she welcomed a flutter of relief. "But many innocent people are going to be hurt."

"What makes you think they're so innocent?" He cocked his head and his left brow.

She took a tiny sip of wine, enough to wet her lips. "She can be very persuasive. Can you not send an envoy there to force her surrender, or just put her under house arrest and order her followers to disburse?"

He shook his head. "'Tis hardly necessary, my dear. The matter will end at Shrewsbury. She'll crawl back to Warwickshire in disgrace and 'twill be the end of it. If in the unlikely event she does make it to London with her sniveling milksops, I trust 'twill be to beg my forgiveness on bended knee. Which I shall or shant grant, depending on my mood."

He'd emphasized that last word, accompanied by his rise from the table. He stretched, yawned, and held out his hand to her.

"Topaz hasn't ever bent her knee for anyone, sire," Amethyst warned him as they walked over to the window seat. A stream of raindrops began rapping on the panes. Her insides churned with fear. Her sister's life was in danger, but she hesitated to tell Henry how far she believed Topaz would go. His not taking the matter seriously was a curse and a blessing to her. Lack of retaliation on Henry's part would provoke Topaz even further. Oh, if it would end at Shrewsbury!

"Then be it in her best interest to learn, as she shall be planting a big kiss right smack on my crupper!" He smacked that crupper with his hand, then he sat, pulling her down alongside him. He unclenched her fists. She hadn't even realized how tightly clenched they were.

"This actually upsets you, my darling?" He seemed surprised this even fazed her.

I must be a better actress than Anne Boleyn, she thought. "Yes, it does. In fact it makes me ill."

"Fear not; your sister is merely a wrinkle on my gooser. The minute my generals appear on the horizon, her ragtag army will disperse like they've got firecrackers up their poops." He focused his attention on the pattering rain against the window.

"But what about my sister?" she prodded.

He turned to her and shrugged. "What about her? She'll be banished back where she belongs."

"She thinks she belongs on the English throne." This wasn't the first time she'd told him of Topaz's fantasy.

"And I think she belongs in a lazaretto. But being the kind hearted prince I am, I shall meet her halfway." He chuckled, squeezing her hand. She forced herself to be glad he was making such light of it.

"What can I do to lift you out of this sullen mood, my dear?" He chucked her under the chin. "You barely touched your repast. Would a few cream filled tarts be in order?"

"No." She cringed. "I couldn't eat—"

"What, then? I am at your disposal. Shall I call the jugglers, the mummers? A romp, then?" He tossed his head in the direction of the bedchamber.

"Can we sing, sire?" Music, only music, could dispel her dark clouds right now.

"As you wish." They went to the conservatory and she took up her lute. He sat and positioned his fingers on the harp. She closed her eyes and once again, lived her lifelong dream. Music—Henry—Amethyst—no one else existed.

* * *

Three days later, Norfolk entered the king's chambers and demanded to see him. The Yeoman of the Guard let him through and he entered the outer chamber where Henry was playing dice with three other men.

"Your majesty, I must see you!" He rushed up to the king and dropped to one knee.

"Not now, Norfolk," he waved the duke away with a flick of his hand. "We are playing for St. Paul's Bells and this Miles Partridge rogue is about to win them from me."

"But your majesty," he wrapped his fingers round the king's chair arm. "This is about the war!"

"War?" Henry looked up, the dice cup in his hand falling dead silent. "Has Francis invaded again?"

"Nay, Lady Warwick's uprising!"

Henry screwed up his mouth. "Lady who?" Then as it registered he laughed, spilling the dice out of the cup, watching intently as they tumbled onto the table. "Snake eyes!" He turned to Norfolk. "You mean they are not done with her yet?"

"Nay, my lord, she did not come through Shrewsbury. Word has it they've turned north, looped about the Great Forest and are coming down the east following the River Trent picking up every malcontent in your realm. I fear by the time they get to Lincoln…" He got to his feet as he babbled. "I fear—"

"Aye, she'll pick up support there, all right," Henry cut in. "They still harbor me a grudge since the bloody Pilgrimage of Grace." He turned to face Norfolk, shifting in his large chair.

"I just rolled a seven, sire," Partridge spoke up.

Henry struggled his bulk out of his chair and drained the last drops of ale from his goblet. "Oh, take the bloody bells, Partridge, there'll be plenty more where they came from anyway."

The king led Norfolk into his receiving chamber, musing out loud as he went. "Not a bad plan, as traitorous plots go. First she lands mercenaries near Preston, the last place anyone would expect foreign ships to land." They approached the table where the maps lay spread among the plates heaping with fruits. "Then she has the wits to go north and avoid my Welsh hordes." He traced Topaz's route on the map with his finger. "Now she's threading through every pocket of discontent in the kingdom. I suppose we'd best act now before she musters an army worth its salt. You never know with these looneys. Very well, Norfolk, send an emissary to young Lord Cuthbert Clifford of Tutbury. He can muster eighty-five hundred men, more than enough to take care of Topaz and her meager band."

"Aye, she's known to have just over five thousand," Norfolk informed him.

Henry said, "Clifford has yet to earn his battle scars for all his might at jousting but let's see if he can wield a sharp sword as well as a dull one. If he wants high office in my kingdom, he'd best put a swift end to this rebellion. I'll lose my good graces if I hear of this matter one more time. Now off with you." Henry stuffed a bunch of grapes into his mouth and waved Norfolk away.

* * *

Lincolnshire

Topaz and her army, their scouts ahead of them, continued their march south across the open field dotted with buttercups, daisies and clover. The broiling sun beat down upon them. Topaz wiped her brow with the hem of her sleeve.

The thundering of hoofbeats approaching from the opposite direction caught her attention. The column came to a stop as the rider neared. Vogts squinted and called over his shoulder to Topaz, "'Tis only Muller. I sent him ahead to scout the lay of the land. Let's see what he has to report."

Muller reined in his horse. The sweat glistened on the animal's back and he foamed at the mouth.

"Fetch water for this horse!" Topaz commanded as Muller regained his breath.

"Lord Clifford and his battles are marching to meet us," Muller reported. "They're only a few hours behind me. I know it's Cliff, for one of Lady Topaz's pages recognized the crimson standard edged with yellow. He must have close to ten thousand men with him. We are outnumbered."

"Where is my page? Has he been hurt?" Topaz asked.

"Nay, he's just not a good a rider as I am. He'll be upon us soon."

Vogts glanced about. "Well, if they outnumber us, we'd best dig in and have them come to us. We can't attack if we have the fewer men."

"That valley we just passed through not ten minutes ago would be a perfect place!" Bridgeman offered, maneuvering his horse in twixt Vogts and Muller. "We'll take the high ground on the far side and as they come into the valley we can swoop down upon them."

"I suppose that's as good a place as any," Vogts said. "Pass the word. We shall move on back there. Put the men to digging right away so our earthworks will be dug by the time Cliff arrives."

The army set up their positions overlooking the valley and waited. Finally, Clifford came into sight and thrust his elaborate standard into the soil on the other side of the valley. His column marched no farther but rather began to form their own positions across the valley on the high ground there.

Vogts noticed Clifford's men wheeling cannon into position as all three battles formed a line abreast, the same formation he had chosen. He cursed out loud. He turned to Topaz and Bridgeman and stomped over to where they were sitting partaking of their evening meal in the trench that had been dug for them. "He sets up artillery. We have none. 'Twould be suicide for us to attack now. Let's sit tight. Let him come to us."

Army faced army over the valley, neither wanting to move to an inferior position, each waiting for the other. "This looks like an impossible stalemate, but I know time is on Henry's side," Topaz groused. "If they just sit like this, Henry could move more men to join the fray." As she wondered what the next step would be, something in the distance caught her eye. "Look, a knight just raised the white flag of truce on the other side." The rider threaded his way down the valley and up the incline on her side. Vogts's men escorted the emissary to them.

"I am sent forth by his honorable eminence, Lord Cuthbert Clifford. His lordship demands your immediate surrender and warrants by his good name that ye will not be tortured and that your execution will be swift and as painless as the headman's axe permits. Your retainers are of no import and may leave in peace. What is your answer?"

Topaz stood to her full height, brushing dirt off her skirt. "I shall consult with my advisors and bring you an answer. Wait here." She didn't say please.

She turned to face Vogts and Bridgeman, linking their arms in hers. "He is a brash youth, Lord Clifford, but he is fair and we are outnumbered," she said, bringing them out of the emissary's earshot.

"And he has guns," added Vogts.

"I could spare my people much pain." Topaz sighed, her eyes following a drifting cloud. "But this is my destiny. I shall not give up now!" she proclaimed her vow once more.

"I knew Cliff's father. The son's no different," Bridgeman said. "He was always proud and vain, full of his own greatness. He can't be trusted. He was a liar and a thief. Never did a Lord mistreat his fiefs and vassals like that man. I fancy their morale won't hold if we can get a good thrust in."

"How?" interjected an impatient Vogts. "With all those cannons! We can't attack, we'd be massacred."

"Then he must be made to come to us!" Topaz rose to the balls of her feet and did a little dance.

"And leave his guns back at his earthworks?" Bridgeman looked at her, grimacing. "But how?"

"A proud man, you say?" Vogts spoke up. "And easily riled, mayhap a few choice insults could spur such a man down from his hilltop! But what could anger his likes, so?"

Topaz turned to Vogts and balled a fist on her hip. "Why, several days hence I met just such a man. Proud and arrogant, his passions easily fired."

"And what did you do?" Vogts's eyes grew wide.

"Well…" she began in a teasing tone, "I told him my fool was more of a man than he, and quickly he set about to show me otherwise, didn't you, Vogts?"

"Why, of course," Bridgeman squawked. "I have it! Is that fool still with us?"

"Easy," Vogts railed. "Watch who you call a fool, old goat."

Bridgeman guffawed. "Not you, you fool, the village fool!"

"Why, yes!" Topaz held up a pointer finger. "How could you miss him in his outrageous garb? But what's the point?"

"Methinks Cliff shall receive your answer now, and a fitting gift besides," Bridgeman said. "Lady Topaz, listen up, here's what we do…" He went on to explain his plan. "…then to our posts, I'll wager there's a fight about to start."

"Archers, form three lines at the head of each battle," ordered Vogts. "Don't loose your arrows till I give the word. We don't have many shafts, they all must be made to count. Lady Topaz, come with me to the middleguard."

* * *

Lord Clifford watched as his smiling emissary returned with a sealed parchment in hand and a handsome carved oak chest under his arm.

"She yields, my Lord!" the emissary shouted jubilantly, as his mount climbed the incline.

"Well, good, let's get her and have this thing over with." Clifford held his hands out for the booty.

"There is a condition, my lord." The emissary held back.

"What is it?"

"I know not, my lord, her answer is set down in this message." He held up the parchment. "All I was told was that she will surrender to you with but one condition. Shall I bring the message to your tent, my lord?"

"Nay, break the seal at once and shout it out. Let all these loyal men see how usurpers quake and grovel before the very name of Clifford. She fears to battle my might. Bah!" He thrust out his chest and his tawdry livery strained against his bulk. "What difference if I grant her one condition on this the eve of her doom? Read on, my good man."

"Very well, my lord." He broke the seal, unfolded the parchment, cleared his throat and read. "I, Lady Topaz of Warwick, hereby set my seal upon this document of surrender. The good Lord Cli—"

Clifford shouted, "Louder! Louder! Yell it out so that all may hear. Come, men, gather about. Go on!"

He cleared his throat again. "I, Lady Topaz of Warwick hereby set my seal upon this document of surrender," he recited in a booming voice that echoed throughout the encampment. "The good Lord Clifford, trusted of King Henry and most honorable of warriors has made this request of me and I concede. The great and noble Clifford is much admired throughout this land and would no doubt have held a prominent position in my court."

Clifford preened, stroking his beard, basking in the praise.

"I will permit his Lordship to come hither and take me into his custody, even as he has implored. There is but one small favor in return I ask and this is it. I, who would be queen, shall receive His Lordship in my hilltop court and surrender myself to him… but only if he comes arraigned in livery…" He looked up. "Livery? Oh, well." He continued, "…livery of that office which I would gladly have given him above all others, though there be much competition in Henry's entourage for this post."

"Not unreasonable a request, I suppose." Clifford kept up the beard stroking. "No doubt King Henry would've given me high office. If she wishes me to dress as the Archbishop of Canterbury, Lord Mayor of London, or High Chancellor of England…so be it! Quite fitting methinks, if only King Hal were as perceptive! Well, go on, my good lad. Which is it to be?" He leaned forward in anticipation.

The emissary took a deep breath and read: "And so my lord, with all due respect, I commission thee to your appointed office in the court of the bear and ragged staff. Within this oak chest, my gift to you, you will find the tunic you must wear. 'Twould fit no man better than thee and my surrender you may have when you appear before me in it."

"Well, open it!" demanded Clifford, flailing his arms. "Let's see which robes of high office I would be granted by Lady Topaz."

The emissary struggled with the tiny gold latch. "'Tis locked, my lord. Nay, wait, the key is embedded in the wax seal…"

He dug the key from the seal with his fingernail and scraped it free of wax. He turned it in the lock and the lid popped open. The men strained forward to see the splendid garments within. Clifford slid off his mount and lumbered up to the emissary, wiping sweat from his forehead. The emissary reached into the chest. He pulled out a white linen cloth and some folded material.

Unable to wait another second, Clifford yanked the chest out of the emissary's hands. "Let me, let me!" he squealed, reverting to childhood. He overturned the chest and dumped the contents to the ground. Grabbing the garment by the sleeves, he raised it high for all to see…

…the green, yellow and blue quartered garb of the fool, bells tinkling as it unfolded, legs trailing on the ground. The men turned to each other, daring to snicker under their breaths.

Clifford flung it to the ground, the bells' final jingles echoing the snorting men.

"She would have me for her court jester, would she!" he roared. "This is the answer you bring me, you oaf?" Clifford's puffy cheeks matched the crimson of his livery, his eyes blazing slits. He grabbed a battleaxe and brought it crashing down on the emissary's head, felling the open-mouthed man with his furious blow.

Leaving the murdered messenger behind, he leapt astride his mount and ordered his men to follow him down into the valley.

"There's a witch roosted on yon hill and by God I'll see her burned alive before this day is done!" he wailed, storming off down the hill, his men scurrying after him. When they reached the bottom they drew up their battle formation once again. Line abreast, they stood, archers in front, exactly like Topaz's men who had already formed high above them.

* * *

"It worked!" Vogts clapped with glee. "He's in a fury!"

"More to the point, his cannon are behind him," Bridgeman observed. "This fight's down to handguns and arrows now."

"Why have they stopped their charge at the bottom of the hill?" Topaz watched, puzzled.

"To exchange arrows, of course," Vogts snapped. "Don't you know aught about modern warfare?"

"Only what I learned as a child languishing in the Tower," she answered. "I learned every account there ever was of Bosworth, for the blood that spilt there is the same that runs through my veins. And every battle of the Wars of the Roses... St. Albans, Northampton, that Wakefield ambush. Towton, Barnet and Tewkesbury, I know them as well as were I there myself."

"Heads down!" Vogts warned. "They've loosed a flight. Look out!"

They scrambled into their ditches as the first hail of arrows darkened the sky.

"Good thing we're up here." Vogts caught his breath. "Their shafts won't carry as far as ours. Look, most are falling short. Let 'em have it, men. See, look there." He pointed. "Our shafts are finding their mark."

"Towton! The battle of Towton!" Topaz's voice pierced the air.

"You already said that one," Vogts snapped. "Forget the Wars of the Roses, you've got one of your own now. Here they come again." He squinted into the distance. "But still short for the most part."

"Hold your fire!" Topaz screamed to her men, scrambling out of the ditch in order to be seen, waving her hands.

The men halted, bows poised in midair, looking about in confusion. Vogts stood agape. Even Bridgeman stood silent as another hail of arrows fell about their feet. One or two of the more powerful shots entered the ranks.

"Now fire back!" Topaz commanded. "But only every fourth archer, quick, pass the word. Towton!"

"This is nonsense," Vogts spat, stalking up to her. He clutched her forearms. "We're firing only one arrow for every six of theirs now!"

"That's the whole point, fool," Topaz retorted, clasping his hands and flinging them back to his sides. "At Towton the fight took place in a snowstorm driven by a keen wind. The Yorkists held back their fire just like we are now. The Lancastrians were blinded by snow. They didn't see the wind knock down their shafts. Every time the Yorkists fired a few flights, a mighty hail of arrows was returned, but fell short. Soon the Lancastrians ran out of arrows. The Yorkists advanced and beat them back with their own spent shafts. They just picked them of the ground as they advanced."

Vogts, listening intently all the while, tilted his head, looking at Topaz with a new- found admiration and respect. "Well then, let's see if history repeats itself."

For the next half hour the exchange continued, a few of Topaz's arrows returned by black swarms of Clifford's piercing the air. Finally Clifford's bowmen exhausted their arrows and stood looking haplessly at the legions above.

"All right now, lads, let 'em go!" commanded Vogts. "Loose all shafts now, let's sting 'em with their own darts!"

Their archers moved forward, picking up the fallen shafts of their enemy as they went. They returned them in a continuous deadly volley. An unrelenting storm of arrows eclipsed what light remained in the sky. Mayhem erupted in Clifford's ranks as they panicked and milled about. Some cowards even broke and ran for their lives.

When the deathly shower of arrows ended, Vogts mounted his charge. As the two armies melded in hand-to-hand combat, the clamor of battle rang out. The clash of swords and clanging of mace and axe resounded through the stagnant air as they crushed armor beneath them. More quickly than she'd ever thought, the melee ended. Clifford's panicked troops were routed, fleeing before Vogts and his troops. Within minutes, Vogts captured Clifford and dragged him on his knees before Topaz.

"And what say you now, Cliff?" Bridgeman obviously enjoyed this moment of gloating. "Are ye ready at last to don the cap and bells and swear allegiance to your rightful queen?"

"This rebellion won't last!" Clifford bellowed from down on his knees. "God save King Henry! Your parboiled heads will all rot on London Bridge before this week is out! Surrender yet, before my troops regroup and overrun your sorry band of outlaws!"

Vogts turned to Topaz and Bridgeman, a wry smile on his face. "Methinks his Lordship's wits are addled.

Mayhaps a gentler blow I should have delivered when I crushed his helmet 'neath my mace."

"Nay, 'tis his pride that's broken, not his skull." Topaz cast a hateful glance at her enemy. "That dome's so thick it needs no shield." She tsk'd. Such a stupid bully, too. What say you, Lord Clifford?" She gave him a disdainful sneer. "Do you not know near half your men have joined my cause, sickened of your mistreating ways? Wingfield was a popular young man. When you smote him down, your own emissary, and killed him in blind rage you did yourself no favor. As I said, 'tis turned almost half your own against you. They brought me gifts too...your very own artillery! What say ye to that?" She tossed her head.

"Again I say God save my liege," croaked the embittered Clifford, streams of sweat pouring down his face. "I'm Henry's man unswerved."

"Well that's that, then," Bridgeman declared. "Decided. Vogts, did you note a good spot to let the blood of a fool nearby?"

"Why, there's a good strong tree back yonder side of this very hill," Vogts replied. "A fine gibbet, its sturdy oaken limbs would make."

"Fair Lady Topaz, I implore thee." Clifford fixed his gaze on Topaz, his eyes wide. "You have no need of my death...do not permit these bloodthirsty villains to string me upon the gallows. I am a noble just like you!"

As Topaz was about to speak, Bridgeman's hand shot out and he cuffed Clifford's ear, shaking it violently. "Hold your tongue, scum, ere I rip it out. That is no fit comparison. The kind and gentle Lady Topaz loves her people. You! You cleft your own almost in two for bringing you a message that was not to your taste. Speak to me not of mercy."

"Well, if he doesn't want to hang, we can cut off his head instead," Vogts said. "Right now. What's your fancy, Cliff?"

Clifford's jaw slackened and his chins jiggled, his incoherent stammer accompanying the squirm under his captor's tight grasp.

"Enough!" Topaz cried. "There'll be no more blood shed this day. The people of England are about to ruled by gentler hands. No more murder of knights and lords at battles' end. A return to chivalry I would seek. Any that will not join us, we will set free. Only their weapons we will keep." She looked at each of her loyal men—soon to be subjects.

Bridgeman released Clifford's earlobe and Clifford reached out to Topaz. She extended a hand, allowing him to slobber over it, obviously his idea of a kiss. "Thank you, my lady. You have spared me most graciously."

"Oh, no." Topaz snatched her hand away. "One moment more, Lord Clifford. In your case I have but one condition."

"Anything, anything, but let me live." He clasped his hands as if in prayer. "Release me, please!"

"Come with me to my tent." Topaz clasped him by the wrist and led him, like a prized palfrey, to her tent. Vogts followed closely, trailed by an equally bewildered Bridgeman.

"What has she got in mind?" Bridgeman wondered out loud.

"I know not, but whatever it is, I would like to watch." Vogts rubbed his hands together. "I, er...I should ensure the lady's safety."

* * *

Clifford left the camp shortly afterwards. Vogts, Topaz, and Bridgeman watched, helpless with mirth as Clifford took his place at the head of the few hundred men on foot who chose to leave with him. Many of the unarmed men were wounded and limping, all with bowed heads, a defeated army. Clifford stared straight ahead, making eye contact with no one, trying to muster some dignity, for he was dressed in full court jester's regalia, bells jingling with every jolt of his horse's canter. Topaz's men jibed and taunted in an uproar of hilarity. Clifford's face was purple with suppressed rage as he passed Topaz.

"We bid you farewell now, Lord Fool Clifford!" Topaz shouted merrily. "I do hope we shant meet again, I'm not so kind when ired. You fought me to avoid wearing those togs of office and spilt the blood of your own followers to spare embarrassment. Ponder that as you leave me, twice embarrassed, beaten by a wench in battle and adorned now in most fitting garb. No other office could be better suited to a man of your qualities." She waved him off. "Now get ye hence, before my good counsel persuades me yet to override my own condition and put you to the sword."

Clifford's column slowly disappeared over the hilltop. That eve Topaz and her army indulged in a wild celebration, breaking the rationing rules with the added spoils of Clifford's supplies. Ale, cider and wine flowed round the campfire among dancing and singing.

Late that eve under the new moon, so unlike that dark moonless night in the cove, Topaz and Vogts recounted the day's events.

"Ah, yes, Towton! You might yet make a general, Lady Topaz," Vogts complimented his benefactress. "That fair head of yours holds a soldier's wits. Towton!"

"St. Albans, Northampton, Wakefield, Barnet and Tewkesbury, too, don't forget. I know them all!" Topaz replied, chin raised high.

"Marseilles!"

"What happened there?" Topaz leaned toward him with interest. "A big battle? Tell me!"

"'Twas where I first kissed a beautiful woman, Lady Topaz, and I'd sooner show you than tell!"

He also leaned forward, meeting her exactly halfway, where she stole a quick glance over at the snoring Bridgeman. A flagon having fallen twixt his legs, ale seeped out, soaking his breeches.

Topaz looked directly into Vogts' eyes, a deep teal, smoky in the glowing embers of the campfire. Their lips met briefly, fleetingly. She pulled away and pressed her palms on his chemay, against the contours of his muscled chest underneath.

"Let us retire to our respective tents now, Franz. We've got a kingdom to win. There will be time enough for pleasures once I am queen."

"The sooner the better then," he agreed with reluctance. "I care not to deprive the kingdom. I must put their desires before my own."

"Aye, and we all need our beauty sleep," she added.

"It doesn't seem to do Bridgeman much good." He nodded in the old codger's direction.

Bridgeman emitted a loud snort as Topaz and Vogts parted company for the evening.

* * *

The march south continued the next day with a jaunty confidence that gained new followers along the way. Every day hundreds of common folk left their fields and marched alongside. There were plenty of weapons to arm the new recruits, taken from Clifford. Oxen pulled the heavy cannon won in the fight. By the time they reached the outskirts of Northampton, Topaz's army numbered 12,800.

* * *

Whitehall Palace

"So what did we win in the fight, what spoils did we gain?" Henry badgered Norfolk as the harried duke entered the presence chamber with yet another armload of maps.

"'Tis scarcely credible, sire. Topaz's unskilled ranks have routed Clifford's army. He was captured and made to look a fool, bells and all. His men are scattered and Topaz and her minions even now march south upon Northampton."

"'Twas a dire mistake to send Lord Clifford. He was too inexperienced. A better soldier would have done it easily. Let me think." Henry pressed his palm against his head, furiously trying to remember one of the many names that always seemed to escape him. "Aha! That good knight, Sir Cecil Hampstead. An older gent with well-won battle scars, a fighter I can trust. Send him at the head of your own men, you can muster fifteen thousand with ease. When Clifford pulls himself back together with what's left of his battles, he can join Hampstead. We'll have near two to one in our favor, see how the would-be queen likes those odds. Aye, send out the word, we have decided. The honor goes to Hampstead while Clifford gets a chance of redemption. This time they'd better get it right or I'll do the job myself."

It was at that moment Amethyst walked through the door to ask the king where they'd sup that eve. She clutched the doorframe for support when she heard his words, not tinged with the slightest hint of humor this time.

Norfolk turned and gave her a slight bow of recognition. He stammered a few parting words to the king and backed out of the chamber. She stood aside to let him pass, and watched as Henry unrolled a map. He plunked a pitcher on its edge to keep it down, and leaned over on his elbows to study it, following a route with his golden toothpick.

She daren't interrupt him now. Later, after a full meal, she could make him listen to reason. She retreated, crept along the wall, and was just backing out the door when her name thundered through the chamber.

"Amethyst! Stay you here, I've already seen you. Norfolk can blend in with the walls, but you, not quite," he called out, still hunched over the map, his eyes following the trail of his toothpick.

She tried to peer over to see how close to London the toothpick was. "Sire, you're busy, we shall talk after we sup."

He tossed the gold pick aside and stood straight. The map rolled up with the toothpick inside it like a frog's tongue catching a fly.

He lumbered over and sat in one of the matching chairs by the fire. "Sit here," he motioned her to take the other.

His steward brought another wine pitcher, poured the king a gobletful, and disappeared.

"Wine?" he offered.

"Nay, thank you."

"Fruit? Pastry?" He gestured to the table.

"Nay, thank you."

"A romp then?" He leered at her.

She didn't answer that. He stared into the fire, and she could tell by the furrow of his brow and the chewing of his bottom lip that had agreed to a romp, he'd have carried her to bed, raked her, and dismissed her just as quickly to return to his maps.

She knew, just as they all did, that Topaz's uprising was no longer a farce to jest about.

"Sire, you don't really plan on suiting up and riding out to battle, do you?" she ventured.

"That may as well have been me wearing a fool's cap with jingle bells for all the good Clifford made us look, the silly catzo." He shook his head with a tsk-tsk.

"Your personally riding out to battle would be rather extreme, would it not? I know you love your tournaments and jousting." But mayhap this was just another exercise to him, on a much larger scale, of course, but practice nonetheless. "Or is this an excuse to escape the stuffy palace and partake in outdoor sport?" She urged, whether he wanted to hear it or not, "I wish you wouldn't go, sire. We...I need you here."

He took a long swig of wine and looked at her. His features softened and a smile curled his lips. He flung the remaining contents of his goblet into the fire and dropped it onto the rug, holding out his other hand to her. She slid onto his lap and he began kissing her.

She tried to forget Topaz and her army, the king's growing preoccupation with it all, and enjoy the feel of his hands through her hair and his lips on her neck. Only she knew how to handle Topaz. Seize and arrest her; a few years' stay in a sparse Tower cell would bring her to her senses. Armies and political campaigns and cannon fire were not the answer; the kingdom would be torn apart once again. She'd wanted a peaceful end to all this, but mayhap it was too late. He forged ahead without heeding a bit of her advice.

"Sire, you're not going, are you?" she pestered. "Tell me you won't go."

"Go where?" One hand cupped her breast, walking her slowly through a field of warm, gentle bliss; the other crawled under her skirts and slowly slid up her thigh.

She threw her head back, pulled out her combs and let her hair tumble. He nibbled at her neck while his hands teased her to a mounting fit of desire.

"Go...to stop Topaz's uprising," she breathed, as he slid her undergarments down to around her ankles and turned her so that she straddled him. She instinctively moved against his mounting erection, her body flooding with warm moistness.

"The only uprising is 'twixt my legs, and I am helpless to stop it." He brought them both to their feet and whisked her into his arms, through the presence chamber, and into the bedchamber. They tugged at each other's raiment until both were completely naked.

When they lay spent, he held her in his arms until the room grew dark. The muffled voices of some of the staff approached. He reached over and pulled the bedcurtain closed as she began fondling him. Just then Norfolk's voice came through from a few rooms' distance.

"Sire?"

"Not now, Norfolk," he dismissed the duke. "I'm handling another uprising."

* * *

"Disturbing news, my lady." Bridgeman on his mount cantered up to Topaz, sending swirls of dust up from the ground like a sea of funnels.

"Pray tell!" Topaz yanked on her reins and her mount began grazing on a patch of brown grass. Vogts reined his mount alongside her, frowning.

"Those men of Wakefield that joined up today," he began.

"What of them?" interjected Vogts, an abrasive edge to his tone. "They seemed to be good hearted youths, all barrel chests and sturdy, ready to give good account of themselves in any fight. I'm glad to have 'em."

"'Tis what they brought that worries me," Bridgeman continued, his eyes darting about to observe who was within earshot.

"Plague?" Topaz's fluttering hands dropped her reins. "The plague is among us?"

"Lord, no," Bridgeman assured her. "Not yet, at least. Sure enough there is a plague of kinds about to fall upon us. Its name is Cuthbert. Re-armed he is, and devout in the pursuit of his vengeance. I'll spare repeating what he plans to do to you, my lady, should he succeed in capturing your royal person. That is the news those Wakefield lads brought with them."

"Well, he'll have to get by me and my sword first!" A snarl twisted Vogts's lips. "I knew we should have killed the viper."

"London soon will be within our sight, she'll be in our grasp ere week's end and Henry knows it," Bridgeman declared. "His support and influence, however, grow stronger the closer we get to the capital. Bare handfuls of men are throwing in their lots with ours now, while hundreds still stream down from the north. The few southerners that have enlisted speak of another army, not a dozen miles from here, led by Sir Cecil Hampstead and endowed with over fifteen thousand men.

Cliff is rushing to join them with another six thousand, new blood mixed with the remnants of the force we shattered at Lincoln. If the two merge we're done for." He shook his lowered head.

"Why then, it's obvious," Vogts said. "We must attack before Cliff gets here. We're almost even in numbers but it won't be easy. I've heard of Hampstead. His knightly exploits are legend throughout the whole of Europe. He fought beside Henry at the Field of Cloth of Gold." His lips spread into a lusty grin. "This will be a real fight."

Topaz gathered her reins and spurred her mount on. "Enough of talk. We must press on. Lord Clifford will not wait and we are wasting time."

"We'll need to march through the night with all God's speed," Bridgeman urged, his voice taking on a preaching tone. "Earthworks must be dug before first light."

"You're right, Paddy," Vogts admitted. "Our only chance is a dawn attack. We must rise with the sun and breathe just as fiery a breath."

* * *

The next morn dawned with the twittering of the sparrows and thrushes mingled with the singing of the larks. Topaz could also discern the unmistakable cawing of crows all in blissful concordance throughout the copse of trees that sheltered their encampment. The sun peeked over the horizon, giving way to another tranquil morn, undisturbed by human voices, stomping feet and clattering hooves. She enjoyed these halcyon moments of quietude before the others arose, waking to yet another leg of her journey towards the crown. Removing her chemise and underclothes, she sank to her knees in the stream behind the camp. She let the invigorating ripples engulf her body as her arms floated weightlessly in the flow. She splashed water on her face and rubbed her eyes, gazing out over the small fertile hillocks in the distance. Trees graced the landscape, their graceful boughs sweeping the ground like satin veils.

She dried herself off and dressed quickly, as the stirring of the men alerted her.

Returning to the excavations, she surveyed the troops around her, a melting pot of her people. Only two distinct groups stood out: Vogts's band of mercenaries with their outlandish foreign dress and the two thousand crimson-crested troops still dressed in the livery of Clifford, their former liege. Topaz made a note to herself to burn those brash uniforms as soon as possible.

Having breakfasted and in position before Hampstead's army stumbled out of their tents, Topaz's men unleashed a deafening fusillade of cannon balls. Unlike Clifford's raw recruits, Hampstead's men, though taken by surprise, reacted quickly. She laughed as she espied them pulling on their breeches and scrambling for their weapons, then rapidly forming a well-organized defensive formation. The first charge of Topaz's army pushed them back, but Hampstead, a veteran campaigner, consolidated and retaliated. The tide of battle stabilized, each side trying to outmaneuver the other. With the sun directly overhead, the battle raged on, neither side giving quarter.

"Hampstead lives up to his reputation, my lady." Vogts approached Topaz in their earthworks and knelt beside her, keeping an eye on the men charging forth around them. "What a fighter! He screens his maneuvers in the trees and hillocks. We know not where they are, or where they'll hit us next. We're in a fight that won't be long forgotten."

Topaz wound a tourniquet round a wounded soldier's leg. He winced as she pulled it tight. "We're holding our ground now, but what will happen when Lord Clifford arrives?" she asked Vogts, her eyes not once leaving the festering wound. "He can't be far."

Bridgeman shuffled up to the ditch, tumbling in, landing on his backside. He scrambled to his feet, brushing himself off. "They've turned our vanguard, the line is breaking. And Cliff's been sighted. He'll be on us within the hour. Doth not bode well, I fear we're losing."

Topaz left Bridgeman to finish bandaging the soldier's wound. She and Vogts climbed out of the trench. He protectively guided her over to the next hillock where they saw their vanguard retreating under the pressure of Hampstead's attack.

"I'm not surprised," Vogts admitted. "'Tis mostly Cliff's former army in our vanguard. They're tired and never were well trained, for all their pretentious crests."

"There's another attack forming. Look there!" Topaz pointed to the horizon.

The fighting lulled as both sides turned to watch the legions riding down on the battlefield. Clifford's unmistakable crimson crest streamed from the incoming army's banners. A cry rose up from Hampstead's ranks. "Treachery, Treachery! Cliff rides against us. More of the red crested devils are upon us. Treachery!"

The cry of treachery echoed down the line. She saw Clifford and his men as they were met with a hail of arrows and gunshot from both sides. Within moments they were forced to defend themselves against Hampstead and fight one another. Hampstead, already in retreat, panicked by the seeming reinforcement of the rebels.

Vogts called for a charge. Topaz's entire army pushed as one into the field of battle. The enemy was soon routed and cut down as they retreated.

Bridgeman clamored up the hillock, limping towards Topaz and Vogts. "What is going on? I thought we were being pushed back. I come up here and see we're routing them."

"Even you won't believe what happened. This is even better than one of your tall stories, Bridgeman," Vogts replied. "Just as we were being pushed back, Cliff rode down upon us. We all thought we were done for. So, too, it seems, did Hampstead. He'd been there battling Cliff's red crest all morning long and must have thought he joined our side. As soon as Cliff came into view, Hampstead attacked him and they ended up fighting each other instead of us. We just waited and finished them off. We turned a narrow defeat into a crushing victory but a hard-won one."

Topaz scanned the battlefield, shuddering at the sight of the corpses, arrows thrust through their chests, strewn about the ground mingled with the wounded, crying for help.

"So this is real war." She took a deep breath and closed her eyes. "'Tis not so glamorous as the old timers tell in their stories of the Wars of the Roses. We lost many good-hearted and valiant men today."

"'Twould have been much worse if Sir Cecil had not thought that Cliff was with us," Vogts retorted.

"'Tis a good thing he saw Lord Clifford's ostentatious crest all over our ranks," Topaz said. "With so much of his livery alongside ours, 'tis only natural he'd think the worm had turned."

"Henry's armies are in disarray. London is ours!" Bridgeman crowed, throwing his head back, nearly tipping over.

"We're all tired now." Vogts helped Topaz to her feet. "Let's tend to the wounded and rest this night. On the morrow, too. We'll bury our dead and rest our spirits. I fancy then we'll be in a mood for London."

* * *

Topaz awoke the next morn in better spirits. Despite the heavy casualties much was captured: more cannon, fresh supplies of powder, balls and arrows as well as handguns, swords, maces, poleaxes, pikes and battleaxes. They'd also procured spears, leather jerkins and iron helmets for the archers. The plate armor, helmets and shields were of the finest quality. Her army was now re-equipped and strong.

Vogts reported that their army was still 7,400 strong and better supplied than ever, enabling them to begin the march on London.

"One step closer to the crown," she whispered, kneeling to pray.

* * *

Whitehall Palace

"A message for your majesty." The page timidly held out the parchment. Henry snatched it out of his hand, breaking the seal without bothering to observe it.

"From Norfolk? Does he not have the mettle to deliver it himself?" the king muttered.

The page stood rigidly, staring up at the king as he scanned the message. He crumpled it, waved the page aside and stomped back into his privy chamber. “Heads will roll!” His voice echoed through the corridors of his chambers as the page turned and scampered away.

* * *

Kenilworth Castle

Matthew entered his solar, drawn to the cream colored parchment atop his desk. Stepping closer, he focused on the seal stuck to the center of the parchment. Lord above, could that be the royal seal? He tossed his cloak aside and snatched it up, broke the seal and tore into the letter.

From Amethyst: *“Please call on me immediately. I beg of you a visit of just a few days. The king himself is riding out to battle to thwart this insane plan of Topaz’s.”* He looked up past the letter, mentally running through his list of tasks for the next fortnight. Could he make it to London and back in time to finalize his purchase of lands from the Duke of Gloucester? Never mind; business could wait. Amethyst needed him.

Wasting not another moment, he ordered his servers to pack some trunks and ready fresh horses. Before nightfall he was on his way.

* * *

The thought of her nearness made all thoughts of banqueting vanish as he strode past the great hall and watched servers scurrying around readying it for that eve’s meal.

He waited in her receiving chamber, already having bathed and changed from his traveling clothes. A maid opened the door and Amethyst appeared, resplendent in a gown of midnight blue shot through with gold threads. Sapphires glowed at her throat. He stood, consuming her with his eyes. Oh, how he wanted her!

“Matthew.” She rushed into his arms and he fought the impulse to devour her with his frustrated passion. Struggling against a surge of raw desire, he gently broke their embrace.

"Tell me what has happened. I heard no news on the way here. Has the king led an army out?"

"Aye, Topaz is planning to march on London." Her voice trembled. "The king rode north just this morn."

She led him to her solar and he kept a respectable distance. He refused all offers of food or drink, but listened intently as she poured out all her anxieties. "If she does not perish in this battle, the king will have her head, Matthew. She will face the axe as Anne Boleyn is doomed to do so."

"'Tis out of your hands, Amethyst," he attempted to assure her. "The king wouldn't heed your advice. Now 'tis all up to him."

"But I worry for my sister's life." Worry lines marred her smooth features. "She's outnumbered two to one, she's bound to spur Henry's temper. She doesn't know his temper. One wrong word and he'll..." She cradled her head in her hands. "Oh, God," she moaned He ached to hold her, but still, he kept his distance. "She's made her decision, you cannot control her fate," he tried to comfort her as best he could from where he sat. "She knew when she went ahead with this, that her life would be in danger. She knows all that. She also knows Anne Boleyn's fate. And I am sure she will be more careful than our ill-fated queen, as not to share that fate."

"But I worry for Henry too." She gazed past him. "He did not have to ride out into battle to personally defend his crown! I keep thinking of my great-uncle, King Richard."

"Amethyst, this is hardly the same thing."

Her eyes met his. "You don't know what this is like, to have two people you love going out onto a battlefield, fighting each other with armies. With swords and maces and cannon." Her eyes darkened and tears slid down her cheeks.

"I'm sure it will be all right. All we can do is pray, 'tis all we can possibly do now. We can do nothing else." He could no longer sit at this distance. He reached out and gathered her in his arms, inhaling her flowery scent, running his hands over her satin gown. Her body relaxed and softened against his. On a reckless impulse, his hand roamed upward, his fingers playing through the ringlets that escaped her headdress.

She pulled away slowly, their eyes met and she managed a smile.

"You feeling better now?" He struggled to keep his voice steady, for he was close to losing his senses.

He had already admitted it to himself, what he'd been planning on telling her for so long—he was very much in love with her.

"Let's go to the chapel and pray, Matthew." He followed her out of the apartments through the splendid palace. They reached the chapel, and he knelt and prayed...for peace, and to one day have the woman he loved.

* * *

St. Albans

King Henry marched north, clad in Milanese plate armor, gathering supporters, the sons of those who fought beside his father at Bosworth, through every village and hamlet along the way.

Clifford and Hampstead gathered the remnants of their routed armies and joined Henry there. The next morn Henry's army gathered on the outskirts of the town, numbering thirteen thousand six hundred by now. They were poorly armed since Clifford and Hampstead's men had lost most their weapons, but well equipped with cannon. Henry set up his battle lines on a ridge, a perfect wide open field of fire for his heavy guns.

"We'll let the traitors come, then blast them where they stand!" Henry ordered from atop his armored mount, slamming his visor down. "That Warwick witch won't find my crown so easily plucked."

* * *

Topaz's army continued its march south to capture London, her long-coveted crown nearly within reach.

"St. Albans lies just fourteen miles south, then London!" Bridgeman shouted over the rhythmic clatter of hoofbeats.

"My dream is coming true," Topaz proclaimed, to whomever was listening. "Soon cruelty and treachery will be cast out. Wisdom and kindness will sit on the throne instead of a despot and all England can rejoice. The rightful ruler will see her people better served. For 'tis not the people that should serve their sovereign but the monarch that must serve his…or her…subjects."

"Ho!" Vogts halted. "Save all that, the column halts and here comes Derbyshire. What news?"

"You'd best come see for yourself, Vogts," the soldier replied.

Vogts, Bridgeman and Topaz followed Derbyshire to the front of the column of mercenaries. "See you yonder, the milestone!"

Carved into the limestone marker was the number 12 slightly larger than the "St. Albans" carved above it. Next to the milestone stood a gaggle of men surrounding two poles, eight feet apart. As they neared the scene, she realized the poles were pikes set on end, a head mounted atop each blade. She gasped in horror at the sight of the familiar face on the left, pale and bloodless in death. Clifford! A banner tied twixt the pikes read "Death to all Traitors."

"'Tis Henry's welcome!" Bridgeman cried.

"The king himself?" asked an incredulous Vogts.

"Look closely at this pike." Bridgeman pointed to a blood-soaked emblem below each head. "That is the royal seal on each of these pikes."

"'Tis Cliff on the left, but who is the other one?" she whispered, her mouth as dry as the scorched road before them.

"Hampstead." Vogts gave a solemn nod. "Henry erred in killing him. No better man could lead his troops."

"Why, you forget Henry himself," Bridgeman said. "For all his faults he is a lion in battle. He'd slay a dragon and need no help from St. George to do it. He'll make Hampstead look like a knight's squire in comparison."

"I fear you underestimate me and my men," Vogts snapped, casting Bridgeman an annoyed glare. "We'll make Henry wish he had gone hunting doe. Why, we've cannon enough now to breathe fire down old Hal's neck from dusk 'till dawn."

"My, my." Topaz tsk'd. "He'll think he is fighting a dragon. We'll be sure to scorch him with the flames. He may as well taste them now, so he'll be prepared for hell this time tomorrow."

"His lines cannot be far away." Bridgeman shielded his eyes from the sun with his hand, squinting out over the fields. "We'll pitch camp here, rise before dawn and attack at first light."

"No!" Topaz shot back. "Let's go on now and get it done. I am so near the throne I can fairly taste it. I cannot wait. My England needs me."

"The men and the oxen are tired," Vogts said. "A good long rest will do us all good. This oppressive heat wears on man and beast. I can't recall when last it rained. No, hell can wait a day for Henry! England too must wait for you. Lady Topaz," He lowered his voice but Bridgeman sneaked up closer to hear. "Come to my tent tonight. We need discuss my booty. I've some pretty plunder in mind for myself."

"Wait till I'm queen, Franz, then I'll give you a royal screw," Topaz quipped, spurring her mount on, leaving Vogts and Bridgeman in an angry swirl of dust.

* * *

Topaz awoke and roused her men in the darkness. They marched to the field of battle in a ghostly muffled silence, setting up their lines in the stone-gray shadows fused with a muted pink flicker of daylight. Soft light diffused through a silvery mist cloaking the battlefield. She sensed an ominous presence nearby; that had to be Henry's men beyond the nearest hill.

* * *

Henry's grooms strapped the last of his plate armor in place. Holding out his hands, they slipped the cumbersome gauntlets over his meaty forearms.

"Tell me again, you've heard the maneuvers of man and beast in the fog below?" the king asked one of the lookouts, still panting from his run to Henry's tent.

"Aye, my lord, I'm sure of it. There's an army moving in the valley below."

Henry left his tent and lumbered over to his row of cannon, the gunnery crews preparing them for their first firing of the day. "Well, men, shall we greet our guest? Let's see how she handles the king's balls, eh? Let her have the first volley."

Thundering booms shook the earth as the first cannon shots disappeared into the mist.

The fusillade of cannonball tore into Topaz's ranks. A second volley followed quickly, falling harmlessly to their rear. The third fell even further back.

"We must fire back! Why aren't we firing back?" Topaz implored Vogts as the mist dampened her cloak.

"Our guns are not yet readied and in this fog we can't see where to shoot anyway." Vogts strained to see. "Henry's men are guessing. They hope we'll reveal our position by firing back. That's why the second salvo missed us, they fired over our heads that time. They'll keep trying different spots until we give ourselves away, or the mist lifts and they see us."

"This pea-souper won't give way for hours yet, I'll wager," Bridgeman observed.

"Well, we can't just sit here and be shot at while they range the field!" Topaz grabbed Vogts's sleeve, nearly tearing the linen. "We must do something!"

"We must sit tight and keep our position mum," Bridgeman answered for him.

"Barnet!" Topaz did that same little dance as before. "The Battle of Barnet!"

"Not again, Topaz," Vogts groaned. "Leave the war to us, we'll serve you well."

Topaz ignored him. "At Barnet," she rattled on, "the Yorkist artillery was set up under cover of the night. In error their line was misaligned. They were set up too close, right in front of the Lancastrians. All night long the Lancastrians put up a barrage of cannon, firing for all they were worth at where the Yorkists were supposed to be. By morning the Lancastrians' supplies were spent, overshot and wasted."

"What would you have us do, Lady Topaz?" Vogts asked.

"Why, move forward, you puttock!" Bridgeman cuffed him on the jaw. "In front of the line of his shortest fire. Set up our own guns there, right under their nose."

"Then what?" came from the exasperated Vogts.

"Why, just sit and wait," Bridgeman said. "While he wastes his balls and powder we save ours."

"And when the fog clears we have him, at the end of our guns," Vogts concluded, brandishing a grin at the nodding Bridgeman.

"Aye, point blank." Bridgeman nodded.

"Quite a surprise for Henry." Topaz let a satisfied smirk cross her lips.

* * *

Under cover of the heavy mist, Topaz's army stalked forward into a new position, as quietly as possible, until they formed immediately below Henry's guns. Salvo upon salvo flew over their heads, landing way behind them. Slowly the heat built and the mist burned off. Now they could vaguely discern Henry's battery. When they saw Henry's gun carriages silhouetted against the horizon, Vogts ordered his men to open fire. Fired they did, with deadly accuracy, smashing Henry's guns to smithereens. His men reeled back as Vogts and his mercenaries charged at them without warning. Within a half hour, Topaz's army had taken the plateau. Gloating, she raised her standard instead of Henry's. The heat and humidity continued to build as the armies faced each other.

"Look at the army he's assembled," Topaz said. "They're twice our size."

"But we hold the plateau and all the cannon," said Bridgeman. "That offsets their numbers."

"Let them try and take the guns," Vogts dared them. "We'll cut them down as with a scythe."

Henry, now forced to the bottom of the hill, rallied his men about him. He realized he was in the same position as Richard at Bosworth. His army had lost the high ground, their cannon had been destroyed, and every time they mounted an attack on this plateau, they would suffer heavy casualties. He couldn't try and defeat Topaz's army; he had to do what Richard did—lead a direct assault onto the enemy. If he could slay Topaz, he would be the winner.

The cannon pounded his troops unmercifully as he climbed the hill, but he still got within 50 yards before being driven back, actually exchanging blows with Vogts. With the clanging of mace, sword and shield all about them, neither men yielded, until Henry fell back with his troops.

Topaz watched as Henry gathered his men about him for another attack.

"He's strong as an ox, old Hal," said Vogts. "Almost had me down before I knew it. And where did he learn to curse? That raging bull did not sound very kingly to these ears."

"He paid dear for that charge," Bridgeman said. "Dead men litter the field, and they're mostly his."

"He'll come again," Topaz warned, fighting to keep the doom from her voice. But a surge of courage spurred her on. "Oh, no, I will not lose, not after all this," she vowed.

Vogts turned to her, smiling. "I'm banking on it, we've found our range. He ventures here again and he'll be sorry. Yet stay where he is and he'll be pounded all day long by our guns."

"Why doesn't he retreat?" Topaz's frustration tightened her muscles. "Why doesn't he set up for another fight closer to London?"

"If he were to run from a wench in the heat of battle, all England would disown him," Bridgeman said. "I'll vow he'd rather die a king than live in exile."

"He's massing for another charge," Vogts predicted. "It should be over soon."

"Henry's doom is upon him." That same courage brought Topaz a surge of confidence. "And look! The very sky itself has darkened in portent. As if the gates of hell itself are opening now to receive him. Come on, Henry. Come upon my guns," she goaded. "Let me speed your journey."

"'Tis black as night," Vogts observed, looking across the sky. "Yet here he comes and what a rumble do they make as they charge upon the hill."

"Wait!" Topaz hushed them. "'Tis not their feet, 'tis thunder. Aye, hell awaits ye, Henry. Your doom is upon you and I am to be your queen."

Henry and his men charged on under the black clouds. Topaz could barely make them out in the thick gloom. "Oh, how I have lived for this day," she chanted. "The crown restored to the House of Plantagenet!" A sudden fork of lightning tore through the heavens. The first volley of cannonballs followed. As the thunder and the roar of the cannon mingled, spatterings of rain began falling, developing into a torrential downpour. The wind rose, swirling the deluge all around them. By now the lightning flashed with every few heartbeats. The thunderclaps drowned out the sounds of battle. Some of the cannon started to sputter and misfire, allowing Henry and his men to advance once more. Fierce combat ensued, but finally Topaz's men drove Henry and his troops back down the hill.

As the sudden tempest passed, the sides regrouped, each taking stock of the other.

"How did we fare?" Topaz asked Vogts. "Their attack was so fierce. Why didn't they fall before our guns?"

"The tempest," Vogts said. "It soaked our powder, it will not fire."

"The guns are useless now!" cried Bridgeman. "Alas, we've lost our advantage."

"We came off badly in that last exchange," admitted Vogts. "We lost many men, we've got less than five thousand left. How can we fight him now? His force yet numbers nine or ten thousand."

"He's right." Bridgeman wrung out his cloak. "We can't survive another charge. The day is lost." He coughed and spat upon the ground.

"Methought the storm told of Henry's doom," Topaz proclaimed with a dramatic flair. "'Tis I that is undone."

"Lady Topaz, most of my men still can fight," Vogts said. "Come with me. We'll break through Henry's ranks and make a run for Scotland. I could use a woman like you. A lady of breeding with fire in her belly. I'll even marry you if you want. I've never seen your like before and I can't let you go now. I need you, Topaz." He clasped her hands, kissing them with a desperate hunger.

She drew her hands away. "Control yourself." She took her flask and splashed wine in his face.

"Aye, go!" Bridgeman urged, a droplet of rain glistening in his eye, or was that a tear? "We can hold King Hal here for a while. Every one of us would gladly die for you. Mayhaps you'll fight another day with more worthy retainers at your side and win the day. Go, make haste."

"No monarch since time began had worthier subjects," Topaz rebuked him. "I could not, will not leave you here when never more you needed me. I cannot let my people suffer for my deeds whilst I bide my time in some foreign palace. No!" She stomped her foot upon the earth. "This thing is at an end and I must save my people from Henry's retribution. He knows not that our guns won't fire and surely cannot relish another charge. Bridgeman, sir, ride down to the king under the white flag of truce. Give him this, my message: my forces will lay down their arms and I will surrender to him with but one condition."

"Always one condition!" Vogts raised his arms and dropped them at his sides. "You want him to switch with the court fool, Will Somers?"

Topaz smiled sadly. "Nay. Henry must let all my followers return in peace to their homes. If the king will give his royal bond that my people not be harassed, then he may do as he will with me."

She sat, gathered a few men and calmly played dice games til Bridgeman returned. "The king accepts your surrender. He gives his word that all who fought with you may go their way unharmed but must lay down their arms and leave their horses."

Two of Henry's knights strode up the incline just as Topaz took her leave of Vogts and Bridgeman.

"They are coming to take me?" Topaz stood and stoically bade farewell to her loyal followers. "Then I suppose this is goodbye. Mayhap we shall meet again, mayhap not." She held out her hand for each of the men, and they clasped it fondly.

"In the Tower, mayhap?" Bridgeman mumbled, "Although I'm in no hurry to get back there again."

Vogts slipped him a sideways glance, shaking his head. "What is it that you would have of her?" Vogts stood, facing the knights, his hand on the hilt of his dagger.

"Nay, Vogts, let them take me." Topaz approached the knights in their hateful Tudor livery, straightening her skirts, standing straight, shoulders back, chest out. "Go now, but never forget me. Take care of Bridgeman for me."

"Aye, Lady Topaz, I shall heed your wishes. You will always be queen in my heart."

"Don't worry about me," Bridgeman spoke up. "I can take care of myself."

The two men turned and joined the ranks of the defeated army, already streaming away from the plateau.

"His majesty the king has sent us to take you into his custody," one of the knights addressed her.

She stepped forward as each knight took Topaz by an arm and dragged her down the hill. It was there that she and Henry Tudor met for the first time.

Their eyes locked on each other. She stood, expressionless, feeling no hate, no remorse, no sense of accomplishment. She was drained of all emotion.

He, however, leered at the shapely figure in the way that would degrade her the most, ogling the breasts spilling out of the low-cut bodice. He then glanced at his toadies. "To the Tower with her, in the same cell her moronic father rotted in." He swept past her and stalked away.

* * *

Topaz entered the Tower on a barge through Traitor's Gate. She disembarked, refusing a helping hand, and the guards led her across the grounds. As they passed the timber-framed Queen's House, she looked up at the small window under the gabled roof in the north wing. There she caught two black eyes following her as she walked. It was Anne. She knew it. As she continued to walk, their eyes locked and the two heads nodded in unison. Topaz held her head high, determined to exit this prison alive, not carried out headless in a pine box as would the unfortunate soul up there in the confines of her quarters.

She saw that they were heading to the far corner of the Queen's House, in the direction of the adjacent Bell Tower, where she'd spent the first four years of her life... where they'd dragged her father, limping, to his death... where she'd been born, and where she was fated to die... coming full circle, to born and to die within the Tower of London.

She held back and the guards nudged her along. They reached the top of the winding staircase and she halted. She breathed the musty air. It was still there, it hadn't escaped. The dampness invaded her lungs, mingled with the odors of fear, sweat and misery. It sent her reeling back in time, back, back, till it seemed as if she'd never left. Once again she was that terrified little girl. The clanking chains scraped the ground as guards dragged the prisoner past her, her mother's hand trembled in hers, panic pierced her. It all happened so fast, and she saw it, heard it, smelled it, felt it all over again.

"Papa!" she shrieked, as she had that day so long ago. She escaped the startled guards, tumbled down the stairs. Her hands scraped the rough stone. She stumbled, slammed into the stone alcove, gasping for air. A ribbon of light shone through the narrow arrow slit. They caught her and dragged her back up the steps, yanking her hair, tearing her scalp.

"No! Not here! Anyplace but here!" Her cries echoed against the stone walls and died within them, confined there forever.

They shoved her into an airless cell and she crashed onto the splintered wooden floor. The iron gates clanged shut and the guards shuffled away. She felt something mushy under the rushes but she didn't dare look. She huddled into the corner and stared straight up at the peaked ceiling, counting the beams, one, two, three, four, five, where they peaked. She saw initials carved into the wood. How they ever got up there, she'd never know. A crossbeam hanging about four feet below the ceiling was crudely carved and full of holes. *If only I had a rope*, she thought...

The fireplace was closed off with a rusty spiked gate. From where she lay on the floor she could see into the black void of infinity, not a speck of blue sky or sunlight beyond the thick wall. Centuries of ashes, cooking smells and the remains of fat and grease coated it with grime. She finally stood, stretched, as it was the only pleasurable thing she could do, and walked over to the window. Bloody streaks smudged the dusty leaded glass. She tried to push the iron latch to open it, but it wouldn't budge. Straining to see, she could glimpse the Thames, a stream of greenish-gray in the distance.

She walked back to the fireplace and jumped up on the ledge next to it, made from a solid block of stone. She reached up and ran her fingers over the smooth wooden beams. A splinter caught in her finger and she yanked it out. At least she could exercise, keep her blood flowing. She skipped in a circle, along the edges of her cramped prison, humming as she did, stretching her arms way up, letting her muscles go free.

She stopped in the center of the cell, heart ticking rapidly, and spun round and round, faster and faster. The dankly lit window flew by, then the fireplace, then the door, window, fireplace, door, in rapid succession. Her head reeled in dizziness, her breath increased. Her legs folded and she collapsed, falling through a funnel of blackness until she felt nothing.

* * *

Hampton Court Palace

Dinner had just started in the great hall when Amethyst's maid of honor rushed in, bustled up to the high table, and whispered in Amethyst's ear, "Lord Gilford is here, Madam. He says he must see you. It is urgent."

The meal forgotten, she ran to the palace entrance and found him pacing up and down like a caged lion.

"Amethyst, I must see the king," Matthew begged. He grasped her arms and collapsed into her embrace.

"My God, Matthew, what's happened? What?"

"The lads!" His voice broke. "The king has taken the lads to the Tower!"

She gasped in horror. No, how could he be so cruel? "Oh, God, no! When?"

"Two days... no, three... I don't know. I left as soon as they did, skirting Warwickshire so they wouldn't run into me. They must be there by now." He grasped her arms. "Please, you must let me see him!"

Fear and anger shot through her in savage battle. This time she couldn't control herself. "That bastard!" she spat, using that word for the first time. "Why would he do this to them? Topaz received her just desserts, but why the innocent boys?"

She led Matthew through the entrance and left him there, dashing back into the great hall. She approached the dais, glancing at the plates piled with red meats, carrots, squash, goblets spilling with wine... the whole scene made her want to retch. The king was busy talking with one of his nobles. "Your majesty, I must see you," she cut in, against protocol, against etiquette. At this point she no longer cared. Damn his court manners. He hardly had any himself!

The courtiers took no notice as the king made a big display of excusing himself and exited the great hall with Amethyst.

They found a dark corner and she faced him. "My lord, you've locked my nephews into the Tower?" To have referred to them as Topaz's sons would have raised his ire. Hers was raised enough for the both of them. "Why?"

"I had to, love," he answered with an uncaring wave. "As a precaution."

"Precaution?" she shrieked. "You still haven't answered my question. Why?"

"To keep Topaz in line. Worry not, my love. They are quite comfortable, in a spacious suite, are being waited on by many attendants, and want for nothing."

"But they are prisoners nonetheless!" she spat, knowing if she raised her hands, she'd clamp them round his throat and strangle him.

"Political prisoners," he corrected her. "Not criminal prisoners."

"As were my father and cousins!" She sounded like Topaz, but couldn't help it. All her self-control had vanished, reducing her to a raging she-wolf.

"Hardly. I am not Richard the Third. I am your Prince Hal and I would never let any harm come to your nephews."

"Matthew is here. He is beside himself." Mayhap he had enough heart to spare the boys' father his agony.

"Ah, then fetch him, as we are about to have our meal. We are having…" He began counting on his fingers, "crayfish, oysters, carp, lampreys, crane, swan, quail, goose, duck, rabbit, lamb, and fruit custard this evening. That will ease his mind."

She forced herself to regain civility as she repeated, "the boys are fine, the boys are fine…"

Henry welcomed Matthew, slapped him on the back, and gave him the same story he'd given Amethyst. Was it true or another of his calculating deceiving plots? As they sat at the high table forced to obey protocol, they could only guess.

* * *

Amethyst stepped off the barge and passed through the Tower gates. The green was thronged with people, craning their necks to see the scaffold. She hadn't come to see the execution; she'd come to visit Topaz. As she threaded her way through the crowd toward the Bell Tower and crossed the courtyard, she stayed at least ten bodies away from the execution site. But as guards led the condemned to the scaffold, the crowd suddenly rushed forward. A tight jumble of bodies crushed her, mere steps from the scaffold. Then a subdued hush swept over the crowd as she turned to see the prisoner, dressed in black, climb the scaffold steps.

"I pray you, Mr. Lieutenant, see me safe up, and for my coming down let me shift for myself." The crowd tittered at his poke at humor in the last moments of his life. She froze to the spot where she stood and a swell of sickness rose to her throat. The condemned was Sir Thomas More, Henry's Lord Chancellor, and Topaz's primary advisor and supporter in her quest for the crown. Amethyst shoved her way through the crowd, away from the revolting sight, and bolted through the entrance of the Bell Tower where Topaz was imprisoned. As she ascended the uneven stone steps, winding to the top in a dizzying spiral, grasping the rough center column for support, she tasted the fetid air and felt its moisture. She would have known where she was even if she'd been blindfolded, for she'd been told of the close confines and stifling mustiness so many, many times, as Topaz recalled each detail. Amethyst, age two at the time of her father's death, remembered none of it.

Cannon shots boomed around her as she reached the top of the stairs. Thomas More was dead.

Topaz was sitting, writing, when the guard turned the key and swung the iron bars open to let Amethyst in.

They did not embrace. "You look well enough," Amethyst commented.

"I am well enough. And I shall exit here alive." She placed her pen down and sat straight up in her chair.

"No one ever has, and I told you not to do this—"

She cut Amethyst off. "I did it and it is done."

"Thomas More is dead."

"I heard the whole thing," Topaz replied. "I heard the head fall into the straw basket as well as the deafening cannon shots. My hearing is quite acute."

"Why did you call me here?" she asked.

"Amethyst, do you love me?"

Topaz's sudden question struck her odd. They'd never spoke of love for each other. She wanted something. Flowers, mayhap? "What kind of stupid question—"

"Just answer me. Do you love me?"

Amethyst put her head down. "Of course I love you. You're my sister. But I am so utterly disappointed in you and vehemently hate what you've done...yes, I love you, in spite of myself."

"Will you help get me out of here?" She approached Amethyst.

Amethyst stepped back. "No. Never. I shall not follow you up those cold steps, into this room where our father—"

"I am not asking you to betray your precious king. I am asking you to ask him a favor. I have repented, Amethyst. I am truly sorry for my doings, and I wish to be set free."

Amethyst had to laugh. Only her sister had the boldness, the audacity, to even think of such a thing. Not even Anne Boleyn, the supposed 'witch,' walled up beside her, would dare to appeal to the king for her release.

"So were Fisher and More, and all the others who betrayed the king," she berated her sister.

"More was not sorry," she stated. "More was all too glad to help me."

"Then why all of a sudden are you so full of remorse?" Amethyst wanted to know.

"This was not my doing, Amethyst. I was forced into it." She turned and faced the wall.

"Oh, pish posh," she scoffed. "You talked of nothing else, all your life, Topaz, all your damned life. This was your dream, remember, to be queen. Your dream. Who forced you into it?"

"Our father." She turned and looked her dead in the eye.

"What?" Amethyst shook her head, she couldn't be hearing this.

"I never told anyone this, but his spirit talked to me, all my life, telling me to do this, to carry on his name and regain the crown," she blathered. "I did it, not for the glory of being queen, but for the kingdom. For the poor, for the commoners...and for our family. But I've had all this time, locked up here, allowed to walk nowhere but along the skinny ramparts twixt here and the Beauchamp Tower. So I've been praying." She clasped her hands together. "I've prayed to father, almost every hour of the day, and he spoke to me again, telling me to appeal to the king through you—"

"Oh, so I'm the royal messenger, then. Funny, father didn't ask me to do any of this."

"You never knew him the way I did," Topaz said. "I've been speaking to him all my life. Now he tells me to repent. Beg the king for his forgiveness." She paced the cell in circles. "That is why God made you, my sister, the king's closest confidante, so you can appeal to him on my behalf." She stopped pacing and faced Amethyst. "Of course, the king would never harm you. You're his special one. You are dearer to him than Catherine or Anne were, or even his daughters. He will listen to you. Please, Amethyst. Tell the king I shall relinquish all my claims to the throne if he lets me go."

"And why should he trust you?" she asked warily.

"No traitor has ever appealed to him this way," was her fast answer. "No traitor has ever repented and admitted his wrongs. More went to the death fighting for his beliefs. Please, sister, tell him I am sorry. Here." She handed Amethyst the parchment she'd been writing on. It was her appeal, in writing, relinquishing all her claims to the throne.

Amethyst looked into her sister's eyes. They were rounder than usual, and brimming with tears. "Do you really mean this, Topaz?"

"I swear on our father's and grandfather's graves." She crossed her heart and held up her hand. "I am asking you to save my life."

She looked at her bedraggled sister, her eyes pleading with a pathetic quality Amethyst could only discern as genuine. "Very well. I shall give it to him."

"Oh, Amethyst, thank you!" She rushed up and hugged her. "You will not be sorry, the king will not be sorry, the kingdom will be all the better with me helping out my poor souls once more." Amethyst returned her embrace.

* * *

Sitting in the barge gliding up the Thames back to the palace, Amethyst considered the wisdom of her decision. She didn't want to see her sister die. She knew Henry was keeping her alive simply out of his love and devotion to Amethyst. After all, he was about to execute his own wife.

She nearly dropped Topaz's parchment in the river as the boat docked. She then tucked it securely inside her bodice. She would hand the message to the king. The decision was still his.

Chapter Thirteen

The Tower of London

Jolted awake by enraged shouting outside, Topaz rose from her pile of straw. Shivering in the frigid cell, for she'd been denied firewood, she pulled her ratty cloak round her shoulders. Dawn struggled to break through a pewter-gray sky as she went to the window. Peering through the tiny crack, she watched the rabble surround the scaffold below. The pushing and shoving mob bellowed and spat curses as they jostled for a clear view.

This was to be the spectacle of the century. Anne's final moments had come.

The executioner, clad in a black robe, a hood covering his head, climbed the steps carrying a long sword. Amethyst had mentioned that Henry imported a French swordsman to spare Anne the agony of repeated axe blows. How considerate of him.

The crowd hushed and all heads turned to the right. Topaz watched Anne, shrouded in a robe of black damask covered with a white mantle, emerge from the Tower's interior and walk across the courtyard. Four of her ladies accompanied her, two of them clutching her arms as if she hadn't the strength to walk herself.

The ladies stepped aside as Anne climbed up the scaffold to the platform in solitude. Topaz pushed the window open on its rusty hinges and pressed her head against the opening, a bit sideways so one ear faced the courtyard. She wanted to witness this, but she knew Anne would make a final speech, so she wanted to hear it, too. The frigid breeze blew into the musty cell, further chilling her.

Anne stumbled on the top step and with no one to help her, struggled to regain her footing. She turned to face the silent mob as all eyes stared up at their queen in her final moments. "Good Christian people…" The breeze carried Anne's voice to Topaz's ear, and she heard every word clearly, for Anne spoke out as if to reach the far corners of the kingdom. "I am come hither to die, for according to the law, and by the law I am judged to die, and therefore I shall speak nothing against it. I am come hither to accuse no man, nor to speak anything of that, whereof I am accused and condemned to die, but I pray God save the king and send him long to reign over you, for a gentler nor a more merciful prince was there never, and to me he was ever a good, a gentle and sovereign lord. And if any person will meddle of my cause, I require them to judge the best. And thus I take my leave of the world and of you all, and I heartily desire you all to pray for me. O Lord have mercy on me, to God I commend my soul."

Those were the last words she would ever speak. The Bishop stood by, muttering a silent prayer. The painful silence dragged on as one of her ladies climbed the steps and approached her. She removed Anne's headdress and tied a blindfold over her eyes. The swordsman bided his time, swinging the blade to and fro like a pendulum. Anne knelt, lowered her head to the block, he raised the sword, she jumped up and turned…

One downward stroke severed her head. Blood spewed forth, soaking the straw, spattering the Bishop's robe, the swordsman's cloak. The crowd rushed forward in a crushing charge to dip cloths in the dead queen's blood, sopping it up like gravy from a trencher. Topaz stared in morbid fascination at the macabre spectacle. *That could have been me if Henry had hated me this much,* she realized, shivering—on account of that thought rather than the cold. But all she'd tried to do was seize the kingdom. She'd never brought forth a dead heir.

Anne's maids clamored up the scaffold steps hauling an arrow chest, for no one had thought to provide a coffin.

She pulled the window shut in despair at the senseless death. *Oh, if only she had been a witch*, Topaz mused.

* * *

As the cannon shots signaled the moment of her death, the king crumpled up Topaz's letter and passed a sentence of life imprisonment. Her sons also remained imprisoned—for security. He followed Richard the Third's example of keeping his two nephews secured in the Tower during his reign. Those lads vanished from the face of the earth, vilifying Richard and destroying his reputation forever. But Henry wouldn't let history repeat itself.

* * *

"Thank you, my lord, thank you! You don't know what it means to my mother and me to have Topaz alive!" Amethyst rushed up to the king, dropped to her knees and kissed his ring as if he were Pope. Topaz's spared life eclipsed Amethyst's heartbreak for her sister confined within a filthy cell.

"I did it out of my love for you, my dear heart." His tone carried not a hint of kindness, however. "I could not bear to see you lose your sister. She will live, but she must stay imprisoned for her heinous deeds. But one slip and up the scaffold she goes."

Oh, how cruel and heartless of this man! But still, she knelt, bowed and scraped to him. Such was his power over her. "No, sire, she will not, I know my sister better than anyone. She is truly sorry."

"Then show your king how much you appreciate his generosity. Make those cannon shots stop ringing in my ears."

Why was sex his remedy for every incident, from a broken lute string to a woman begging for her sister's life? But she knew Henry's voracious appetites. Burdened with affairs of state and his personal disasters, they hadn't been together since Anne's incarceration. During this fraught time, she'd felt that pang of longing for his touch, to unite in feverish rapture.

He whisked her into his arms and dipped her, then lowered his lips to meet hers in a warm and intriguing kiss that she returned, matching his hunger.

"Oh, my Amethyst, 'tis been such a long time," he moaned, guiding her over to his bed, parting the draperies. Velvet brushed her thigh as he lifted her skirts, tickling the soft flesh with his fingertips.

"Amethyst, there is nothing stopping us now," Henry murmured into the strands of her hair wound around his fingers, his breath ragged with desire. "I am free, and you are to be my queen."

"So soon? But—" How could he think of this now?

He cut off her protests with a crushing of his lips to hers. His arms encircled her bare shoulders, his warmth seeped into her skin, setting her afire. His eyes pinned her, searching her face, her hair, exploring her features one at a time. Her fingers extended and touched the red-gold stubble on his chin. Her lips parted, her mouth watered, wanting to drink in those luscious lips, to explore his face, his hair, once more, to show him know how much she wanted him.

His parted lips touched hers so softly, fitting perfectly with hers, as always. They kissed more deeply, in as perfect a rhythm and coordination as any they danced together. Her arms wound round his neck. His arms encircled her waist and he brought her ever so gently to him, their bodies conforming like plaster to a mold. His head tilted to one side and his tongue penetrated further. She struggled to breathe, her heart tripping, wild splashes of color and sunbursts behind her closed lids. His manhood grew more rigid as his desire mounted.

"You are beautiful, Queen Amethyst," he lavished his praise as softly as the lapping of the Thames against the palace walls.

"My lord, I am not yet…" she whispered, her lips brushing his. As his mouth devoured hers, his hands traced the curves of her shoulders. Her hand landed lightly on his thigh and she gently stroked the smoothness of his hose. Then they united in a tight, clinging embrace.

She let him mold her to the contours of her body and make her his own, once more. He covered her body with his, as she yielded to his caresses and hungry lips.

As he fondled the sensitive tops of her thighs, she craved the feel his flesh against hers, within her. He teasingly peeled her undergarment off her, his fingers probing her moistness, flattening her palm against her straining body, as she pressed herself against his hand. He pulled his hose to his knees and their lower bodies met, her thighs separating as he crushed them with the mammoth blades of his wide pelvic bones. He plunged into her, again and again, her back arching. She melded with his flesh as they became one.

They cried out together at their shared climax, and he remained within her, growing soft.

"Amethyst," he panted, "I love you like I have loved no other woman. I cannot wait for you to be my queen."

"Sire, please, there is one thing I must do first…" Her breath regained its steady rhythm as their bodies calmed. He lifted damp tendrils of hair from her neck, brushing them back onto the pillow. "Please hear me." The aftermath of lovemaking wasn't the best time to discuss his children, but she hardly got to see him anymore. It must be now, before he jumped up, threw on his clothes and rushed back to his relentless demands. "I know now that Mary and Elizabeth are both bastardized, once again the future king or queen could be my child."

"So what is the problem, my dear lady? I am free, I want to share my life and my kingdom with you, and I need an heir." He rolled over on his back and reached for a goblet on the side table. "The entire kingdom ridicules me as never having chosen a queen who could provide me, but more than that, the kingdom needs a queen, and my throne is incomplete without a queen perched atop hers." He quaffed his wine. "Not only that. My life is incomplete without you by my side. The time is now, Amethyst. The coronation can be within a fortnight." Propped up on an elbow, he gazed down at her.

"Sire, I want nothing more than to be your wife." She pulled the sheet over her breasts. "But before we marry, I must ascertain one thing. I would not dare disappoint you again just as—as your other two wives have done. When I become your wife and when the crown of England is placed on my head, I want to be carrying your child, the future king. I want to ensure that your wish for a son comes true, and only until I am sure the future King of England is within my womb, I will refrain from marrying you."

He traced the goblet's rim with his thumb. "But that is not necessary. We will bring forth many princes...and even a princess or two if you desire. We needn't wait."

She ran her fingertips down the smooth contours of his muscled chest, brushing over the springy mat of red gold hair. "It will not take long, sire. I had the pebble removed by the same physician. And I know my body just like any other woman, and my longing for your child will be fulfilled before the next full moon lights up the sky. I just know it."

He chuckled, holding his goblet to her lips. "You must be thirsty after that exertion. Very well," he spoke as she sipped. "We've waited this many years, another fortnight or so shan't matter all too much. As long as we can spend every night in the throes of passion that will ensure the creation of our first child, I can certainly wait. The past is over, I want to cast those two disastrous marriages into the Thames and consider tonight with the woman I love a fresh beginning."

"Speaking of fresh beginnings...we have a life to create." She set down the goblet and slid her body over his, wrapping her legs about his waist, feeling his urgency once again.

* * *

A fortnight later, she faced a shattering disappointment: she was not yet breeding. Or a month after that. Two more moons waxed and waned, and still the miracle of a newly created life did not bloom inside her.

In desperation, and without telling Henry, she called on his private physician, Dr. Butts. Certain the king was tied up in council meetings, she took a barge to the physician's home in Chelsea and sprinted up the bluebell-lined path to his door.

A servant led her into his private chambers. He sat behind a huge desk, scratching pen across parchment. Floor-to-ceiling shelves held bottles of every size and shape, mortars and pestles, jars of powders and herbs.

He put down his quill and focused his pale gray eyes on her. "Lady Amethyst, what can I do for you? What ills you?"

She approached him as he sat back in his creaky chair. "Dr. Butts, we must keep this entirely secret. No one must ever know."

"You have my word as a doctor. All my patients' visits are kept strictly confidential. Now tell me…are you in pain?"

"Nay, not yet. It is a common affliction among women, Dr. Butts. I am unable to conceive," rushed out of her mouth in one breath.

He tapped the desk with clean fingernails and motioned for her to sit. "How long have you been trying?"

"Several weeks now, Doctor." She took the chair across from him. "We know it is not him. He has sired several children already. 'Tis I. And I cannot bear the thought of being barren, of never giving him what he desires most. Whoever gives him a son will be the one forever. I want this so badly. You must help me." She clasped her hands beseechingly, as if he were Saint Jude.

"Mayhap you are trying too hard." He folded his hands across his chest. "You are obviously very anxious and it is keeping you from conceiving."

"But the anxiety is all up here." She tapped her head. " What has that got to do with my womb?"

"Quite a lot. It is not widely believed, but several Italian physicians have theorized that illnesses…divers ailments, from the sweat to ague to simple fatigue can be brought about by anxiety, manifesting itself in an illness in a completely different part of the body."

"Fascinating." She shook her head in wonder. "Aye, it is true, I am ever so anxious. But there must be something you can dispense in the meantime, some mixture of herbs to hasten pregnancy."

"I shall see." He stood and plucked several bottles from the shelf along with a mortar and pestle. He mixed the herbs and powders together, pounding away with the pestle, and poured the concoction into an empty bottle. He sealed it with a stopper.

He held it out to her. "Clary and hyssop to calm you, anise and coriander to rid your system of any invaders that may be blocking the way. Drink this in hot water like tea, three times a day and if you are not with child in two months, come back to me."

She took it, wanting to pour the entire dose down her throat. "Two months! Oh, Dr. Butts, I simply cannot wait that long."

"We mortals can only do so much, Lady Amethyst." Dr. Butts brushed the fine brown powder from his hands. "The rest is up to God."

"But how can God not want me to have the child I so desire?" She cradled the bottle in her hands as if it were a magic potion deciding twixt life and death.

"We know not why He punishes us," the doctor replied. "I am but a physician. I carry out His work, I am His mere servant. He picks up where I must leave off."

With the reason for Anne's doom foremost in her mind, she pressed on: "Is there anything you can give me that will guarantee a boy?"

Dr. Butts' opaque eyes smiled at her as he shook his head, chuckling. "My dear, I am a physician, not a magician. But try a lot of violet and rose oil."

"You mean drink it?"

"Nay, dab it on your pulse points. Sprinkle it on your bed linens. It gets me growling." He wiggled his brows, closed his eyes and leered at a secret thought she hoped he'd keep secret.

"Thank you, Dr. Butts, I appreciate the advice, but raising his…his level of interest is not my problem." Amethyst turned to leave. "'Tis the result I am desperate for." She said a silent prayer that those results filled the bottle she now held.

* * *

Within a week, she reached the last dose, swallowing it full-strength, without the dilution of hot water this time, grimacing as its coppery metallic taste assaulted her tongue. She then licked the inner rim in order to get every last trace into her system—but, alas, to no avail. Another visit to Dr. Butts and a stronger potion yielded the same results—and she remained barren.

"My lord, I am as desperate to produce an heir as you are," she sobbed into Henry's robe, crushed at the onset of her fourth flux since vowing to give him what his wives couldn't.

"'Tis all right," he sighed. But as he stroked her hair lovingly, she detected the distress in his tone.

Still she refused to become his queen until she was sure she carried the future monarch within her. So he stopped asking her to marry him.

* * *

"I know what I must do, sire," she declared one eve after a session of lovemaking that had become a necessary duty to produce a desired effect. Naked but for the circles of rubies about her throat, waist, and fingers, she separated their bodies and pulled the sheet around her.

"What? Do a fertility dance out in the garden?" His voice carried weariness coming close to defeat.

"Nay, you must take another woman as queen consort." Her prepared words tasted like vomit as they emerged from her mouth, but there was no alternative.

"I shall not!" He glared at her. "You are the only woman I want. I will not cast you aside again whilst another woman parades around here as queen consort."

"I did it before, didn't I?" She slid up to a sitting position. "But those other times it was against my will. Now I am doing it willingly. I want you to have your heir, sire, I know how desperate you are. And I love you too much to stand in your way. I am not being fair to you, or the kingdom. I must step aside." This noble proposal offset her sorrow of having to watch him cavort with another woman, knowing he was bedding her whilst she lay in her cold bed alone.

He gathered her into his arms. "Oh, Amethyst, you are the most understanding, compassionate woman God has ever created. When those other women did nothing but take from me, you've been so willing to give."

"As a matter of fact, I have someone in mind," she said. "I've thought this out carefully. This is no whim."

"Who? There is no one at court I desire. She cannot be one of those dowdy cows lumbering round here." His eyes were two spikes of light as he studied her in the darkness.

"Neither dowdy nor a cow, but a fitting breeder, young and healthy. My new lady in waiting, Jane Seymour, Anne's former lady-in-waiting. She's a genuine, friendly soul, always so eager to please." Dispensing with the heaped praise, she added the reality: "She's a plain, homely girl, but she would be a perfect consort for you, sire."

"Jane Seymour?" He wrinkled his nose as if cauliflower were cooking in their bed. "She is such an insipid little creature. I could never see her as queen. She is too meek, too unassuming." He wagged finger at her. "No, no, do not play matchmaker with royal blood, I won't have it."

"But she's exactly what you need." Amethyst's efforts weren't all selfless; she needed to assure own safety, for she could stay barren for life. And she knew how Henry dealt with barren concubines. "With all due respect, sire, look at your former wives. Jane is as unlike them as night is to day. Just remember the only reason you would consider taking Jane as your queen. You need an heir."

"Oh, Amethyst, I do not want to admit it, but you are right," he caved in, rubbing his temples. "But remember, naught betwixt you and I will change. Jane, if indeed she does become my queen consort, will not impede you and me."

"Of course, my lord." After all, she thought, Amethyst would be changing Jane's life forever. "Looking the other way while her husband dallies with the woman he loves is part of her wifely duty."

"A most compassionate woman, a saint among mortals, you are," he murmured, showering her with kisses. "And every time I bed Jane to create my heir, I shall imagine it is your body I am caressing, you I am making love to, you who are creating my son. You must let me show my gratitude, Amethyst. What would you want of me? More jewels, castles, lands, titles, name it and it is yours."

"Nay, my lord, just be there for me. I do not need any more titles, I've already got one, I've got Warwick Castle and any other castle would pale in comparison. I do not need any more things. I need you. Just you." She snuggled up to him.

"All right, but let me give you something. I must," he insisted.

Amethyst calculated rapidly. "All right, consider this proposal, my lord. If you make Jane your queen, and she produces your male heir within a year, will you let Topaz free?"

"What an idea indeed." The king guffawed, his amusement not quite reaching its usual apex, a guffaw overshadowed by the tragic events of his reign. She knew how desperately he was trying to forget it all. "And only you would think of it."

"That is all I want, my lord," she stated her request in a calm tone, not at all demanding.

"Granted," he sighed.

"Do you wish to meet your future queen now?" She sat up and slid off the bed, clutching at her undergarments.

"She can wait." He pulled her back into bed, began stroking her hair, then lightly touched her face and neck with his fingertips. She took his wrist and ever so gently brought his hand up to her neck, guiding it over her breasts in small circles. His other hand wound through her hair, fanning it over her shoulders. She spoke once again in that soft, velvety tone reserved only for him, in the candlelit privacy of the most inner chamber.

"Tell me you want to ravish me. Violate me, Henry. I want you to pin me to this bed and possess me till I can't take any more. Torturously tantalize me until I explode in a volcanic climax." She touched his half-open mouth with hers, forcing his lips apart with her tongue. She kissed him deeply, leaning against him until her pelvis was straddling his, her knees against his ribs, his hand sliding up and down her thigh, the strokes now faster, more urgent. She circled her hips, easing him into her. She pushed him back down on the bed, brushing her breasts over his lips as she rode him. She pressed one firm, round breast against his mouth and he instinctively started to suck. Her cheeks and lips grew feverish. Her pulse soared. She groaned. She eased herself up and down on him, thrusting gently at first, then more furiously as she felt that familiar explosion where her body and mind rocked in spasmodic ecstasy. She called his name, over and over, conquering him, the king. He cried out for more, his breath swirling hotly around her ear as he cried, "Oh, Amethyst, I am so helpless…so helpless…" She had his hands pinned down at his sides, and her thrusting became so rapid that he could barely keep up with her frenzied rhythm. Finally she slowed to a stop and lay still as he grew soft inside her. She lifted herself up and stroked his member until it became sufficiently aroused once more, then lowered her head to touch its delicate head with the tip of her tongue, nibbling ever so gently with her teeth, sending him into spasms of ecstasy.

"Yea, Amethyst, yea. Oh, Lord Jesu, you are a vixen."

Inside she jumped for joy, knowing she would deliver good news to her sister on the morrow.

* * *

Amethyst was bursting to tell Jane about her new role in life—in effect, her real life. She planned to tell her on the morrow, Jane's day off, but why wait?

Jane was busy preparing Amethyst's bath that evening, pouring rose oil into the warm water.

"Jane, stop that a moment and come here." Amethyst dismissed her chambermaid who was undressing her, not asking where her undergarments had gone.

"Jane, your life is about to change within the next twenty-four hours," she announced with no preamble.

"What do you mean, Lady Amethyst?" A look of fright crossed the dull round eyes and a splotch of color surfaced on the pasty cheeks.

"The king wishes you to be his queen consort," she delivered with a huge smile. After all, this was a momentous occasion. How many chances would Jane get to marry—much less marry a king?

Jane almost smiled, straightening her headdress, fingering her necklace, eyes darting everywhere. "That is impossible, Lady Amethyst. I am but a servant."

"He thinks quite highly of you," she poured it on.

"After all, your father served in the Tournai campaign and accompanied the king to Field of Cloth of Gold. Sir John holds a prominent position here at court. You are more than a mere servant. Not only will you be plunged into wealth and comfort beyond aught you could ever imagine, this means more to me than you will ever know." She didn't tell Jane the other part of the bargain. She did not mention Topaz at all. "The kingdom will grow to love a queen such as yourself. And you will give the king many princes, I know it." *Within the year, I hope*, she thought.

"Myself? As queen?" Jane turned to face herself in Amethyst's looking glass, as if visualizing herself in that most lofty position. "Queen..." Her eyes appeared fixed into the mirror's depths, reaching back into her soul, as if asking it to guide her.

"Aye, Jane, the king would be so honored," Amethyst flattered the mousy lass, tipping her chin up with her index finger. "There. Head held high, regally!" She pushed the girl's shoulders back so the timorous slump became the erect carriage and bearing of royalty. "Like a queen more every minute. Do you see it, Jane? Do you see yourself on the throne beside the king, a crown glittering atop your head, dripping in the queen's jewels, commanding the realm alongside your husband, the king?"

Now a smile parted the thin lips. Jane turned, thrusting out her small breasts, sneaking a sideways glance at herself, smoothing her skirts. "Of course I thought of it, as does every young lass in the kingdom. But never did I believe it would ever happen."

"Come, we shall make you look like a queen." Amethyst removed Jane's cumbersome headdress, letting her light auburn hair tumble round her shoulders. They switched places, just for the night, and Amethyst let Jane bathe in the softly scented water, dressed her in a splendid violet gown with flowing sleeves and low square neckline. She fastened one of her necklaces around Jane's throat, the dark rubies setting off her hair's fiery glow as Amethyst brushed it till it shone.

Aye, all would be happy. His new queen would give him that desperately needed heir, and he and Amethyst could continue their relationship with no pressure.

Henry and Jane were formally betrothed the next day. Ten days later they were married privately with Amethyst as witness. There was no jealousy, no resentment—and no coronation. Henry's desperation for an heir precluded any further ceremonies. That eve, as Amethyst lay in her bed alone, she had one wish: for Henry and Jane to be conceiving the future King of England this very moment.

Chapter Fourteen

Amethyst went home to Warwickshire for a short visit, to let the king and his new queen have some private time.

Bluebells lined the path and the grass smelled sweet with fresh spring dew as she set out early in the morn for home. Dismounting Honey, she walked in the grass alongside the rutted path for a while. She removed her shoes, letting the springy blades cushion her feet as her groom guided Honey along. The sky, a warm azure, beheld creamy clouds stretching out over the horizon, beyond the velvety hills.

As they entered Warwickshire and the castle came into sight, she remembered that first day she saw her ancestral home. A flood of misty sentiment tugged at her heart; she belonged at court serving her king, but something kept pulling her back here, causing her to long for it when she was away. Was it the castle itself, the imposing fortress looming before her with its cavernous entryways and vast gatehouses, or the people she'd left behind to lead this coveted life of a courtier? It was both, she knew—and something—rather someone.

She spent but a day at Warwick, telling her mother of the king's marriage to Jane, of Anne's demise brought about by her misjudgments, and Amethyst's bargain with Henry to let Topaz free.

The following day, after a stroll round her beloved Peacock Gardens and a picnic along the bank of the Avon, she mounted Honey and rode off to Kenilworth. Her heart singing with every hoofbeat on the short journey north, she pictured his eyes, his lips, an embrace as warm and gentle as the breeze that fondled her hair. His image vanished as she rounded the final bend and glimpsed the red walls peeking through the copse of cedars before her.

She crossed the moat, passed through the gates, and she was there—Kenilworth, her very own escape from court, from home—from the world.

A page greeted Amethyst and her groom, led Honey to the stables, and she headed for the private apartments. She knew her cheeks were flushed and her hair was tousled, streaming down her back in golden waves, just the way he liked her, natural and uncourtly.

They were finishing up the evening meal in the great hall when she entered. Servitors scurried about, clearing tables, clusters of guests here and there, a circle of nobles sporting clipped hair and beards, fine satins brandishing rich embroideries, sweeping plumes, clever tongues—and Matthew.

He stood at the center of a group, engrossed in conversation, his head bowed in concentration, one toe straight out, the other pointing to the side. Her eyes ran up and down his length, recording every detail of his appearance. He looked up and noticed her, his eyes blazing an exuberant green as his face brightened in recognition. He excused himself and approached her. She went to him, arms outstretched, the surrounding voices converging into a blur as he, too, came towards her. Hand clasped hand, cheek touched cheek, and she drew a deep breath, emitting it in a contented sigh.

"Amethyst, what brings you here? I've been thinking of you." He spoke as if to a goddess he worshipped.

She thrilled at that, beaming. She so badly wanted to blurt out just how much she'd been envisioning... dreaming... fantasizing about him. "We have a new queen, Matthew. Lady Jane Seymour. She and Henry were wed the other day."

"But Amethyst, I thought... according to your letters—"

"I refused the king's marriage proposal." She did not want to tell him why, but one look into those trusting eyes, and she began pouring the entire story out to him. "I gave Jane to him, I knew that I must, knowing that I can never give him an heir. He is desperate for his heir, and Jane was a wise choice indeed." She lowered her voice and lifted her lips to his ear. "She had just become my lady-in-waiting. I introduced them. I prettied Jane up to regal standards, made her look like a queen, and Henry was delighted. She will make a wonderful mother for our future prince, and nothing twixt Henry and me has changed." But something twixt her and Matthew was changing. Her heart fluttered in anticipation of his nearness; she'd taken extra care with her hair, her dress, her choice of fragrance. She shivered with longing for a light touch of his hand on hers, a casual brush across her cheek. She constantly wrote him letters in her head and most of all, missed him. But she didn't share this with him—not yet.

"Well, I say, the king is right, we do have a saint about us," he praised. "Your giving another woman chance to be queen was very noble indeed." He clasped her hand and guided her to the balcony overlooking the courtyard. "Another chance you passed up to be queen." They stood alone among softly chirping crickets.

"A barren queen will never last long in this realm, Matthew. I am protecting myself as well. I have accepted the fact that God does not want me to be queen. Let us just hope Topaz has accepted that same fact. About herself, that is."

"I would have thought life in the Tower would serve to humble her." He finally tore his eyes away from her to gaze out at the stars.

"And a more loving queen we can never have than Jane. Her lineage is impeccable, her father is a noble, a great admirer of Henry's. She is worthy of the position," she gave him the same pitch she'd given Henry, having practiced it enough.

"And what of you?" He returned his gaze to her. "Are you leaving court now?"

She sensed the hope in his tone. "Nay, I shall stay on. Henry has never confided even in his queens of certain matters, and even if I never become his wife, I am glad to hold my post as long as he wants me there."

"So, have you seen your sister?" His eyes left hers and swept over the grounds before them.

"Yes. And I made the most crucial bargain with Henry." She had to set it up, for this was bigger news than the realm having a sudden new queen. "Topaz's freedom hangs on it. He wanted to repay me for giving way to Jane. He offered me castles and gems and titles, but I told him I needed no more of that. What I wanted was intangible. So I asked him for the greatest gift he could ever give me. I asked him, if Jane produced a male heir within one year, to set Topaz free."

"Oh, Amethyst." He emitted a curt, ironic laugh. "The odds are so great."

"Not really." He obviously didn't know the ways of women. "Jane is nowhere as anxious as I was. I believe he'd *will* Jane to start breeding and overrule God's wish if it is not to be. He is so desperate for that male heir, he agreed. Well, almost immediately."

"And how much coaxing did it take on your part?" His eyes twinkled under the night sky.

"No more than a few minutes. These days he is becoming quite coaxable."

"Your magic powers do beguile even a king, Amethyst." He took a step towards her and a breeze lifted her skirts nearly to her knees. He reached out to smooth them down and her hands captured his. He drew her closer and slowly, hesitantly, began stroking her hair, as if he'd wanted to do it for a long, long time. He tilted her head to meet his gaze.

"Oh, Amethyst," he whispered, parting his lips to meet hers in a desperate kiss. She'd wanted so badly to fulfill the dream she'd been nurturing in her mind and in her heart—and to make it reality, to be Henry's consort, to sit beside him, to give him his beloved heir. She now transferred this desire to the man before her, the confidante to whom she'd always bared her soul. She brought him to her, searching his lips with hers, her hands nimbly exploring the thick locks of hair, his taut arm muscles. She felt a consuming arousal by the strangeness of it all. He responded instantly, returning her kiss, his searching lips smothering hers.

She withdrew her arms and pulled away, as if they both knew it had to end. They loosened their embrace, their eyes still locked.

"Matthew..."

"Aye, I know. Forgive me, I could not help it. I have been wanting that to happen for such a long time—"

"Just because I am not going to marry the king doesn't mean I am free. I am sorry, I never should have started this." She touched her fingertips to his lips.

He looked at her, his eyes darkened with desire. "Please, Amethyst, promise me one thing."

"What?"

"That you will consider me your closest ally," he said.

"Of course, Matthew. You are my only ally. I love Henry with all my heart. But I can never marry him, we both realize that. I can never bear Tudor children. You will always hold a very special place in my heart."

"Please, Amethyst, let me kiss you, just once more... " he whispered, his voice drenched with longing.

"Matthew, you have a castle full of guests." She inched backward.

He sighed, took her hands and gave her one last despondent gaze before he departed to fulfill his duties as host.

* * *

Matthew had business to attend to, so Amethyst left Kenilworth with a promise that she would return as soon as possible. The vision of his disheartened face as they said goodbye lingered before her eyes and in her heart. She missed him already. *No,* she prayed. *Please don't let me fall deeper in love with him than I already am!*

* * *

After sending a message to Topaz in the Tower telling her of the bargain she'd struck with the king, she went to visit her. Topaz had grown pale and thin, her gown hanging on her emaciated body, but she'd been moved to a comfortable suite in the Queen's House, one floor down from where Anne had spent her final hours. A subtle warning, mayhap. Henry was a very subtle man.

"Do they not feed you here?" Amethyst asked with disgust as Topaz idly twirled a strand of hair round her finger, which looked even bonier than usual.

"Indeed they do." She waved a hand over at the table across the room. Amethyst looked upon plates piled with food.

"Mutton, sweetmeats, fruits, an entire loaf of bread...why are you not eating?" Amethyst could have helped herself to one of those juicy apples, but her sister needed every morsel.

"I am anxious, Amethyst, anxious to see what this queen is going to bring forth, if anything, for she is the deciding factor of my fate." She rubbed her hands together in a washing motion.

"You will continue to live should Jane not produce a male heir, you just will not be free," Amethyst told her.

"I would be dead than spend the rest of my years in this dungeon!" She dragged herself to an overstuffed chair and plopped down, propping her feet on the footstool.

Amethyst looked round, at the overstuffed feather bed, the rich tapestried rug, the lacy pink curtains opened to let the spring sunshine spill through. "I would think you would be thankful to me for talking the king into entering into this bargain instead of complaining like an old shrew, This is far from a dungeon, Topaz, and considering what you've done, you are lucky your head is not atop London Bridge bumping alongside your cohort, Thomas More's."

"Aye, I appreciate it, all right?" She looked over with a sneer. "At the end of the day it is your power over the king that keeps me alive. It is Jane's reproductive abilities that will set me free. And if indeed he has been cursed by the Almighty, as he has been so far, my fate be cursed right along with him." She crossed her ankles, playing with the tassel hanging from the chair arm.

"I shall keep you well informed, sister. Now eat." She pointed at the feast. "You are positively scrawny. I shall go now to visit my nephews."

* * *

Henry's only son, Henry Fitzroy, died in July at age 17. "This is her final curse, and she is cursing me from the grave!" The king shook his fists at the heavens as he and Amethyst walked the grounds together.

"And Jane will give you another son, I know it, sire." Amethyst tried desperately to soothe him, for now she had a personal stake in this. "She's young and is so devoted to you."

The king stopped, plucked a rose off a nearby bush, and handed it to her. "A pink rose, roses I had especially bred just for the grounds here at Greenwich. To symbolize the union of the Yorkists and Lancastrians, the red and the white. Pink, a perfect blend of the two colors, the two royal houses. They have been united all these years, and still I haven't got an heir. Oh, Amethyst, how much longer must I wait until my prayers are answered? I should have a palace full of princes."

"Oh, you shall, my lord. Jane will come through."

"I have begun to count on Jane, to put my every hope in her, every fiber of my being begs her to give me a son." He shook his head with a frustrated sigh.

"And she shall."

* * *

The Tower of London, 1537

When Jane announced that she was with child, the bonfires blazed and prayers went out for the safe delivery of the long-awaited prince.

Topaz clung to her Bible like she never had before. "Please let it be a healthy boy, heavenly father. I have relinquished all my claims to the throne, I surely have. I shall never try to oust Henry again, or you may strike me dead."

She begged, she implored. She meant it.

* * *

The queen, the royal heir within her womb, now sat at the king's side on the dais. Amethyst had no place there anymore, so she resumed her duties in the gallery with the King's Musick. Although they all knew she'd introduced Jane to the king, she offered no explanation as to why. No one knew about her barren state except the king and Dr. Butts. She could almost see the courtiers looking at her with questioning eyes—why had she let Henry marry her lady-in-waiting? It was a most bizarre happening. The smugness of her secret appeased her misery which intensified every time she saw Queen Jane, her ever-increasing confidence in her new position, and her ever-expanding abdomen. A blade stabbed at her heart every time she saw Henry touch Jane's cheek or take her hand with a tender affection he'd once saved only for her. Jane's shyness was giving way to an outgoing congeniality, and she made friends with the courtiers like Anne or Catherine never had. She treated them as equals, and they loved her for it.

She was becoming quite a dancer, too. Even with her advancing pregnancy, she leapt about the floor with the king like a graceful swan. Natural color flushed the queen's cheeks, more radiant than the rouge Amethyst had slathered on Jane's face that first night—and her eyes gave off a sparkle that matched Henry's when they met. Amethyst hadn't expected any of this—this critical match that had blossomed into companionship and mutual affection. *That should have been me*, she lamented as she strummed her lute, eyes brimming with the tears that turned her king and his queen into two shapeless blurs. But at least she still had his love—something Queen Jane would never have.

"Jane fairly glows, does she not?" he gloated one eve as he and Amethyst played cards in her chambers, piles of food and jugs of wine before them.

"She looks hearty," Amethyst mumbled into her hand, tossing a card a little too carelessly onto the table.

"Haven't you gotten your mind on the game?" Henry attacked his cards and dice and tennis as competitively as he ruled his kingdom. "This is the fourth hand you've lost."

"Is that all I have lost, sire?" The tears, which flowed more freely these days, were welling up again.

"What do you mean?" He finally laid his cards down on the table and directed his attention to her.

"I have seen you but twice in the last fortnight. We have not made love since you married Jane," she unleashed her frustrations, longing for a mere brush of his hand.

"Well, Amethyst, I own but one privy member. Had I two or more, then—"

"Since when has that ever stopped you? However, that is not the point. I am not bothered about the lack of lovemaking, although now that she is with child, more coupling with her is hardly necessary. You and I hardly see each other anymore. You are always with her," she vented, holding back even more pent-up vexation. Had she released all she held bottled up inside, she'd have caused a tempest.

"Well, Amethyst, she is carrying my child, I must see to her needs, see that she is comfortable—"

"You can easily provide for her every comfort with the hundreds of servants at your feet," she broke in, although his need to explain himself to her, a mere subject, alleviated her disgruntlement. "You mustn't be there every second. And you certainly needn't sleep with her."

"You adamantly refused to sleep with me during my first travesty of a marriage, when in effect I was still a bachelor," he reminded her. "Now that I am lawfully married, you complain I am not sleeping with you. Sheesh, woman, what do you want?"

His patronizing tone further boiled her blood. "That was different; you were pursuing me. I did not know you had any feelings for me other than those of lust. We are far past that, Henry, our feelings are those of true love, they are out in the open, and you are depriving me. Remember, it was I who introduced you to Jane."

"Only because you proved barren and you insisted," he reminded her of another fact.

"So you are going to hold that against me now?" She jumped to the defensive.

"Nay, I am trying to play a hand of cards!"

"Oh, go to your wife, play cards with her." Amethyst gulped the last of her wine.

"That I will!" He quit the room before she could even think of a retaliation.

She sprang to her feet and dashed to her writing table.

"My dear Matthew," she wrote, *"It has all come back to hit me in the face. He is becoming infatuated with Jane. I feel so betrayed. What would I do without you?"*

* * *

Henry returned to her chambers the very next eve, and they made love tenderly, leisurely, without the frantic urgency of a couple desperate to conceive. But she noticed a certain detachment on his part; he was there in body, but not in mind. She sensed something missing, but did not badger him about it. Later, he quietly slipped out of her bed when he thought she was asleep. She knew he was going to join his wife.

* * *

"Why don't you go home for a while, Amethyst?" Henry suggested one eve after he tucked his very pregnant wife into bed. "I have some matters here I need to attend to, Jane will be entering her confinement soon—"

"And you want me out of the way," she answered for him, sparing him the trouble.

He inhaled a sharp breath, ready to retort, but she held up her hand. "'Tis all right, sire, you needn't explain yourself. I am clearly in the way. I can use a break anyway. My fingers are all calloused from lute playing, and need to be softened up a bit. I can use some time in the quiet of the country, without blasting voices and shrill viola strings ringing in my ears."

"Now that is not you, Amethyst. Music has always been your passion, and you must not think you need to escape it. I am simply very fraught with worries right now. The French—"

"I understand, sire. I shall obey, pack up and be out of here by sunrise tomorrow," was her curt reply.

"Please come back for the christening. Dr. Butts says Jane should bring forth the child by the first of October," he extended the invitation with a brotherly pat on her arm.

"I shall be here, my lord. I heed and obey." But she wondered why he wanted her at the christening. Surely Jane didn't want her to be Godmother! That would be rather awkward.

"I am inviting Elizabeth to court for the christening, too. I was even thinking of having Mary stand up as Godmother."

That came as a relief. "She would be honored. So you will have all your estranged women around you."

"What do you mean estranged? You and I are not estranged. I love you as much as I always did, Amethyst, I am just very preoccupied right now," came that lame excuse, sounding like an ever-repeating refrain of a folk song.

"I understand, Henry. You needn't explain yourself to anyone. After all, you are the king," she said sardonically, turning her back on him to begin packing.

He slipped out silently and she departed the palace at daybreak.

Chapter Fifteen

Amethyst entered the gatehouse of her beloved Warwick Castle, grabbed a messenger and sent a message to Matthew. From her perch at the top of Guy's Tower early next morn, she saw his mount flying over the rich soil. She called and waved down to him. As she strode the ramparts bursting in excitement, he reached her minutes, hardly out of breath.

He clasped her in his arms, lifted her off the ground, twirled her round. Their laughter sang in the soft summer breeze. He placed her down and they stumbled dizzily over to the edge overlooking the Avon.

"What a lovely view, I have never been up here before!" He unlaced the front of his shirt with one hand. She found that gesture so very sensuous, although she knew he wasn't trying to be.

"Aye, it is my very favorite part of the castle. I've been up here in the dead of winter, at night when the stars are strewn across the sky."

"On top of the world." He returned his gaze to her, his eyes sparkling like the sun's rays glinting off the river.

"I could have been," she sighed, taking his hand as he pulled her closer to him. "He has Jane now. That is why he sent me home."

"For good?" His eagerness was so obvious, it excited and saddened her at the same time.

"Nay, just until Jane brings forth his heir. He is ever so anxious."

"Well, I can understand that. I would not want to be in his position." He brushed a few strands of hair from his eyes.

"I feel lost, Matthew. I feel so empty," she poured forth. "Pushed aside, like a used rag. He has become so infatuated with Jane, he's gotten silly. He makes up silly songs which he sings to her, he gathers flowers from the garden and shoves them into goblets and gives them to her like a little boy. He has become a child."

"Well, then it is obvious. He is in love with her." He didn't want to seem to look her in the eye as he said this. "There is no reason for you to feel lost. You have your home, your castle, and your family here. You have the lads. And..." A breeze rumpled his shirt and she glimpsed the golden hairs on his chest, the color of buttercups sprinkling the fields. "You have me. I will always be here for you. I married the wrong sister. It should have been you. I love you, Amethyst. Oh, God, I love you so much." Now he looked her in the eye, capturing her face between his hands.

So he said it...what she'd been holding back for so long. Although she'd already fallen in love with him, she didn't feel that spiraling thrill of the expected revelation. It was ruined now. "Matthew, I am barren, I never would have given you those two beautiful lads."

"It doesn't matter." His hands slid from her face down to her shoulders. "Amethyst, leave court and marry me. I'll talk Topaz into giving me a divorce."

Oh, how her heart would have leapt and danced had this happened before. But now, it was simply too late. "Matthew, I've had enough of these married men and waiting for divorces. I wasted away half my youth waiting for Henry to divorce Catherine. How many times do you think I can go through that again?"

"Well, I am not King Henry, I will hardly need to start my own church." He grasped her hand twixt his own. "Please, Amethyst. Say you'll stay here where you belong and be mine. And when I divorce Topaz, marry me."

"You mean if you can divorce Topaz." Her cynicism irked her, yet she needed that protective barrier.

"Then you would consider it? You would leave court and the king...for me?" He moved closer to embrace her, and she felt his heat seeping into her, the warmth of his desire.

"If the king's affection for Jane continues to grow, I shall come back home," she agreed, unable to force a joyful note into her voice.

She knew she must leave court, for she could not remain there if she was to marry Matthew. She also began to seriously wonder if Henry's love for her was waning. "But I cannot consider marrying another man who is already married. I have had enough of that."

"Then I shall seek a divorce, I must." He looked her square in the eye. "I know you've heard that before. But I love you so much."

Her eyes left his and wandered down, drank in the unlaced shirt, the strong chest and the muscled arms that held her so fervently. And when he tilted his head to touch her lips with his, she responded, her arms winding round his neck. With the summer sun blanketing them in warmth, they locked in an embrace that spoke of everything they'd been holding back.

* * *

The Tower of London

"Topaz..." Amethyst approached her sister, clutching a scroll, her face expressionless. "The day has come. It is October, nine months since Queen Jane announced her impending arrival."

"I know you bear the news. What is it?" the trembling Topaz implored, her fingers intertwined, her face drained of all color.

Amethyst held the scroll out. "The queen has brought forth a prince. You are free."

"Oh, dear God!" Topaz dropped to her knees, lowered her head to the floor, stringy wisps of hair coiling around her. She sobbed, her body in convulsions. "Oh, thank you, God, thank you, God!" Her muffled voice was barely audible as she gasped and thanked the Lord again and again.

* * *

Amethyst and the newly released Topaz attended Prince Edward's christening in the chapel at Hampton Court three days later. The Princess Mary, honoring her father's request, stood Godmother. The four-year-old Princess Elizabeth, having taken a shine to Amethyst, held her hand. The radiant king beamed with an exultation Amethyst had never seen in him. Through her sorrow that she couldn't have brought him this elation, she shared his joy. All his life he wished for a closeness resembling a family. Now he had another daughter, a new wife, and that most cherished, most wanted prince. She smiled through her tears, happy only because he was finally happy. He had his heir, Topaz was appeased, and peace once more reigned over the kingdom.

For nine short days.

Amethyst sat with the king as he sobbed his heart out. "Jane is dead. She has left me. God has taken my sweet dear Jane and has left me here to suffer on earth," he wailed, bursting with grief.

Jane had attended the christening, weak and unsteady. She withstood the rigors with great difficulty, all the ceremonies and festivities from which she'd never fully recovered. Henry kept a vigil by her bed for nine days, during which she passed in and out of delirium. He was there, at her bedside, when she slipped away.

"I was there, Amethyst, I was there. Why could I not have brought her back? All the while, I held her hand, did not let go, and she left me, while still connected. As I held her one hand, God snatched her away by the other, right from my presence." He shook his fist. "My physical bond with her could not keep her here with me. Oh, how powerful we kings think we are until God's will enters, then we realize how weak and mortal we all are. God cares not that I am a king, for I am a mere servant. Should it be His will to take away what is mine and make it His, then it is to be!" He rambled on and on, and all Amethyst could do was stay by his side and let it gush forth until spent, as she had through all his other tragedies—and they'd added up to quite a few. Her duty was to comfort him with her presence, should he not desire words of condolence. Then he began to blame Anne, once again.

"She curses me, continues to plague me. Why, even if I had her rotting body exhumed and burned like the witch she was, as I did with that deplorable Becket, her soul would continue to plague me, for it is her soul that lives. Her body is but a headless putrefying corpse, but her soul...oh, her soul is very much alive, intact, and will not leave me alone!" He faced the wall and began screaming at Anne, visible only to his mind as he beheld her, and irrationally but continually entertained her presence. "Cease to control my life, Anne, quit me and my family, go on to another victim, just leave me and let me live my remaining years in peace, free from your evil spells and doings!" he shouted to the blank wall. "Revenge is what you wished, I know, and you have achieved your ends. I stand here in defeat, I acknowledge your power, I have relinquished you from your earthly restraints, so go about the spirit world among your fellow demons and let me live in peace among the living."

"Sire..." Amethyst held a goblet to his dry, cracked lips. "Please drink some wine, you must calm down."

He took a gulp, and she wiped a trickle from his chin. She didn't even know if he was aware she was with him. It mattered not to her whether he remembered; the important thing was he'd called for her and she was there.

She wanted to remind him that he had a strong, healthy son, the son he'd prayed for, the son Anne could never take away. How could he be cursed when the heir he'd always longed for lay alive and breathing, in the very next room? But she did not speak, for he would not hear her.

She simply held the goblet to his lips, let him drink, and when his meal came, fed it to him. He took it in, reflexively, chewing, swallowing, yet not tasting, the food he so vehemently relished and enjoyed as a sensual interlude, now merely sustaining his body. He then closed his eyes and slept, as did baby Edward in the next chamber.

* * *

Jane's body was interred in Windsor Castle's St. George's Chapel. "When my time comes, I shall rest next to her, the mother of my only prince, to lie side by side with her throughout eternity," he sobbed.

* * *

He retreated into his chambers for several weeks, and emerged only to attend council meetings. One eve, he summoned Amethyst to his chamber and she obediently complied, sensing that he was ready to make love to her.

She realized she'd guessed correctly when she entered his retiring room and found him hunched over a wine goblet at his writing desk. His burly arms supported his head, his eyes stared straight ahead, not turning to look her way when she entered, but fixed steadily on the dying embers in the hearth. She could tell he was engrossed in thought and did not disturb him until he was ready. She guessed he was thinking of Jane.

A minute later, he heaved a deep sigh and, running his hands over his ever-thinning hair, gave her a half-smile, motioning her to sit.

"Amethyst, I did you a terrible disservice and I beg you to forgive me."

"Do not apologize, my lord. You are in deep mourning and I am here to comfort you." She sat across from him.

"I would have died of loneliness had you not been here when I needed you. I need you, my love. Like I never needed another human being. Through it all, you have always been by my side. And that is where I want you to stay. Become my queen. I have my heir, the kingdom is secured. All I want is for you to reign with me through the rest of my days."

"Please, my lord, Jane is only dead a few weeks. You mustn't think of remarriage so soon," she chided him gently, emphasizing the "please".

"I must! I must have you by my side." This was not a romantic marriage proposal; it was a desperate entreaty.

"I shall marry you, my lord," she agreed, without the elation of a first-time bride-to-be. Sadly, that was not in her destiny. "But not while you are still in mourning."

"Oh, Amethyst..." he sighed, a deep heavy sigh from the depths of his soul. "I don't know how it happened. Jane had been a mouse, so plain and quiet, then she blossomed into a beauty, and I simply could not stand being without her. She was so sincere, so soft-spoken...lacking in your fire and passion, of course, lacking your spirited allure, but that is what I found so compelling about her. I simply wanted to take that wilting flower and watch it bloom, and bloom she did. I did not mean to turn you away, but when you were gone, I missed you more than ever."

"Please do not bother, Henry. You asked for me, and I am back. I shall help you through your period of grief, and then mayhap later we can discuss a marriage, after Christmas, after the new year. At least let a new year enter our lives."

"Aye, as you wish. Just make me feel young again, Amethyst," he implored her.

Of course she knew what that meant. He did not want to whip out his lute and begin dancing a pavane. With practiced acquiescence she sat upon the king's lap and began stroking his hair. She parted the ermine-trimmed robe and kneaded the rigid muscles beneath his linen shirt, feeling the tautness relax under her fingers. They both stood up with precision timing and he led her over to the bed. He removed her bodice, unfastened her skirts, letting them spill to the floor around her feet. He lifted her as if she were his precious crown itself, and placed her on the bed amidst the velvet coverings and down pillows strewn about.

He kissed her and she returned his kiss, mechanically, dutifully.

She closed her eyes, and suddenly, at the unbidden vision of Matthew, her pulse quickened and she let herself be taken away into the realm of pure fantasy. She straddled him, as they no longer coupled in the missionary position, for his massive bulk atop her would have crushed her bones. She tried to forget his overpowering corpulence as she moved against him, running her tongue over his earlobes, over the thick neck, down the colossal bulkiness of his chest.

She took his member twixt her fingers and realized it was not fully engorged, but pliant in her hand, lacking the erect, throbbing urgency on which the king usually prided his sexual prowess.

"Sire…" she whispered. He was mumbling something incoherent, controlling their movements, slow at first. Then as he too realized his passion was not aroused, he began thrusting more rapidly, in a circular motion, his breathing labored and heavy. She lay atop him, her thighs firmly locked around his huge girth, accommodating his every move. He grabbed her buttocks and futilely tried to push himself into her.

"Oh, Lord, Amethyst," he moaned as he held her trapped in his grasp and began shoving himself against her wildly. She waited for him to explode within her, but felt nothing. "Just finish me, finish me…" he panted as she buried her face in his shoulder and felt him straining desperately to fulfill his obligation to her as a man to a woman. But still nothing happened.

It amounted to a sputtering, stammering apology that embarrassed them both. He blamed his impotence on his preoccupation with his matters at hand, wondering if he could please his future queen if duty demanded it. The only thing that reassured him was that he no longer had Anne to blame for his impotence.

It bothered Amethyst not that the king was unable to perform, for she knew he was still in deep shock and was not yet ready to function normally. The thought of being his queen gladdened her, but she no longer felt the spark of excitement as in the beginning. Her duty to him would be as a wife first—she would be queen simply because he was king.

* * *

Amethyst traveled home to Warwick Castle for Christmas at the king's insistence. The mourning continued through the holiday season and though she would have stayed had he wanted her to. But she heaved a relieved sigh when he ordered her into a carriage on the first of December and sent her north, for the mood around court depressed her greatly.

"You will be all right, sire?" Their breaths came in puffs in the frigid air. She pulled her ermine wrap closer to block out the biting chill that had lain frost upon the ground. Branches and bushes hung laden under its crystal encumbrance.

"I shall be fine. This is my idea, remember?" He blew into his hands.

"Are you sure you will not come to Warwick with me?" She knew he wouldn't but she had to ask once more afore departing. "You would be in warm, welcoming company, and the folk would be so honored by your presence."

"Nay, I shall stay at court, but thank you for the invitation, I shall promise to visit your fair Warwickshire on my next progress. I shall stay with my son, as it is his first Christmas, I would like us to spend as much time as possible together." His eyes lit up at the mention of his son.

She grasped his hand. "Sire, I am so sorry the way it all happened, so sorry."

"No, do not be." He took her other hand, warming them both. "I had my Jane for the short time I did, and for that I shall be eternally grateful to you for having given her to me."

"I did not give her to you, my lord—" She wanted that misconception corrected.

"Had it not been for you, I never would have considered Jane. 'Tis in that regard that Prince Edward is partly yours, Amethyst. Think of him as the son you and I shall never have."

She reeled back with that, shaking her head. "Oh, sire, Edward belongs to Jane! She lost her life in order to give him life, to give him to you, she knew how desperately you needed him—"

"Always think of Edward as part of you, Amethyst. Why do you think I named him Edward?"

She gasped. "Surely not…not for my father, sire!"

"Just do not tell anyone." He lowered his voice, although only the coachman was present, and he was nodding off in his seat. "Any son that would have been born of our love would have been named Edward. So why not my Prince? Just do not mention it to any Warwickshire folk, especially your sister, for I believe her head would swell."

Amethyst assured him, "Topaz's head is well set, my lord, and she has settled back into the Warwickshire country life quite fittingly, with her menagerie and her caring for the poor."

"Well, you bid her a fond greeting from me, for she has been behaving impeccably since her release." He handed her a bag of gold coins. "For the people of Warwickshire."

"Why, thank you." She took it from him and dropped it into the pouch at her waist. "She will be pleased. my lord, I know my sister. Nary a word of a rebellious nature has escaped her lips since she once again set foot upon free soil."

"Mayhap this means she and her husband will reconcile," he rattled off casually enough—of course. He knew naught of her growing love for Matthew.

An unexpected stab of jealousy shot through Amethyst. She tore her gaze from the king into the outlying meadows, following the fluffy white dots in the distance as the sheep grazed, simple and aimless as they were. "Mayhap, sire. There is naught keeping them apart, now, is there?" But she knew better.

A blatant contradiction ran through her head as her mouth formed the words she felt she had to speak to the king. Topaz didn't want Matthew back, she'd never loved him and all he wanted was to be free of her.

He glanced at the thick clouds. "You must be gone, lest you encounter a storm on the way. I daresay these clouds look fraught with heavy snowflakes. I bid you Godspeed, my Lady Amethyst."

They kissed, lightly, quickly. She waved to him as the carriage lumbered through the long inner courtyard and past the gates of Hampton Court Palace. She strained her neck to watch as the gatehouse flanked by its crenelated towers shrank into the distance.

She was on her way to her family, her beloved Warwick Castle, and—Matthew.

Chapter Sixteen

Warwick Castle, 1537

"Please fetch my mount if he is up for a journey to Kenilworth," Amethyst instructed a groom.

"Why do you wish to visit *him*?" Topaz tossed out with a matching toss of her head.

Why, indeed? Amethyst thought. The boys were no longer there. As much as she loved to see her nephews, they had been the only logical link twixt her and Matthew.

"He's the father of my nephews and we are friends," she offered an explanation, then berating herself for feeling the need to do so. "He is entertaining the Duke of Norfolk and his retinue this Christmas and invited me. Does it bother you?"

"Nay, not in the least," she sniffed. "I've no use for him. We are civil to each other, that is it. We do not associate otherwise." Head held high, she looked down her nose at Amethyst.

"Then I shall be on my way. I shall see you in a few days' time." The groom led her mount to her and patted the brushed mane.

"Fit as a fiddle, my lady," he announced.

The fact was, Matthew had invited Sabine as well, but she'd declined, offering her duties at Warwick as an excuse. However, Emerald was already at Kenilworth, for she and Norfolk had just been betrothed.

* * *

Matthew greeted her carriage at the gatehouse. He lifted her out and gathered her into his arms before her feet even touched the ground. His eyes sparkled against his ermine cloak, which blended with the newly fallen blanket of snow sprinkled over the ground. He lifted his face to the sun and its rays glinted like chunks of gold in his eyes. A sunbleached streak running through his hair caught the sun's radiance as his lips parted in a gleaming smile.

His body strained to come closer to her through the layers of robes and wraps. His eyes conveyed that unspoken message. As their lips met, her mind traveled back to that evening...once again she was with him before the fire, stroking his hair, his lips hot and demanding.

"How fares the king and our new Prince?" he asked as they entered his solar, candles ablaze, echoing the two roaring fires on either side of the oak-paneled chamber.

"Oh, Matthew, he is in a bad, bad way. The loss of Queen Jane has put him into a state of melancholy even I cannot fetch him out of. Pray God the company of his son, along with Elizabeth and Mary will bestow upon him a speedy recovery."

"Aye, that was quite a shock to all of us, the death of Queen Jane. Had she not attended the christening—"

"Of course we all know that is the reason. She was not strong enough to withstand all that pomp and ceremony. But the king blames Anne. That's all he rambles on about now, Anne still casting spells from beyond the grave. I cannot reach him, Cromwell cannot reach him. I worry for him."

"Has it affected his physical health?" Matthew gestured to a chair before the fire.

"Well, his appetite has returned, with a vengeance." She sat and smoothed her skirts. "He's become quite...well, portly." She never thought she'd hear herself admit that her revered king, her lifelong idol, would be described with anything less than splendor.

"Well, that is a good sign." He sat beside her as two servitors laid out plates of cheese, bread and fruit. A steward brought a jug of wine and two goblets. "He would be in a bad way indeed were he not eating at all."

"But he uses it as an excuse, a comfort...he's lost interest in all his favorite activities, tennis, hunting, even music... " What she couldn't tell her dear Matthew was that the king had lost interest his favorite activity of all—lovemaking. Even her enticing overtures, her lace and Chinese silk chemises, the jasmine and violet oils, no longer aroused his interest. She offered this much: "When I try to reason with him by telling him that Jane would have wanted him to go on with his life and not mourn her so terribly, he simply scowls and sinks his teeth into another chicken leg or cherry tart."

"Is another wife in order?" He looked at her questioningly, and she could detect in his eyes that silent plea. Her heart surged with warmth as she received his unspoken signal.

"He...asked me to marry him, but I told him to wait until after the Christmas season, for he is still in shock from Jane's death and should not be contemplating remarriage right now." She lifted her goblet and took a sip. "He's got his heir now, two daughters who love him dearly, he's got Cromwell and his fool to cheer him and...of course, myself for companionship and comfort. He must help himself out of this. Then mayhap discussions of marriage would be in order."

"So you're going to marry him," came out flat and defeated.

"Well, Matthew," she jumped in, "He may not even ask. I am not counting on it, put it that way."

That seemed to brighten him up, for he happily plucked up a wedge of cheese and ate it with gusto. "The main meal will be in the great hall when Emerald and Norfolk get back. My, she's turned out to be quite a lady."

"I haven't seen Emerald since my last visit, nearly a year ago. Aye, she is indeed a beautiful young lady. Our mother marvels at how much she resembles a young Margaret Pole. Holding their miniatures up side by side one could barely tell the difference."

"Have she and Norfolk decided on a wedding date?" he asked.

"Nay, but she said something about wanting a winter wedding, with the newness of the chaste virgin snow around her." She smiled in great pride of her sister, for she guarded her virginity like a chest of gold. "That's Emerald. The family poet."

"As you are the family beauty." He said evenly, not in a flattering way.

"That is debatable," she countered.

"Do you...do you intend to remain at court? If you do not marry the king, I mean," he hesitated, and she wondered if he was afraid of sounding too brusque. "I mean...do you ever find yourself longing for Warwick Castle?"

She wanted to tell him how she found herself longing for him. "Aye, all the time. But the king needs me more. Especially now, with the loss of Jane."

"He does depend on you, doesn't he? Do you consider it a burden at times?" he asked, helping himself to a chunk of bread.

"Nay, I do not consider it a burden. He has done so much for me...made me a member of the court when I was but a young novice, brought me under his wing, showed me how to love...he spared Topaz."

He finished his bread and looked over at her. "Topaz's saving grace was Queen Jane's birthing of Edward. But it ultimately was your idea."

"Ah, aye, but he told me he would never execute her. Had Jane not brought forth Edward, Topaz would simply have remained a prisoner. A comfortable prisoner, but a prisoner nonetheless." Not having eaten since that morn, she swept up some bread and cheese.

"Amethyst, do you truly believe Topaz was sincere in her forfeiture of the crown?"

She nodded. "Oh, aye, Matthew. She got on her knees and thanked God with racking sobs when I delivered the news that Jane had given the king a male heir. I never saw her humbled so before God or any man. Topaz humble herself? Never. She always held the loftiest position in the land. Until now. Aye, her quest failed and it is history."

"You were right when you said I did not know my wife at all," he admitted. "All her anger, her resentment, I thought her incessant wailing was her only outlet. I never knew she would carry out her plans. She seemed to ebb and flow like the tide..." He inhaled and refilled his goblet. "After one of her tirades, she would calm down, be almost jovial, her sense of humor would come shining through, she would sit with the lads and read to them, we would spend hours laughing, joking, she would be on an even keel until...it seemed to go with the phases of the moon, or her monthly flux at times. After a while it got to be like the moon dial on the clock. "He sipped. "I would dread its full face coming round to show itself, for that was when Topaz would begin her tantrums, and keep it up for five or six days, till the moon would wane, then her mood would languish right along with it, until the next time around."

"How about when she was breeding?" Amethyst plucked a few grapes from the stems.

"Then she was subdued...not jovial, not sprightly, but cool and aloof. I could not get near her, then during her confinement she became nearly invalid. She implored me to hold her hand or rub her belly. But I never knew her, I never really, intimately knew her, the way a husband and wife should."

"Mayhap you are lucky." Amethyst smiled over the rim of her goblet. "Do you have any regrets?"

"Nay, I have not. Topaz and I were never meant to be." His voice did not betray any sadness or remorse; his eyes sparkled in the firelight just as they always did. She knew Matthew hid no contrition; that sparkle was genuine, and no remorse could show through without dimming them.

She felt confident enough to mention the king's surmise. "The king wondered if a reconciliation was in order now that Topaz has mended her ways."

He laughed, a full-throated guffaw, shaking his head resolutely. "Never, never could we ever exist together in peace. Her ideas, her ways, are much too reformist and perverse for me. I admire what she does for the poor, for she seems to have boundless energy with which to travel dusty, nearly impassable roads with wagonloads of food and clothes, but she and I shall never exist on the same plane, not here, not in any other unearthly life. Besides..." He turned his thoughts inward and his eyes darkened. "I could never forgive her for what happened to the lads. If it weren't for her relentless quest for the impossible, the boys would be here with me...free, not locked up as ransom for some future rebellion that might never happen."

"But Matthew, they are quite comfortable. They do not live like prisoners. They have books, they have servants, they have food and drink aplenty—"

"They have confinement, Amethyst," he broke in sharply. "They have four walls, that is their home, that is their world. They shall grow up like..." He halted immediately and thrust the cup to his lips.

"Like my father?" she finished his sentence.

He shot her an embarrassed glance.

"Nay, Matthew. My father had but one day of freedom from the time he was locked up at age eight. One day. He spent his years in the Bell Tower, a small, musty, ancient prison that afforded no comfort. I was born there, but remember none of it. The lads are treated like princes by comparison. The king made sure of it."

"The king cannot be too sure of Topaz, can he?" Matthew cupped his hands round his goblet. "He obviously still considers her a threat. Otherwise he would let the lads free."

"I told you, Matthew, the king has not been..." How to put it? "...not quite in his right mind since Anne began wielding her dubious allure. He let Topaz go because I convinced him she was honest. I dare not ask him to set the lads free, not yet. But of course I plan to, when he regains his keen perception and becomes the great ruler we all adore."

He cast her another glance, cocked his brow and shook his head. "Amethyst, are you sure you do not see the king differently than the rest of us do?"

"What do you mean?"

"With all due respect, after all he is the king, and has treated me with nothing but kindness and high regard, but he has survived several tragedies, has lost wives and children, and is advancing in age." That last observation wasn't something subjects dared voice out loud. "Do you believe his condition will be reversed?"

"Oh, aye, Matthew," she assured him, and herself at the same time. "Living through tragedies and striving to gather the pieces of his life is no reason to give up on him. Look at what Henry's been through. A lesser man would have expired from much less of a strain than Henry's endured." She sat forward. "You do not see him, Matthew.

You do not see how ingenious he is, how resourceful. Why, when he wanted to be free of Catherine, and the church would not grant the divorce, he declared himself head of his own church. No king has ever done that before. He knows what he wants, and most of all, knows all the intricacies of how to go about getting what he wants. He will survive this, Matthew, wait and see. He will once again be the lean, fit, sharp Henry we all once knew." *Oh, I hope*, she added silently.

His eyes looked into hers. "I admire your convictions, Amethyst, and I hold your reverence for the king in the highest esteem. But I need to ask you one more time... should the king not recover... or God forbid retreat into a worse state of health... please come back home." He reached across the table and grasped her hand. "Come here to Kenilworth. I want you here."

"I cannot offer you an answer until... and if... the time ever comes." Of course she couldn't commit herself, but, oh, how she longed to throw herself into his arms and cry "Yes, yes, I want you, too!"

He went on, "I want you here now, but you seem to believe your fate lies elsewhere. I have wanted you here with me for a long time now. I am in love with you, Amethyst. I want you to marry me." His grip on her hand tightened and his gaze intensified.

The goblet grew warm in her other hand, as her body responded in ardor, so unlike her feelings for Henry. She felt as if she possessed two hearts, one for each of these different, very unique men, each extraordinarily special in his own way, one a king to be revered and venerated, the other to be melded with her own existence, to share the joys and sorrows of plain Warwickshire folk.

She knew she could love both, for she did, in different ways. But could she be everything to both these men…the regal courtier, as well as the mistress of an esteemed yet provincial noble's castle?

"Matthew…I cannot expect you to wait for me…not whilst I am still in service to the king." It pained her to say this, but she could not in all fairness dangle him like a puppet.

He let her hand go but his gaze stayed on her. "There, listen to yourself, the way you put it… 'in service'. Like it is a task you must perform, like working his fief or trundling off to Calais with his navy. Is that true love, Amethyst? Do you love the king?"

She nodded in all honesty. "Aye, I love him, yet, he is the king and I am but his humble servant, and even if I became his queen, I would only be queen consort, still a subject, and he cannot ever—"

"Say it, Amethyst," he demanded. "I want to hear you say that you no longer love the king the way you once did, what you once had is gone, dead, buried along with his martyred wives and unborn children, never to be resurrected. You are fooling yourself if you think you can return to court after all that has happened, and still be to him what you once were. Go back to him if you wish. But you will return here in due time, and I shall be waiting."

Matthew had said exactly what she had been afraid to even think. Even though Matthew knew that she and the king had been lovers, he touched on a nerve that went straight to her heart and made her realize what she'd been fighting all along. Yet, she couldn't leave Henry, finally free and about to make her queen—once more.

"Tell me, Amethyst." His eyes, darkened to a deep green, were riveted to her so that she dared not look away. "Tell me what you and the king had is over, and that you want me."

"All right!" she blurted. "You are right! I no longer love him the way a woman loves a man. If I marry him it would be out of love, but not in love the way I once was."

He sat back and made fists. "I knew it! Amethyst, he is becoming an old man. He has his heir, he does not need you…mayhap he does need you in one way, but not the way I need you. Amethyst, I love you so much, oh, how I want you!"

She could hold back no more. She jumped up and sat atop his lap. He embraced her, crushing her body to his. He slid her skirts to her thigh tops and caressed her sensitive flesh, seeking, winding though all the lace and satin. They explored, searched, and finally found the core of each other's desire.

He lowered her to the soft bearskin rug in front of the fire, one of many soft warm comforts he'd been denied by Topaz. Then he began kissing her, slowly at first, but seemed to know her most receptive spots; the tips of her earlobes, the hollow of her neck. He removed her robe and moved down to her breasts, kissing, licking, torturingly slowly. He continued this way, running over the sensitive backs of her knees with his fingertips, trailing hot kisses down her stomach. He removed her chemise and brushed it over her naked body. She ached for him. "Matthew," she could only raggedly gasp, for her voice was gone. Slowly he removed his doublet, shirt, breeches and hose. She was ready, dizzily gasping, yet he continued in his calm, slow manner, further torturing her with each deliberate kiss, each flick of his fingertips over her burning body. She panted, yet his breathing stayed as cool and even as if he were tending his garden.

As they made love she exploded into a searing frenzy of ecstasy. She lost her senses and let eternity carry her away.

He wouldn't let her stop to rest, although she was panting now out of exhaustion. Her leg muscles were giving out. Shifting her body so that they were now on their sides, she clamped her thigh around his back and stroked him from behind as they made love with powerful intensity. She erupted again, this time from within.

As she felt him growing soft inside her, she clasped her hands round his head, bringing him to her in a long, lingering kiss that incited her desire once more.

"I must rest, Amethyst, I must rest." He spilled out of her, lying beside her, their mingled moisture glowing on their bodies. "My, what have they taught you at court!"

* * *

The lovers entered the great hall hand in hand. His magnificent plate of silver adorned the trestle tables. The candles glowed, the minstrels tuned their lutes in the gallery. Present were nobles from the neighboring shires, and since Norfolk and Emerald were the guests of honor, several of Norfolk's relatives had been invited, including his sister, her husband, and their flighty daughter Katharine Howard.

Katharine Howard seemed enchanted with Amethyst, and begged her to tell some stories of the court.

"What is it really like there? Is Hampton as sumptuous as we hear it is? How does the king spend his free time? What time does court retire for the evening? Is there dancing and merrymaking at all times? Is there any hanky panky in the deep dark passageways?" she inquired, giggling the whole time. Amethyst told her only of the happy times, of the musical evenings when everyone sang and danced, the mimes, tumbling jesters, bawdy jokes and flowing wine. She didn't relate the tragedies of the last few years, of Anne's disastrous end, for Anne had been Katharine's cousin. She omitted to mention the grief the king now suffered over his beloved Jane. Court was not a place the feisty Katharine Howard would want to be right now, but Amethyst didn't relay her true thoughts to the impressionable youngster, who only wanted fables of cavorting knights and maidens.

"Nan never told me much about court," Katharine said, her eyes darting over to size up every young male that entered the great hall, from the Duke of Buckingham to the small and wiry marshal seating the guests. "Her reign was so short," she said, her voice taking on a serious tone Amethyst didn't think the girl was capable of.

"Did you know your cousin well?" Amethyst asked.

"Not much, though my father and Anne's mother were brother and sister. She was nearly twenty years my senior. But I tried to follow all the happenings at court when she was first brought there, to her last days as queen. Such a fool, my cousin. She had naught but her charms to entice the king, had she not?"

"It was Anne's biggest tragedy that she did not give the king the son he wanted," Amethyst now opened up, that pang of sorrow still surfacing in the small piece of her heart she'd reserved for Anne.

"Had I been Nan, I would not have borne him any children, for that seems safer than bringing forth a girl," Katharine declared. "Look at the way Catherine of Aragon wasted away, and the way he saw fit to dispose of Nan. I say 'tis safer to remain barren, then no one can be blamed."

Oh, Henry certainly would have blamed a barren wife just as much, Amethyst thought, precisely the reason she'd stepped aside for Jane. No one knew that better than she. But why reveal Henry's darker side to the likes of Katharine Howard, who would likely be married off to some social climber who'd squander her meager dowry.

"'Tis a pity the way your cousin Anne met her end, and I am truly sorry," Amethyst offered her sympathy. "I always felt sorry for her."

"Think naught of it," Katharine replied. "For now I believe the king needs a queen who can coddle him in his old age, a genteel wife of his own generation who cannot outdance him nor outride him, but who will see him through to his final moments, and finally…outlive him."

"My, you have the king halfway to his grave already." Amethyst tried not to let this simpleton annoy her, for she knew the king not and never would.

"Nay, Madam, he seems old to me because I am but seventeen, same as the Princess Mary. I see the king as a father…no, a grandfather!" She giggled, then focused her fleeting attentions on a young rogue with plumed hat jauntily cocked to one side, the feather's end brushing his green doublet.

"Excuse me, Madam…for I see someone with whom I have some unfinished business!" She flounced away in a cloud of heady perfume and that boundless energy of the young.

Amethyst remembered wistfully when she was Katharine's age, not quite so flighty and emptyheaded, but she remembered, as it was not that long ago, how the king took a fancy to her, invited her to court, made her his own…just at that age, radiating youth, naivety, and the promise of a thousand tomorrows.

She pondered Katharine's insight, surprising as it was. Maybe Henry did need one of his contemporaries to accompany his slide into senility. Or could she still be what he needed to rejuvenate that spark she knew was still within him, veiled by his shroud of grief? Ironically, now that he was finally free of any wives plus the burden of producing an heir, the prospect of marriage to him had become just a bit dimmer.

* * *

Emerald and the Duke of Norfolk arrived, and Amethyst barely recognized her sister. She'd grown so tall; with her headdress she was nearly a head taller than Amethyst, her gawky body had blossomed into that of a curvaceous woman, her breasts swelled beneath her low neckline, and she carried herself with the grace worthy of the title she bore.

They embraced warmly, and Emerald introduced her to the Duke. "This is Thomas Howard, Duke of Norfolk. Thomas, my sister Amethyst, Duchess of Warwick."

He took her hand, they exchanged pleasantries, did not mention Topaz, the king, or his tragedies. It was not the time. It was Christmas, and Amethyst was basking in the afterglow of lovemaking. None of the guests commented when she sat beside him on the dais; it seemed so right and natural, but it stirred up an element of surprise when she announced her return to court on the day after New Year's Day.

"But Amethyst, we thought you would stay on with…with us here at Warwick," Emerald said as Amethyst supervised her maids in the packing of her gowns and delicate undergarments. "You and Matthew…you seem to get along so well together, and we all know what is amiss with the king."

She faced her sister, reached out to touch the young face, the fresh skin, so unblemished, aglow with the cold country air and unmarred by life's tribulations. "Emerald, no one knows what's really amiss with the king, himself included. Anyone calling themselves as faithful a friend as I would not dream of leaving him now. Matthew and I... we have become close, for we share a common bond, the lads, and I have arranged for him to visit them in the Tower, and I inform him of their condition, but to leave court now would be unthinkable."

"Oh. I thought you and Matthew shared something much more deep and special than that. I was hoping you would return to Warwickshire as Lord Gilford's mistress."

Was her sister especially perceptive as were so many precocious youngsters, or had Matthew revealed his feelings to the family?

She managed an ineffectual laugh. "That, my dear, is outlandish! What would Topaz think?"

"Who cares?" Emerald echoed Amethyst's thoughts, that she, so well versed in the art of diplomacy she'd learned at court, didn't dare speak. "She stated one time that if you ever marry, she hoped it would be a respectable time after King Henry's death."

Amethyst shut the lid on one of her traveling trunks. "Oh, Emerald, it gladdens me to think that Topaz cares so much for the king... after all that had transpired, I believe she has finally mended her ways... finally."

"Oh, it has nothing to with her caring for the king, Amethyst."

"Well, what then?" She turned to Emerald. "Why not, then out of respect for his memory?"

"To ascertain the legitimacy of your child," Emerald stated.

"What cheek!" Surely Topaz could not have guessed of the depth of her relationship with the king. "She is overly presumptuous and should learn her place once and for all! And for you to go repeating it... Emerald, I am surprised at you. Surely you do not think—"

"Oh, no, Amethyst." Emerald's eyes grew wide, capturing that youthful innocence that had not given way to her tall stature or curvaceous figure. "Why... you and the king? The thought is absurd." She laughed, her young voice cool and clear as the virgin snow capping the trees.

"Aye, the idea is absurd," Amethyst now agreed. "The king is who he is and I am... who I am. The thought of carrying his child is..." She remembered what she'd thought of it, how badly she'd wanted to give Henry the one wish he was living for, but now, especially now that he had Edward and her desire to bear his children had given way to a simpler wish to comfort him, she felt that burden lift off her shoulders. "... it matters not, he has his male heir and is happy... enough."

"Aye, I believe the king will be happy to see you again." Emerald gave her a smile that faded as she added, "but I'll be sorry to see you go."

"I'll be back soon," she answered her sister, but put a question mark at the end of the sentence when she repeated it in her mind. "I shall be happy to see Hal again."

* * *

She bade farewell to Matthew on the eve of her departure, for he was leaving before dawn to inspect his tenant cottages in Dumbarton and would be gone before she rose. They met in a chamber in the north wing of the castle that he used when it was overflowing with guests; for it was small and afforded no view of the surrounding countryside. In fact, it faced a corner of the inner courtyard. He was waiting for her, under the covers of soft wool trimmed with ermine. She slipped twixt the sheets and removed her robe, her only garment. She'd braved the drafty halls just to surprise him. He extinguished the one small bedside candle and as her eyes adjusted to the dimness, the room brightened in the whitish glow of the fallen snow in the courtyard below.

"Amethyst, so many things have changed since I realized how I felt about you. I perceive things, I can hear, I can feel, I can taste the wind right now. You've made me feel that there's more to life than running a castle and shouting orders and making crops grow. You've made me realize I'm alive."

His words were so enthralling, it was a wonder he hadn't hired a lyricist to put them to music. If he'd been able to play an instrument, she was sure he'd have serenaded her with those very words.

"No one has ever told me that," she told him the truth.

"Well, that is the way I feel. I went outside today and for the first time I can see how beautiful it is. I can tell you the shape of every cloud that was in the sky today, I can tell you which way the breeze was blowing. I can tell you how many birds I saw today and what colors they were. I want to enjoy life before it is too late. I want to awaken my senses and let the world inside. I never want to lose you, Amethyst. If there is any way we can work things out, we must try."

"Matthew, I will always be a part of your life, but I could not leave Henry, not now." That truth stood twixt them like a castle wall.

"But he is not here," Matthew dismissed his king with a wave of his hand. "It is us tonight. Let us make it last."

"Aye, Matthew. Tonight." She wrapped her arms round him with their gazes locked. She saw every feature in the moonlight beaming down on them from the heavens.

He smoothed her hair, his fingers playing along the back of her neck, making her quiver all over. Wordlessly, he kissed her. The scent of his body was clean, and aroused even her taste buds.

His hands were so nimble and skillful, she let herself float away as their mouths locked together. He tossed aside his linen shirt and peeled off his hose. His body then covered hers and all she could hear were their gasps and moans of delight and their heartbeats quickening together. Her hands found and massaged him until he throbbed under her touch. She eased him inside her and he started thrusting slowly, gyrating and moving with her, stroking her, fondling her, playing her like the strings of a lute. He put her to music. Their bodies pulsated like a giant drum; their bodies attuned to each other in an exquisite blend as they exploded into crashing chords and soft, tender harmony, fading into oblivion as the music ended.

He wasn't finished yet. As his fingers teased and circled, thrusting gently, she felt him explode as another climax intensified into a shuddering crescendo.

She leaned over and kissed him again, her gratification giving way to another wave of arousal, as she ran her tongue over his supple body.

The covers spilled to the floor and now a bluish-white glow bathed their naked bodies as he started to respond. She pulled him to her once again, and once more the music leapt and swirled in an encore to a breathtaking performance that consumed them both. For the first time in her life, music appeared before her eyes. Then, once again, it faded.

At the edge of a dream, not quite asleep, she thought she heard Matthew talking to her. "Hal and I have not made music quite like that in a very long time, Matthew," she thought she mumbled.

When she next opened her eyes, the brightness of morning blinded her and Matthew was gone.

She noticed she had on her finger a gold ring set with a brilliant pear-shaped amethyst surrounded by tiny diamonds. She slid it off as easily as he must've slid it on in her sleep, and read an inscription inside. "wait I shall wait I shall wait I shall…" all around the circumference of the band, in an infinite circle of eternity. Would she make him wait forever? It was not her decision to make.

Chapter Seventeen

"Come here, let me hold you," were his first words to her as she entered his audience chamber. His next words were "get out" to the grooms and a steward.

"How did you do while I was away, sire?" He embraced her—how different his heavy bulk felt from the trim Matthew, how much more demanding and possessing was the king's touch. But she had missed it—aye, she had, and she found comfort rather than passion in his arms again, at Hampton Court, surrounded by regalia and splendor.

"My son has an appetite like a horse," he bragged about his second favorite possession after the kingdom. "He suckles on the wet nurse's duckys like the world is coming to an end!" he boasted with pride. She sighed in relief at hearing him put it this way. "I got out and did some riding on the warmer days, walked miles and miles, and felt my blood flow through me for the first time since October."

"Your leg ulcer is better then?" She glanced at his leg, wrapped as always, but it didn't seem to distress him.

"It seems to be subsiding." He lifted his leg and patted the infected area. "But I'm sure it will be back to haunt me."

"Oh, sire, you seem so much happier now, the folk in Warwickshire as everywhere...they worry about you so!"

"No need to worry any more, for I have provided them with an heir. The kingdom shall not go kingless." He raised his head and gave her a haughty grin.

"Nay, they love you, my lord," she piled on the praise he craved. "They are doubly pleased about Prince Edward."

"I must get him betrothed." He chuckled, and she knew his sense of humor had once more blessed him.

"Speaking of betrothed, my sister Emerald is to marry Thomas Howard, Duke of Norfolk." She removed her cloak and tossed it on a chair, slipped out of her shoes and sidled over to the window seat.

"Ah, Thomas. Good man, good man." He followed, stopping to fill a goblet with wine. "How about your other sister, Genghis Khan?"

"She is somber and quiet, tending her animals, no one has come round to court her." *That report should make him even more joyous*, she thought. The fewer thorns sticking in his side, the better.

He laughed. "No one has the brass whirligigs to court her. A repressed queen would make a right tyrant of a wife."

"You are right, my lord." She nodded. "She is not interested in marriage."

"But I am, Amethyst." He sat next to her in the window seat, a seat for one, so they were a bit crowded. He pulled her closer and lay her head on his chest. "The new year is upon us and I want us to finally become man and wife... king and queen."

"Are you truly over Jane, sire?" She had to bring this up, not wanting to rush into marriage if he wasn't ready. "I want you to think about that carefully. Mayhap we should wait until she has been gone a year. That would look more respectful in the eyes of the kingdom as well."

"Nay, I do not want to wait. Jane would have wanted me to carry on with my life, and she knew how you and I feel about each other. I have never stopped loving you, and the passage of another year will only serve to waste more time." He lifted her headdress off and removed the pins himself, flipping them on the floor.

"All right, sire," she sighed, wondering where that spark of excitement, that thrilling rush had escaped to. But she let him gather her hair in bunches and when one thing led to another, she forced Matthew from her mind.

* * *

Then she realized that her life was going to take another turn, possibly a tragic one.

She was carrying Matthew's child.

She'd missed her monthly flux twice, and now by March, she was sure of it. Her dresses didn't fit, she vomited every morning and could barely keep anything down except milk-soaked bread—sometimes. Sharp biting pains like none she'd ever known pierced her lower abdomen.

She went to the only person she could possibly tell, the person she trusted, the person who had the power and the understanding to help her.

She went to Henry.

"My lord, I must speak to you of an urgent matter," she whispered as they sat on the dais, Henry tucking into a pheasant wing. She couldn't stand the sight of the feast spread before them.

He rarely danced anymore, for his leg ulcer now plagued him unmercifully. The dais was empty, the courtiers going about their dance like there was no king at all.

"Please, I need to tell you something." She couldn't wait until they reached their chambers. She was desperate to tell him, desperate for his help.

He swallowed and emptied his goblet into his mouth. With a burp, he turned to her. "Well, what is it?"

"I am with child, my lord."

He blinked and stared at her with bugged-out eyes. Before he could utter a word in response, out rushed, "Sire, it belongs to Matthew Gilford. I am at my wits' end. I know not what to do. He is still married to my sister, although he is in love with me. I love him, but…" Unable to hold back any longer, she began to cry, as she did so easily these days. "I so wanted to marry you, but I could never do you the disservice of expecting you to act as father of another man's child…"

To her relief and astonishment, his look of shock gentled to that of compassion. He patted her hand. "I am not upset, for I have my own problems and this pales in comparison. I shall take care of it for you."

"What will you do, my lord?" She knew he could help her—surely he had an answer she hadn't come up with, but Hal would know.

"Go to your chambers and I shall join you forthwith." He brushed her away as he grabbed another wing from his plate.

"But, sire, the meal is not yet over and I still have got to play my music—"

"Go to your chambers! Now!" Pointing towards the doors with his hand holding the wing, he pounded his other fist on the table. A few courtiers turned, but no one paid attention. They were used to the king's short temper and bouts of shouting.

But he'd never blown up at her this way. She cowered if he'd slammed her in the face with a rock. Obeying his command, she rose from the dais and, head held high, the train of her gown wound round her arm, exited the great hall with quiet dignity.

She paced her empty bedchamber. The fire sputtered out to a bed of glowing coals, but she did not feel the cold seeping through the leaded glass. She pulled the velvet curtains shut and watched them billow out to the tune of the wind that rattled the panes. The shock at the king's thundering reaction had given way to numbness as she sat, fingers laced over her abdomen and the life growing inside her, and waited.

He flung open her door, slamming it behind him. She did not rise, did not greet him or kiss his hand or embrace him. His burning anger seared her, as imposing as his physical presence.

He strode up to her and pulled her to her feet, his fingers in a tight grip round her arm. "I want the entire story from you now. When did this liaison begin?"

"Just…just this past Christmas, my lord." Her mouth went dry, her tongue thick. She needed liquid desperately but did not dare rise from the chair. "We were together on this visit, and that was the only time."

He took the final step that brought them nose to nose. She flinched at the sound of his pendants rattling. She waited for a stunning blow but it didn't come.

"All the while I thought you were barren and now you are carrying Matthew Gilford's child?" His grip on her arm intensified. It hurt. But she didn't dare pull away.

"I thought I was barren too, sire. You know how hard I tried. I even went to Dr. Butts who made up some concoction for me, but it never worked. You know how badly I wanted to give you an heir."

"My confidante, my lady, my special intimate, with whom I share everything, and you go behind my back whoring around Warwickshire, lying on your back and spreading your legs for your sister's husband?" He shook her arm, causing her entire body to rattle.

He may as well have struck her, for his words plunged through her heart like a dagger.

"It was not like that, sire." Her dry throat caused her voice to crack. "We—we love each other, the way you and I did, er—do..."

"Do not sass me, you whoring wench." He flung her backwards and she stumbled. "You refused to become my queen because I was married, and now you go and share another married man's bed?" He stomped over to the far side of the chamber. She waited for him to fling open the door and slam out. But he stayed. She prayed he'd leave without another outburst. Mayhap on the morrow he would think more clearly. Anne Boleyn's tortured soul invaded her mind, how his false accusations of that innocent victim cut short her life. But Amethyst had not committed adultery!

"Sire, I am your concubine, your mistress, but never have we exchanged vows in the eyes of God or the church," she tried to reason with this man half-crazed with jealousy, desperate to reason with him. "You and I are not married." Her voice calmed as she laid out her defense. She knew Henry intimately enough to know he admitted when he was wrong. She saw past the commanding monarch. She'd seen him stripped of his jewels, his crown, his regalia. She knew the man underneath. *He'll listen to me*, she assured herself.

"And never shall we be," he rasped. "You committed this…this act behind my back. Without telling me." His eyes were narrowed slits, spewing forth sparks of fury. "You knew of every wench I ever shared my bed with, wife or not. You knew everything. Do you take me for a fool, Amethyst?"

"N…nay…" No, her reasoning wasn't getting through to him. *Will he come to his senses tomorrow?* She feared not. A rash decision hit her—she needed to leave court, to plan a future far from here, far from danger. She would not let history repeat itself. She would not follow a headless Anne Boleyn to the grave.

"There is only one thing to do." Now his voice carried composure, but this frightened her even more, this unruffled dispassion. He was past the initial anger and working on the punishment.

She awaited the dreaded words and immediately began preparing herself for imprisonment in the Tower…the endless prayer for her soul's salvation…the walk up the scaffold steps to muffled drumbeats and gawking eyes…the black-masked executioner…his blade glinting in the sunlight…the block with its cup for her chin…the slash severing her life from earth…

"I shall marry you off," his words cut into her horrid thoughts, stunning her. "He will be a nobleman, worthy of your rank, for appearances' sake, although to me, you are nothing more than a common street whore." His sneer carried all the loathing he'd harbored for Anne. "That is the way I feel about you. You will raise your bastard child and I shall go on with my life."

The relief flooding through her prompted her to rush up to him. But she reeled back at the sight; his brows were drawn together in a furrow of rage, his lips drawn and tight, his fists clenched.

"Thank you, my lord, I…please find it in your heart to forgive me. Please do not punish the child. It is not his fault. It is God's will."

"God's will? God told you to lie on your back and fling your legs up into the air?" he spat. "You insult me, and you shall insult me no more. I shall marry you off, all right. To someone you rightfully deserve."

"Who?" she dared ask, knowing he must have someone in mind.

He answered her with a hateful snarl. "Just get yourself a wedding dress. And do not dare wear white."

"But please just tell me his name!" she dared demand this time.

"Sir Mortimer Pilkington." He hadn't hesitated for a second. He'd chosen her husband twixt the time she told him of her pregnancy and now. A nobleman. At least he wasn't casting her off onto some London fishmonger. His eyes raked over her one last time, as if to print her image into his memory, then he stomped from the chamber with a resolute slam of the door.

She was too numb with shock to even weep. She simply sat and thanked God he was letting her live.

She considered running after him, begging him to forgive her. She knew why he was punishing her like this. He no longer had her to himself; she carried another man's child, and this fact undermined the intimate closeness, the belonging they shared. She no longer belonged to him and him alone. He was insulted. But she could not go to him. Her time as the king's special one had ended.

* * *

He ordered her to stay confined to her apartments, and she took her meals there. He banned her from the great hall and dismissed her from the King's Musick. No one save the king knew she was carrying Matthew's child, but they knew a rift had occurred twixt her and the king. But no one dared to ask her why, after the passion and tragedies they'd endured together, the king suddenly expelled Lady Amethyst from court functions.

He would not let her see her betrothed until the wedding day. She begged his closest associates, the Duke of Norfolk; his favorite groom, Henry Norris; his personal jester, Will Somers; but no one dared spill a word about this Mortimer Pilkington.

With packed trunks and a teary farewell to her ladies, she donned her simple wedding gown of beige satin, the underskirt of embroidered satin dotted with pearls. Atop her head was a pearl-lined caul, her hair pulled back underneath. Around her neck she wore Henry's first gift to her, the teardrop pearl she so treasured. Matthew's ring stayed on her finger. With his image clear in her mind, she exited her apartments for the last time. She held back tears as she walked through the corridors, past the king's chambers. She ached to see him, to say goodbye. He was nowhere in sight.

There was never a sadder, more sorrowful bride.

A carriage took her to St. Margaret's Church in Bromley, south of London, where she was to be married to the man she'd never seen. She was allowed one maid, Harriet, and they sat wordlessly as the carriage rattled over the rutted roads, over the bridge spanning the gray choppy Thames, the wind biting and vicious. The sunless day lashed out at her from the sky, a leaden shroud of tarnished pewter.

Her stomach churned as they reached the small church, its thatched roof bare in spots like a desolate stretch of abandoned ground. Mortimer Pilkington, her betrothed, stood at the altar with a priest, both dressed in black. As she walked up the aisle, his face came into focus, his features sharpening as she approached him. He was short, his white hair thin, bald on top. His sharp black eyes glared at her with complete absence of interest in the dull candlelight. His cheeks sagged into ruddy jowls that brought down the corners of his mouth into a frown. She halted and stood beside him. He nodded and without giving her another glance, turned to the priest and commanded, "Marry us and be done with it."

His accent was that clipped chirp of the titled nobility that sounded condescending even when uttering soft endearments.

She recited her vows as if by rote, and it was over before she even realized she was there. He jammed a thin band on her ringfinger, grasped her arm and led her back down the aisle to her coach and her new life as a married lady.

"What is the name of your manor, my lord?" were the first words she ever spoke to her husband.

"Cleobury. It is the primary residence. I own another house in Chelsea, for I travel to London quite often," was his clipped answer.

"What...what is your occupation?" She knew nothing of this man—absolutely nothing. She did not know what he knew of her, either, but she was sure the king had informed him of her maternal status.

"I am a wool merchant. I own several farms out East Anglia way. I keep busy." He turned to her, those stony eyes regarding her with an apathy bordering on distaste. Mayhap he owed the king a favor, and that was why he'd agreed to marry her. He certainly didn't seem in the least pleased at the turn his life was taking.

"Are you...widowed?" she ventured.

"Aye. Esther died giving birth." His voice softened a fraction and he cleared his throat.

"Oh...I am terribly sorry." Mayhap he was capable of loving another human being after all. Her heart indeed went out to Esther, doomed to go to her grave in service of this dispassionate rock. "Did the child survive?"

"Aye, the miserable sod. He killed her. He is the one who should have died," he snarled with venom.

His words jabbed her like the point of a dagger. How could he speak of his own son this way?

She turned away and watched the cold gray landscape rush by. She could no longer speak to this man. He seemed happy enough with the silence as well.

Cleobury was a stone manor house in the popular shape of an "H" in homage to Henry. It looked as gray and dismal as the day surrounding them, and of the years that lay ahead of her. The child inside her, Matthew's and her creation, was her only thread of the life so heartlessly wrenched from her.

After a meal of cold meats in what he called the great hall, a dining room with shabby furnishings and a sputtering fire, he led her up the stairs and ordered a groom, "bring her trunks up to her chamber." Were they to have separate bedrooms, then? She heaved a sigh of relief.

But her relief vanished just as fast.

With his open palm pressed to her backside, he led her to a bedchamber she knew had to be his, for his clothes lay strewn about and hung in an open wardrobe. "This is where we shall spend the wedding night," he declared, and her hopes plummeted. The chamber dwarfed the bed. A white marble fireplace held three candelabra on its mantel. His family coat of arms was carved into the wall above in black, red and white, trimmed in gold. Although the rest of the house was furnished sparsely, his private chamber was certainly worthy of expenditure.

She sat down on the bed and sank into its feathery softness. How different from Henry's beds. As huge as they were, they were always firm. She literally bounced upon them before they would mold to the contours of her body.

She removed her cloak and placed it on the chair next to her. She looked up at the unfamiliar coat of arms, at the high ceiling arching above her head, out the window into the darkness, ran her hand over the cold sheet. She longed for Matthew, for Henry, for her past as she fought back tears, lightly touching her palm to her midriff, where the life grew, the life she now protected with her body and her warmth.

She heard the shuffling of feet and looked up to see Mortimer standing at the foot of the bed. "Take this wine, it will warm you until the groom lights the fire."

"Thank you, my lord."

"And call me Mortimer when we are in private. You are no longer in the bedchamber with King Henry," he ordered, his tone disdainful.

"Aye…Mortimer." Oh, how she longed for Matthew's loving arms.

He'd already taken off his riding habit and wore a simple linen robe. No satins, no ermine trim, no gems glittered at his knuckles. He was indeed an austere nobleman. The band he'd placed on her finger seemed to mock her with a defiant wink in the candle's glow. She wanted to slide it off and fling it out the window.

After a groom lit the fire and vanished, Mortimer snuffed out the candle and climbed into bed. This was the dreaded moment. She gritted her teeth at the thought of making love with this cold unfeeling person. But she could not curse the king, for she knew he was lying in his enormous bed, alone, feeling betrayed, hurting just as much as she was. Mortimer turned to her. "All right, let us consummate this marriage." Each movement was slow, deliberate. He plucked the caul from her head and tossed it to the floor. "Take that off," he commanded, and waited while she removed her gown, chemise and petticoats.

"May I get under the blankets?" she implored, her voice small. "It is cold."

"Nay. I want to see what my wife looks like naked. You shall perform your duty. Then I care not what you do until I summon you again."

She obeyed, removing the rest of her undergarments, and lay before him, exposed, completely unclothed. He ran a hand over her breasts, down her slightly protruding stomach.

"How far along are you?" he asked with obvious scorn.

"Nearly three months, my lord." Her voice shook as her body shivered.

She shut her eyes and tried to form a picture of Matthew as Mortimer grappled twixt her legs, awkwardly, roughly, as if he'd never caressed a woman. He knew nothing about female anatomy, all the secret folds and intimate spots, the art of stimulation. She yearned for Matthew's feathery caress, his gently probing fingers inside her, his circling thumb, his masterful hands with his gentle touch, bringing her in pulsating waves to the heights of ecstasy. Her husband roughly jabbed two fingers inside her. She felt as if a doctor were examining her. He lowered himself next to her, struggling out of his breeches and hose. He moved his face close to hers, touching her lips with his in a tentative, halting kiss. His tongue jutted out and probed twixt her lips until she reluctantly yielded, opening her mouth as he thrust his tongue inside. His rough tongue probed ineptly. He did not know the technique of kissing, either. One hand stroked her cheek with the back of his hand like a man deciding if he needed a shave. Squeezing her eyes shut, she conjured up Matthew's face, his eyes, his silky hair under her exploring fingertips, his soft moans, his angled cheekbones. Finally she probed his mouth with her tongue, taking him a bit aback.

He guided her hand down to his soft, limp member. She tried her best to stiffen the folds of flesh, to make him respond, and finally his manhood stirred. He leapt on top of her as if mounting his prized palfrey, and awkwardly tried to thrust into her. She responded slowly, as it was not him, but the cold surroundings that intimidated her. She didn't belong here in this stone manor house. It was not the white-haired Mortimer Pilkington atop her, his barrel-chested torso and bony ribs digging into her, but her beloved Matthew, his rugged body thrusting as they clung wildly to each other, her legs wound around his firm buttocks, her gasps and moans and cries of his name, her fingers twined through the mat of glossy hair, his sharp profile in the hollow of her neck as she turned to look at the man she loved atop her, inside her.

She eased him in, and she and Mortimer Pilkington joined as man and wife, slowly, as their uncertainty and remoteness demanded. She opened her eyes once and glimpsed a man she knew not, a man she loved not, not wanting to know what was going on in his mind and his heart, not caring whether he loved her, for the life inside her filled her thoughts, the gift Matthew had given her. She clung to that one attachment to him. After one, two, three, four thrusts he emitted a half-groan, half-cough, cleared his throat and dismounted her.

Their coupling finished, Mortimer showed her to the privy, and he promptly fell asleep, huddled closely to his side of the bed, nearly hanging off the edge.

Shivering, she climbed in and pulled the cover up over her head, clutching Matthew's life within her. Tears poured from her eyes, down her cheeks, into the corners of her mouth, sweet and salty at the same time. Warm, like mother's milk, soaking the pillows, the fluid of her emotions spouted out of her body. Her heart ached for Matthew, the shock he would feel, the betrayal he would harbor. "Please forgive me, Matthew," she whispered into the pillow again and again, twisting his ring around her finger with the hand that now wore her wedding ring. She would write to him and explain that the king had them married—she would then give birth quietly at one of Mortimer's other residences and announce the birth three months later. As her new husband slept at her side, she prayed for her child's future.

* * *

The first room she had wanted to see at Cleobury was the library, so Mortimer showed it to her the next morn. A servant scurried by as they walked down the long hallway, past more bedrooms and a roomy solar, to where the library jutted out from the landing of an oaken staircase. The walls were a rich paneled oak, another white marble fireplace displaying his coat of arms above the mantel. Brilliant sunlight poured through the leaded windows, below which were bookshelves stuffed with volumes of all heights and widths. A brass telescope stood before one window, pointed outward towards the heavens. Plushy chairs faced the center of the room, surrounding tables covered with thick and thin volumes, a tilted reading stand beside each chair, holding open volumes. A thick Persian rug covered the floor, a profusion of pinks, turquoises and golds. A writing desk stood against the far wall, stocked with parchment, pens and ink.

The parchment, those pens…these were her only connection to Matthew. "I wish to write a few letters, Mortimer, to…to the family, if you do not mind."

"As you wish. I shall be behind the house, in the stables. Join me there and we shall go riding."

She nodded dutifully as Mortimer turned and descended the stairs. She was relieved he did not ask any more questions, further relieved that he'd left her alone. She crossed the library, glancing at some of the volumes—history books about Greece and Rome, grouped according to subject matter. On the next shelf stood books of science and anatomy. Natural history and botany followed on the next shelf, and astronomy books after that. She guessed the farthest shelf contained the theological section. She approached the desk and pulled the chair out, careful not to make marks on the delicate rug. She sat down to write the most difficult letter she'd ever had to write in her life.

My beloved Matthew,

It pains me greatly to tell you this. Knowing deep in my heart that you and I could never be, I did what the king, in his infinite wisdom, bade me to do: I married. I am now the wife of Mortimer Pilkington, and am expecting his child in December. Mortimer is a devoted husband and a kindly gentleman, and I shall learn to cherish him with the affection and fondness he deserves.

I shall never forget the moments we shared and hope you will hold our precious moments in your heart as you do your first love.

Forever, Amethyst

A tear plopped onto the sheet and smudged her name.

* * *

A week later she lit a blazing fire in the hearth of the solar. She strummed her lute, losing herself in her music, her fond court memories her only escape from the bleak travail that was now her life.

She began to sing softly, eyes closed, her voice in perfect tune and concordant harmony with the soft tones she strummed with her plectrum. Sensing a presence behind her, she abruptly stopped and spun around.

A tall lad of about twenty stood at the entrance, his doublet embroidered with crimson thread, a red ruffly chemay peeking through, his breeches and nether stocks black, edged with red and silver sarsenet. Sloping atop his head was a black velvet cap with curled brim, which shaded his dark eyes, but she could tell they pierced straight through her. His pointy patrician nose crinkled in mild antipathy, the lips a thin slash. His dark hair was cropped in the French fashion and he sported a neatly clipped beard, another fashion statement the voguish King Henry had started.

He crossed his arms over his chest and stood silently, as if waiting for her to rise and curtsy to him. She knew instantly who he was—those discerning black eyes were Mortimer's, the hostile gaze learned only from years of watching it being stared down at him, the height, the stance, everything.

"So you must be Mortimer's son..." Having taken an instant disliking to him, only by virtue of who he was, she decided there would be no peace unless she made the first magnanimous move. She instantly realized Mortimer hadn't even told her his son's name, having referred to him only once, in the carriage, the obvious loathing deepening his malevolece even more. "I...haven't been told your name."

"So...you are my father's new wife. I expected a more mature woman...a stepmother, not a stepsister." He eyed her up and down as if she were a side of beef.

Any other man would have meant that as a compliment, but he certainly did not.

"Why, did he not tell you anything of me at all?" she asked.

"He did not know anything of you at all. Except you did a spread with some Warwickshire hayseed." He sneered, his eyes landing at her breasts.

Then his sharp gaze traveled to her abdomen, and a look of contemptuous disgust curled his lip. "Now I've got to share my home with a squalling bastard and pretend that he is my half-brother."

By now she was seething, and wanted to smack that smirk right off the Pilkington lips. "Listen, you toad. I am your stepmother and you will treat me with respect. You will speak to me only when spoken to, and regard me with the reverence worthy of a gentleman."

"Oh...and you are a lady, I presume? Letting yourself get poked by some country clodhopper all the while dallying round court as the king's whore? I shall treat you with the respect you deserve...you half-guinea slut." He spat into the fireplace.

She stood and the lute slid to the floor and hit the rug with a thump. Hand outstretched, she lunged for him, ready to land a crack across his cheek. He caught her wrist in his and squeezed so tight, her hand numbed.

She squirmed under his grasp, but he held her fast. He was much stronger than he looked. "Let me go, you bastard, let me go!"

"I am not a bastard," he hissed, teeth clenched, yanking her closer to him until barely an inch was twixt their lips. She could smell ale on his breath, could see tiny beads of sweat spurting around the rim of his hat. "I was legitimate, I have every right to be here, you are the intruder. And as long as you and your Warwickshire urchin reside in this house, I am going to make your life a living hell."

He released his grip on her wrist and flung her aside. She missed crashing into the fireplace by inches.

"You're drunk!" She regained her footing. "You are a drunken sod with a pathetic life. Just be gone and stay out of my way."

He stared her down for another moment and said, "I hope your bastard turns to stone inside you and you bring forth a hideous monster. Then we will be free of your clutches and you can go back to whoring round the palace."

She grabbed one of the andirons and flung it at him. He leapt out of the way and stormed out of the solar.

She still hadn't found out the creature's name.

* * *

"Mortimer! Mortimer, I must speak with you." She met him at the stables as he tossed the reins to his groom. Brushing the dirt off his hands, he walked past her up the path to the house.

"Go to the bedchamber and wait for me." He waved in her direction. "I feel like partaking of my wife before supper."

She ignored him. "Mortimer, your son... I must speak to you of him."

He stopped at the foot of the staircase and turned, not making eye contact, never having looked her directly in the eye since their wedding day. "Do not ever speak to me of that wretch. I hate the very ground he walks on. He killed my Esther and he is doomed to rot for it."

"But Mortimer..." She grabbed his sleeve and he yanked it away, slapping her lightly across the face.

"Do as I say, go to the bed and await me." He pounded up the stairs, leaving her cheek stinging from the blow and her eyes stinging with tears.

* * *

He climbed atop her, forced her legs apart, positioned his pelvis twixt her thighs and began thrusting. She lay beneath him, passively, eyes shut tight, desperately creating that picture of Matthew in her mind—first the blond head, then the green eyes, the chiseled bone structure, the lean, hard body. It worked, Matthew's image appeared, and she felt a surge of desire, making Mortimer more ardent. He pumped away as if she weren't there, satisfying his urges, and she knew he hadn't had his arms around a woman in a long, long time.

He wheezed and puffed, galloping away, sliding in and out of her, his tongue thrust into her ear, his saliva dripping down her neck. She lay beneath him, clinging to Matthew's image. Her husband rolled off her, smacked her bottom, and ordered her to dress for dinner.

* * *

She finally learned his son's name was Roland, asking one of the cooks after Mortimer left for his daily ride.

"But we don't speak of 'im to Sir Mortimer and we don't speak to Sir Mortimer of 'im...and 'tis a cold day in 'ell when they speak to each other."

"But why, Martha?" she badgered the cook. "And why is Roland so mean?"

"All 'is life Mortimer told 'im 'e killed 'is mum, she died when she birthed 'im. 'E told Roland 'e should never been born. The lad lives with that all 'is life." The cook shook her head sadly and returned to her dough-rolling.

She went back to the solar and her music. She could almost feel sorry for the louse.

* * *

Mortimer's business kept him three to four days a week—the inspection of his sheep or his haggling with London buyers of his wool. He never took her with him on business. On his days at the manor he saddled up one of his palfreys and she saddled Star, the gray palfrey Henry had given her. They rode through the countryside, over the ancient network of sweeping, forking Roman highways branching out from London. She gazed over the meadows dotted with grazing sheep, upon strips of gently sloping earth in an array of greens, from the light chartreuse of the apple orchards to the deepest emerald, the color of Matthew's eyes. She felt him there beside her, knowing he was breathing the same fresh spring air, the same sun following him on his journeys.

They rode through snug hamlets, peaked roofs and towering church steeples enclosing the bustle of the folk as they scurried about their business, shouting over the screech of cartwheels, neighing horses, squealing hogs and the sloshing of the waterwheel.

Her mount galloped alongside her husband's. They hardly exchanged a word; her mind was entranced with thoughts of Matthew—*Where is he? What is he doing? Is he smiling?*

They would return home and sup at opposite ends of the table, then engage in a game of chess or he would retire to the library, leaving her alone with her lute to retreat to her private world of music.

She wrote letters home, many letters, to her mother, to Emerald, to her Aunt Margaret Pole, giving Princess Mary her regards. When Mortimer demanded his conjugal rights, she complied.

Roland made an occasional appearance, yet he was never there during mealtimes. She hadn't seen him exchange more than two words with his father. The tension twixt the two men chilled her like the biting wind on a frosty winter's day and made her flesh crawl. The obvious lack of love in this house made the very flagstones on the floor seem colder, even with a blazing fire in the hearth.

Chapter Eighteen

Sabine sent Amethyst an invitation to her fiftieth birthday celebration at Warwick Castle. She mentioned in the letter that she was eager to meet her new son-in-law.

Her son-in-law was at least ten years older than she. As much as Amethyst pined for her home, she dreaded this awkward visit. What would Mortimer and her family possibly talk about? He was not the talkative type. The entire trip would be a disaster.

A surge of emotion moved her and she sobbed at the sight of her home up ahead of them. Mortimer looked at her with a questioning look and she did not offer an explanation. How could he possibly understand how much she loved Warwick Castle?

* * *

The next day she took a solitary walk over the castle grounds. Mortimer had gone riding with Sabine and her retinue, as he was acting the true nobleman. The cool spring breeze carried a promise of the warmth and rebirth the earth was about to bring forth. She faced west and saw the sun peeking through a patch of clouds. The bottoms of her shoes sank into the moist earth; recent storms had soaked the ground and drenched the gardens, leaving the flowers wilting and spent.

She saw a rider in the distance and slowed. He came into focus, pulled his reins and turned his mount in her direction, then begin a canter towards her. The blond glow about his head and emerald green eyes took shape. Oh, God, Matthew. She couldn't face him, although she stood frozen to the ground, unable to tear her gaze away.

He caught up with her. He'd already captured her eye. She had no means of escape. Her heart pounded wildly as their eyes met. "Amethyst! What are you doing here?"

"Visiting. It is my mother's birthday."

"Why did you not tell me you were in Warwickshire?" She detected the pain in his voice.

"Why, Matthew?" She looked away, unable to bear the sight of the man she loved so much. "It would serve no purpose." If she had her wish, she would let him sweep her onto his mount and gallop into the sunset together, never to return.

"I am not upset with you, Amethyst. You did what you had to do."

She met his gaze and it all rushed back to her, the love in his eyes, the way he still adored her, beckoned her. Oh, how to tell him the truth without breaking his heart? "Matthew, we mustn't meet again. It does me no good, it does us no good. Our paths crossed briefly, and have diffused."

"How about now? Our paths crossed today…or were you barely a mile from the Kenilworth grounds for another purpose?"

Was she that close? "I've been walking a few hours, I didn't realize…"

He dismounted, approached her and placed his hands on her shoulders, his fingers searing the flesh where they touched, sending hot flames coursing through her. Her gaze drank in all of him, the sun-bleached hair tousled by the wind, the brows knitted into a furrow of stupefaction, the lips moistened by his tongue, so invitingly.

"It matters not how we met today." He moved even closer. "We did. Can you not at least be thankful for that?"

"There is nothing to be thankful for, Matthew. I am sorry I came so dangerously close to your grounds. Now I must go, I must return to my husband." She tried to break free of his grasp, but his fingers clamped fast to her shoulders.

"Amethyst…"

She turned away. "Matthew, I am a married woman now."

"This meeting was planned. I know it. You came this way deliberately," he stated with certainty.

"No, I did not. I could not." Her gaze roamed the ground.

Without another word, he brought her to him and his lips closed on hers, crushing them. She laced her fingers behind his head, gathering locks of his hair, running her hands down the back of his neck, crushing her breasts to his chest. He arched his back and she felt his growing desire, hard and demanding. She raised her hips to meet him. He pulled her gently to the ground and lay upon the sweet grass dotted with clover. Their arms wound around each other, their bodies joined with a desperate urge. He moaned with longing and she yielded to his passion, with every beat of her heart.

"Come back to Kenilworth with me, just for a short while, I need you," he murmured twixt light kisses on her neck, her throat, her earlobes.

"I cannot do that. Matthew, please..." She tore herself away and caught her breath, pushing him away with her weakened will. "Please, let me go, this is wrong."

"It was wrong for you to marry a man you do not love, when you love me," came out like an accusation.

"Nay, I do not love you," she forced out, the words bitter on her tongue.

All went quiet. The breeze stopped rustling the leaves, the birds stopped their melodic twittering, and his panting ceased.

"You cannot mean that." Another accusatory reprimand.

"You are not the right man for me, you are too placid and genteel, I need someone impetuous and tempestuous like King Henry," came the words she did not feel, loathing herself for saying them.

"You cannot tell me you still love him. You admitted to me that you no longer loved him that way. He married you off to a man you do not even know. Now you're saying this? And you expect me to believe it?"

"I...I am confused. I do not know how I feel. You are just making it worse. Do not make me betray my husband. They can come upon us any time now. Just get back on your horse and leave, for your own good." Her mind formed the words that her mouth spoke, but her heart denied it all.

She avoided his face, for she did not want to see the pain in his eyes. He brushed himself off, adjusted his breeches, mounted his palfrey and galloped away.

One final glance engraved in her mind his sorrowful expression, his mouth open to shout a call that never came. He did not say goodbye. She turned and ran back to Warwick Castle, where her family awaited her.

* * *

The day after they returned to Cleobury, Roland entered her chamber without knocking. Mortimer was in London and the servants were tending to their duties about the pantry, stables and grounds.

They were alone.

"What do you want?" She stepped back as he advanced, seeming to delight in her disdain. But now it gave way to fright.

"What do you think I want?" He leered at her breasts, his lip curling to match the brim of his feathered cap.

"Get ye gone, you are drunk. Get out of my sight!"

She backed up further, further, till she hit the wall.

"You are mistaken. I am sober. I have not had a drop today. I find that drink impairs my ability to perform." He advanced further, licking his lips.

She slid along the wall sideways as he took another menacing step. Now at arm's length, he gave her cheek a rough caress. "I want to sample a piece of what the royal pork sword plunged into." He sprang upon her, his hands sliding the bodice from her shoulders. She reached up to slap him away, and he caught her hands.

"Get off me, you piece of filth! I shall scream!"

"Go ahead. No one will hear you. These walls are made of stone. Now…" He worked his knee in twixt her legs, trying to separate them as he dragged her across the chamber pushed her onto the bed. "If you can wag your tail for the king and my father, you can do it for me."

He mounted her, raising her skirts, trying to push his growing boyhood twixt her thighs.

She struggled, spat, and bit his arm through the billowing linen sleeve. He yelped and landed his open palm across her cheek with a loud crack that sent her head reeling. "Wanton bitch! Give me a tumble, wench, show me what made the king's sap rise!"

"No! Get off me!" She bit and kicked.

"Very well, we'll go nose to tail then."

"No! Get away from me, you miserable bastard!" She worked her leg free from under him. She had a great amount of mobility there. She drew it back, slamming it into his crotch. His hands flew off her as he bellowed, staggered back and fell onto the floor, writhing in pain, hands twixt his legs, choking and gagging like a hanged man.

She leapt from the bed, tore out of the room, out of the house and to the stables, mounted the nearest mare and sped off.

She returned at nightfall. Mortimer sat in the great hall, supping alone. His son was nowhere in sight.

"Where were you?" he asked twixt bites and chews.

"Out riding." She sat at the other end of the table as a server placed a goblet before her.

"You do not go out riding unless you clear it with me first." He chewed and spoke at the same time, reminding her of Henry's lack of manners.

She stood, walked the length of the table and met the black steely gaze that penetrated her like a bloodletting needle. He held a leg of mutton in his hands, picking at it.

"Your son tried to rape me today. I want you to get him out of here."

"Did he accomplish anything?" He chewed without looking at her.

"Nay, I kicked him where it hurt."

"Then what are you complaining about?" He chewed and spoke, wiped his mouth with his hand, belched.

"Did you not hear what I said? He tried to rape me!"

"And he did not succeed, and I am not going to have to look at that wretched sod's face and speak to him over a simple canoodling." He waved her away. "Now get ye upstairs, your husband feels like a bit of four-legged frolic."

"You are disgusting! I hate you!" she spat as she turned and fled up the stairs, locking the chamber door behind her. He did not come to her that night.

* * *

The next morn, she went out to the stables to saddle Star. She was nowhere to be seen.

"Kevin, where is Star?" she asked the groom as he returned, leading a white mare by the reins.

"Master Roland took 'er this morning, Lady Pilkington. I know not where."

"Why would he take my horse?" she cried, as Star was the only living thing from Henry she owned, and she'd grown ever so attached to her. "What has he done with her?"

Roland returned an hour later, on a young brown palfrey. Star was nowhere in sight.

"What did you do with Star?" she demanded as he stabled the horse, spitting in her direction.

"Sold 'er," he answered over his shoulder.

"You sold my horse? You sod!" Her fists clenched in rage. "Why?"

"I needed a few sovereigns. My ale money was running low." Pushing past her he headed for the house.

"Where is she? I shall buy her back. I should sell you, you twisted snake, ship you off to San Salvador and sell you into slavery!" She caught up to him and gave him a shove.

He shoved her back and laughed a deceitful laugh, his smile twisted. "You'll never find her."

"I shall tell your father and he will beat your cracker until you cannot sit!"

He halted and faced her, an ugly grimace crossing his face. "It was his idea, milady. We have too many bloody horses already. You shall get over it." He cracked a riding crop in her direction, causing her to jump with fright, and strode away, heaving a glob of spit in the path twixt them.

* * *

Mortimer departed for a three-day trip, leaving her in their chamber, not bothering to say goodbye. As she watched his carriage trundle off down the rutted path, she jumped up and down, unable to contain her excitement. She was taking a trip of her own, to her beloved Warwickshire, to escape this wretched gloom for a few days. She pressed her palms to her unborn child and wished for another chance encounter, Matthew's arms around hers, the life they created out of their passion growing twixt them. Closing her eyes, she envisioned Warwick Castle, the sprawling grounds, her cozy blue boudoir…

She turned the doorknob but it would not budge. She yanked on it, kicked the door, pushed it, pulled it, but it held fast. "That bastard," she whispered, turning her back to the door, sliding to the floor, putting her head in her hands. She was a prisoner in her own chamber.

She tried to ram a chair through the door to no avail. She was too high up to escape through the window.

An hour later a dish of food slid under the door. She kicked it aside, banged on the door. "Let me out of here!" she wailed, to no avail. The footsteps faded into the night and once again she was alone.

* * *

When he returned, she didn't confront him about his locking her in; she couldn't stand the sight of him.

All she cared about was the life inside her. She marveled at the kicking of tiny legs against her middle. It felt like a gentle flutter at first, then within weeks it became a burst of energy. In her mind she shared it all with Matthew. She didn't dare write him any more letters.

Next morn as she did needlework by the solar window, Mortimer entered and crept up to her. "We are going riding," he announced.

"I would rather not." She spoke without looking up from her work. "I shall be approaching my confinement in but a few weeks. Any jostling would affect the baby. I would stay here and give up the riding from now on." These were the first words she'd spoken to him in days.

"But you rode less than a fortnight ago," he countered.

"Aye, but it is at the point where it is too dangerous. I would stay here."

"You are riding today," he demanded.

"Nay, I am not." Though she loathed his very presence, she looked up from her needlework and glared. No longer did he intimidate her. He simply disgusted her.

"You are riding with me." He flung the needlework to the floor and yanked her to her feet. "I am your Lord and you do as I say. Do you want a beating?"

She struggled to break free but he held both her hands. He began dragging her from the chamber.

"Please, Mortimer, it is much too dangerous, I do not want to harm the baby," she made an attempt at reasoning, appealing to what few human traits he had.

"Sod the bastard. I give not a toss for your Warwickshire whelp. We are going riding."

He led her down the stairs and she grabbed the banister for support, almost tumbling over. She dared not run away; she could no longer boast the physical agility she had before her growing expectancy. Before, she could have jumped the banister and fled, or climbed out a window. Now she could barely walk at a quick pace.

He stood beside her and boosted her up into the saddle. She considered leading the mount away and losing herself, but that would do no good. She did not know this horse, he did not know her, and Mortimer would surely find her.

They began a light canter down the path and across the fields. Mortimer led her down a rough detour from the highway, a seldom-traveled route across a sweep of gloomy marsh. He spurred his mount on, and hers followed as she held the reins for dear life. The bumpy tracks jostled her, and they reached an ancient wooden bridge that looked like it could barely hold their weight. She squeezed her eyes shut, held the reins for dear life and prayed to God for her baby's life as they crossed it.

Hedges sped by on either side of the path, overgrown with brush. Highwaymen as well as natural disasters vexed these deserted roads. She had no idea where they were. Terrified, she trembled as the sun disappeared behind a cover of clouds and cast a shadow over the path. She did not see the ditch ahead of them. Mortimer reared his horse and skirted it just in time, but her horse slid into the ditch, losing his footing, his legs giving way under him... she went tumbling into a muddy open void, her hands clutching her middle as the ground rushed towards her to smack her in the face.

* * *

She awoke in a strange bed. A woman wearing a white cap was propping her up on pillows. A fire glowed at the other end of the room.

"Where am I?" she managed to sputter.

"The Hare and Hounds Inn. You took a tumble off your horse," she answered with a country accent.

"My baby..." she gasped. She felt a warm stickiness twixt her legs and pressed her hands to her middle. The baby was there, but she did not feel that familiar thump of little legs against her. "Oh, no..."

She heard someone speaking of a physician and as a black-cloaked man approached her bed. He forced her legs apart, grappled around, shoved his fingers inside, and covered her up. She felt wine trickling down her throat, tasted a powdery mint.

"Did I lose the baby?" she whispered. No one answered.

* * *

Someone placed her in a litter and she dozed to the swaying motion. Someone led her up steps and into a bed. The sweet scent of lilacs surrounded her. "Did I lose the baby?"

No one answered.

A day passed into darkness, then another, then another as she realized she was back at Cleobury. Her husband didn't come near her. Martha the cook brought her all sorts of delicious pastries, breads and finally some sliced turkey meat. She drank milk, lots of milk. The bleeding had stopped. She prayed. Mortimer did not enter the chamber once. Then the life inside her began to stir, and she let forth a stream of tears, for she had not lost the precious life she and Matthew had created.

* * *

With the time of her confinement approaching, she retired to her chamber, the secret of the baby's paternity confined within the walls of Cleobury.

With a midwife in attendance and wrapped in wallflower juices, she brought forth a baby boy. "His name is Edward Henry," she whispered. He was tiny and frail, not robust and strong like Topaz's sons at birth. As the midwife and serving maids coddled him and fussed over him, her heart ached for Matthew.

When she was able to walk about, she sat down and wrote Henry a letter. She poured out all her feelings of remorse for what had transpired twixt them, begging him to reconsider their relationship, for they had been through so much. Before she closed, she told him of Harry, as she called her new son. She had no reason to mention her husband.

She also wrote Sabine with the announcement that she was a grandmother once more. But once again, she didn't dare write to Matthew. She couldn't trust anyone in this house, her husband most of all.

Harry had Matthew's eyes, always widened in wonder and awe at the beauty and the world's sensations about him. His dusty blond hair glinted like gold in the sunlight. *Will Matthew know this boy belongs to him?* she wondered. Did men possess that instinctive nature always accredited to women, when it came to a first-time meeting with their sons? It mattered not; her son would never have any reason to meet Matthew Gilford. Harry's father was Mortimer Pilkington, and although Mortimer avoided the child whenever possible, she hoped the one small corner of his heart would soften when in the presence of this innocent new life.

* * *

She was gently rocking Harry in her arms when she heard clopping hooves and a horse's neigh. Looking out the window, she saw a messenger saddled on a mount, caparisoned with the royal livery—a message from King Henry! Her heart leapt as she lay Harry on the bed and bounded down the steps. She flung open the front door, ready to greet the messenger. There stood a drunk Roland, grasping the door frame for support, his eyes glazed over, the message crumpled in his hand. She glimpsed the royal seal twixt his fingers.

"Hand me that message, it is for me." She held her hand out to snatch it but he held it up over his head.

"This is my house 'n any message from royally or whoeverr i's from b'longs to me!" His slurred words ran into one another. She barely understood what he'd said.

"You're soused, you lush, now give me that message or I'll kick you in your bag so hard, you'll have to open your waistcoat to find it." She yanked up her skirts and drew back her knee, ready to deliver a blow to his crotch. He staggered backwards and fell against one of the great oaks lining the path. He slid into the dirt, his face flushed and bloated with drunken senselessness. The message fluttered to the ground. She swept it up, broke the seal and read its contents.

The king was inviting her and Mortimer to court for Christmas. The intoxicated oaf forgotten, she entered the house, clutching the message to her heart, a prayer of thanks on her lips.

She'd waited the duration of this disastrous marriage for this moment, all the while planning how to beg Henry to grant her an annulment. If he had any compassion in his soul, he would take pity on her and free her from this horrid situation.

* * *

She eagerly packed her trunks in anticipation of the court festivities that she so sorely missed. She felt as if imprisoned for years, although it had been merely months. But the time had dragged on with agonizing slowness. Her heart leapt as she awaited the twinkling candles, the joyous music, the dancing, the eating, the drinking, all accompanied by the lively court banter and intrigue that had been the nucleus of her life so long ago.

As she packed her favorite velvet cloak, she heard shouting beneath her window. She looked out to investigate and watched two shadowy figures shoving at each other, heard them screaming and cursing, knowing it was Mortimer and his son.

She snuffed out her candles and peered out the window in the darkness. Mortimer's stout figure overpowered the taller but lankier Roland's. Then she saw a fist fly through the air and strike flesh and bone as Mortimer delivered a blow to his son's jaw, sending the boy reeling, knocking him off his feet. Roland's hands protectively covered his eyes as Mortimer straddled his prostrate son and began smashing his fists into the boy's face. Roland kicked, flailing his arms with helpless awkwardness. Mortimer clasped his fingers round the boy's throat and began choking him.

Amethyst fled down the stairs, flung open the front door and ran to the dreadful sight. The icy wind whipped about her skirts, slapping her hair across her face. She leapt on her husband, pounding on his back with her fists in a frantic attempt to pry him off his gurgling son. "Mortimer, get off him, you'll kill him!"

"Stay off me, wench!" He elbowed her in the ribs. "This bastard wronged me for the last time!"

Roland's hand shot out, his fingers splayed as if they would break, as he made a desperate reach for Amethyst. His eyes bulged and his face turned blue in the dim light sifting through the foyer's leaded windows.

"Mortimer, please!" She brought back her foot and landed a kick in her husband's head. He released his grip on Roland and rocked back on his son's loins. Roland screamed in agony trying to shift his father's weight off his crushed genitals.

She backed away as Mortimer staggered to his feet, rubbing his head, still straddling his son, a foot on each side of the boy's ribcage.

"Mortimer..." Amethyst gasped with fear, wondering why she'd even interfered. How would he punish her for this? "What happened? What did you do this to him for?"

He turned to her and spat, "That despised bastard, he took thousands of crowns worth of plate and sold it behind my back to pay for his loathsome ale and his filthy whores! He has never been a son of mine and he never will be." He lifted one foot and kicked his son in the ribs. "Get out of my sight, you pox-ridden sod, I should have killed you!"

Roland rose to his elbows, dazed, as Mortimer delivered a swift kick, this time to Roland's crotch. The boy rolled over, clutching his nether region.

She approached her husband and pulled him away from Roland. "Mortimer, he sold Star from under my nose, and as upset as I was at the loss of my dear pet, I did not resort to such abhorrence. You nearly killed him!" She pointed to the writhing figure on the ground.

"I should have, and I shall!" His eyes crossed in rage as he turned to his son. "Get ye gone from here, or I'll have you swinging from this oak by sunup, you scurvy bastard!" With that, her husband stalked away, leaving Amethyst standing beside her despised stepson, still wondering why she needed to save this pathetic figure.

He echoed her thoughts. "Why...why did you save me?" His voice squeaked as he winced in pain with each utterance. "You hate me as much as he does." He looked up at her through swollen eyes, a trickle of blood dripping from the corner of his mouth onto the frozen ground.

"I do not hate you…I…know not why I saved you. I…just abhor violence, I'd heard so many things, of my father, of…" She ceased rambling and held up her hands. "Never mind, just get ye gone, or he really will kill you."

She stood over him for another moment and instinctively reached out to help him up. He clutched her hand and stumbled to his feet, his face contorted in pain. Instead of its usual tight grimace, his mouth gaped in a noiseless scream of agony. He limped over to the oak, holding his side, his other hand cupping his tortured crotch, and leaned against the trunk, watching Amethyst intently. "Who is your father?" he asked in a hoarse whisper.

"He was Earl of Warwick." She plucked a lace-trimmed cloth from inside her bodice, approached him and blotted the blood congealing on his face. He took it from her and gave an almost undetectable nod of thanks. "He was imprisoned for all but one day of his life in the Tower and was executed when I was two years old. My sister and mother saw him dragged off to his death. My sister never forgot it, and will not let the rest of us forget it, either. He was in the way of the throne, and the Tower is where I was born and lived the first years of my life," she shared more with him in this moment than she ever had with her husband.

He wiped his face with the cloth, balling it up and pressing it to his mouth. His breathing was softer and even, and his eyes, though swollen nearly shut, still stared at her with renewed interest. "They…they kill for their bloody thrones…they kill everyone in sight…they stop at nothing," he spoke, his voice so low, she had to strain to hear.

"Aye, and my father was but a pawn in a sick power game. A more woeful life was never led on this earth," she spoke to this boy of her beloved father who she never knew.

"Oh, you are wrong, Lady Amethyst, you are wrong," and that was the first time he'd addressed her in a decent manner, "The biggest waste of life on this earth is I, I am the most unwanted, pitiful creature you will ever know. I was a mistake from before birth, I am the living personification of shame. And as I live, so shall I die, a wasted, meaningless soul…with nothing…now go back to your husband, before he beats you for talking to me. Get!" It was more of a warning than a command, and she obeyed, leaving him leaning against the oak to sop up his blood with her lacy cloth.

* * *

The next day he was gone, leaving a section of the flagstone path leading to the house stained with his blood. She never mentioned his name to Mortimer again, he never talked of his son, and the matter became history as they left Cleobury behind for their journey to court.

* * *

Hampton Court Palace

The palace blazed, abuzz with preparations for the Christmas festivities when Amethyst and Mortimer approached the gatehouse in the falling dusk. Candles glowed in every window and the brisk wind carried lively tunes to their ears.

They dismounted and a page led them through the courtyard up to their apartments. "Tell the king that Lord and Lady Pilkington are here," she ordered the page, who scurried off to deliver his message.

"They are getting younger and younger," she commented to her husband, removing her cloak and draping it over the bed.

"Or are you getting older and older?" Mortimer countered, sitting on the edge of the bed, yanking off his boots.

"Let a chamberlain do that, old bean, you may break one of those brittle hips." Amethyst reached for a wine goblet, not offering him any.

"I like doing things for myself." Mortimer pushed a white lock of hair out of his eyes. The miserable old codger must have been handsome in a rugged sort of way back in the day, she decided, regarding his ruddy cheeks, weatherbeaten from too many winters of riding. His rough masculine appeal would have turned a few female heads in the days of his youth. The bitterness over his wife's death seemed to exhaust his joy for living, turning him into a seething pillar of resentment.

The page returned the message that the king was holding a council meeting, but wished for her and Mortimer to meet him in the great hall for the evening meal.

It was the first time she would see Henry since leaving court in disgrace, and she trembled, her heart tripping. How would he react to seeing her again, how would he act towards her? The tension mounted as she descended the staircase and headed for the great hall. She longed for his company, as she knew he missed her.

She approached him slowly, holding out her hand. He'd gained a considerable amount of weight, carrying even more corpulence than before, but to him all it probably meant was another yard of velvet, another ermine pelt for a longer trim. His red hair had grayed and thinned out more. Lines appeared in his forehead. He regarded her with a frosty eye. The gold orbs did not sparkle as they once did when gazing upon her. He displayed no hint of a smile, no cordiality in his welcome, his hand cold and unyielding as they touched.

"Sire." She dipped in a curtsey. She did not hold her hand out. He did not take it.

"Lady Pilkington."

Oh, how she hated to be called that, and she was sure he knew it. Their reunion was formal, reduced to forced adherence to protocol. She so longed to rush into his arms. She looked up at him and captured his gaze. She knew she had him; aloof and distant as it was, he couldn't tear his eyes from hers. Like the unfolding of a rosebud into flourishing bloom, warmth replaced his cold glare as his eyes softened and began to glow. She drowned in that look of longing she knew so well. She'd never forgotten it in all those unfeeling, loveless nights in her husband's bed.

"My lord, it is... so good to see you again," she whispered so only he could hear, as Mortimer stood off to the side. He all but disappeared as she looked into Henry Tudor's eyes, seeing the jewels glitter upon his hulking chest as he heaved a great sigh.

"'Tis good to see you again, Amethyst." He'd saved that low, intimate tone for her.

She moved a step closer, her head just reaching his shoulder, and took his hand. His fingers tightened round hers and squeezed, his eyes widened, and she blinked back tears bunching her lashes into wet clumps. "I missed you," she confessed.

"We shall speak later, Amethyst." He released her hand, a forced sternness returning to his voice. "Now is not the time. Go sit with your husband."

* * *

Henry summoned her to his chambers that eve and she could barely contain her excitement as she left her stodgy husband behind and scampered through the familiar corridors to be with her king.

He sat sipping from a golden goblet, a matching goblet set on the table for her. She approached him with reverence, fighting the urge to leap into his arms and feel his enveloping warmth, the touch that only he could give her. She knew he felt the same way; she noted the anxiety in his eyes, his restless shifting in his chair as he fingered his pendant.

No, there is no reason to hold back any longer, she decided. She strode up to him. He stood. Their lips met briefly, lingered for but a second, then pulled apart. He grasped her hands. It was like a slow, courtly dance, as their gazes locked once again. She saw the golden fire in his eyes, sensed the longing, the many months of loneliness, the remorse.

"I am so sorry, my lord, the way it all happened." She was the first to speak of it.

"Never mind. How is your child?" He motioned for her to sit.

"He is fine. His name is Harry."

"I know. I received the letter." He sat across from her.

"Why did you not answer it?" she asked in puzzlement.

"Answer it?" He halted his goblet midway to his mouth. "I wrote to you divers times, on the anniversary of Catherine's death, when

I was sure you were going into confinement, when I sat here bored and lonely, after they all leave me alone for the evening…I wrote to you over and over, Amethyst. Not only that—not a day went by that I didn't think of you."

Her heart took an elated leap. Then it plunged as she realized what had happened. "That miserable sod, he intercepted your letters!"

"Mortimer?"

"Nay, Mortimer would never care enough. His son, Roland. His mother died giving birth to him and Mortimer condemns him for it, making his life miserable. In turn, he spreads misery wherever he goes. Oh, sire, he has made my life hell! He has made advances toward me, and I worry so about Harry, I am so afraid he will poison him…he took all your letters, it had to be him!" She clamped her lips into a tight grimace as her blood began to run hot.

The king turned away, deep in thought. Then he turned back to her. "I am sorry, Amethyst, that it worked out this way. But you cannot return to court with a child. Mortimer is your husband and you must learn to live with him. His son will grow out of it, I am sure."

"Nay, my lord, he will not!" She slapped her palm on the table. "It is because of your jealousy that I am married to a man I loathe and who has no respect or regard for me. Do not make it any more of a hell for me." She tried to steady her voice but simply couldn't. All the sorrow, the rage, the indignities of these last months came to a head, rendering her emotionally spent. "I waited all my life to get married because of you, now I am married to someone I despise. I do not deserve this added humiliation. Please take that miserable creature of a son of his away from me!"

"Mayhap I should marry him off," he pondered as if raffling off a horse.

"Nay, my lord, I would not force him upon anyone. He would make anyone's life miserable."

"I can send him off to sea," he suggested. "He may make a good sailor. The French are always threatening, and our navy is still but very weak." With a resolute nod, he concluded, "I shall take care of it.

Luckily, of late, I have had another matter to contend with. I am about to be married again."

This she hadn't heard. There was no lady next to him on the dais, no one flitting about. He dined alone, he danced with no one. "Who is she, sire?"

"For a long while now, there have been some at court who seem to believe another alliance is in order for their king." His tone and his words lacked his youthful command.

"Just because of what they want, you considered marriage again?" she asked. "Since when do you do the bidding of mere subjects?"

He shook his head. "Cromwell considered this marriage, and it makes good sense…twixt me and the first available princess from the continent willing to depart from her homeland and brave the Channel."

"The Channel is not all she would have to brave, my lord." She gave him her cheeky grin of old.

"She need not worry, Amethyst. My days of madness derived from passion are over. I seek only an alliance with Europe, as we have been isolated since the break with Rome, and therefore vulnerable." He took a sip of wine. "We need an alliance, but not with Spain, God forbid, for I wish not to relive a nightmare twice in one lifetime. I ordered Holbein to procure likenesses of several ladies, Mary of Guise being the first, and then he is going to the Imperial court to paint the portrait of Christina, the duchess of Milan. She need not be beautiful, but she need be appealing enough…for appearances' sake, you see."

"Aye, my lord." She stifled a laugh, for she knew her Henry never lost his eye for a pretty wench. He would not settle for a queen that did not please his discerning eye.

"I traveled to Calais, for Francis lined up some of the ladies of his court for me to inspect. Such tedious tasks," he sighed.

"Aye, my lord, imagine, the King of England going out to the market square!" She didn't bother holding back her laughs. This was more amusing than the antics of the court fools.

He slipped her that sideways glance as they chuckled comfortably together.

"So what happened? I'm anxious to hear if you made any progress in this quest for a French courtier." She sincerely doubted he would have met anyone who would strike his fancy; after Anne, how could he bear to involve himself with another lady from the French court, even if she was English?

"My search for a suitable alliance and simultaneous acceptable queen lagged on, as it seemed every eligible maiden in the land found the perfect excuse not to marry me." He finished his wine and poured another. "Cromwell's original choice, Mary of Guise, immediately upon hearing of my interest in her, pledged herself to James the Fifth of Scotland. Christina of Milan remarked that she would only have married me if she had two heads!"

Aye, his reputation had become tainted. That vexed Amethyst, for word of mouth round the kingdom and the continent was unreliable indeed, at the mercy of village folk who embellished their stories and shaped them to the folds of their imaginations until they oozed with untruth. She'd heard rumors to the effect that Henry was everything from syphilitic to crippled, having whacked Anne's head off at whim in order to marry Jane. How far from the truth that could have been! But how could they know? No one knew Henry the way she did. Even Cromwell used to call for her when the king was in a melancholy or difficult mood. So many, many things she missed terribly.

"So how did the journey to Calais fare, my lord? Did any eligible courtiers jump at the chance of crossing the Channel to the open arms of our queen-less kingdom...and our king?" she asked, burning up with curiosity.

"Bah." He swept his hand through the air. "They were all petty balls of fluff, with their pomanders and their unsullied manners covering their licentious lust like the satin brocades and heavy perfumes they douse themselves with. God Jesu, I can still smell it!" He wrinkled his nose and took a swig of wine, wiping a stream of dark red liquid off his chin with the back of his hand. "I decided I would have to seek elsewhere, mayhap the Low Countries. The Netherlands mayhap. A nice elderly woman of the Netherlands, fair of hair and skin, with a robust laugh, older than even I mayhap, and at least two heads shorter than I."

"What a radical change from your former taste in women," she remarked. None of his wives or mistresses, save for Bessie Blount way back at the brink of his manhood, had been fair. Or elderly, if one did not count Catherine at the very end. "That is a great departure from your usual proclivities, sire. That must mean your taste is maturing as you mature."

He looked right at her. "Age, my dear, as I age, just admit it. Wines mature. Kings... and other mortals... age. But you... " He held out his great hand and she took it in hers. How it engulfed her, consumed her in its warmth. "You haven't changed one iota since the day we met. The ravages of age demolished Catherine, right before my eyes, and she was but the same age when I first set eyes on her as you were when we first met."

"I am not quite the age Catherine was, sire. Besides, I believe the stress of the divorce aged her quite a bit." She needed to remind him of that.

"It aged us both," he admitted. "It did not have to, though. If only she had been more agreeable, she would certainly be alive today. However, let us not dwell on such matters."

"So who is she, sire?" She nearly sprang from her seat.

"Anne of Cleves. A pretty young thing, according to the portraits." A hint of pleasure brightened his eyes, but approached nowhere near the passion they'd always shared.

"Has she arrived in England yet, sire?" she asked.

"Nay, she waits at Calais for the weather to improve before she sets sail." He swiped a cold turkey drumstick from a heaping plate and tore into it.

"Are you nervous, sire?" she prodded, for she knew Henry; as adamant as he was about the unimportance of this new liaison, she knew he was as anxious to feast his eyes upon her.

"Nervous? Nay, I wish her a safe and speedy arrival, that is all." He seemed more interested in his drumstick than his next wife.

"What does she look like, sire?" She remembered his request that she be 'presentable'—but Henry always had a special weakness for beauty and grace beyond what he would ever consider 'presentable.' She was sure Anne of Cleves would more than meet his requirements.

"Her portrait belies her true beauty, I am told, but I gather from the likeness that she is of fair complexion, with huge round eyes and graceful features. I believe she will do." He shrugged off this impending fourth marriage and continued gnawing his late night snack.

"'Tis a wise choice you make to choose a lady of Cleves, sire. 'Tis a much needed alliance and we will all feel much safer indeed."

"Aye, I am doing this for the realm, instead of for my own selfish needs, for once," he declared. "Of course, if she turns out to be a stunning beauty, all the better. I look forward to meeting her. You will be present at the wedding, of course, you and Mortimer?"

"Aye, sire, we would be honored." How many of his weddings had she witnessed now? She tried to count. Had it been two? Three? And how tragically they all ended. "We wish your majesty and the new Queen Anne a long lasting and happy marriage," Amethyst spoke for the entire kingdom.

The king smacked his lips as a servitor entered with yet another plate of meats and cheeses. "I am not a young man, Amethyst. As God is my witness, this marriage shall be my last."

* * *

Amethyst and Mortimer stayed on at court for the king's wedding to Anne of Cleves. Rejoining the King's Musick brought tears to her eyes. "Oh, tis like old times!" She shared warm hugs with her fellow musicians in the gallery, so happy to sit at her virginals as she had so long ago. As she looked down over the sparkling aura of the great hall, it seemed mere moments had passed since the last time she'd sat here. But so many lives had passed in and out of this world, and her life had taken a most unexpected turn.

Forgetting her wretched existence at Cleobury, she lost herself in the joy of music.

* * *

Amethyst sat before the fire in her chamber, deciding what to wear to the king's fourth wedding—or was it the fifth?

A page announced his majesty's arrival in her presence chamber. She rose to greet him.

He looked every bit the beaming bridegroom, dressed in muted tones of gold, velvet doublet and breeches, embroidered with the sharp gleam of citrines. Gold enhanced the glitter in his eyes and the lustre of his thinning but shining hair and beard.

"Sire, how good to see you this morning." She dipped in a curtsey, though that was no longer required in private—not twixt them. "May the new year bring you and your new queen much happiness."

"Bah!" He no longer beamed at the mention of his new queen. He scowled and heaved a deep breath, clenching his fists. "That blasted Cromwell! That Crum! I shall personally… " His fists made a twisting gesture as gurgling sound escaped his throat. "…wring his scrawny neck for involving me in this…travesty of a marriage!"

"What happened, my lord? Have you met Lady Anne? What did she do, what did she say?" She followed him round the chamber as he circled, stomping his feet as if trudging through snow.

"Naught, Amethyst." He turned and faced her, his cheeks flaming. "She did naught, said naught. She simply scratched her hoof in the dirt and whinnied."

"Whinnied? Whatever do you speak of, my lord?"

"Have you never heard a horse, My Lady?" He placed his fists on his hips. "Have you never heard the sound it emits from its mouth, from twixt its yellowed and protruding buck teeth?"

"Oh, sire! Anne of Cleves looks like a horse?" She blinked in disbelief. "After all that—"

"Whoever said she has no relatives in England was liar! She indeed has relatives. Identical. They live in stables and pull carts all over the kingdom!"

"B—but—the likeness," she stammered. "They spoke of her fair beauty—"

"Fair! Bah!" He swept his arm in an arc across his chest. "That pasty-faced excuse for an artist Holbein is next! For I shall make sure he never gets another commission as long as he lives. He is beneath incompetence. To look at her likeness and then to look at…at her, one would refuse to believe it is one and the same…person, and I use the term loosely."

"Oh, sire, how bad can she be?" She stood next to him as he halted at the window.

"I'll tell you how bad she can be. There's a saying the Italians have: *'Brutta come la fame,'* she's as ugly as hunger. I never fancied those Germanic women, finding them too husky, too manly and harsh. But this one…hers must have been the mold from which every woman in that part of the world had been cast. Her skin, Amethyst, her skin…" He dragged his fingers over his cheeks to illustrate. "It is pitted and marred, like the craters of the moon. 'Tis not pink, not the olive-tone of the Latin women, not even that sickly pale blue of so many northern women…'tis the hue of muck after a wild tempest, of a swollen peach that has been left on the tree to rot…" He strode over to a bowl of walnuts on her table. "This is the exact replica of her face!" He held a walnut up, pointy side down, and turned it to face her. "Draw eyes, nose, and mouth on this homely nut and there you have it. Cap it with a hideous headdress, like a box placed atop her head, and there you have her, Anne of Cleves! My future wife. Oh, woe is me," he drew out his words with a dramatic flair.

She shook her head with disbelief. "Surely Cromwell wouldn't have deceived you deliberately. Mayhap they sent the wrong one—"

"Oh, if it were only so," he groaned, tossing the nut back into the bowl. "An ugly sister, at the very least. Nay, it is none other but she, and I must devise a way to get out of it."

Her jaw dropped. "You cannot send her back at this late date. All the plans have been made, all has been finalized—"

"I cannot face her in a marriage bed." A server entered the chamber, saw the king, and no doubt heard the king. She bowed out backwards, muttering apologies.

"I shall admit, I am not the dashing young prince I once was... I carry a bit of extra weight..." He placed his hands round his girth, "and a few strands of gray sprout from my scalp, but never can I perform any marital duties in a bed filled with such repugnance and revulsion." His expression echoed that same repugnance and revulsion.

"Then mayhap you can compromise," she suggested, eager to help. "How does she feel about you, my lord, having feasted her eyes upon your majesty for the very first time?"

He must have noticed that extra weight, for he sucked in his gut. "I know not. I did not speak to her. She knows not a word of English. Her ladies were all around her, all dressed in that same boxy headdress, those cumbersome gowns, folds and folds of cloth reaching up to their very chins," he mimicked the ladies' raiment with his hands to his chin, "as if they had gold in there to guard. We are unable to communicate, except by facial expression, and that, I daresay, will suffice more effectively than words of any common language."

"So you plan to spend your wedding night glowering at each other?" She approached him, knowing he'd knock down any pragmatic solution she brought forth.

"Nay, I shall simply shut my eyes and think of England."

* * *

Richmond Palace, 1540

And went ahead with it he did. The King of England and Anne of Cleves entered holy matrimony on the sixth, as planned. The following morn, Amethyst and Mortimer's servers loaded up their carriage to return to Cleobury. But she had to see the king and bid him farewell. *When will I see him again?* The question haunted her as a page granted her passage.

"And how are the new bride and groom?" She entered his chamber as servants scurried about, cleaning up the remains of his breakfast. The new queen was nowhere in sight.

"Must you know?" asked Henry, still at table.

"I was just asking out of courtesy, my lord. I wish not to hear all the intimate details." She tried to hide her grin, but under the circumstances, that was impossible.

"There are no intimate details, of course." He scowled into his cup. "I am seeking an annulment. That will be easy, for it will never be consummated."

She approached him. "You didn't…"

The king picked a morsel out from twixt his teeth and flicked it onto the floor. "I couldn't have raised anything had I been a lad of sixteen sowing his first wild oats. I would like to think I still have some juice within me, but fruit spurts forth no juice unless it is adequately squeezed."

"I suppose so, sire." She nodded her agreement. Who was she to question the veracity of his metaphors?

"Nay, there is nothing the Flanders Mare possesses that sparks the slightest bit of desire within me. I have done my duty to my kingdom. No one can deny that." He glanced round the chamber as if looking for a diversion such a chess board, and crossed his good leg over his bad one.

"Do not fret, sire," she made an attempt to appease him. "You must get to know each other. She is quiet and shy, and must be frightened. You must make her feel at ease. Teach her how to dance, how to play your favorite card games, how to play the lute. She is from another world, and must be made to feel welcome. An annulment is too harsh for her."

He shook his head, distracted. She wasn't sure he'd heard a word she said. "Just think, if you and I had married, what would have happened?" He looked at her and asked out of the blue.

She shuddered, for that thought had plagued her many times, racked her with guilt. Anne…and as a result of that disaster, Jane would still be alive today had Amethyst stayed on at court and been more patient instead of running home, driving him into Anne's arms. The thought forever plagued her as did her reveries about Matthew—what if, what if...

"A marriage twixt you and I was not meant to be, my lord. We know that now," she stated, wanting to ask why he'd even brought it up.

He gave her a sad nod. "Now you must go to your husband and I must go to my wife. I bid you Godspeed, until we meet again."

He stood, they embraced and the king's arms enveloped her tightly. His embrace enclosed her, only to end too quickly. "I truly do still love you, Henry."

"And I you. Now get ye gone before I take you right here before God and everybody." He shooed her out and she bade farewell to the court. *Will I ever return?* She tortured herself with wondering.

* * *

Hampton Court Palace, June, 1540

A messenger brought King Henry a sealed message. He tossed it aside to read later, but something about the seal looked familiar. So he opened it.

"*My dear king,*" it began, "*I am truly sorry to hear that your marriage to Anne of Cleves is to be dissolved. I wish to atone to your majesty for all the trouble I caused you and the kingdom. Therefore, within the next fortnight, I shall send your majesty who I trust will be your next wife: Katharine Howard, niece of the Duke of Norfolk. At eighteen, the lass is eager to please your majesty and willing to learn court protocol to become a respected and popular queen. Katharine is spirited, young, fair...*"

Her enclosed miniature did depict her as quite comely, but he was past trusting miniatures. "*...and she will bring back a youthfulness and joy the court hasn't seen in many years.*" He halted reading and his thoughts drifted back in time, to Anne, the parties, the dancing, the endless nights of merrymaking. He'd been caught up in it all, too, for he had been in his prime. But at his advanced age, he no longer desired nor had the physical stamina to romp with the younger generation, to dance all night, to frolic with the courtiers. He was an old man. He was tired of it all. He would seek no more wives. His sexual desire had diminished with the increase in his appetite. He wanted to eat when he was hungry, drink when he was thirsty, sleep when he was tired, and rule his kingdom the rest of the time.

His eyes skimmed the next several lines, more praise for this Katharine lass, then skipped to the signature—Topaz Plantagenet.

Ah, firebrand Topaz. A weary smile spread his lips. *Will you never settle down?* The idea was quite thoughtful on the agent-provocateur's part, but the timing was entirely wrong. She was mayhap fifteen years too late to offer him a potential bride of such spirited youth. She should have thought of this instead of trying to seize his kingdom.

He made a mental note to jot off a line to Topaz thanking her for her kindness, but to please leave Mistress Howard in Warwickshire or wherever she belonged.

* * *

Topaz had her own reasons for pairing plucky Katharine with the aging king. Norfolk, Emerald's husband, as well as Topaz, were enemies of Cromwell, whose scheme sealed the Cleves marriage. This royal alliance with Henry and Katharine would snatch Cromwell from the warmth and security of the king's favor.

Upon hearing of that doomed Cleves marriage, they planned Cromwell's downfall. They groomed and drilled Katharine in the manners of court—as Norfolk tutored her in conversational French, Topaz drummed the mores of protocol into Katharine's mercurial little head. "Flirt with the king all you like," Topaz warned the pretty young thing, "Arouse his passions, tease him, drive him mad with desire for you, but do not give in until you lay twixt the sheets of the marriage bed."

Katharine, an incorrigible flirter, having had several dalliances already, did not need much coaching in the area of feminine wiles.

The entire matchmaking incident slipped Henry's mind, and on June 23, his marriage to Anne of Cleves was formally dissolved. He and Anne parted company on amicable terms, and she would always be regarded as his 'sister.' He granted her a generous annuity as well as lands and plate. She was forever grateful her marriage to Henry VIII ended with her life intact.

The ambitious Norfolk packed his giggly niece into a coach for her journey to meet her future husband, King Henry.

Topaz watched the coach depart, returning Katharine's wave with a smug grin.

* * *

Roland Pilkington received a summons from his majesty the king.

"The king is going to war with France," he chose to inform her rather than his father.

"Oh, God above, please watch over him and keep him safe." Of course she referred to her king, not Roland.

Amethyst's last look at Roland was from her chamber window as he galloped away to serve in the king's navy. She wrote to Henry immediately, thanking him for summoning Roland from Cleobury as well as giving him a reason to live.

* * *

"I must admit, I have developed somewhat of a fancy to the young Katharine," Henry wrote Amethyst as they were now corresponding on a regular basis, and he'd invited her to court a few times, without her husband. "Your presumptuous sister took my forgetfulness as permission to send the lass here, so she showed up one day asking where her chambers were. How could I refuse such a sprightly slip of a thing? She really does bring a spark of life back into this tired old court. I had thought she would be all wrong for me, with our vast difference in age. But au contraire, she makes me feel young again."

"The news is wonderful, sire!" she wrote back, relieved he had found someone to occupy his time and help him forget his troubles. The feisty Katharine would certainly do that, and grooming her for royal

life would certainly take up a fair bit of his time. *"Topaz will be so pleased to hear that!"*

Topaz was more than pleased when Katharine Howard became queen three weeks later.

Chapter Nineteen

Warwick Castle, January, 1541

Two horses galloped through the gatehouse entrance. A stable boy met them in the courtyard. The travel-weary man and his groom dismounted, their shoes clapping the frozen earth as they hit the ground. A servant rushed outside and led the man up the stairs into Topaz's receiving chamber. The groom went off with the stable boy.

Topaz emerged from her inner chamber. Her eggshell velvet gown was split at the front to reveal a dark maroon underskirt embroidered with tiny roses. The hem swished over the floorboards as she approached her visitor.

"It is such a pleasure to see you, Cousin Geoffrey. Do come in and sip some ale. How fares the weather?"

"'Tis getting darker and colder." He stomped his feet and rubbed his hands before the fire. "The northerly wind pricks the skin like needles."

"Do warm up and partake of some ale, then. When you are sufficiently thawed out, we shall discuss business." She gestured to a chair by the fire.

"But first I need to know a few things." For this she didn't wait till he was sufficiently thawed out. "How fares my dear Aunt Margaret?"

"Oh, mother is her usual self, she never talks of the king anymore, since her banishment from court, but she still fondly speaks of Princess

Mary, as if she's her very own." He knelt and leaned closer to the flames, splaying his hands.

"So she and the king have become enemies, then?" Topaz goaded.

"Not enemies, as such. I believe she will die with her head attached." He turned and looked up at her with an uneasy smile.

The chuckle they shared was not a comfortable one.

"So, what brings me to Warwick Castle, dear cousin?" He stood and plopped into the chair she'd offered.

"Geoffrey..." Topaz displayed a dazzling smile, knowing her teeth were as white as the garland of dried hyacinths round her neck. "I am the first to admit my aborted attempt to regain my rightful control over the throne has been the biggest setback of my life. A lesser person would have considered it a failure, but not I. I do not give up. It was but one method, and it did not work." She gave a casual 'oh, well...' shrug. "There is more than one way to skin a cat, as the saying goes. There is more than one way to spell a word, there is more than one way to make love..." She hesitated, awaiting her cousin's reaction, but he just sat, transfixed, his eyes bright with anticipation.

"Ah, yes, worry not, cousin. Your journey in the biting cold and slamming wind will prove worthwhile after all," she assured him. "There is more than one way to reach one's goal, in other words," she concluded. "Geoff... as my cousin, and my most faithful ally since the death of dear Thomas More, I am soliciting your help."

"Topaz..." he regarded his cousin with a look resembling that of a pilgrim gazing upon his patron saint. "Your silence all this while, your monastic retreat back into the folds of Warwickshire life—the entire kingdom, the king included, took it as acquiescence."

"How naive of them," was her flippant reply, plucking her goblet off the table, holding the stem twixt two fingers as she sipped. "Certainly I fooled you not, Geoffrey."

"Why, I had a feeling you would rise again." He nodded his assurance. "You were never easily restrained. Even when we were nippers, you took charge at all times. You were the leader."

"Lest you question my integrity, let me assure you my integrity is intact." She accompanied that with an unblinking stare. "I relinquished my claim to the throne upon my release from the Tower and I intend to keep my word. I would not betray the subjects of my kingdom and the people I was born to lead. They would have every reason never to trust me again. I would not blame them. No, I have given up all rights to the crown and am forever grateful to the king for having granted me my freedom. But that does not mean I have given up. I may have relinquished my personal claim. However, I do have a son."

"Topaz!" Geoffrey's smile widened. He uncrossed his legs and leaned forward. "What plans have you in that scheming mind of yours? Why, had you been a friend of the king's, you could have executed his divorce in half the time Wolsey did, and with greater aplomb."

"Aye. Much more forcefully, too. I simply would have marched on Rome, hung the Pope in chains and seized the Vatican." Her words echoed her confidence.

"No doubt you would have." Geoffrey cocked his head to one side. "So...what do we do?" He licked his lips hungrily, and she was sure it wasn't because of the good-tasting ale. His lips may as well have formed the unsaid words "What's in it for me?" as clearly as if the words had come from his mouth.

She concealed her smugness. Ah, yes, he was easier to reel in than a tiny minnow—and just as eager to beat the rest of the school to the bait.

"I am using a different approach this time, a more subtle and contriving approach. We are not going to engage any military personnel. There will be no soldiers, no cavalry, no weapons. What I have here, Geoffrey, is a straight path to the throne...the crown gets placed on my son's head and we shall rule through him a new kingdom, a happy kingdom, a rich kingdom." She crossed the chamber and held the door open for him to pass. He stood and walked past her into her bedchamber.

She rolled a trunk out from under her bed. It rested on a low wooden wagon with four wheels and a handle. She slid a key into a its lock and popped it open.

Stacked inside were letters, folded and sealed with wax. They filled the trunk almost to the top.

"There must be a few thousand letters in there," he commented.

"Three-thousand-six-hundred-fifty, to be exact." A wry grin turned her mouth upwards. "Having written five per day for the last two years…two years since the rebellion, I now possess this number of letters."

"What are these letters?" he asked.

"They are messages…messages to my previous supporters. The majority of the messages are to neutral citizens, who will be more pliable and susceptible to what I have in mind."

"What do the messages say?" He knelt and ran his hand over the top layer. "Is it a pack of lies about Henry to turn the kingdom against him?"

Topaz laughed, leaning over to pat her younger cousin on the cheek. "We need not spread lies about him…he has saved us the toil. Look at him." She scowled. "No one trusts him, no one wants to go near him. It is a miracle Amethyst is still alive. She must be canonized for putting up with him all these years. Nay, we need not spread lies. My son Edward wrote the letters. I am the true author, but they are signed with his name written on his parchment. They solicit support to put him on the throne.

They state simply, 'As my mother Topaz has relinquished her claim to the throne, I am the rightful king, by virtue of her father, Edward Earl of Warwick, executed by Henry Tudor, father of the present king. As my faithful supporters, and believers in the reforms my mother planned to put into effect, you will be rewarded when I ascend the throne as King Edward the Sixth.' Short and sweet."

"Do you think you will gather the support, Topaz? Look what happened in the battle. Even with the mercenaries, Henry's army came through victorious." He stood and brushed dust off his breeches.

"It cannot fail," she assured him. "This is not a military exercise. There will be no need for fighting. At the time of our battle, he was just about to do away with Anne Boleyn, and the church was in upheaval, yet the people still trusted him. By now the king has proven himself to be a tyrant." She held his gaze and his interest. "He has confiscated the monies that previously went to Rome, and kept it himself, to finance his wars with France, to build his tawdry coastal forts and decorate his palaces with garish furnishings, to stuff his corpulent face with food while his subjects starve." She had him nodding in agreement. "Furthermore..." She took in enough air to rattle off more offenses. "He has shamed his people with his succession of so-called wives, with his two bastard daughters, and with his sickly excuse for a prince. No one wants the Tudors on the throne anymore. We have had two generations of Tudors, God forbid there should be a third. Should his son inherit the throne, with his Lutheran ways, it would cause civil war all over again. We need unity." She held up one finger. "We need fellowship." She added another finger. "We need harmony." A third finger sprang up. "And we have had none of that with the Tudors."

Geoffrey applauded his cousin, flipped the lid of the trunk shut and sat upon it. "Henry will go wild. He will retreat to one of his hunting lodges to live out his old age in staggering defeat." Geoffrey's eyes wandered off, betraying a hint of fear as Topaz's plan fermented in his mind.

She pinched her cousin's ruddy cheeks and cupped them in her palms. "We shall not fail, Geoffrey. This will be a peasant's revolt and a dissension of the nobility and a coup d'etat all rolled into one. Best of all, it will be peaceful. The age of chivalry will return yet."

"Who will be delivering these messages throughout the kingdom?" Geoffrey asked.

"My pages, your pages, every servant and squire we can spare, and of course, we shall personally deliver them to our fellow nobles. And, Geoffrey..." she hastened to add, "when you reach Kenilworth Castle, keep on going. That is the home of my former husband."

He stood and clapped his heels together, taking Topaz's hand in his. "As the faithful future subject of King Edward the Sixth, I am at your service, Queen Mother."

* * *

Topaz arrived at Gosfield Hall, the stately manor house of her closest neighbor and ally, Edward Hardwicke, the Earl of Arundel. Arundel had secretly provided her with funds for her first rebellion. She knew Arundel and his wife were in Scotland for a fortnight or so, as he'd asked her to keep an eye on his grounds and servants while he was away. To save her messengers' time, she delivered the message herself, for him to read when he arrived back home.

She dismounted, walked up the path lined with graceful elms and rapped the brass knocker against the oaken door. "Please deliver this message to Lord Hardwicke when he arrives back from Scotland," she told the insipid looking fellow who answered the door, whom she took as a servant.

She handed the sealed parchment to the man who took it with a feeble grip. "Aye, Madam, I shall."

She turned, climbed atop her mount, and rode off.

* * *

Hampton Court Palace

"That Warwick boy? No, it couldn't be. Has he actually inherited his mother's brass balls?" Henry implored Archbishop Cranmer, who entered the presence chamber with another fistful of letters.

"These are from the homes of the Earl of Westmoreland, the Earl of Wiltshire, and the Earl of Huntington, among others, your majesty," Cranmer announced.

The king's personal fool, Will Somers, came forward. "Sire, did these lords say who delivered the messages to their residences? Was it a man? A woman?"

Cranmer nodded. "Aye, most of them told me it had been a young boy, a servant, or a stable hand. Certainly no one of any importance."

Will turned to the king. "Your majesty, I just had a penetrating thought."

"Not now, Will, I am in no mood for any droll—"

"Nay, your majesty!" Will interrupted the king for the first time in his life. He had to, for he must enlighten the king before it was too late. "I was visiting my sister last week, remember, at Gosfield Hall."

"So what?" Henry rolled his head about in his hands.

"I answered the door, for Lord Hardwicke and my sister were not in residence. The messenger was not a young page, nay, sire. It was a beautiful woman...in a dark green velvet riding cloak with a bright circlet of flowers about her head and about her neck..."

Henry looked up and knocked a plate of chicken to the floor. The servitors scrambled to clean it up. "A woman, you say? Wearing...flowers?" His mind made rapid connections, unraveling his past. His memory sped backwards as if falling into a void... *beautiful woman, flowers, flowers about her hair, her neck, green, her color*...he remembered Amethyst telling him of Topaz shunning jewelry for flowers, favoring green, for it so accented the burnished lustre of her coppery hair...

Topaz.

"Will...Will...help me up!" the king strained in the huge chair made especially for him and Will sprang forward to help the king rise. He brushed the crumbs off his cloak and limped over to his writing desk, opened the top drawer and extracted a sheet of parchment. "I received this fairly recently. The note Lady Topaz, though I use the 'Lady' bit lightly, wrote about sending me Kathy Howard." He held it up to the candle, then called to Cranmer. "Bring over those other messages, will you?"

Holding the letter up next to one of the messages, he noticed a similarity in the handwriting. His eyes scanned each leaf, then whizzed down to the signature.

"The boy did not write this." Henry shook his head. "It was his mother, it was Topaz. Tell me, Will, what did she look like? Describe her to me, and do not leave out one detail."

Will racked his memory, trying to picture the fleeting image in his mind's eye. "The encounter had been so brief, Sire, I barely held the door open halfway, but I'll convey the few details I do remember..." He squeezed his eyes shut. "She had much dark reddish hair, a mean kind of look and, er..." He held his hands, palms up, level with his breast, and gestured. "She had a rather ample pair of... you know... heavers."

"Aye, I noticed the same thing when I met her," the king replied, his index finger pressed to his lip. "I shall seize her and you shall identify her." His voice regained its resonant tone. "If it is indeed she, she will go back to the Tower. She will rot there yet!"

* * *

Two guards escorted Topaz to the king in the council chamber. Will stood at his side, head erect. Topaz averted the king's hard stare, but upon looking at Will, a look of alarm registered in her features. They looked at each other for a split second, then both looked away as mutual recognition lit their eyes.

Will's gaze slid down Topaz's stony face, the lips set in a determined grimace, the long neck, and heaving under her low-cut bodice, the ample bosom...

"It is she!"

"Are you sure, Will?" the king asked, but it was not necessary. He knew she was guilty as sin and once again she was coming forth to admit it.

* * *

Later that morning guards dragged a struggling, whimpering and sobbing woman from her cell in the Tower to East Smithfield Green. There was no scaffold, only a low block. The hooded executioner stood by while the lord mayor and a few others gathered about.

Her writhing, twisting body broke free from the guards and she fled across the courtyard, leaving the stunned guards holding torn cloth from her sleeves.

The guards and the hooded executioner ran after her, each in a different direction, so that they surrounded her and dragged her back to the block, her knees buckling beneath her, her feet dragging, back to the spot where she was to die. The guards shoved her head down to the block.

The executioner wielded the axe, bringing it down only to embed the blade in the wood, for she had broken free again, inches from the blade's swiping blow as she writhed in the exasperated guards' arms. Her screams pervaded the courtyard as they slid her back down once again. The axe fell a second time, and split open her neck. Blood spewed out of the open wound. Her screams diminished to a strained gurgling, yet her arms and legs thrashed as she made a final desperate attempt to cling to life. The axeman wielded another blow, and another. Finally the body ceased thrashing and lay still. The arms dropped limply to the ground. The severed head rolled into the basket. The struggle was over. The executioner lay down the axe and wiped his hands, drenched with sweat, over his robe. He tore off his hood and breathed a sigh of relief.

The sixty-eight-year-old Countess of Salisbury, the last pretender to the throne and charged with treason, lay dead.

* * *

Word of Topaz's second attempted rebellion reached Cleobury, and Amethyst received an invitation from the king, so she rode by herself to the palace. She was not sure Henry would let Topaz live this time. A sickness pervaded her, and her mount's jostling gallop did not help.

She returned the courtiers' polite but curious nods as the king's guards led her to his chambers. He welcomed her, in a pale blue robe wrapped about his corpulence, a dark wine stain splashed across the front.

She rushed up to him, shunning protocol. "What happened to Topaz, sire? Did she rouse another army? Was there another battle?"

"Nothing of the sort." He shooed at her questions like a fly. "She merely had messengers send notes throughout her former followers and neutral subjects, in her son's name, to rally around him in a non-military coup. I expect she was counting on the neutral subjects, but many of them sent the messages right here to the palace to inform me."

His eyes lit up, and she knew he was getting to the good part. "Then my fool, Will, answered the door of his sister's house where Topaz went to personally deliver one of the messages. It was then we seized her. She has been taken to the Bell Tower where she will remain this time."

"Oh, God..." She wouldn't dare beg him for mercy. Even she believed Topaz had gone too far.

"The sad part is that it aroused such a great deal of support. But that is my fault, and my fault alone. My people have sent me a message, and in the remaining years I have as king, I must make amends with my subjects." His voice gathered volume. "I plan to go on more progresses, and mayhap even take Edward with me. After all, he is the next king. The people should get to know him." He swiped a chicken wing from a pile on a dish and gnawed on it.

"We seized several men along with your sister," he informed her, chewing. "Among them was your cousin Geoffrey Pole. Another was Roland Pilkington."

"But...I thought you sent for Roland to serve in the navy."

"He never showed. He resurfaced just yesterday, as one of your sister's supporters." He gnawed and chewed some more.

"Where is he now?" she asked.

"In the Salt Tower, with your cousin Pole, awaiting execution," he gestured out the window as if showing her the garden.

A wave of unexpected sadness washed over her. She took several deep, rapid breaths. Roland was going to die. What a terrible waste of a human life was this boy.

She gathered her courage and took one more of those deep breaths. "I...I wouldn't even bring this up weren't it for the history you and I have shared. But I hope you will let my sister live, sire. Not to give her freedom this time, just that she be allowed to live. She is a disturbed woman. She isn't evil, only troubled. As long as she is imprisoned, she cannot be a threat to you, so please...let her live, to spare my mother the grief...so that the lads will still have a mother."

Henry tossed the wing onto the table, wiping his hands on his robe. "Princess Elizabeth once asked me where her mother was, and I tried to explain, saying she'd gone to heaven. But she didn't quite understand where heaven was, or why her mother had gone there."

Amethyst pitied that poor child for all the hurt and resentment that would flood through her in her life, not to mention the hate she would harbor for her father…

"Out of my love for you and respect for your mother, I shall let Topaz live. But never to be set free."

She nearly collapsed with relief. Her heart calmed. "Thank you, sire. I know my mother will be forever grateful."

"Now I must make amends with you. I have wronged you time and again like I have never wronged another human being, and the tragically sad irony of it all is, you are the one I've cared about the most. You are the one person who would never deliberately cross me or harm the succession to the crown in any way. I acted impulsively when you told me you were expecting Gilford's child. I am growing old, Amethyst, all those who have betrayed me in the past have left so many scars, I cannot think straight anymore." He ran his hand over the last strands of hair on his head. "My jealousy of you made me react irrationally, but in my mind I felt you'd betrayed me when you came to me bearing Gilford's child. I want you to know how truly sorry I am. Tell me what I can do to make it up to you. Give me your wish…and I shall grant it."

That was simple. "Let me out of this loveless and horrid marriage, sire," was Amethyst's prompt request.

He nodded. "Very well, your wish is granted. I shall obtain a dispensation for an annulment. Although I can never right the wrong I did you, I can at least do this." He hesitated and ceased looking her in the eye. "But, Amethyst, there was one person whose life I was not able to spare."

"Who?"

"Your Aunt Margaret. She was imprisoned here in the Tower in March and she was executed this morn for treason."

A dagger went through her own heart. She sank into the chair before her.

"I am so sorry, Amethyst. It had to be done."

She heard his voice from a distance. *Aunt Margaret.* The aunt that had helped raised her since the day of her father's death, and for many years a second mother to Mary. As the last claimant to the crown, she and her sons had to be eliminated.

"I am sorry, too, my lord." But she couldn't bring herself to resent him for it. He did what he had to do. Wearing a crown was a dangerous job.

"I cannot risk having any more traitors threatening me or Edward," he went on, though she didn't want to hear any more of it. "I am letting Topaz live because of my love for you. But I simply could not help the others. Treason is punishable by death and so must it still be."

"I understand, sire. I must leave you now, I've...got chores."

She exited the palace and took the barge to the Tower to visit Topaz at the place where her sister was destined to be born and die.

Chapter Twenty

Hampton Court Palace, February, 1542

Amethyst sat in Princess Elizabeth's apartments giving her a lesson on the virginals. Henry entered and embraced them warmly.

"It is so good to see you, my lord." She stood and curtseyed. "How was the progress?"

"Splendid, my lady. Your fair Warwickshire truly loves their king," he gushed, giving Elizabeth a pat on the head and letting her grip his finger.

They left Elizabeth with her ladies and headed for his apartments.

"I have ordered a dispensation for your annulment, Amethyst. I will let you know when it will be final." The king held out his arms for his Esquire of the Body to remove his cloak. "Fetch me my black satin robe, Patrick." He began twisting and yanking the rings off his fingers, a laborious endeavor, as his fingers had grown so fat and thick, the ruby on his thumb was permanently stuck on. His last attempt to remove it had been two years ago.

"Thank you, sire. And when should that be?" Of course she wanted the exact date and time.

"As soon as I get round to it. Just be patient with me, Amethyst." As hard as it was to even think patiently, relief washed over her.

"That should go fast indeed," she said. "I have been busy with Elizabeth's music lessons. 'Tis so good to be back at court, sire. Even temporarily."

He smiled down at her. "A better tutor she could never have. And she could have been yours."

She turned away, tears stinging her eyes, tears for what could have been, should have been, but could never be.

* * *

A page delivered a message to the king: "Your majesty is wanted in the council chamber at once."

"What is it now?" he muttered to himself, hiking himself out of his monstrous chair and lumbering towards the chamber doors. "I shall return shortly," he told Amethyst. "Should you see Kathy… er, the queen, pray tell her I have returned."

"I shall, sire." But she knew Queen Katharine was not roaming the palace searching for the king to welcome him back into eager arms and enquire about the success of his progress. She was either in her chambers or those of Thomas Culpeper, with whom she spent a great deal of her time.

* * *

Henry called for Amethyst an hour later and she returned to his chambers. He looked as if he'd been struck down by God himself.

She rushed up to him, dispensing with the curtsey. "Sire! What is amiss? What happened at the council meeting? Are we being invaded by France again?"

"Nay, we are not being invaded by France." His voice cracked, a spitting rasp. She'd heard this tone only once before, when he spoke of Anne. Two days before her death, he'd spat forth fury and rage like a dragon hissing fire.

"What could have happened to make you so livid?" She stood back, afraid he'd strike her in his rage.

"We are not being invaded by France!" he repeated. "My wife is being invaded...by a list of rogues the length of your arm!" He balled up a sheet of parchment and flung it across the room. It hit a goblet, sending it crashing to the floor, a purple pool seeping into his precious Persian carpet.

"Oh, Jesu..." She'd warned Kathy, the uninhibited lass she'd met at Kenilworth that Christmas, whose standing as Queen of England did nothing to alter her behavior. She'd regarded Kathy as somewhat of a younger sister. *"Kathy, please,"* she'd warned her, *"Please be more discreet, meet Culpeper or... whoever else,"* as there were others, *"as far from the Palace as possible, for you are the Queen of England, you must keep your private life strictly separate from court life..."*

But the silly twit continued her dalliances, in her chambers with the king barely two rooms away, practically under his nose, as if in defiance, to avenge him for his flabby body and his lack of sexual appeal. She saw Katharine's end in sight as the ignorant girl couldn't. With that supposed immortality of youth, she continued her romps, her trysts, thinking that her position as queen would grant her immunity to the court gossip.

"She has shamed me, she has ridiculed me, has ridiculed the crown, has ridiculed the entire kingdom! She will pay for this and she will pay with her life!" He flung a goblet to the floor. Wine spilled like blood.

The king showed no remorse, no self-pity, no pleas to God as to why he'd been chosen to suffer. His life was the kingdom and personal relationships were no longer a priority. He displayed rage; pure, indignant exasperation, no longer diluted with those crippling emotions of hurt or grief as one scorned or betrayed by a loved one. He had spent too many years trying to mend ways and reconcile; now, anyone who crossed him, on a political or personal level, paid with their life.

The Queen of England was no exception.

* * *

After Mass the next morning, Amethyst exited the chapel. As she stepped into the corridor, she heard a faraway shrieking, the feral cries of someone crazed with terror. "Hen-reee! Hen-reee!" echoed down the hall, not so much a name, but a howl, long and drawn out, then receding until the cries died in the distance.

"Sire, what was that?" She turned to the king, next to her.

"You heard it too?" he whispered. "I thought it was in my mind again."

Amethyst peered into the long gallery, where all was quiet. The doors running along the left were closed, as were the windows at the right, shut against the harsh cold of winter.

It sounded like someone got murdered!

* * *

King Henry scratched his signature on Katharine's death warrant as he sat in the council chamber. "She is to die by the axe on Tower Hill in one week." His voice sounded as flat and defeated as he felt.

* * *

Katharine lost her head on the same block and upon the same scaffold her cousin Anne Boleyn had climbed six years ago. Her alleged lovers preceded her to their deaths. Once again Topaz watched the spectacle from her cell in the Bell Tower. "I die a queen but I would rather die the wife of Culpeper," were Katharine's last words.

Topaz *tsk*'d with a roll of her eyes. "Come now, you could've done better than that." Even with her last breath, Katharine lacked the diplomacy and eloquence of her cousin Anne, oblivious to how her final words would ring throughout history, not having bothered to deliver a rehearsed speech before the raucous mob now in a crushing frenzy to sop up her blood.

Henry was away at Richmond Palace on the day of the execution. Amethyst, staying in Mortimer's London townhome while awaiting her annulment, had just bitten into her breakfast when she heard the cannon shots. She put the bread down and pushed the plate away, her appetite gone.

The king was a widower for the third time.

* * *

Richmond Palace, June, 1542

King Henry summoned Amethyst to the palace where his groom and mount waited for him to arrive for a ride through the countryside.

She sat on the garden wall, pushing up her sleeves for her arms to get some sun. On this glorious day a few cloud wisps floated through the sky like languorous kites suspended over the earth.

The king arrived in his special litter, dressed all in white, riding cloak draped over his arm.

He sat next to her and dispensed with any greeting. "Amethyst, I need to try to quell this anxiety. I need to gather my thoughts and rid myself of these haunting demons."

"Which demons, sire? What is wrong?" She looked into his eyes, troubled and glazed over, no longer the glistening gold of his youth, but two muddy puddles surrounded by sagging pouches of gray. He looked as if he hadn't had a decent night's sleep in weeks.

"I am troubled and need to speak with someone who I believe has guided me a great deal through my life. I need to rid myself of hauntings, memories, the specters of my dead wives." He spoke in a low voice, not wanting any of the servants to hear him speaking of demons and ghosts. He never cared what servants thought before; throughout the years, they'd seen him at his very worst, but he cared not, for they didn't dare cross him.

Now, his thoughts and fears were for Amethyst's ears only. That was it, she realized. He'd never been afraid of anything or anyone in his life. Until now. And what was he afraid of? The dead, who could not possibly harm him?

"Sire, there are no demons. No one is haunting you. They are all dead and gone."

"You do not see what I see, Amethyst. As close as we ever could be, you cannot enter my head." He pressed his hands together as if begging for release of these demons from his haunted mind. "You cannot hear the voices, you cannot see with my eyes, you cannot see Anne's ghost or see Katharine's blood spewing forth before me."

"Surely someone can help rid you of these torments. Talk to a priest."

"I've given up on the clergy for obvious reasons." He held out his arms for her and she rested her head on her chest. "No, there is something I wish to do, and I want you to accompany me, as you are the only person I would have with me when I do this."

"What is it, sire?"

"I need to visit my parents' tomb in the Abbey. I feel my father...beckoning me, and I must go to him." He pulled away and looked into her eyes. "I've felt his presence about me for some time now. I need go there, for not only his mortal remains lie there. He took such pride in that tomb, I know his spirit will reside there for all eternity."

"How do you feel about his spirit visiting you? I've never known you to be a believer in spirits and such. Did this start with your father, or with...the other departed queens?"

"I feel comfort in his presence, but after I visit his tomb, he'll continue to rest there, knowing I've been there. He needn't beckon me any longer. I shall heed his call and let him rest in peace."

"Of course I shall accompany you to the Abbey, sire. As you wish." Westminster Abbey. It fascinated her in childhood, and she'd promised to return someday. So why hadn't she fulfilled that promise? Life had not bestowed upon her the luxury of much free time to appreciate her country's magnificent history. But now it beckoned her, as Henry's father beckoned him.

* * *

They arrived early the next morn, to visit the tomb in privacy. He needed help in and out of his specially made carriage with the extra wide door. He leaned on two golden canes, two ushers, and Amethyst, and still needed to take painstakingly small steps. It took a long while to alight from the carriage and walk through the West Entrance, but once she was within the shadowy shrine's hallowed walls, she knew where she belonged.

She let the king have his privacy and lingered behind, for she wanted to see it and breathe it all over again. As she gazed upward at the soaring ceiling and at the magnificent ancient effigies, the invading chill penetrated her like a haunting spirit. The growing daylight filtered weakly through the stained glass windows but afforded little light as she made her way down the North Choir Aisle and past the coronation chair.

Knowing this was a privilege afforded to a select few who would ever pass through this kingdom, she reached out and slowly ran her fingers over the smooth wood, reading each scrape and notch the chair had endured over the centuries. She knelt and touched the Stone of Scone under the chair. The sandstone block was surprisingly smooth. As her footsteps on the flagstones echoed throughout the cavernous walls and up through the vaulted ceilings, she turned her head in every direction in order to drink it all in. All around her were marble tombs, inscriptions, chapels, and fan vaulting splaying out above. She walked down the same aisle young Henry and Catherine had as they'd swept by her, remembering how his robe brushed her foot and how their eyes met ever so briefly in total absence of recognition, on his way to becoming king.

She passed through the chapel of Edward the Confessor and knelt at the recess on the side of the five-hundred-year-old marble tomb. Pilgrims had come here through the centuries to beg cures for the plagues and pestilences that snatched away lives without mercy. She said a short prayer and walked further on, past the tomb of King Richard II and his queen, Anne of Bohemia, immortalized in gilt-bronze figures. She stopped to look at Edward III's tomb, his gilt-bronze effigy, and statuettes of his twelve children, next to the black marble tomb and white marble effigy of his queen, Philippa.

She finally reached the Chapel of Henry VII, Henry's father. The exquisite airy fan vaulting spread out above her, the walls encrusted with tracery, niches crowded with statues of saints and martyrs. After watching him back away signaling his private time was over, she approached him. "Can I touch it, my lord?" she blurted out like a child.

He smiled and nodded. "You can enter it if you wish." He limped up to the ornately carved bronze grille enclosing the tomb and opened the gate with a small key. Amethyst peered twixt the bars to get a glimpse of the elaborate tomb. It was of black marble, atop which rested gilt effigies of King Henry VII and Elizabeth of York, their hands clasped in prayer. Two gold lion cubs crouched on sculptured cushions at their feet, the folds so delicate and soft they could have been made of satin. Golden angels with spread wings stood guard like heavenly sentinels at the four corners of the tomb, a gold medallion twixt them bearing coats of arms. More golden angels graced the tomb around its sides.

She followed him inside. Walking to the front of the tomb to the marble pillared altar topped with gilded angels, she knelt and prayed.

Looking up above at the curved arches that framed the delicate fan vaulting like a group of carved wine goblets rising above the arched leaded windows, she swore she could see heaven.

They retraced their steps and exited the Abbey through the North Entrance. She turned around and took one more look at the towering Gothic structure, the house of God and the mortal remains of the great immortals.

"It is the most magnificent place in the entire world, sire," she sighed as Henry's attendants helped him into the carriage. With the king settled, she bounced up with a light boost from one of the men.

"Do you wish to spend eternity within the Abbey walls, Amethyst?" he asked her.

"Oh, my lord, I couldn't! I mean...look at who I am!" She shook her head, the idea amusing her.

"If you so desire it, my darling, you shall repose there. And so will your children. After all, you are a Plantagenet." In granting her this gift, he regained all her trust and respect.

"Oh, sire, that is the most gracious honor, the most distinct tribute one could be given, to be entombed in England's greatest church alongside kings and queens, princes, knights and nobles... such a glorious display of respect. I never considered where my final resting place would be."

"Of course, you're young, you have a few more years left." He gave her a wry grin and she slid over to hug him.

But as the carriage pulled away and the Abbey slid from sight, she no longer wished to speak of death or final resting places. She never mentioned it to Henry again.

Chapter Twenty-One

Cleobury, June, 1542

The sweating sickness broke out again, claiming 50 lives in their village within the first week.

As Mortimer and Amethyst returned from a buying trip to London, Martha the cook bustled out of the pantry, hands clasped, the color drained from her face.

"What is it, Martha?" Amethyst jumped down from the coach and approached the frantic woman. "Why is all so silent? Why is there no one working in the fields?"

"'Tis the sweat, Lady Pilkington. The whole household's gotten it. I am the only one on my feet, for I had it when I was a lass." Martha wiped her hands on her apron and Amethyst couldn't help glancing there, hoping not to see sweat stains.

Amethyst called after Mortimer, heading upstairs for the chambers. "Everybody seems to have the sweat."

"I shall look in on them," he called over his shoulder. "Keep your whelp out of here. Get him to the gatehouse."

She went back to the cook. "Have you tried to fetch Dr. Ashworth, Martha?"

"Nay, I couldn't get any further than the well, all the folk here scream for water every two minutes." She swiped at her forehead with her arm.

Amethyst approached her groom as he guided Lady, her new palfrey, to the stables. "Kevin, I must take her again. I must fetch the doctor. The entire house has the sweat!"

The groom shot her a look of panic and his face whitened like a pale moon behind the clouds. "God's foot, the sweat! Shall I go with you?"

"Nay, go fetch some water from the well. Bring it to the folk in the chambers. I shall be back."

She rode as fast as Lady's strong legs could take her. She breathed in the warm sweet air and tried to appreciate the trees in bloom all about her. Patches of luscious green rose to the hills. A tangle of trees letting in dappled sunlight canopied the narrow road to Dr. Ashworth's residence.

She approached the outskirts of his village knowing something was terribly wrong. No one was about; windows were shut, all was quiet. This was more ominous than the approach to her own home, for here was an entire village deserted. She'd never felt so alone, so mortal.

She led Lady past the empty market square. All shops were shut tight, awnings drawn over the stands, doors closed. A scattering of rotten apples and peaches lay on the ground, the last vestiges of the abandoned hamlet. She shuddered, tightening her legs round Lady's smooth back, the contact with another living being somewhat of a comfort.

She heaved a sigh of relief at the sight of Dr. Ashworth's house beyond the gravel path surrounded by oaks. But as she led Lady up the path, that same dread overcame her. She knew without even looking any further that the house was deserted. Something made her continue on, and she dismounted Lady and tied her to a post. Clapping the knocker against Dr. Ashworth's door, she glanced around. Never had she seen anywhere so deserted. It reminded her of the stories she'd heard about Pompeii buried under volcanic ash.

The door finally opened and a lass appeared, half hidden behind the door.

"Is Dr. Ashworth in?" She peeked inside.

"Dr. Ashworth passed on, Madam. The sweat...got the entire village. Nearly everyone gone, but I stayed here. Me mum, she's abed, not long for this world."

"Oh, Jesu!" Dr. Ashworth, who'd tended Harry during a bout of fever, and cured Mortimer of agonizing gallstones with a simple surgery, gone. "The village...has everyone fled?"

"Aye, either by choice or by death, Madam. It swept through but a week ago. Most fled, but the remaining folk perished, either in their houses or buried by a brave few priests still about." She pointed down the road. "Try the church."

"Nay...nay, I must return home. God be with you, child." She backed away, took a glance at an upstairs window, curtains drawn against the hot sun like a death chamber, the entire village tormented with death.

She arrived back home hot and tired, the sun poised low in a sky strewn with blotches of red, shedding a sloping path of orange light down the hills.

Mortimer sat on the small pallet in the gatehouse, his chin in his hands. His black eyes stared out into space. Harry was sleeping peacefully next to him.

"Is he all right?" She rushed over to him and touched her finger to his cheek.

"He seems all right enough, spitting up and shitting all over the place as usual. What of Dr. Ashworth?" he asked.

"Dr. Ashworth died of the sweat." Harry began to awaken and let out a squall. She lifted him into her arms and rocked him. "The entire village is deserted. I talked to one of his servants. Her mother was dying upstairs. We are alone."

She prayed for this terrifying disease to spare her child. "How about the household?" she asked.

"Martha is wiping them down, going twixt the three of them," he answered, still staring. "She already had the sweat and is immune. And what about you?" He finally glanced her way.

It was the first question he'd ever asked her about herself. "Topaz and I both had the sweat during one outbreak when we were with Aunt Margaret, before the king gave us Warwick Castle."

"I never had the sweat," he declared, as if proud of it.

Oh, God, just what she needed to know. "We shall stay here in the gatehouse where we will be safe. The stablehands are assisting Martha with the other servants. We must get through this. We must!" She clasped Harry close to her heart.

"I worry not." Mortimer calmly rose from the pallet. "Put the baby down." He took Harry from her arms and placed him on the small pallet the baby had been lying on. He led Amethyst by the shoulders over to the larger pallet. "Our marriage has not been dissolved yet. And if I am to die, I want to know my wife in my final moments."

He yanked at the buttons of her bodice. He peeled off his breeches and hose, pulled her down beside him, and there he took her. The baby crawled to a corner, curled up and slept as his stepfather mounted his mother and groaned, writhed and strained on the straw pallet.

* * *

The sun was about to dip below the cedar trees as Amethyst gazed out the window, up the path at the main house. One of the grooms headed for the well with a large bucket. She turned away, took Harry into her arms and nestled in a corner of the pallet, as far away from her sleeping husband as possible.

Only a fortnight, and she would be free of him.

Unless he succumbed to the sweat... she pushed the thought from her mind and held her son even closer.

* * *

She awoke to the sound of moaning and instinctively turned to Harry. He was sleeping peacefully. She peered over at Mortimer and saw his stony features contorted in pain. She pressed her hand to his forehead. It was burning up and drenched with sweat. Oh, God Jesu, her thoughts had become reality.

She reached for the bucket. In the dim light the distant moon afforded, she wrung out the rag and swept it over his face, his arms, his chest.

Mortimer gasped. "Save me, please save me..." Astounded at this drastic change, for she believed he would die with the same stoic frigidity as he'd lived, she filled the pewter cup with fresh water. Holding it to his lips, she propped his head up with her free hand.

"Drink this." She parted his lips with the rim of the cup, but his teeth were clenched. "You must drink this if you care to live!" she shouted. With another painful groan, his head lolled to one side and fell back against the support of her hand. She remembered treacle being a remedy for the sweat, but there was none here in the gatehouse. Should Mortimer expire, she had to protect the life that meant more than her own—her child's. She had no reason to live without Harry. "I'll go up to the main house to see if Martha can rustle up some treacle," she whispered to her husband, unsure if he heard her.

She bunched a blanket in the corner as far from Mortimer as possible and wrapped Harry up. She slipped out the gatehouse door and sprinted up the path toward the main house. She knew that the sweat lasted no more than a few days, and the patient needed be bedridden for twenty-four hours, followed by a week's quarantine. Whether he lived or died, her marriage would soon be over. A sudden revelation hit her: whether he lived or died, she didn't care.

She opened the front door and closed it behind her. Her slippers scuffed over the stone floor as she headed for the staircase leading to Mortimer's solar. She would find Martha down the hall in Amethyst's outer chamber, where she always slept. Shadows crept up and receded as she strode down the long gallery, memorizing the layout of furniture she could not see in the blackness. Entering the chamber, she called out, "Martha...are you awake? 'Tis I, Amethyst. I need some treacle..." The room was as quiet as a tomb.

She descended the staircase, her hand sliding down the rail, guiding her. She turned and bumped into Martha at the bottom. "Martha,

Mortimer has been stricken. Harry will be next if I do not protect him. I need some treacle."

"There is none, Lady Amethyst. The other three...and Kev, they...they done passed on, sometime in the night."

Her gasp echoed through the dark rooms. "Oh, no."

"We have to get their bodies out of here...you and me." Martha started to bolt.

Amethyst grabbed her arm. "No, Martha...wait. I shall ride to Whitehall in haste, and summon the king's help. I shall be back by daybreak. Just go to the gatehouse and look in on Mortimer. Take Harry out of there, away from him. Bundle him in your arms and go to the stables until I get back."

She turned, leaving a stunned Martha, fled to the stables where she saddled and mounted Lady, and rode off into the night towards London.

It was still dark when she approached the palace gates, but she felt as if she'd ridden nonstop for a week. Her bottom ached so badly from the violent whacking against the saddle, she doubted she'd be able to walk.

She left Lady at the gatehouse, tied to a tree branch, for there was not a stablehand in sight. As the yeomen guarding the gates recognized her, she babbled incoherently about needing to see the king. She rushed through the dark galleries, past the great hall, silent in its slumber, devoid of all the glowing candles, music and voices, and headed for the king's apartments.

At the door to his privy chamber, his yeoman-in-waiting gave her a nod and let her pass. She burst into his bedchamber, tripped over the two sleeping yeomen on palliasses and fell onto Henry's Persian rug. "Sorry! So sorry!" she stammered over her shoulder, scrambling to her feet, gathering her skirts, fumbling in the dim torchlight as she approached the king. His enormous bed dwarfed even his huge frame beneath the covers. She stumbled up to him, tripping over the edge of another rug.

"Sire! Sire, please wake up, 'tis a matter of life and death!" She shook him gently, then more forcefully, as he was a deep sleeper, especially after a night of heavy gorging and feasting.

He turned over to face her, trying to focus in the weak stream of daybreak peeking through the window.

"Amethyst? What is it?" he mumbled, his words garbled and sleepy.

"Sire, Mortimer has the sweat, it has just killed my entire household, and my baby is going to be stricken next!" her voice shook with sobs. "I need your help. Please get Dr. Butts to come at once with some treacle, for my baby is in mortal danger."

He reached out to her and she collapsed into the warm cocoon of his linen nightshirt. "It will be all right, I shall find Dr. Butts."

He rose and roused his grooms, who stumbled from their pallets sleepily and scurried around to get dressed. Moments later they summoned the doctor, and Henry ordered his Esquire of the Body to dress him. The clock struck the hour of five. He would have been rising soon for Mass anyway. However, this morning, he ordered another groom to go to Cleobury, fetch young Harry and bring him back to the palace where he would be safe. He then sat with Amethyst and tried to calm her.

Exhausted from the ride and weak from hunger, she fell into the king's bed and drifted off into a dead sleep. She did not wake until noon, when bright light flooded the chamber with the scurryings and sounds of another ordinary day.

She asked an usher to find the king and he appeared a while later with Harry in his arms. "He was safe, Amethyst, Dr. Butts looked him over, found him fine and brought him here. He's been fed and he fares well."

"Oh, thank God!" She clasped her son and he wrapped his chubby arms round her neck as she crooned to him softly, rocking him back and forth. She lay him on the bed and the king sat next to her.

She had to ask the next question. "And how is Mortimer?"

The king's face told her. His eyes, usually mean slits of deep thought and concentration, were darkened. "Mortimer has left us, Amethyst. May he rest in peace."

"Yes." A thunderous flood of emotions, sorrow, pity, relief, all converged in her heart. As her eyes filled with tears, she began laughing hysterically. Sobs racked her body as tears poured forth, and the king's warm comforting arms wound round her. She felt as if she had come full circle, and somehow it all felt right.

* * *

Mortimer was buried with his family in the graveyard adjoining St. Stephen's Church down the road from Cleobury. There was no one to give a eulogy. The villagers had either died or fled the epidemic.

Amethyst slid the thin gold band off her finger and placed it upon Mortimer's chest just before they shut his coffin and lowered it into the ground. She did not say goodbye.

Sabine turned to Amethyst at the burial site, just as the first shovelful of dirt fell atop Mortimer's coffin. "Matthew could not attend, but he extended his condolences."

Hearing Matthew's name unleashed a rush of emotions she could no longer harbor deep inside. Leaving the small party standing rigidly at the graveside, she turned and fled into the church, rushed to the altar and knelt. "Give me strength, Lord," she prayed. "Give me the strength to raise Harry in Mortimer's name and live with this terrible lie. Let me always be respectful to his memory. Let me be the best I can be."

She inherited Cleobory as well as their London home, his money, jewels and plate, and there was a great deal, as Mortimer had been miserly his entire life. She wanted nothing from this marriage, so she planned to sell everything and donate the proceeds to the poor.

She took her wedding gown, folded it tightly and placed it in her hearth. The flames consumed it, turning it to charred blackness as she turned and walked away.

* * *

The king invited her to join him on his summer progress through the shires. "Oh, sire, you don't know what this means to me!" And she made sure he didn't know. This journey would take her mind off Matthew and the unforgiveable way she'd wronged him. When Mortimer was alive, she spent those endless nights in her fantasy world, reliving those blissful moments with Matthew. She cherished that memory, a precious jewel in a velvet box, and closed the box when real life summoned her.

Now she purged Matthew from her mind as the royal carriage jostled over dusty roads, fields of bluebells and East Anglia's dark marshy fens in the distance.

After dinner one eve at Eltham in Kent, one of Henry's boyhood homes, they sat and chatted. Henry steered the conversation to a serious topic she'd avoided up to now.

"Amethyst, I believe you should tell little Harry of his true parentage by his next birthday. You cannot deprive him of his heritage. You created a living legacy that belongs to the Gilfords. It is wrong to deny Matthew and Harry the joy they deserve in one another...and you and Matthew should also be together."

"But he is still married to Topaz," she reminded him of that one detail.

Henry traced his finger round the rim of his goblet, deep in thought.

Please force her to divorce him, she silently begged. *You can do it—you managed to divorce Catherine by breaking with the church! Why not a simple divorce twixt two subjects?* She decided to speak up. After all they'd been through, she was entitled to this simple favor. "Henry, can you grant Matthew a divorce, on the grounds that Topaz was unfaithful? Not to him, of course, but to the crown, when she staged her rebellion." Her heart stopped as she held her breath awaiting his answer.

"Hm..." He stroked his beard. Those golden eyes narrowed into calculating slashes as she'd seen so many times. She did not dare interrupt him; for to break Henry's train of thought could mean the very doom of the kingdom. "I'll send her a letter appealing to her kinder nature—and she does have one hidden under those skirts somewhere, doesn't she?"

"Oh, yes, of course!"

He started to prop his bad leg on the chair next to him. Watching him struggle to lift the enormous weight, she got up to help him, but he waved her away. He sat back and said, "Your son and his father must suffer no longer. It is especially unfair to the child. I never meant any harm to the child. All I wanted to do was punish you and Gilford. I never would have wanted to go through life not knowing who my true father was."

"They do deserve the truth. It's been tearing me apart inside. But I held back because I know how difficult life is for illegitimate children. They suffer during adulthood also. I thought it better for Harry to believe he was a Pilkington, the product of a marriage, rather than the product of..." she needn't finish.

"I won't force a divorce on your sister. But I shall put her to the test of her life—to decide if she loves her own sons more than the husband she refuses to set free. I shall give her what no other prisoner languishing in the Tower will ever have...a choice."

* * *

Topaz received a simple proposal from the king: *if you grant Matthew a divorce, you will be allowed to see your sons.*

"My darling babies in exchange for that mindless buffoon? Aye, I shall grant him a million divorces!" The decision required no pondering, no weighing of consequences, no thought whatsoever.

* * *

Henry, going about his royal duties, paused for a moment. *Will she pass my test?*

Chapter Twenty-Two

The Tower of London, September, 1542

Streaming banners atop the White Tower's four peaks fluttered in the breeze. Matthew entered the imposing structure, suppressing a shudder. Oh, what misery and torture these walls beheld.

His eyes avoided the scaffold site as two guards escorted him across Tower Green. Approaching the round Beauchamp Tower, he glanced up at the small openings cut into the stone. These narrow slits provided the only view of the world outside. His heart went out to those doomed prisoners he'd never met—most prominent of all, Edward of Warwick confined here for life. He so admired Sabine's stoic tolerance to a lifetime of imprisonment, only because her husband was a helpless victim.

The guards led him inside and up a winding staircase. Slices of light spilled in from those narrow slits in the wall.

They approached a rotting wooden door bolted with a rusty lock. One of the guards opened it with a skeleton key from a ring jangling with keys.

The door swung open and the guards motioned him in. He stepped into a small stuffy cell, one window crossed with bars, letting in barely enough light to see a straw pallet and battered table. Claustrophobia panicked him as the walls closed in on him. His eyes adjusting to the dimness, he saw a pile of logs smoldering in a pit. A small figure huddled before it.

He knew that dark auburn hair, even in the gloomy shadows. It hung about her shoulders, ratty and unkempt. He saw the outline of bones jutting out from the thin shawl wrapped about her shoulders.

She stood and stared straight at him. Hit with sickening recognition, he stepped back in shock. Sunk into her pallid face, her eyes no longer beheld that spark of conviction and life. They were dull; defeated. She gave a slight nod, as if waiting for him to speak first. He looked into the lifeless orbs unmasking the shadow of the woman he once loved.

He heard the door clang shut behind him and the guard clear his throat.

"Topaz...I come to thank you." He did not step any closer.

"Have you seen my sons?" Her feeble voice echoed her defeat and ruin.

"Aye," he answered. "A little while ago."

"The king is going to let me see them. Do they fare well?" She approached him and he stepped back.

"They are quite comfortable," he informed her. "They do not complain. They keep well occupied with their books and their prayers."

"Lutheran prayers, no doubt." She stopped and spat upon the filthy floor.

"It matters not how they worship, Topaz." *Why would she care about that?* he wondered, but didn't want to get into a religious discussion. "They are prisoners here and shall never escape these confines."

"You come to thank me for granting your divorce, and begin bellowing about the fate of our sons." Her voice gathered volume and struggled to regain its characteristic chiding tone.

"Amethyst's husband died from the sweating sickness in June." He took a breath to sneeze but the foul odors made him choke.

"Oh, I am sorry to hear that. I know nothing of the family's goings-on since my imprisonment. How is their child?"

He refrained from holding his nose. He realized with horror most of those foul odors came from her body. "I have never seen him, but

I trust he is well," he said. "I have not heard otherwise. Amethyst and I have not been corresponding."

"I suppose she is going to return to court, since Henry is a widower again." She slipped her shawl off and swept it back round her shoulders. A wave of body odor hit him. "That information I was able to procure first-hand, from this very window." Of course she referred to Katharine Howard's beheading.

He breathed through his mouth. "I know not if she plans to return to court. That is why I have come to thank you for granting me the divorce. I plan to marry Amethyst. I am in love with her and wish to be free of the marriage you and I entered."

"You finally admit it then?" She came closer and he backed up against the wall.

"What do you mean?" He kept breathing through his nose. "You knew?"

"Emerald told me you two were…rather cozy. But the joy of seeing my babies outshines any further benefit I derive from being married to you." Her breath reached him, stale and odorous.

"It did not happen until much later," he made sure she knew. "You and I had been estranged for quite some time."

"And now you want to marry her, you say." Now she stood within half an arm's length.

"Aye." He turned his head sideways. "My love for her has waned not one bit over the years, for I miss her even more now. I was hurt when she married Mortimer…but I knew it was on the king's orders and she had to obey."

"Aye, a more obedient servant there never was," she remarked.

"She and Henry were as close as two people can be, but do not share the love she and I now do," he emphasized that so it would sink in to her stubborn head. "So I ask you to set me free to marry her now. She arranged for your release the first time. I gave you your beloved sons. Now that the king has given you this choice, you have no reason to hold onto our marriage any longer."

To his relief, she turned away and went to the window. He gulped the musty air, clearing her odors from his nose and mouth. Watching her, he observed her profile. It was sagging, haggard. She had aged so many years since he'd last seen her. She'd taken many years off her life fighting for her cause. He could almost admire her for it.

She faced him. "You are right, Matthew, there is no reason for our marriage to remain intact. You are granted the divorce. Go and marry Amethyst. And hurry, before she marries the king. Then you will have to wait another year or two before she is widowed again."

"Thank you again, Topaz..." He forced himself to approach her, kneeling as he took her hand in his. It felt like the papery surface of parchment upon his lips. Eager to escape, he bowed out of her cell as if she were royalty, to grant her that one last dignity, then nearly fell over his feet getting out of there.

He exited the Tower gates, jumped upon his mount, spurred it on, and tore down the road to Warwickshire.

* * *

Sabine led her grandson Harry on his new pony, Maggie. She gripped the reins with one hand and wrapped her other arm protectively around the spirited toddler, thumping the horse's sides with his pudgy legs, as if to spur her on. "Nay, she's only a pony, Harry." Sabine laughed with delight at her precocious grandson. "When you get to be a bigger boy, then you can ride a stallion through the countryside and jump fences and ford streams. But all little Maggie can do is walk round the grounds, after all, she's a baby just like you."

The clatter of hoofbeats approached the stables. Sabine turned to see who her visitor was, for she was expecting a delivery of fabrics from Paris.

The rider swept his hat off as he came into focus. She saw the wind slapping the dark blond hair across his face. He grinned, waving his free arm in greeting, calling out, sounding very joyful indeed.

"Sabine!" He jumped off the mount and ran to embrace her.

"Why, Matthew! Whatever brings you here?"

"I must see Amethyst! But first..." He looked at the boy, approached him and held out his hand. "Hello, little fellow," were the first words he ever spoke to Harry. They clasped hands and studied each other for a long moment with equal curiosity. Matthew regarded the life Amethyst had created—of the same flesh of the woman he loved. A pang of remorse weighed on his heart for this fatherless boy. "I am Matthew Gilford. You must be Harry."

As Matthew clasped the boy's hand an instant bond melded their souls. *I am going to be this boy's new father.* Tears sprang to his eyes at the thought.

He turned to Sabine. "Is she here?"

"Aye, she is." She waved in the direction of the gatehouse. "I believe she is in the solar playing the virginals."

Sabine called a stable boy to take Matthew's mount and with another smile at the child, he broke into a run—to Amethyst, his future wife.

A servant led him through the corridor and knocked on the solar door. As the door opened, light flooded the darkened corridor. There she stood in the doorway, her silhouette blocked out by the rays of light glowing from inside. He knew every detail—the waves of her hair, the curve of her shoulders, the cinched waist, the billowing of her skirts about her hips, lying in graceful folds about her feet.

Her eyes widened in wonder, with nearly as much awe as when she'd floated through the rooms of Warwick Castle for the first time. It took no more than a split second to take him all in—his glittering eyes, his muscular arms, his hair feathered over his ears, his trimmed beard shading his squared off jaw and parting lips, which broke into a dazzling smile.

He entered the room and her features converged before his eyes. His loving gaze met her dumbfounded stare. "Matthew..." That one utterance spoke not of their past denial, but of wonder, gratitude—with a longing he hadn't sensed since their last night together.

They fell into each other's arms.

She was dressed entirely in black widow's weeds. It looked so unnatural on her, turning her skin to a sallow paleness, so unlike the bright hues that reflected her ebullient nature.

They pulled apart and he cupped her face in his hands. "Amethyst…I am free!" He spoke the words he'd been bursting to tell her, during that agonizingly long ride from London, the words he'd spoken in his mind over and over again, over so many years…

"Free? How?"

"She granted me a divorce." The words rushed out of him. "I spoke to the king at Greenwich and then went to the Tower to see her and to see the lads."

"They are well?" she asked.

"Aye! Though it breaks my heart that they are prisoners, I am glad they are alive." He spoke between rapid breaths. "I told her I was in love with you and wanted to marry you. We both knew there was no reason for us to remain married. I shall get the dispensation…by then you will be out of mourning and we will be married!"

She clasped her fingers together, gazing up at the heavens. "Oh, blessed King Henry! He must have finally convinced her."

"She did not mention the king at all," he said. "She made it sound like it was her decision."

"Pish posh!" She shook her head. "This is Henry's doing, I know it! He wanted me to…" She stopped dead in her tracks, for she was rushing ahead of herself. "Oh, Matthew, that is wonderful news!"

"You look happier than I have seen you in a long time, darling. Please tell me you love me…it would make it all complete if you just let me hear those words I've been longing to hear."

"Of course I love you, Matthew. I've loved you for such a long time, but what good would it have done to tell you? I was married, you were married—"

"But now we're free. We must tell your mother…and Harry!"

"You…met Harry?" She searched his eyes for some sign of perplexity, but saw nothing but the brightness of love and happiness, as brilliant as the crisp autumn air.

"I just met them by the stables with his pony." He beamed. "He's going to be quite a man."

He'd already met his son. But she was finally free to tell him. She could not deny this man his son any longer. She dreaded his reaction, hoping their love would supersede his resentment. "Matthew, there's something I must tell you."

She clasped his hand and he circled her palm with his thumb, remembering Topaz's skeletal claws as they curled around his hand, baring her frailty.

"Let us first tell Sabine and Harry the good news." He tugged her towards the doorway.

"Nay, Matthew..." She grasped his arm and guided him over to the window seat where she saw Sabine guiding Harry around on the pony. "I must tell you this, but..." Her gaze permeated his, begging him to forgive what she'd done to him. "Please, you must understand, it was the only thing I could have done."

"What?" he questioned, unable to imagine anything that would diminish his love for her.

"Harry...Harry is your son."

His gaze flew down to the courtyard, straining to see the figure that had just ridden through the gate, out of his sight. "Harry? Mine?"

"Matthew, we conceived him that Christmas when I visited you at Kenilworth."

He looked at her, not with anger or resentment, but with awe, as if she'd just healed a wound that had plagued him for a long time.

"You were married to Topaz, I could never have told you then," she said. "The king flew into a rage, because he and I were about to be married. So to punish me, he married me to Mortimer. I went into confinement and didn't emerge until three months after the baby was born, to quell any suspicion..." She inhaled deeply and bowed her head. "Oh, Matthew, how it tore me apart to have kept this from you. But Topaz wouldn't let you go..." She covered her face with her hands and released the anguished sobs she'd harbored for so long. Now it all poured forth. The truth finally dispelled the lies she'd been living.

"Amethyst, my darling…it is all right. What matters is now, the future. Now…let us go join our son. He did take a bit of a fancy to me." Matthew wrapped his betrothed in his arms.

* * *

One week later to the day, Topaz fired off an impatient note to the king asking when she could see her sons. She had granted Matthew his divorce. Now she demanded Henry uphold his half of the bargain. Her note went unanswered. The boys remained in their cell, Topaz in hers.

* * *

Hampton Court Palace Queen's Closet, 1543

On the day Matthew was granted his divorce, King Henry and Katherine Parr exchanged wedding vows before Archbishop Cranmer. He'd chosen this educated, wealthy, twice-widowed woman of thirty-one to care for him, coddle him and nurture him through his old age and eventual infirmity. Never was a woman so different from Katharine Howard and Anne Boleyn.

Amethyst sat with the king on the eve before his marriage in his inner chamber. She strummed her lute and they sang together as they always had, not forgetting a word, not missing a note. His bloated and painful body restricted his movements, depriving him of most of the sensual pleasures he once knew. Although he was no longer able to strum his lute or harp, his voice still retained the sharp and melodic tone of his youth, and they still harmonized beautifully.

"I am so glad you are taking Lady Latimer as your wife, sire." She toasted him with a goblet of May wine.

"She seems so kind and understanding…"

"…but much too young, I am afraid," he finished. "I hope I can make her happy. I believed I needed someone of my own generation to walk with me through these final stages, to grow old and sluggish with me, to sit when I cannot dance, to walk when I cannot run, to retire when I can no longer stay awake. But in the end I just could not. An old man like me, and here I am with that ever-roving eye for a pretty young lass."

"But you are not old, sire." Her voice gathered that encouragement he craved. "Why, my mother is older than you and she is as sprightly and energetic as ever."

"Ah, yes, and she has regained her youthful figure. Look at me, Amethyst." He ran his hand over his ample torso. "I am a huge mountain of a man. The days of my youth are gone, and I have not many days ahead of me. I would be a fool to think otherwise."

"Do not talk like that, sire." It upset her so, knowing that the end of his reign would mean the end of an era...and the end of the lengthiest, most significant chapter of her life. How tragic that it could ever possibly come to a close. "You have many years ahead of you."

"I just hope I can make Kate happy. Lord knows, all my other marriages were such mismatches...except Jane, my dear Jane." His eyes shut and she knew he was fighting back tears. "The first two were not even marriages in the legal sense, they were mockeries of the holy sacrament of matrimony. Not one of them had a happy ending, Amethyst. Five times married, and every one ended in tragedy." He shook his head, his voice laden with regret.

"You have Mary, and Elizabeth, and Edward. You shall leave quite a legacy," she never let him forget what his children meant to him.

"And if God be with this kingdom after my departure, I trust he will make Edward the greatest monarch it will ever see." These words emerged with a bit more hope.

"There have been queens who have been great, my lord. There was Matilda, and Eleanor... "

"Aye, Amethyst, and do you know what the Boleyn witch told me just days before her death?" His eyes settled upon her. "That Elizabeth would be the greatest queen that ever lived. Ha!" His laughter ended in a fit of coughing. "That sprightly minx, a great queen? Already she is an incorrigible flirt. She will willingly offer her hand to the first dashing rogue that captures her heart and damn the kingdom. Nay,

Elizabeth is out of the running. She's got too much of Anne in her to ever give a passing glance to the crown."

"Aye, I suppose you are right, my lord." There she had to agree. "Elizabeth's heart is just itching to be captured. She is such a bright girl. She would have made quite a skillful leader."

* * *

Topaz screamed for the guard and he strolled up to the iron bars separating the prisoner from the outside world, for he had nothing else to do.

"Cease your bellowing, wench. What is it that you want?"

"I want you to send a message to Henry Tudor, a verbal message, for written ones do not seem to get to him!" she shrieked. "Tell him I want to see my sons. He told me he would reunite us when I granted my simpleton husband his bloody divorce. He is about to marry my sister, and I still have not seen—"

"Cease!" His voice cut the musty air like a sword.

Topaz's shrill wails and the guard's command echoed in clamorous discord and faded.

"The king will grant you your wish when he sees fit. It is not my duty to cater to prisoners. I am not a messenger." He spun on a heel and marched off. She reached twixt the bars to grab his cloak but he yanked it away, his footsteps dying into silence.

"I want to see my sons!" Topaz screamed, at no one, banging her fists on the iron bars, shaking them, rattling them on their rusty hinges. "That Tudor bastard! He will rot for this!"

* * *

Amethyst and Matthew were married in the Hampton Court chapel one year to the day after Mortimer's death. The king gave the bride away, and this time she glowed with the promise of a new and happy life with her beloved.

As the Archbishop said, "You may kiss the bride," she placed her hand on his forearm, feeling the quivering passion as they shared their first kiss as man and wife.

* * *

On that same day, Geoffrey Pole and Roland Pilkington were executed on Tower Green for treason.

The Pilkington line ended as Amethyst's new life began.

* * *

Henry's wedding present to them was the gift of Pendennis Castle, a fortress on the Cornwall coast.

"You will take care of Pendennis, Matthew," Henry told Amethyst's new husband, "and make sure she is always well-fortified. It is in a most strategic spot, a mile from St. Mawes, my other fortress guarding the mouth of the River Fal. They are a mile apart, overlooking each other on opposite points on the coast. It will do you some good to escape this heat...and Lord knows our souls can use a cleansing now and then."

"That sounds grand, my lord." Amethyst curtseyed to him and kissed his hand. "It is so generous of you. I haven't been to the coast in such a long time, and we will take meticulous care of our new little fortress."

With a cook, a groom and two of their chamberlains, the newly married couple headed west.

Pendennis was a round fortress built specially to guard against the French during sea-battles. Exquisitely cut granite stones boasted grotesque gargoyles and embattled turrets carved into the tower. The central round keep held several gun decks, and the lower battery held fourteen more gun positions. Lodgings were inside a separate entrance block attached to the main tower.

As Henry had told them, the castle was built at the end of a tiny peninsula jutting out into the sea. She looked out towards the craggy shores and felt the misty sea-breezes of Cornwall. The sea crashed up against the shore and the spray washed over her like a cleansing of the soul.

Across the narrow inlet she could see St. Mawes, its high round keep rising out from three semicircular bastions in the shape of a clover leaf. It was barely visible behind the mighty stone wall that surrounded it, built into the jagged boulders jutting out into the sea.

She stood in the small but comfortable lookout post, gazing out towards the sea. Pink and purple fingers of alabaster streaked the sky. The sun sank before her. Matthew walked about her in circles, surveying the lower battery beneath them, marveling over the five thousand pounds the king had spent on each castle. He shaded his eyes and looked over her head beyond the sparkling River Fal to an even more distant horizon.

"A place like this will keep the bastards at arm's length," Matthew proclaimed, his frustrated warrior's spirit ringing in his voice. "Firearms, that is." He ran his hand over one of the brass cannons facing out to sea.

* * *

In the small dining room glowing by a roaring fire, servers arranged the round table so that they sat next to each other. The steward poured them each a glass of wine and he proposed a toast: "To Lady Amethyst Gilford, my new wife, many years of happiness within the realm that we are about to create."

They clinked glasses and she sipped the cool wine, turning warm as it passed her lips. She caught his gaze twinkling in the fireglow as the yellows and oranges flitted about his hair, creating an aura around his head.

This wild barbarous land surrounded their citadel, giving her a feeling of recklessness. She wanted to act impulsively, to behave in a primitive manner unrestrained by court etiquette and the stuffy mores of the society in which they'd been bred.

"Matthew, let us be as wild as the land around us!" she purred, taking his hand and lifting the velvet robe off his shoulders, letting it spill to the floor. His fingers laced through her hair and it tumbled out of the headdress which she tossed aside. She ran into the bedchamber and yanked off the coverlet. They ran down to the beach, where all was silent except for the hammering the waves bruising the rocks below. A spatter of stormclouds stained the sky. The sweet wind flowed, the perfect backdrop to the wild expanse of rugged coastline and uninhabited land, its few native dwellers speaking the primitive Cornish language. The stars lit the sky like multi-faceted diamonds and enhanced the landscape of velvety blues and moss greens, the expanse of the dark seas about them.

He watched as she ceremoniously spread the coverlet on the cool sand on the terraced platform overlooking the sea. She shivered as goosebumps broke out all over her accompanied by a hot thrilling rush. She batted away his roaming hands; her eyes spoke her desire to play the dominant role. Beside her on the coverlet where she had pulled him, his arms rested above his head. He moaned when her mouth tasted his lips and throat, and her darting tongue flicked down his chest and lower still.

Her passion was uncontainable. He was finally her husband and she wanted all of him, everything he had to give. She wanted him to feel with her as he never had with another woman. As she tossed her hair, tickling his chest and stomach with her silky ends, their explosive coupling shattered the night.

The surf clamored at their feet as it slapped the shore, the sweeping sea air soothing their hot, entwining bodies. They became one with the sand, the sea, and the heavens. A cloud passed in front of the moon, like a curtain drawn against the silvery glow, filtering out all but the palest bands of light. Gulls cried plaintively, then soared away into the night. Once again all was silent but the lovers' delighted breaths, in unison with the feathery breeze. The man in the moon looked down and smiled upon them.

* * *

Hampton Court Palace, 1544

Henry sent Amethyst and Matthew an invitation to court to celebrate his first wedding anniversary to Kate Parr. Leaving Harry in the care of his nurses, they packed their most ornate carriage and began the journey to London.

She hadn't seen the king in several months, and could barely conceal her shock upon seeing him. He sat, leg propped up, in an enormous chair in his audience chamber, his ushers and gentlemen of the chamber clamoring about him offering him more wine, more grapes, more pillows for his leg, another cloak to keep warm.

"Amethyst, I cannot rise easily, for my leg pains me so greatly, I can barely stand it."

"Of course, sire." She approached him and he held out his hand to clasp hers. The Regal of France ruby was nearly embedded in the folds of his skin, barely visible.

"Does the ring not bother you, sire?" she asked, at a loss of anything else to ask him, knowing his body was a column of pain and burdensome weight.

"They cannot remove it without removing my finger along with it. Mayhap I can grasp a chicken leg with only four fingers, but why hinder myself any more than necessary?" He emitted a wheezing laugh that erupted into a coughing spell. "Oh, Amethyst, I am not well. Kate cares for me so well, I would be lost without her. But of course it is always a joy to see you."

"Thank you, sire."

Queen Katherine came in and Amethyst curtseyed to her queen. Then she got out and left them alone. She just didn't belong here with the king anymore.

Chapter Twenty-Three

Whitehall, January, 1547

Henry ordered his Esquire of the Body out of his dressing room and sat for a few moments, letting his leg drain, enjoying a rare moment of solitude. After a few breaths of fresh morning air at the open window, he summoned his brother-in-law Charles Brandon, one of the few remaining nobles that he trusted. All the others were either dead, in prison or fallen into disfavor.

Brandon entered the chamber a while later, swept off his plumed cap, knelt before the king on bended knee and bowed his head.

"Rise, Suffolk, this is not a marriage proposal."

Suffolk stood, brushed off his knee, and placed his hands and hat behind his back. "What is it that your majesty would have of me?"

"Suffolk, I have been having nightmares, the worst of nightmares. Oh, Jesu…" Henry held his palms to his head, heaving deeply. The throne shook as he coughed, sputtered and cleared his throat.

"What about, your majesty?" Brandon trembled, dreading another of his king's fits of rage.

"Everyone…those who are gone from this earth, yet do not cease to haunt me. Anne…I can see her black eyes like two nuggets of coal boring into me in the darkness of my bed, in the dead of night…then Katharine's laughter, she and Culpeper continue to laugh at me from the grave, I can take it no longer." He uttered a whimper as Brandon took a step forward.

"Mayhap you should speak to Dr. Butts, your majesty."

"Bah!" He swept at the air as if a mosquito buzzed in his face. "He has done naught for me, naught for my festering leg wound...no, naught will release me from this torture but death." He looked up with pleading in his eyes. "I have endured so much, Brandon. I need to make my final peace with the Lord, but before I do, I must protect my son from any possible threats to his rightfully inherited crown. He must not endure what I did, fighting these tenacious pretenders, defending my crown with my very life...nay, Edward must never suffer the indignities of a usurped throne..." His fist pounded the chair arm, "or even the slightest doubt that he will reign as true king until his own death. I must eliminate them."

"Who, sire?" Brandon's voice rose just above a whisper.

"The pretenders!" His voice filled the chamber, as large as his presence. "The ones who pose any threat to my son's rightful inheritance. They must die, they must be eliminated."

"Well, then...who would that be, sire?" Brandon found his voice, but wished he hadn't.

"Those two boys in the Tower...I want them executed immediately." He waved his fingers, the names escaping him.

"Which two boys, sire?" Brandon cocked his head in surprise and confusion.

"Oh, you know..." But mayhap he didn't. Even before Topaz had begun to fade into obscurity, the existence of any offspring was not widely known, or considered, throughout the kingdom. "...the grandsons of Warwick. Edward and...oh, what is the other one's name?" He waved his hand about impatiently and pressed it against his forehead, not wanting to tax his brain too heavily with such inconsequential trivia.

"Oh, those two. I believe the other is Richard, your majesty. But they're hardly boys. They must be in their twenties now."

"Already?" Henry rubbed his temples. "Jesu, where does the time go?" he muttered.

"They're still imprisoned in the Tower, are they not?" Brandon fetched a clean cloth from the shelf and gently placed it on the king's leaking leg.

"Aye, the two of them. I took no chances letting them out, just as my father did with their grandfather. Sometimes history cannot help but repeat itself." He fixed his eyes on Brandon. "This is not to be documented, nor is it to be signed as a formal act of execution. I want you to go in there at the stroke of midnight tonight and do away with them."

Brandon recoiled. "But how, sire? Do you wish poison to be dispensed to them?"

"Any way you wish." He shut his eyes and rubbed his temples. "Smother them in their sleep, dunk them in a butt of malmsey like their great-grandfather met his end, do whatever you want, I don't give a fig. Just do it quietly and non-violently. No blood-letting, no bone-crunching, no skull-bashing." He met Brandon's astonished gaze. "After they have ceased to breathe, lay their bodies out upon the beds in which they sleep. Then go to their mother's cell and inform her that the king has granted her wish... she is finally to see her sons."

He blinked. "After they have been... after they pass away, sire? Do you not want her to see them alive?"

"No, I do not!" Another fist thump on the chair arm produced a loud rap as his ring struck the wood. "That is the whole point. Is your memory that short? She tried to kill me and usurp my throne, you dunce. The only reason she is alive is..." He waved Brandon away. "Just heed my wishes and be done with it. I told her I would let her see her sons, and she shall see them. I did not specify, however, whether they would be alive or dead. Her wish was simply to see them, and see them she shall. Then..." He reached over, took a swig from his goblet and scowled, spitting the liquid back into the cup. "This is water, damn it all. Bring me some wine. What do you fools think I am, a bloody infirm? Bring me some Verney and make haste. Then... what was I saying—"

"She shall see her sons' corpses, sire," Brandon refreshed his memory.

"You need not put it that way." The king rolled his eyes. "'Tis not as morbid as it sounds. I could have dragged them off to the scaffold as my father did with their grandfather and whacked their heads off into a bloody basket for the pretenders that they are, just as I did all their other relatives. I want this incident kept quiet." He reached forward and rubbed his leg. "Let her see them, as she so plainly requested. Keep her restrained, however. Lead her out with four guards, one at each arm, one in back and one in front. After she is finished gazing upon her children peacefully sleeping in the throes of eternity, as long as you keep her restrained and do not let her fly into hysterics, toss her back into her cell. Quietly. Sedate her if need be. Dispose of the bodies in an equally surreptitious manner. I must rid them of this earth." His voice went hoarse. "I cannot let my son go through what I have. Those children are dangerous and must be eliminated."

"Aye, sire. It is done." Brandon positioned his knee for the exiting sweep downwards.

"I am not finished!" Henry bellowed. "Now for the disposal of the bodies...bury them. Do not cast them into the Thames. It will be necessary to get grime under your nails, but I do believe it is a desirable alternative to blood.

They must vanish from the earth without a trace. When it has been ascertained that they have been adequately and unquestionably disposed of, come back here and I shall grant you a small but sufficient token reward."

"Aye, sire!" Brandon's face split into a smile as he rubbed his hands together. "Is there anything else you wish, sire?"

"Only some bloody wine." Henry held out the chalice and flung its contents out the window.

Brandon bowed. "I shall summon your Lord Steward, sire. I shall report back to you after midnight." He bowed again and again, bowing himself out of the chamber.

Henry sighed. "Now they are all dead," he muttered to an uncaring world. "All the pretenders to the crown are gone. With the exception of Topaz, but I must keep my promise to Amethyst. 'Tis a pity the way history is doomed to repeat itself, 'tis such a pity..."

* * *

At two o'clock in the morning, four guards stopped in front of Topaz's cell and opened the iron gate. They approached her bed and one of them shook her awake. She turned over, the torch glaring in her face startling her. At first she didn't know whether she was still dreaming or if they had come to drag her to her execution, or...

"What!" she screamed, scrambling under the covers. "No, I do not wish to die! Bring me to the king, bring me to him!"

The guard yanked the blanket off the trembling figure. "We come to bring you to your sons," he said. "The king has granted your request."

She lowered the blanket and took several gulps of air. "What...now? In the middle of the night? Are they sick? Are they ill?"

"Nay, they are not ill," the guard in the far corner replied. "They are quite restful."

"Lord Jesu, what is the idea of this then, why do you come barging in here like barbarians, to scare—"

"Do you wish to see your sons or not?" The front guard flailed the torch about wildly.

"Aye! Why would I not, having waited all these years..." She climbed out of the bed and pulled on a robe. Two guards each seized an arm, the other two walking in back and in front. They led her from her cell and down the winding stairway out to the courtyard. The dewy earth was spongy under her bare feet.

They led her into the Beauchamp Tower and up another staircase to the stuffy room where the boys had spent the last few years. By the light of the torches in their flambeaux, she saw her sons lying in their bed at the far end of the room, side by side, quietly.

She tried to break away from the guards to run up to her sons, hug them, kiss them, throw herself into a tearful, emotional reunion…but they restrained her.

"We shall guide you," the one at her left said, and she struggled again.

"I am capable of walking to my sons' bed myself. Unhand me, you monsters!" she spat, keeping her voice low as not to wake her two sleeping angels.

"We have orders to restrain you." By then they'd nearly reached the bed. Now she could make out their features, Richard's blond hair falling over his forehead, Edward's complexion paler than she'd remembered…

"Do you never let them see sunshine?" she murmured, as she held her hand out to brush Richard's hair off his face, the guard holding her steadily by the elbow. "They sleep so deeply, they always did," she whispered, then touched Richard's cheek. "Richard, honey," she cooed, her hand moving down, fingers extended to rouse her beloved son from sleep. She felt the smooth cheek. It was cold, the skin hard and waxy, unyielding to her touch. She gave his head a gentle shove. "Richard," registered nothing, just outward confusion as her mind blanked. "What's wrong here?" She thrust out the other arm, the guard now holding her by the waist as she leaned over and shook him by the shoulders, the still, lifeless body not moving, not breathing.

"Edward!"

Her other son also lay still and quiet, his body stretched out stiffly upon the sheet, hands at his sides. "Richard! Edward! Wake up!" She shook Richard violently, tugging at his nightshirt, lift his head off the pillow. Yet the eyes remained shut. She dropped him back down, letting out a high-pitched scream. The guards loosened their grip in surprise. "No! You killed them! You killed them, you bastards!" she wailed, backing away from the death bed, falling into a dead faint, spilling to the floor, bringing the guards down with her.

* * *

Warwick Castle

The message arrived as Amethyst and Matthew were leaving for Kenilworth. They'd spent January at Warwick, for Emerald had gone into her confinement here. She'd insisted her first baby be born at their ancestral home, insisting equally adamantly that her sister be there. Now that baby William was nearly a week old, they readied their servants and horses for the journey back home.

Both the royal messenger and his mount, caparisoned with the royal livery, breathed puffs of steam into the misty air. She asked them to wait while she broke the seal and read the message. It was from the king, but it was not in his hand. He wanted to see her immediately, for he was gravely ill and wanted her by his side.

"I must go, Matthew. He needs me."

Matthew let out a sigh of frustration, unable to go against his king's wishes, yet resenting the king's frequent summations of his wife.

"Must you go running to court every time he calls you?" He took her wrists and placed her arms about his waist. "Just this once, tell him you've other things to do."

Her heart fluttered under her heavy cloak. "You're wrong, Matthew. Henry wouldn't summon me this way unless it was of the gravest importance." It was then she knew—some primitive instinct that forewarned of death, one of the body's natural defenses, mayhap—a preparatory signal to guard against the shock and grief that would follow—it alerted her. "Henry is dying. He is nearing the end and wants me there with him during his final moments."

She broke free of her husband's grasp and looked up at the royal messenger, breathing warmth into his cupped hands, rubbing them together against the cold.

"Tell the king I shall be there. I am on my way."

"Aye, Madam." Without another word, he spurred his horse on and galloped back down the frozen road to London.

"Amethyst…" With his pleading eyes, Matthew looked so much like their son, she resisted the urge to reach out and pat him on the head.

"Let me go to him, Matthew," she tried to appease him. "I have not seen him since our wedding. This is the longest I've ever gone without seeing him…I must go."

"He's got his wife, what does he need you for?" he persisted.

She could never explain to her husband the special bond she and the king shared, the knowledge that each would always be there for the other, no matter what the reason. She simply could not refuse Henry his final wish, after all they had meant to each other. What she and the king shared, although common knowledge throughout court and a fact even his wives had learned to accept, had been of the most intimate and personal manner, confined to his private chambers, known to no one but each other.

"I must go." With that, she turned and headed for the stables to saddle up Lady for the ride to Whitehall.

* * *

She arrived on the evening of the 27th. The guards led her straight into his bedchamber. The close, musty air smelled of sickness, dried sweat, and the stinging stench of vomit. She took tiny breaths in order to accustom herself to the foul odors as her eyes adjusted to the dimness. Although it was barely sunset, the velvet drapes were pulled shut. The candles' eerie glow pulsated angrily and let up thin streams of smoke as she swept by. A fire roared in the hearth, its orange tongues flicking at the charred bricks around it.

She approached the giant bed and steadied herself against one of the bedposts. Her fingers fidgeted over the carvings as she clasped the post, gathered her skirts and hoisted herself up onto the bed, her feet dangling over the edge. At first she could not see him; he was covered with the velvets and the furs he so loved to burrow under. But as she strained to see, she could discern a figure, a head against the pillows, a nearly bald head, the eyes slits under folds of puffy yellow-gray skin. This was not her beloved Henry, not the strong, willful man she'd given her life to, the man she'd nurtured and loved. His face was puffed up to grotesque proportions—only because she knew him so well did she recognize him. His breathing was raspy and irregular, every other breath a wheezing gasp that made his chest rise and his face strain in agony.

He opened one eye and saw her gaping at him in disbelief, her jaw slack, her lips parted as if to trying to form comforting words and soothing thoughts. She hadn't meant to let him see her staring at him so. But the horror of seeing him this way, like a helpless invalid dragging the last breaths of life, could not be concealed with a mere smile.

"You are here..." he croaked, his voice thick and muddy with the fluid that bloated his body and pressed against his brain, causing disjointed and distorted thoughts. "You are here, my love."

"Aye, your majesty, I came as soon as I got the message."

"You have been so good to me..." He reached out, his arm puffy and distended, the fingers so swollen she could not see the joints.

Without thinking she reached out one shaking hand and touched his distended limb, as if her touch could comfort him, bring him back to a bearable state. But the skin was stretched, taut, waxy and cold. He could not grasp her hand. His fingers were paralyzed, unable to bend, clasp, or clutch. She occupied her other fidgety hand by clutching a corner of the bedspread for support, her nails tensely raking over the embroidery one stitch at a time.

"'Tis all right, my lord. I am here now," she whispered, not knowing what she could possibly share with him. Should she talk about Harry or the Christmas gifts she and Matthew had exchanged? Would he even hear her?

He began to speak, and she had to lean forward to hear, for his voice was faint and weak. "My dear Jane, you've come back to me..." The sentence ended in a sigh and he struggled to open his eyes again.

"Jane, I missed you so...Anne killed you, I know she did, she killed our son, she killed you, when you were so young and beautiful, Jane, my dear Jane..."

Her breath caught in her throat and she sat paralyzed as his hand groped for hers once more.

She placed her hand inside his as he continued to mumble names, first Jane, then Anne, then calling Cromwell over and over. She sat, stupefied, unable to help him, for he was beyond help. He was slipping from this world and she would not leave his side until he had departed completely.

She sat with him through the remainder of the night, not stirring. The chamber was quiet except for the tiptoeing of the groom of the chamber as he rekindled the fire.

At one o'clock a.m., the door opened and shut. She jumped, startled, turning to see a rangy lad walking up to her. "I am Anthony Denny, come to tell the king he must prepare for death and ask him if he wishes to confess."

"Now?" she whispered, for she still wasn't sure if the king would regain his senses and comprehend what was going on around him. "Why not before?"

"No one dared before, but the physicians tell me now that it is their opinion that the king has not long to live." He spoke brazenly, as if of someone not present. Ignoring Amethyst's tug on his sleeve, he approached the king from the other side of the bed and put his lips to the king's ear, shouting, as if to someone at the other end of the room, "Sire, is there anyone to whom you wish to confess?"

The king did not reply.

Denny tried again. "Sire, you are in man's judgment not like to live, you must prepare yourself for death."

The king lay still. She thought he'd slipped into a coma, but at length he finally spoke: "The mercy of Christ…could pardon all my sins, though they were greater than they be."

"Sire, do you want to see a priest?" Denny persisted, in that high-pitched voice that nearly shattered the windows.

After another long silence, the king spoke once again. "Only Cranmer, but not yet. I will take a little sleep, then, as I feel myself, I will advise upon the matter." His eyes fluttered, then shut as his head lolled to one side.

"Cranmer! So be it!" Denny rose from the king's side and scrambled out of the room.

"I love you, my lord. I will always love you," she whispered into his ear. Although he registered no response, she knew in her heart that he'd heard her.

She sat with him for another hour, listening to his raspy breathing, his labored sighs, alternating with incoherent babblings about Anne and Charles, calling her Jane, cursing the Pope, Anne, Catherine, or was it Katharine? as his jumbled mind slipped further away. At one point she tried to press a chalice of wine to his lips. He slurped at the cup, sputtered, swallowed and sighed, as if knowing this taste of the beloved wine he'd savored so much throughout his life would be on his lips in death.

Cranmer then burst through the door, rushed up to the bed, and leaned way over, trying to extricate a confession from the barely breathing king.

"Your majesty! Your majesty!" he spoke just above a whisper. When the king did not reply he glanced up at Amethyst helplessly.

"He is incoherent," she said. "I do not believe he hears you."

Cranmer leaned over the bed, climbed upon it halfway, one leg astride the huge mound of mattress, and supported himself on his elbows. "Your majesty, it is I, Cranmer!" he shouted, as if raising his voice would enable the dying man to comprehend. "You sent for me. Do you die in the faith of Christ?" he asked several times with no response. "Give me a sign that you hear me. Let me know if you die in the faith of Christ and that He has redeemed you."

Amethyst hadn't moved her hand from the king's and felt a slight gesture. The fingers had tried feebly to grasp at hers. "He moved his hand, I could feel it," she whispered to Cranmer, and she knew that was the last touch she would ever know of her king.

She sat quietly, watching as his lips formed a word. She leaned forward, nearly bumping heads with Cranmer, his ear pressed up against the king's lips.

"I... I love you..." the king whispered.

Who was he speaking to now? Jane? A young and long-ago Catherine that he had indeed loved, his childhood love, the first wife whom he later denied and cast aside?

Cranmer lifted his head, cleared his throat and discreetly looked away, fingering his cloak.

"I love you…Amethyst," the king said with a feeble sigh, his final farewell to the cruel world that he'd passed through so briefly.

"Farewell, Henry. Farewell, my lord," she whispered, as his face became a blur through her tears.

She looked over at Cranmer and saw tears in his eyes. "He is with Our Lord now," she said softly. Cranmer, gazing down at his departed king, nodded.

After another moment of silence, Cranmer looked up. The courtiers came busting into the chamber, wanting to know if indeed he had slipped away, shouting like a deranged mob, "The king is dead! Long live the king!"

"You shall remain for the funeral, Lady Gilford?" asked Cranmer. He still hadn't left Henry's side, oblivious to the shoving courtiers who wanted a chance to gape at the king's corpse.

She was still holding his hand. It grew cold beneath her fingers. She knew he was at peace now. A strange kind of relief washed over her and for the first time since entering the chamber, she was able to speak normally. "Aye, of course I shall. Now I must summon his widow." Amethyst rose and covered the king's face with the bedsheet. She wanted to slip off the ring he had given her and place it on his finger, but she knew it would never fit. With one last glance over her shoulder at the rumpled bed bearing the king's body, she shoved her way through the shouting, bumbling fools and headed for the queen's apartments.

* * *

Amethyst entered the queen's privy chamber and the two women embraced. Kate knew as soon as she saw Amethyst appear. "He said goodbye last night then sent me away." Kate finally let the tears flow, placing a candle on her table next to all her Bibles and prayer books. So the queen hadn't slept all night either.

"I arrived late last night," Amethyst said. "I must have just missed you."

"Did he speak to you at all?" Kate asked.

"Nay...he spoke, but most of it was incoherent. He was delirious, Kate, he called out for Jane several times...denounced the Pope, Wolsey, and Cromwell, talked to Jane, cursed Anne—"

"All those people are dead," Kate said. "Did he not speak of anyone alive?"

"He asked for Cranmer. That...that was the last he spoke." Never could Amethyst tell the king's widow that his very last word before departing the earth had been her own name. As Cranmer was not close enough to hear, she and only she would carry that, Henry's last spoken endearment, to her own grave. "That was all, Kate. Then he slipped away."

The two women King Henry VIII had left behind stood side by side. Linking arms, they knelt before God and prayed for his soul.

* * *

Amethyst went back to the king's bedchamber at dawn. The bed was empty, the covers spread neatly over the mattress, the window thrown open, letting in a blast of the raw January wind. The dying fire threw sparks about the fireplace. "Where is King Henry?" she asked one of the Yeomen of the Guard.

"They've taken the body to embalm it, my lady. "The body will lie in state in the king's Privy Chamber while the Chapel Royal is being readied."

She took one final sweeping look at the bed in which she'd shared so many passionate nights with her king. The guard was watching her, so she fought the dreamy mist that began to fill her eyes. Aware of what he must be thinking, she quickly turned and exited the chamber for the last time.

* * *

She borrowed a sheet of parchment and a pen from Kate and wrote to Matthew, asking him to join her immediately. He would certainly hear of the king's death by the time the note arrived, but she wanted him there with her for the funeral.

She then thought of Topaz, wondering if her sister was now expecting to be set free. But of course the decision belonged to the nine-year-old King Edward.

* * *

Alone in the Privy Chamber, Kate knelt and sobbed quietly before the blue velvet-draped coffin as Amethyst approached the guarded doorway. The coffin rested upon trestles under a pall of cloth of gold. Dozens of candles gleamed in the darkness, casting a long shadow from Kate's unmoving figure.

Amethyst tiptoed away, leaving the queen alone with her husband.

* * *

On the thirteenth of February, after twelve days in the Chapel Royal, the unwieldy coffin was hoisted onto the black-draped hearse for the journey to St. George's Chapel in Windsor. He would be laid to rest in the grave next to Queen Jane, as he'd always wished.

Matthew sped to London upon receiving Amethyst's note. With a comforting embrace but few words to exchange, they joined the funeral procession bearing torches in the wet, gray, but warm day. The breeze promised that first breath of spring and carried the clanging of the churchbells throughout the kingdom.

Two days later, the procession reached the king's final resting place at Windsor. Pallbearers removed the coffin from the hearse to be lowered into the grave in St. George's Chapel. Amethyst did not enter. As the Aldermen of London, the lords of the Privy Council, the archbishops, members of the king's household and other nobles crowded the chapel, she stood in the biting cold for the duration of the short service.

She did not want to see his coffin being lowered into the ground. Witnessing the cold reality and truth of his death and burial would eradicate the memories she held of him healthy, passionate, and alive. She heard the squeaking groan of the pulleys as the Yeomen of the Guard lowered the coffin. She heard and the final plunk as it hit the bottom. She heard Bishop Gardiner leading the funeral service, *"Beati mortui qui in Domine Moriuntur,"* "Blessed are they that die in the Lord."

She heard the vault sliding shut, then Gardiner shouted, "King Edward the Sixth, by the grace of God King of England, Ireland, Wales, and France, Defender of the Faith!"

The crowd echoed his words, and Amethyst mouthed them silently with her husband's arm tightly clasped about her shoulders. Then she and Matthew turned away to begin their journey home.

"Would you like to stop at the Tower and see the lads?" Amethyst asked as they approached their mounts.

"Nay," he answered. "Next time. I have had enough solemnity for one week. I trust they fare well."

"Oh, I am sure, Matthew."

They spurred their horses on and headed down the frozen road to Warwickshire.

* * *

She did not set foot in St. George's Chapel until many years later. When she found herself passing through Windsor one rainy day, she rode up to the castle and entered the chapel. Looking around for a magnificent tomb to rival that of his father, she wandered the chapel in the weak light. He'd always spoken of taking Wolsey's tomb for his own after the Cardinal died. He planned to spend a fortune on a tremendous monument, much more massive and imposing than any other. She approached a few tombs, but his name was not inscribed on them. "Henry, where are you?" she called out as she strolled over the flagstones. Without warning something made her halt in her tracks. She looked down and what she saw beneath her feet startled her: a polished stone slab inscribed with a few lines in small lettering. She had to kneel to read it:

IN A VAULT
BENEATH THIS MARBLE SLAB
ARE DEPOSITED THE REMAINS
OF
JANE SEYMOUR QUEEN OF KING HENRY VIII
1537
KING HENRY VIII
1547
AND
AN INFANT CHILD OF QUEEN ANNE

"'Tis only I, my lord," she whispered, and left a long-stemmed red rose on the grave.

His daughter Mary was by then Queen of England. Although this may have disturbed Henry, she knew Catherine would have been pleased.

Chapter Twenty-Four

The Tower of London, March, 1547

Topaz boarded a barge at the Tower, which took her to Whitehall Palace. King Edward had finally answered her plea for an audience with him. Flanked by guards, she walked through hallways and chambers to the Council Chamber. At the end of a long stretch of red carpet sat the king upon a platform, the enormous throne dwarfing his tiny figure. A somber face peeked out from a plumed cap sprouting tufts of reddish hair. A fur-trimmed crimson robe draped his shoulders, spilling down the platform's first three steps. A heavy gold chain hung round his neck, and he tugged at it as if it bothered him. His dark hose sagged around the skinny knees and ankles, his feet swung to and fro, the shoes flapping off his heels.

As she approached him, his young but troubled features came into focus. He was Henry's son, all right; she saw the Henry she remembered in Edward's gold eyes, his tight lips, his erect posture.

Yet he was a boy—a boy who should be romping in the grass, climbing trees and skipping stones on a pond—a boy thrust onto a king's throne.

She halted at his feet and curtsied against her will. She never dreamed she'd pay homage to a Tudor. But because her fate had taken too many wayward turns, this oaf, the offspring of the fat, monstrous and dead Henry, held her very life in his sweaty little hands.

"Rise," he ordered, his voice cracking. He cleared his throat, trying to cover up his embarrassment. She saw a hot flush burning the pale cheeks as Edward tugged at the top button of his doublet.

"Lady Topaz," he continued, "The council informed me that you have been imprisoned in the Tower since your rebellion to overtake the throne from my father, King Henry the Eighth."

"Aye, sire." This was probably the first he'd heard of it. How old had he been when she'd fought for her rightful crown? Four? Five? A toddler in nappies? "I live the remainder of my days in great remorse and regret for having betrayed such a kind and thoughtful king," she began her memorized speech. "I greatly mourned his majesty's passing, and wish to appeal to your majesty for mercy. I have realized the error of my ways, I live with the grief and torture of having my sons torn from my arms, and I plead with your majesty to have pity on me and let me live out my days in freedom." She wanted to add further pleas that she hadn't prepared and this was her only chance. Her life depended on her choice of words, her tone of voice, her ability to convince this child who'd spent his pitiful brief life behind palace walls, being groomed for kingship. It was up to her, a woman who had seen the birth and death of two sons and led out a battle to capture England's throne, to convince this nine-year-old she deserved to live.

She took a breath to speak, but too late.

"I shall confer with the Council," his high voice rang out, "and relay my decision within a fortnight," he stated flatly, his eyes darting from this wall to that, from the ceiling down to the shoes slipping off his feet.

"But—" She held up a hand.

"Remove Lady Topaz back to the Tower," he commanded. The guards lunged forward to seize her.

"Your majesty…" she called over her shoulder, struggling out of the guards' grasp, to run back to the throne, to throw herself at this boy's feet, to beg for her life. But it was over. "Let me go!" she spat at the guards, twisting her arms that they held fast in their grip.

They ushered her out of the chamber and back to the waiting barge, where she would pass once more through Traitor's Gate.

* * *

Hampton Court Palace, Christmas, 1547

Amethyst, Matthew and Harry received an invitation to spend Christmas with his majesty King Edward VI at Hampton Court Palace. Overjoyed for Harry to meet the king, she accepted.

As they readied their household for the journey to Hampton, another royal messenger arrived. Amethyst broke the seal and read the contents of the letter. Its subject matter concerned King Henry's will. She hadn't expected him to bequeath her anything; she'd passed on all the jewels he'd given her, with the exception of the teardrop pearl necklace, to his daughters Mary and Elizabeth. She wanted no more manor homes, lands or titles.

Her eyes filled with tears at the beautiful, simple, but most meaningful bequest.

He'd granted her and her family the honor of interment in Westminster Abbey, to lie in eternal rest with the immortals of history, to come full circle with her own history and to repose in her beloved shrine.

* * *

The palace blazed with candlelight shining through the clear cold night as they passed through the gates. The stars lay sprinkled about the heavens, twinkling over the kingdom. The North Star like a glittering jewel paved the way for the rest, bringing the earth to the close of another year.

Festivities filled every corner of the palace. Revelers sang and danced past them, servers carried cups of ale and wine. Fires blazed in every hearth.

A heavy cloud of sadness hung over Amethyst as they headed toward their apartments. She wiped back tears she didn't want her husband and son to see. It would be too tedious to put her emotions into words, and she didn't want to spoil this most special Christmas for Harry, gurgling with excitement.

She knew her first Christmas without Henry would be sad, but she had no way to prepare for it. Especially here in Hampton Court Palace, where they'd spent so many happy times. It all came rushing back to her, those many evenings with him at the high table, the nights of love in his bedchambers—chambers that she would never set foot in again, which now belonged to his son.

Matthew sensed her sadness as they changed out of their traveling clothes. "Do you want to talk?" He held her, stroking her cheek with his knuckles.

"Nay, Matthew. 'Tis just... being here, that makes me sad, that is all."

"Mayhap we shouldn't have come," he said.

"I could not disappoint Harry. Besides, I want Harry to meet King Edward. Who knows when he will have another chance to meet him, with us living at Kenilworth..." She was trying to tell Matthew that this chapter of her life, of her years in royal company, of her royal surroundings, trumpetings and fanfare, were now over. Kenilworth was her true home, and that was where she belonged with her family.

She wiped away a final tear and they headed for the great hall.

* * *

Princess Mary sat alone at the high table, her eyes dull, her lips tight. Amethyst knew she was struggling to hold back a bursting dam of sadness. It was a sad time for her, too. Although her succession and Elizabeth's had been restored, nothing would ever be the same. Amethyst embraced Mary warmly, giving her a final squeeze of the hand, knowing they would probably never meet again.

"Mary, please do come visit us at Kenilworth..." she extended the invitation out of courtesy.

"I would like that..."

A hopeful gesture, an empty promise, but it would hang in the air nonetheless.

Next she saw Kate Parr. She had recently married Tom Seymour, the true love of her life. Princess Elizabeth was at her side, at the brink of womanhood, her red ringlets bouncing in time with her jaunty step, a cornet dangling from her hand.

She embraced Elizabeth and turned to Kate. "Is all well with you, Kate?"

Kate glowed, and Amethyst did not begrudge the former queen her happiness. She had not loved Henry, just as Amethyst had not loved Mortimer. One did not choose whom to love in this life, she'd realized long ago. Kate had done her duty by the king, and he'd set her free.

"Everything is superb, Amethyst!" She grabbed Amethyst's hands and held them to her middle. "I am expecting!"

She glanced down at Kate's tiny waist, no bigger than Elizabeth's. "Are you sure?"

"Tom and I want this baby so badly. I so enjoy caring for Elizabeth and Edward, but to have your own..."

She understood Kate's every word. To be reunited with Matthew and to share their son had been the one joy in her life to which nothing could compare. She wished Kate a safe and healthy birth.

They finally made their way to King Edward, a tiny dot among a retinue of advisors and councilors clamoring about him, wanting to serve his every need. She knew the boy simply wanted to enjoy the music; he'd had enough of being king, this was Christmas and he wanted to revel in it like any other child. He looked hot and uncomfortable in his regalia of robes and furs, gold and gemstones dripping from his neck. She remembered Henry's words: "Edward should have been ours, the product of our love, the life we should have created together, our prince, our living legacy."

But the boy knew nothing of her many years with his father, the bond that held them close, the unspoken vows that bound them together although they had never exchanged any pledge before man or God. She did not want to see Henry in his eyes, but there he was, in the gold sparkle, in the red-tinged hair, along with Jane's delicate build. Edward would never be the sturdy athlete his father was, but she wondered if he'd inherited the Tudor mind. *What kind of king will this boy be?* she wondered, glancing at Elizabeth laughing merrily with other youngsters, playfully slapping one across the cheek. *And what kind of queen will Elizabeth be?*

She presented little Harry to the king and the two boys looked at each other with that blank but curious look peculiar to children. Harry knew this boy was his king, but his young mind didn't comprehend quite what that meant. To Harry, he was a boy in fancy robes. To Edward, Harry was the only child in the entire palace younger than himself.

The music played on, the mimes and masques came out, the banquet began, and King Henry VIII was all but forgotten as the kingdom lived without him.

* * *

Amethyst and Matthew rode a royal barge to the Tower to visit Topaz. She had mixed feelings about seeing her sister. Of course she still loved her. But she didn't look forward to this. She hoped Topaz had dropped all her grudges and gotten over her all-consuming anger.

"I shall go see the lads, you can go see Topaz," Matthew said as the barge bumped up against the riverbank.

"Nay, let us both visit her together," she countered, not wanting to listen to any of Topaz's remaining rants alone.

"I do not care to see her, Amethyst," he stated with a finality she didn't care to argue with.

But she couldn't accept his refusal. "She granted you the divorce so that we could be together. She is the mother of your children. She deserves one last visit from you."

"Oh, all right," he reluctantly agreed, and the guard led them across the green to the comfortable quarters where she was lodged.

Flanked by guards, they approached her cell and saw her slight figure hunched over a writing desk.

"Topaz," Amethyst called, and she turned. Amethyst's hand gripped Matthew's arm in reaction to the sight of her sister. Her face was even more drawn than before, her eyes two dark pools of pain sunken into gray sockets. She had to grab on to the edge of the desk for support as she stood. A shadowy haze behind the iron bars, she squinted and cautiously approached her visitors.

"It is Amethyst, and…Matthew is here with me."

Clutching her shawl around her bony shoulders, she shuffled up to them, unsteady on her feet. She stood before them and stopped, staring at the floor. "He killed them," she murmured, her voice a weak echo of her frail body.

Amethyst wasn't sure she'd heard correctly. "Killed who?"

"Your stinking rotten dead king, he killed my babies." She looked up, her eyes narrowed to slits of hate.

Matthew slapped his palm against the cold stone wall. "Oh, no," he moaned.

"What?" Amethyst gasped. "What are you talking about, Topaz? Where are the lads?"

"Didn't you hear me? Dead!" she shrieked. "He killed them, he… " She broke down and turned away, scurrying back to her desk, lay her head in her arms and babbled between sobs.

Matthew ran up to the guard and shook him by the collar. "Where are the two boys, the Gilford boys? I demand to see them at once, I am their father!"

The guard stepped back and looked away as Matthew released his grip. Instantly Amethyst knew Topaz had spoken the horrible truth. A numbing shock tore through her and she clutched at her heart.

She barely heard the guard's next words: "They died a natural death, just before the death of King Henry."

"Natural!" Matthew's anguished cry tore through the depths of the corridors. "Where are they? Take us to their place of burial!"

"I know not where they are buried," the guard said. "They expired suddenly and were interred somewhere, I know not."

"Who would know?" Matthew flailed his arms. "Does King Edward not know?"

"Nay, King Edward knew nothing of this." The guard shook his head.

Matthew buried his face in his hands, shaking his head in quiet despair. Amethyst grasped him and they clung together in shared grief.

* * *

They approached every Yeoman within the entire fortress, from the sentinel at the White Tower to the guard at Traitor's Gate. No one knew where the boys were buried.

"I do not suppose King Edward would know," Amethyst said as the barge took them back to the palace. "He was not even king yet when they died. He never even knew the boys."

"Topaz said Henry killed them." Matthew wiped away a tear as the barge slipped into the stream of traffic traversing the busy waterway.

Amethyst shook her head, anger and sorrow building up inside her. "Oh, Lord Jesu...how could he have done this to two innocent boys? How could he?"

He turned to face her. "Simple...he ordered one of his henchmen to carry out the atrocity, just like his father did to your father. Regard for human life does not seem to run in Tudor hearts." Bitterness and pain tortured Matthew's voice.

She took his cold fingers in hers and warmed them twixt her hands, bringing his hand to her lips. She drew him close and whispered, "We will find out what happened." She vowed to find out, even if it took her dying breath.

The Tower receded into the black mist of the night and faded into the distance. She bade a final farewell to that hideous monster sliding into the blackness of the past, farther and farther away—the place of her birth and of so many deaths.

Turning her back on the great yellow monster, she let the memory fade into the clouded void of her past, to die with her past, to leave her in peace.

She couldn't help but wonder if Henry had taken the boys with him to his grave.

The love she'd once held for Henry became tainted as the Tower and all its horror slipped away. She knew he'd committed acts of mindless cruelty, but the shock paralyzed her as she grieved over her nephews. She'd once believed Henry to be infallible, perfect and without sin. But now, looking at the unspeakable pain her husband bore, she vowed to find the answer…why had Henry done this?

* * *

Within the promised fortnight, a guard stopped by Topaz's cell to deliver a message from King Edward. Her heart leapt, for she knew not what the boy king had in store for her, the only remaining threat to the crown.

Hands trembling, she tore at the royal seal. She gasped gulps of air as she unfolded the parchment and mouthed a silent prayer, "Let the child uphold his father's word and keep me alive."

She scanned the page looking for the fatal words: death or execution. Her eyes zigzagged down the page, taking in each word, not yet putting them together to comprehend the message.

She started at the beginning again and read it through. It slipped from her fingers and fluttered to the floor. She clasped her hands to her breast and heaved a heavy sob from deep inside.

Tears sprang from her eyes and ran down her cheeks. She looked up, at the patch of blue beyond the panes of leaded glass, coated with years of dust. She glanced down at Tower Green, at the cobbled square marking the scaffold site where queens and traitors had met their deaths. She gazed at the chapel beyond, where Anne's and Katharine's remains now lay. Her eyes swept over the minute speck of earth she was privileged to behold. She took what would be one of her last looks at England.

By order of King Edward VI, she was to depart this world as she knew it.

He was sending her to the New World—to America.

Chapter Twenty-Five

Portsmouth, June, 1548

The gulls cawed lazily and the sea breeze sprayed a salty mist at their feet as Topaz, Amethyst, and Emerald stood on the swaying dock. Amethyst gazed up the gangplank at the Searchthrift, the New World-bound vessel. Her black hull glinted back the sun's rays, her sails surged against the wind, her masts soared into the sky. The galleon rocked gently, nudging the pier, as if urging Topaz to hurry and embark on her voyage, never to return.

Topaz had regained the color in her cheeks, her clear eyes sparkling with visions of her new life to come. Her hair, spilling down her back and graced with a velvet circlet, let off a fire of its own in the sunlight.

"Well, this is it, sisters." Topaz clasped their hands. "I am on my way to my very own world."

"The king just wants you the hell out of England once and for all." Amethyst let a smile play on her lips.

Topaz smiled back, cocking a brow. "Aye, but I am to leave England alive. Thanks to you, of course, dear sister," she hastily added.

"Have you no fears of journeying to this unknown world?" Emerald asked. "The Ocean Sea is so large, it can swallow you whole, and the New World is known to be so cold and harsh, with savage natives tramping the wilderness."

"I am not afraid, as I was not afraid of Henry Tudor," she stated adamantly. "King Edward has made a most wise choice. 'Tis better to be leader in an unknown land than to be a mere subject in this old, corrupt, and tired kingdom." She glanced round with a scowl. "With me as leader, the New World will be the greatest kingdom on earth, mayhap not in my lifetime, but I shall certainly be the one to start it all. You will see, I shall do it the proper way. There will be no religious persecution, no heavy tax burdens, no tyrant monarchs ruling from a lofty jewel-encrusted throne. My New World will have what this kingdom has never had…freedom. And as of the moment I set foot on that ship, I shall no longer be English. I shall be American."

Amethyst blanched. How strange that word sounded to her ears. How alien. Only Topaz could rattle off such an eloquent speech minutes before their final farewell. But she saw the sincerity in her sister's eyes, the knowing that they would never meet again, yet needing to have the last word.

"I know how badly you wanted the crown to descend back upon our family. Just be thankful we are all still alive," Amethyst said.

A man emerged from the galley. A blue velvet and fur cloak flowed about his slender form as fluidly as the waves slapping the shore, clinging, reaching, then swirling back again. The threads of his trim winked in unison with the colored gems about his neck. As he walked, his hose glinted like the radiant strings of a harp.

He descended the gangway and Amethyst caught Emerald's astonished gaze. They all turned to face him.

"Sebastian!" Topaz greeted him brightly. "Pray do say hello to my dear sisters Amethyst and Emerald."

So this was Captain Sebastian Cabot, the intrepid explorer of worlds beyond the common folks' wildest dreams, revered as a trailblazer guided by God himself to reach those wild, barren shores, to unite two worlds, the old and the new.

"Captain Cabot." Amethyst curtsied before this exulted adventurer. She remembered Henry financing his expeditions, boasting, 'This man will do for England what Columbus did for Spain' and reveling just as much in Cabot's talent as a cartographer. One of Henry's yeomen of the crown aborted the first voyage, and Cabot sailed for Spain instead.

He took Amethyst's hand and swept off his plumed hat, revealing a full head of silver-streaked hair. His eyes matched the ebullient blue-green of the sea, and his jagged smile creased the weatherbeaten ruddy skin, dusted with a light silver beard.

"It is my pleasure, Lady Amethyst."

Topaz introduced him to Emerald next, and her eyes widened with wonder.

"So how do you feel about Topaz's voyage to the New World?" Captain Cabot asked them.

"It is astounding beyond my belief, Captain," Emerald replied. "But Topaz has always been the brave one in the family. I am forever grateful to King Edward for granting her this gift of life in a new and unspoiled land."

"I, too, am forever grateful to the boy king, for launching this expedition," Cabot said. "He has just advanced me to the grand pilot of England, a high honor indeed. However, I do miss good Henry the Eighth. He were a fine and noble king, and I only wish he could be here to revel in the joy of exploring new lands, of connecting all these very different worlds and peoples under the unified banner of mankind."

Topaz, standing idly aside, elected to change the subject back to her own idol, Captain Cabot. "Amethyst, Emerald, do you remember the Dun Cow, the rib of the cow whale in the entrance to St. Mary's church in Bristol?"

"Why, yes." They nodded. "On every visit to Oakengates, our Aunt Margaret's manor home in Bristol, we heard Mass there many times," Emerald said.

"That's from a whale Sebastian captured near Newfoundland," Topaz bragged as if she'd harpooned it herself, her admiring gaze sweeping over the captain's form.

Amethyst turned to the aging but sprightly captain, her astonishment meeting his shrug of nonchalance. "No one ever told us. I never would have known to ask where it came from. It had been there all our lives. Forever, it seemed..."

"Aye, since 1497, to be exact," Cabot said. "Since before you were twinkles in your mother's eye I am no longer a young man, but Lord willing, I shall see many new lands and open up more passages of trade, uniting the world."

"You are not old, Sebastian," Topaz sang in a mildly chiding tone, caressing his arm. Sebastian returned the affectionate gesture with a quick but endearing hug. "He is but seventy-three years young, and still has to lose but a hair on his head," she gushed, her flattery as frothy as the wave caps nuzzling the ship.

"Madam, if you think seventy-three is young, then you are but a babe, and much too young to make a voyage over the high seas," Cabot teased.

"I am sorry, Captain, but the infant king hath given his orders!" Topaz bantered back.

They both tittered together, Topaz covering her face like a giggly girl, displaying a mirth Amethyst had never seen in her stoic, pensive sister. She and the captain obviously shared a genuine rapport, and Amethyst said a prayer of thanks Topaz had finally achieved a degree of contentment—in this last chapter of her life.

"Well, my ladies, the tide will be ready to launch Searchthrift on her way shortly. I must retreat to the galley to make final preparations. Lady Amethyst, Lady Emerald...I do hope we shall meet again in this life." He gave them a bow and circled the air with his hand.

Amethyst reeled at a stab of melancholy, for they all knew that would never be. "Aye, Captain Cabot, and I bid you Godspeed. My prayers shall be with you and your crew throughout your voyage."

The captain turned and climbed back up the gangway, his swirling cloak and plumed hat trailing obediently behind him.

The sisters stood silently, putting off the inevitable. "Well, dear sisters," Topaz finally spoke, "I must embark also."

"Please make sure Captain Cabot takes good care of you. And please do write and let us know of your progress," Amethyst said.

"Sebastian and I have become fast friends, as you can see. We shall comfort each other and fight the seas together when they become hostile. And of course I shall write. No one has heard the last of me!" Topaz proclaimed as if battling for the crown once again.

The three sisters embraced one last time, and Amethyst detected a hint of reluctance in Topaz, to relinquish her family and country, to be torn away across that dark tempestuous void and thrown upon unknown soil.

"Farewell, sisters. I am on my way to Utopia." Then she pulled away, twirled round and climbed the gangway, not looking back. The last sight Amethyst ever had of her sister was the sweep of her coppery hair receding into Searchthrift's galleys.

As Emerald walked back up the pier, Amethyst stopped and gazed upon the flag fluttering atop the mast of the Great Harry. Stepping off the pier, once more onto her beloved native soil, she heaved a sigh of relief.

Chapter Twenty-Six

Kenilworth, January 1559

Amethyst sat down and wrote one of the most important letters she would ever write in her life: to her new queen, Elizabeth.

She toiled over draft after draft, crumpling each page onto a growing pile on the floor. This had to be polished. This had to be concise. This had to be perfect.

I humbly beseech Your Majesty to ascertain the final resting place of my nephews Edward and Richard Guilford, who died so suddenly at the apex of their youth in the Tower of London...

That was the easy part. Now she needed to ask of her queen to find it in her heart to answer the most haunting question: why?

After ten drafts and a floor strewn with scribbled-on parchment, she held the final product in her hands, folded it and pressed her seal upon the wax.

She prayed the queen would answer her someday. Through the following weeks, the months, the years, she never gave up hope.

* * *

Kenilworth, November 30, 1559

Amethyst's chambermaid handed her a folded letter embossed with the royal seal. This was copied by no scribe. This was the writing of

Queen Elizabeth herself. She read the letter four times before the shock wore off.

My dear lady Guilford,

I harbor elation and sadness at dispatching this long-awaited news about the fate of your nephews Edward and Richard. I just returned from Lady Frances Brandon,

who, on her deathbed, handed me a journal to keep as my own. Her father, Charles Brandon, Duke of Suffolk, bequeathed her this journal which he began when my father reigned. As you know, Charles and my father were quite close, as Charles was husband to my father's sister Mary. At the entry for 10 January 1547, Charles wrote that my father summoned him to carry out a most heinous deed. As this is of much more importance to you than it is to me, I enclose Charles's original journal pages of which I speak.

Amethyst unfolded another page the queen had included with her letter. She read Charles Brandon's very own words:

The king summoned me to his chamber this eve, more distraught than usual. He ranted on about protecting his son from any possible threats to his rightfully inherited crown. He would not suffer his son to fight pretenders and defend the crown with his life as the king had...Edward must never suffer the indignities of a usurped throne. He declared that to eliminate the slightest doubt that Edward will reign as true king, he must eliminate these pretenders.

The pretenders he spoke of were 'those two boys in the Tower' and he declared he wanted them executed immediately, I being unaware of which two boys until he refreshed my memory...the grandsons of Warwick...one of the name Richard, the other of Edward...at which time the king ordered me to go to their chamber at the stroke of midnight and do away with them. Upon my asking what method of execution was his pleasure, he left the decision up to my own discretion. But he specified to do it quietly and non-violently...at which time his majesty then issued orders to lay their bodies out upon the beds in which they slept, reach their mother's cell and inform her that the king has granted her wish to see her sons.

I was not to tell the mother her sons were dead.

With a very heavy heart, I carried out the royal orders. I confess I do not know how the bodies were disposed of.

She turned the page over. Nothing was written on the other side.

Amethyst folded the pages just as the queen had sent them and went to show her husband the truth. Their long wait had ended.

Chapter Twenty-Seven

The Tower of London, 1674

As excavators were digging up the stone stairway in the Bloody Tower, the bottom step was overturned. A worker glimpsed what looked like a human bone jutting out of the ground. Several minutes later they unearthed two skulls, mostly intact, but broken into fragments on the top and sides. Further excavation revealed two skeletons.

Although these weren't the only skeletons excavated from Tower grounds, their location was close to Thomas More's decription of where the princes were buried. When the discovery was made public, the majority of English subjects concluded they were the sons of Edward IV, Richard and Edward. Upon taking the throne, Richard III had sequestered his nephews in the Tower, the elder boy briefly known as King Edward V.

Richard and Edward, the sons of Topaz Plantagenet, had also been imprisoned in the Tower and murdered there. Any of the numerous remains found buried on Tower grounds could be those of Richard and Edward. After all, Henry did order Brandon to "bury them. Do not cast them into the Thames. They must vanish from the earth without a trace."

Today the bones found in 1674 are interred in an urn in Westminster Abbey. They remain unidentified. But at the time, their unearthing satisfied the English subjects who believed the bones finally received the royal burial they deserved.

THE END

Epilogue

Cape Cod, Massachusetts

I walked down the tree-lined street in the charming town of Chatham, slowing my pace every time a particularly quaint item caught my eye in the windows of the long row of antique shops. My gaze stuck on a huge writing desk. I did a quick about-face, entered the shop, and stepped up on the platform in the front window to study it closely. Of dark mahogany, the finish was scratched and worn, yet its character gleamed through, displaying a rich heritage and boasting pride in its longevity. I ran my hand over its bumpy, knotted surface. It contained rows and rows of deep slots and drawers like those in the old apothecary shops. I noticed a set of initials carved into the center in elaborate script. "T.P." Who could this person have been, whose etchings survived the ages? It was a grand, majestic piece, a tribute to the artist who'd built it. I had to have it.

Nestled safely in the corner of my living room, it became the catch-all for my trinkets, my papers, my files, a nook for virtually everything I needed all in one place. It became a source of entertainment as I opened and closed the drawers, placing items in the compartments like a little girl playing house. It was then I discovered one of the bottom drawers was stuck. I tugged and yanked, but it would not budge. Finally, I pried it open with a butter knife wrapped in velvet. It came loose, then popped open. I stuck my hand inside, groped around and extracted a square object, a book of some sort, a manuscript wrapped in heavy layers of cloth. It was covered with a film of yellowish dust, looking withered, feeble, and old—very old. I slid it out cautiously, freeing it from its musty tomb, carefully unwrapped the cover and gazed at its contents: several pages of yellow parchment covered with old or middle English writing. Cradling the delicate pages in my hands, I riveted my eyes over the text, which, aside from a word here and there, I could not understand. But when I looked at the top of the page, I saw the date: July 30, 1571. I held someone's life story in my hands. Someone who had sat at this exact same desk, had touched the same papers I now held, who breathed the very air I was breathing, had left their memoirs in a time capsule, to be found—and read—and shared with the world, more than four centuries later.

Dear reader,

We hope you enjoyed reading *To Love A King*. Please take a moment to leave a review in Amazon, even if it's a short one. Your opinion is important to us.

Discover more books by Diana Rubino at https://www.nextchapter.pub/authors/diana-rubino

Want to know when one of our books is free or discounted for Kindle? Join the newsletter at http://eepurl.com/bqqB3H

Best regards,
Diana Rubino and the Next Chapter Team

About the Author

Diana writes about folks through history who shook things up. Her passion for history and travel has taken her to every locale of her books, set in Medieval and Renaissance England, Egypt, the Mediterranean, colonial Virginia, New England, and New York. Her urban fantasy romance, FAKIN' IT, won a Top Pick award from Romantic Times. She is a member of Romance Writers of America, the Richard III Society, and the Aaron Burr Association. When not writing, she owns CostPro, Inc., an engineering business, with her husband Chris. In her spare time, Diana bicycles, golfs, does yoga, plays her piano, devours books, and lives the dream on her beloved Cape Cod.

Visit Diana at:
http://www.dianarubino.com/
http://www.DianaRubinoAuthor.blogspot.com/
https://www.facebook.com/DianaRubinoAuthor
and on Twitter *@DianaLRubino.*

Author's Note

Astute readers will notice that I needed to adjust some events to suit the story's timeline: the sacking of Rome was in 1527 and Thomas More's execution took place in 1535. The reason I write historical fiction rather than biography is because fiction gives novelists flexibility, and our imaginations can fill in where the historical record doesn't provide us with the indisputable facts and of course, the dialogue that took place behind closed doors. Hence, I always say my books are based on historical facts—the facts I was fortunate enough to excavate from the dusty archives of past generations who were thoughtful enough to record them, so we can marvel at them many centuries later.

All the characters in this book are true historical figures, with the exceptions of the Jewels, their mother Sabine, Matthew Gilford, Mortimer and Roland Pilkington, and the Jewels' children. The events leading up to Richard III's ascending the throne, George of Clarence's death by drowning in a butt of malmsey wine, his son Edward of Warwick's execution and Henry VIII's accession to the throne did take place, and the fate of Edward IV's sons, the Princes in the Tower, is still not known. The bones that repose in the urn in Westminster Abbey have never been proven to be those of the Princes.

Edward, Earl of Warwick, whom Henry VII executed at age 25, was the last male in the Plantagenet line. In real life, he did not have daughters named Topaz, Amethyst and Emerald. He died without issue, lived his entire life from age 8 in the Tower, and was thought to be simple-minded. Upon becoming king, Henry VIII posthumously reversed the attainder against Edward and bestowed titles and riches on Edward's sister, Margaret

Pole. She then fell out of favor and died a brutal death by the axe of a fumbling executioner.

King Edward IV's marriage to Elizabeth Woodville was declared invalid, bastardizing his son, so his brother, the Duke of Gloucester, ascended the throne as Richard III. Henry Tudor's army defeated and killed Richard at the Battle of Bosworth to begin the Tudor Dynasty with King Henry VII.

Richard's corpse, beaten and bloody, was flung across his horse, carried to the House of the Grey Friars in Leicester and buried in the Collegiate Church of St. Mary's. Eventually, Henry VII erected a monument to Richard's memory, which was subsequently destroyed during the dissolution of the monasteries in Henry VIII's time. In February 2013, Richard's remains were discovered and excavated under a car park in Leicester. DNA testing determined a match between the remains and a living descendant. Now only Edward V, the nephew he was believed to have murdered, is the only English monarch with no known final resting place.

The Battle of Bosworth is dramatized in Shakespeare's "Richard III" when Richard, upon losing his horse, utters the famous cry, "A horse, a horse! My kingdom for a horse!" although in reality he insisted on fighting the remainder of the battle on foot. According to legend, the crown Richard had worn at the battle rolled out from under a hawthorn bush and was placed on Henry's head as he became King Henry VII. Upon his death, his son became Henry VIII. Towards the end of Henry VIII's reign, his daughters Mary and Elizabeth were relegitimatized and each reigned in succession after the death of sixteen-year-old Edward.

The Duke of Clarence's son Edward, Earl of Warwick (father of the fictional Jewels) spent all but one day of his life imprisoned in the Tower by Henry VII to keep him out of the way, until he was executed.

So it's plausible that Henry VIII could've kept Topaz's sons imprisoned there throughout their lives.

Topaz accompanies Sebastian Cabot to the New World, but it is not known whether he brought any female passengers on his voyages. His next voyage did not occur until 1553, during which he accidentally discovered what is today known as Russia while looking for the northeast passage to Cathay. However, his discovery of Newfoundland did take place, and the Dun Cow, the rib of the cow whale he brought back as a trophy of that discovery is preserved in the western entrance to St. Mary Redcliffe Church in Bristol.

Many of Henry's palaces are still standing and open to the public, such as Hampton Court Palace, the Tower of London, and Windsor Castle, which is Henry's final resting place, where he is buried next to Jane Seymour, the mother of his only legitimate son. Westminster Abbey, having reached its 900th birthday, holds many centuries of history within its hallowed walls and is a magnificent shrine, Henry VII's opulent chapel being a splendid work of Gothic architecture. Warwick Castle, up the road from Shakespeare's birthplace of Stratford-upon-Avon, is one of the few medieval castles in England that is still intact. It is one of the most beautifully preserved castles in England, and the private apartments are adorned with Madame Tussaud's wax figures depicting a Royal Weekend Party in 1898, decorated with the lavish furnishings of the time. The castle also has beautiful grounds, staterooms, a dungeon and many towers to climb, affording a sweeping view of the Warwickshire countryside and the River Avon. The gleaming red Kenilworth Castle is close by, but is mostly in ruins.

Bibliography

Albert, Marvin, The Divorce
Ashdown, Mrs. Charles H., British Costume During Nineteen Centuries
Banks, F.R., The Penguin Guide to London
Bowle, John, Henry VIII
Braudel, Fernand, The Structures of Everyday Life
Burke, John, The Castle in Medieval England
Doherty, P.C., The Fate of Princes
Durant, Will, The Story of Civilization
Elton, G.R., Reform and Reformation
Gies, Joseph and Frances, Life in a Medieval Castle
Griffiths, Arthur, The Chronicles of Newgate
Harrison, Molly, How They Lived, 1485-1700
Jenkins, Elizabeth, The Princes in the Tower
Kendall, Paul Murray, The Yorkist Age
Kendall, Paul Murray, Richard III
Markham, Clements, Richard III
Newark, Timothy, Medieval Warfare
Quennell, Marjorie and C.B., History of Everyday Things in England, 1066-1799
Read, Conyers, The Tudors
Sorell, Alan, Medieval Britain
St. Aubyn, Giles, The Year of Three Kings

Stone, Lawrence, The Family, Sex & Marriage in England, 1500-1800
Story, R.L., The Reign of Henry VII
Warnicke, Retha, The Rise and Fall of Anne Boleyn
Whitaker, Terence, Haunted England
Wood, Margaret, The English Mediaeval House

Acknowledgments

I would like to thank the Medieval Heritage Society, who at Goodrich Castle, patiently answered my many questions and gave a fine performance.

Many thanks, as always to the Richard III Society, for everything else.